Relish In the Tread

Steven Keith Hunter

First paperback edition April 2023

Edited by Joseph Doucette
Cover Design by Dan Fowler

Map by Alice Wang

ISBN 978-1-7389129-0-2 (paperback)

www.relishinthetread.com

Thanks to Reka for introducing me to pilgrim life
Thanks to Lisa for kicking my ass
To Ciaran for sending me a bit of money in Istanbul
To my Family and the few friends who've stuck around
To Mira for so much support getting this book out into the world
To Dan Fowler coming in at a clutch moment
And to All the Dead Writers that inspired me to be literary

Special Thanks to Everyone who
showed their hospitality across Europe

Vatican

Marino
Artena
Alatri
Arena
Cassino

Ceprano
Mignano

Baia Domizia
Viaggio Coppola
Napoli
Pompei
Sorrento
Priano
Maiori
Salerno
Eboli
Potenza

Ripa Candida
Spinazzola
Bitoni
Bari

Dubrovnik
Trebinje
Herceg Novi
Tivat
Zanjic
Radanovici
Bar
Sveti Stefan Beach
Sukobin
Skoder
Bushat
Lehze
Plazni San Pietro
Rinia
Durres
Kavaje

Paqin
Elbassan
Frangovo
Orhid
Qukes
Koziak
Bitola
Budje
Stenje
Niki
Herakleae
Florina
Veye
Hot Sp
Arnissa
Edessa

Thessaloniki

2000KM DE ROMA

hillipi

arou
avros
Loutra
Kavala
Xanthi
Komotini
Alexandropolis
Feres
Ipsala
Kesan
Malkara
The Farmer
Tekirdag
Marmara
Silivri
Buyukcekmece
Avcilar

Hagia Sophia

A ISTANBUL

Pilgrim

What little remained of morning fog hovered through the old courtyards and village square of St-Jean-Pied-de-Port. The foot port of St. Jean, or St. James, and the beginning of the Camino Francés. People of all kinds walked out from the doorways of many small houses onto the pebbled road to start their trail to Compostela.

"The weather can change quickly," a young woman warned. "And sheets of cloud come in without notice up top. It's easy to get lost. We have to be careful."

A thousand meters of hiking on a road that tens of thousands had tramped before us. "Let one man die from his foolish wanderings," I crowed to myself, "and danger becomes the most pertinent thrill."

The Camino Francés to Santiago-De-Compostela was a 900-kilometre straight line across Spain. A journey surrounded by dozens of other walkers. I'd never carried a pack for more than a couple of weeks. I had also never walked across a country. These trials alone wouldn't be easy. Half of the people in our hostel, or albergue, treated this pilgrimage like the ascent of a Himalayan peak. Their brand of danger irritated me. I walked ahead of them, on my own until another huge group arrived.

The sky was azure, and the air heated by 8:30. My pace steadied as my thighs engaged for the steep hill. I mounted the incline moving through a crowd in bulky Gore-Tex hiking boots and carrying walking sticks. I noticed three exceptional characters to my right. The oldest of them had a long, matted beard; the second had bright blond hair, wearing board shorts, baby blue sunglasses, and a glaring smile; the last of them was heavily tanned with peach fuzz along his chin and a fat, cone-shaped spliff dangling from his bottom lip.

"You want some?" he offered.

"Maybe not quite yet, but cheers," I said, giving each of them a fist bump. "I'm Freddi. Nice to meet a few peeps here who aren't wearing 'Columbia' gear. Shit's ridiculous."

Two were Italians – Dani was the elder with the weathered beard; Cosimo had the peach fuzz. They'd started their day at one of the many albergues in Saint-Jean where they had met their new, pale, beachcomber friend.

"I'm Amos – and Canadian," he said cheerfully as he dragged from the fat spliff. "These two Italians are nothing like the rest."

"Holy shit guy, anoder Canadian – how the hell are ya, eh?" We shared an ironic laugh. The route continued to grind. "Well, my dudes, hopefully see you later, maybe we can share a few. I'm gonna keep grindin' here for now, though. Adios muchachos."

Their giggling voices faded behind me. Each time my foot grazed the cement, I focused on my breathing. I took in some air and released it again. I glanced at the cloudless sky and the snake-rattling sun.

"The fog moves in quickly," I muttered to myself.

The pastoral greens brought chimes of paradise into my soul. A cool breeze sliced through the mid-day heat just as I arrived at a spray-painted shack filled with discarded hiking gear.

My broken heart had instigated this journey of a million steps. The aftermath of that crackled, spent relationship left me unglued. Years of travel without returning home. Countries crossed. Continents uncovered. In the wake of shattered love, questions arose. I asked myself if there was a reason to carry on traveling any further. My partner had ditched me and the road we'd manifested together. Another man offered her stability, a life of promise, and a child. My self-worth dwindled and self-pity soared. Travel itself wasn't enough. I needed to find what was important in all this travel. I needed to attempt something unique and make a deeper connection to my spirit. The cadaver of my failed relationship smelled awful. My conscience demanded a fresh start, away from memories that left me hitting the skids. It was time for new direction, new steps, and intentional tribulations. It was time to feel the terrain against my soles, to see whether I was in love with the road or just running from accountability.

From that hut full of old gear, the Way reached a plateau. The short grass smelled fresh. The scent of rich soil seeped into my nostrils. My shoes bothered me. I tied them up and took out my Crocs and walked barefoot. The grass was soft. It felt soothing on the bottoms of my bare feet. Air rushed through the hard bristles of my beard. When the wind hit my eyes, small tears fell down my cheeks. I wanted nothing more until I saw my three compatriots appear behind me. I slipped my Crocs on.

"Thought I'd wait for you guys," I said, putting my hand on Dani's shoulder. "Feel like some company?"

"Yea for sure, and a cerveza – nice shoes."

We walked side by side until we found a huge escarpment. We sat down. An epic viewpoint from the mantle of a cliff, overlooking a dozen snow-capped mountains with Christmas tree beards. Our legs dangled a few hundred meters above ground. We wrapped our arms around one another. Time stood still. Submerged in the belonging I found with these companions, I confessed my fear of being useless and lonely. I admitted my deepest worry: that one day I would realize I'd wasted my life playing around. As the words fell, a weight lifted from my shoulders, just as my backpack had a few moments before. My friends closed their arms against my back. One after the other, they too declared what grievances had brought them onto this reflective pilgrimage.

Dani's fight was against addiction, his search for more. We were of an age and felt our backs against the same metaphysical wall. Amos was still unscathed. He hadn't known struggle or sorrow, but he'd questioned his very existence since his graduation from college. Cosimo was the younger brother of

11

Dani's best friend. Eighteen years old with one foot in a jail cell and a dangerous taste for cocaine. He couldn't speak a single word of English.

"I'm constantly translating for this dick and balls, but he's a good kid. Wait 'til you hear him play guitar."

It wasn't a walk we were on. This was a passageway into knowledge, a chance to listen and learn and share and eat and drink at a long table of united nations. All of us at peace with one another, ready to dance 900 kilometres across Spain in search of incremental wisdom, calm, and humility.

"We are so lucky to be together," I thought. "Here with crisp mountain air and a hot sun." I felt the transformation from weathered traveler to what a Hungarian friend who'd walked this Camino called me. She told me her stories of the Way when we'd met in India and the changes she had gone through.

"You need to go. You will go," she proclaimed. "You're already a pilgrim, Freddi."

Every time I spoke to her, she repeated it for years, including the last time I'd spoken with her, just a few days before I walked off the doorstep of that albergue in Saint-Jean-Pied-De-Port.

"Pilgrim."

She was the first to call me that, but not the last. Everyone became a pilgrim that first day. Our openness with one another created something. We surrounded ourselves with people of all generations and cultures and backgrounds; we were united in exhaustion from carrying our damaged, decaying spirits. Each of us reached for strangers to listen and accept our baggage. Portents arrived like stigmatic flesh wounds, regularly, every hour. The messages were clear: release, release. And it was only the first day. We tilted into the descent from the summit of El Camino towards a town called Roncesvalles. A patch of unmelted snow. Amos didn't hesitate. He leapt joyfully onto his back and waddled his arms and legs up and down, snickering. We fell in beside him.

* * *

Arm's reach from the obelisk at Vatican City, ready for another, different, long walk. One year after that Camino Way.

Everything but confidence. Stupidity led me to early mistakes as my pilgrimage got under-way. It had nothing to do with Christians or Roman Catholicism. It was about two distant landmarks. Two thousand kilometers from the Holy City towards Europe's cusp, at Hagia Sophia, Istanbul. I scowled at the sheer volume of summer tourism in Rome, first at the Fontana di Trevi and then the Colosseo, pushing my head down through acre-long lines of tourists. Nervous chills accosted me whenever I had to cross paths with them in the long barricades of polo shirts and khaki shorts. The crowds left me dizzied with nausea, like having a panic attack in a New York shopping mall on Black Friday. I was busy giving myself a disgruntled speech under my breath when I saw Parco Caffarella. The tourists evaporated. The outskirts of the city took over. A park brimmed with the noise of women and their children. I had lunch under an enormous tree.

This ancient pilgrimage track ran parallel to Rome's new mega-highway. My blind faith said locals could direct me; I didn't consider that they would lead me astray. I looked down the busy highway with 2000 kilometres ahead of me. Where was this ancient trail? Hordes of emotions threatened to overwhelm me. Fear of failure. Inadequacy. Fear scraped through my head, threatening mental collapse. Bitter realization: I'd left without a map. And no one had any knowledge of an ancient road out of Rome. Stuck and frustrated, I longed for that trail to Roncesvalles – and my Camino friends, those people who accommodated therapeutic reflections. I passed an airport gate and considered the guards a perfect target for directions. They shrugged like everyone else. "Appia Antica, no lo so."

I quivered with disdain and hate for their indifferent, ugly faces. Surrounded by thousands of coughing automobiles and big, blaring buses back on the six-lane motorway. Calm retreat became a wayward stranger. I fought with myself, resisting the temptation of a passing bus.

"Dove, Appia Antica? Non scusa, prego, AP-PEE-YA AHNN-TIKA?" Each time, it got more infuriating to repeat, and each time I was pointed to the highway. Sweat seeped from my body and around my 13-kilogram pack. It sopped through my t-shirt. It wrinkled my skin. Sweat burned my eyes. Even my fingertips dripped. Then, I saw a name on a passing signpost. Was it the one I was searching for: Appia Antica? A small arrow pointed down an intersecting road. An African woman in high heels and a tight, dark, reflective outfit stood in a small patch of gravel on the shoulder. She smiled, then leered and swayed her hips as though she were dancing.

This timeless road was lined with finely polished silver blocks, overgrown with propagating trenches of green grass. A road without traffic. The peace I sought between undisturbed, balletic footsteps. This was the first part of the long, ancient road to Constantinople and the first transcontinental highway the world ever knew. An ancient Roman chariot road going all the way south to Formia. My Via Francigena Way led me from this cobblestone route and back into civilization. The terrain grew bare its iconic stone trees, which had been blocking heat in the mid-forties. Carbon monoxide from exhaust fumes made the heat worse until the ascent into my first village, Marino

Closer to the sun than any of its surroundings, the town glimmered. The spires looked like the tips of a royal crown. Skilled artisans had built wonderful, terraced homes and small flats overlooking gardens and fields under a clear cloudless sky. The air was filled with the aroma of eggplant parmigiana being roasted and fried garlic from pasta aglio e olio. Every pantry had a tall, glass bottle of local olive oil and a cupboard full of sugo jars.

Marino's townsfolk gathered in a park area with high fences. A football pitch surrounded by long, metallic benches for onlooking families. Upon arrival, I received the humorous impression that everyone had assembled to welcome me, the pilgrim. Adolescents danced onto the field. They sang in Italian, waving their arms at me. I fell into a space between two proud sets of parents. This was it. A chance to witness normal life in southern Italy. How different, or similar, it was to the place that I called home years ago. Someone at the church told me to come here for the local priest. The man who could arrange a night's sleep in the church. But he wasn't walking around in a black robe, and I hadn't seen anyone wearing a white collar.

Breaded pork paninis in waxed paper sat in huge trays on tables after the show. The people of this country, even with sandwiches, treated food quality as a testament to their integrity. I was so hungry I stared at the large trays. And one man's Coke next to me, perspiring down its steel shell. The groups congregated and volunteered a boy who spoke the best English. He first asked the usual, "Where are you from?" I began to feel like I was a small stopover act that had come through town, shining a little light from the outside world, as they laughed. A figurine in a glass case no one wanted to touch, but everyone wanted to know how it was made. I stood in front of fifty people. A character from Mark Twain's mind once the word spread of why I had come through.

"He says he is walking to Istanbul?" someone murmured in disbelief.

"He walked here from Canada!" People gave me their oohs and ahhs, then returned to their sedentary repose. They tossed me aside like an old toy, but for the priest who peered from the crowd beside my boy with the English.

"Ciao Padre, I came here," the boy translated, "by foot from the Vatican, and I'm headed to Istanbul." He acknowledged my words, though he didn't understand them, and listened with patience. "I don't have much money for a room in town, and I wondered if you," my eyes drooped, defeated after a strenuous day, "had space for my mat and sleeping bag in your church?"

"That is all?" the boy asked.

"That is all," I responded, ignoring my hungry, shaking hands. "Oh, and thanks for coming to meet me, of course."

The priest left, then returned with two sandwiches in waxed paper. The sandwiches were incredible. He passed me a Coke, which plummeted into my stomach like a waterfall after the first sip. My face lit up and my throat gyrated. My stiff limbs surged with energy. The priest left a second time, for much longer. The boy led me to a minivan, but before heading off, I said good-bye to the priest and shook his hand with appreciative vigour. He put his palm on my shoulder and spoke in Italian, then finished with a compassionate farewell. The boy and I climbed into the van. He drove toward the church, but we passed it. We pulled up to the town's albergue. A place I had been. I looked to the boy driving, aggravated. My face was chalked with confusion.

"No, no, no, no, no. I have no money for this. Why are we here? Are you serious?" I said, irritated and tired, through

15

heavy, exhausted breaths, trying to hold it together.

"It's OK, OK, no problem." The boy passed me fifty euro. When the priest had gone the second time, he called ahead and arranged the room. The boy entered and spoke to the clerk. I met the clerk who had told me before there was no kind of reduced rate for pilgrims. He laughed at my question. His attitude improved this time. I gave the change back to the boy.

"No, it is a gift from the Padre to you, pilgrim. It is for your long journey forward," he explained innocently. I caught the tears before they could fall. I cleared my throat.

"Buon viaggio," I said gratefully as he left.

Ep. 2
Stand-Up Kid

A thick stream of sweat poured down my back after an hour of hiking uphill. High up on a mountain slope, a town appeared. Humidity lingered, covering everything like a blanket of meringue. Before me was an ancient, stone fortress. Small homes encircled the town, with stacks of them piled high around the cathedral like vertical Jenga blocks. People in matching shirts were filling huge balloons. Banners draped down over the narrow corridors of the aerial hamlet. A stage had been erected outside of the church. It reminded me of the finish line at a marathon.

Artena was enjoying the last day of a two-week art and culture festival. The inspired hands of artists savagely shook metal cans of paint, ball-bearings rattling symphonically. They blasted large canvases with spray paint and created luminous work that coloured entire laneways. Live bands came to the summit village from Milano intent on blowing up the spot until well after midnight. Stone corridors so congested one struggled for air. It wouldn't stop the surge. Bodies piled into one another in hopes of a memorable night. University students spoke English with me and dapped my fists, snapping photos. Between the little church square and the beer tap, everyone got to know my straw hat, long beard, and oversized rucksack. And no one could ignore the ever-expanding white stains on my shirt, growing since I had left the Vatican.

My hat lay upside down, outside my tent's door as I gasped for air in the morning. I tried to make sense of my recollections of the previous night. The voices of men in a bar rang in my mind. The man who spoke loudest of all was the one insistent on buying me a beer. We couldn't speak, outside of a few common words, but he was a patient and confident man. His weathered face and hands suggested he was a workhorse. He worked for the city, was close to retirement, so he expected little from life other than to have more time with his grandkids. That was all he wanted. Artena was his home and would be until he died. He seemed confused by the choices I had made.

"Why not family? Why complicate life?" he asked in surprise.

I was a lost soul, but he had no idea about that. Everything in life was simple for him, just as it was for his father before him. He never questioned that. He had his morning coffee, believed in God, had a wonderful wife that cooked his meals and took good care of his progeny. He didn't wonder how Cambodians, Malians, Nicaraguans, or anyone else lived or survived. He had to work and provide for his kids. His worldview was founded on routine, stability, and duty, not metaphysical questions or a search for "meaning." He had his weekends and holidays to Chianti.

The same bar was empty in the morning, except for the early faint rays of sun making it through a checkerboard of thin, wood-lined, square windows and a bartender I hadn't yet met. I slammed back an espresso, grabbed two cups of yogurt from the little market, and went back down the hill to the main road. It was time to start walking again.

Tall umbrella pines lined both sides of the road until I reached a golden-faced mountain ridge. On the right side was a ranch with a long, wooden fence and three lovely, chocolate Trakehner horses. They danced over to me and hung their long faces over the fence for my hand. It felt like Artena, a town of swollen hearts, was saying its final farewell.

Sweat dripping into my eyes, I noticed an empty table under an awning. Two men, a few yards away made it obvious they'd noticed me. The common southern Italian grins of

17

disapproval they gave to every outsider shone across the patio. It was an unintentional glare, without malice. Customary dirty looks for the unusual. A girl interrupted my scan across the wide, wooden bar inside.

"Can I help you with something?" she asked affably. Caught off-guard by an English introduction, I cleared my throat.

"Yes, can you lower your prices, please?" My joke sailed over her head. Instead, she sold me a sandwich and milkshake.

Later, she came outside to smoke with her workmate. When I was alone on the terrace, she came out again.

"Was it good?" she asked politely. I resisted the urge to tell the truth. Before I could say anything, she looked at my pen and notebook and queried, "What are you writing?"

"Ah," I moaned. "A story of sorts," I blurted, then nervously added, "I guess you could call it a story."

"Really? I write a little too," she said, somewhat sheepishly.

My eyes widened with interest, "And what do you write?"

"Mostly poems, little things that I think of – nothing serious."

"Who's serious?" I bluffed.

I was lying. I was serious with myself. I hid from her eyes, afraid I would give away my overwhelming and nearly uncontrollable desire to have someone like her to walk with me, even for a little while, on The Way.

She told me about her time on Ibiza and traveling.

"Not like you," she said anxiously, "I mean, I like to travel. It is so nice, so many places for going, so many experience!"

We shared stories back and forth about work life on Ibiza. The debaucherous lifestyle and the drones that stole oxygen. She left for Ibiza with her boyfriend, but they broke up. Then she went home to help with her family's cafe.

"He wanted to keep traveling – even now he is on Canary Islands and going for Thailand soon."

Sounded familiar. I knew all too well how selfish the road could make someone; I believed the sacrifice was a worthwhile one. I even convinced myself that it was valuable for one's development. He wanted to revel in the outside world. He wanted the world he had seen glamourized in photos and folklore, romanticized places he had dreamed about. I knew, it was self-evident: all good things were wild and free, like Thoreau said. Her old boyfriend sounded like a decent bloke. But her, she had more of the pilgrim inside of her. Maybe even more than she wanted to admit to herself. She was a soul seeker, a creator. She was pensive about her coming years; he was a tourist on the hunt for beaches, chasing things that didn't exist outside of movies.

"We tried to long distance, in Skype, maybe visit or two – it's not good." I wondered whether she was lamenting the break-up or just making sure I knew it was over.

"Long distance is very tough," I commiserated, remembering how my last relationship went from sizzling to finished in the same fashion.

"I have to get back to work," she explained. "My name's Ella."

"I'm Freddi Woomba." I must have said it louder than intended, because it caught the attentive stares of the two locals again. She walked away in her black-and-white-striped capris, hips swaying from side to side. Her apple-shaped bum left me entranced, like a child seeing fireworks for the first time. The locals noticed me noticing her.

She came out, one more time, with less ostensible enthusiasm. "Here, I just threw this together." She seemed rushed, and her tone was meek. She looked so charming, yet shy. "It's something I wrote," she whispered, then swung around, in slow motion. Along with the folded page, I was left with her fresh scent of lemongrass. The writing was in Italian with an inscription at the end:

When you learn more Italian, you can read this!

I couldn't understand a single phrase, but the beauty of those Trakehner horses from earlier ran through her prose. Learning enough Italian to translate her poem would take me longer than it would take to walk to Istanbul, so I laughed. My heart hit my chest cavity when I walked in to pay. Money on the bar counter, I tried to look aloof. Ella's eyes sparkled as she spoke with encouragement to my crimson silence.

"Have a great journey, pilgrim!" I turned to leave, then

steeled my nerves, mustered some courage, and turned back.

"Listen, I'm gonna walk to Alatri tonight, no further – it is only twelve kilometers away."

"Yea, ok."

"Yea, so what about you meeting me there after you're done here?"

"Sure," she said without much thought. I was stupefied. Flabbergasted. Could it be that easy?

We arranged to meet in the town square of Alatri at 10 p.m. It was so definite. Out on the Way, my spirit ignited like my grandma had just tossed me a stack of coins for the arcade. "Psht? For real?" I yelped in my mind, "I was sure she'd blow me off!"

The next three hours, I climbed uphill without relent. My knees and ankles ached, but still, I walked on clouds, head in the sky, careless about the cement under my Crocs. At the foot of Alatri, I found a market to buy pasta and a bottle of wine. Up a cobblestone passageway and through a large gate, the narrow, stone lanes were hardly adequate for a Fiat. The old town of Alatri was built within the walls of a castle. I smiled the whole way, waving at every grumpy face that cared to make eye contact.

"Scusa, dit mi per favora, dove sei la centro," I asked a man with growing confidence.

Hordes of barbarian tourists would be invading Tuscany, spellbound by Roman town squares. But here – here, in this corner, I was the only foreigner. I was here, alone, tracing my hand along ancient walls. Walls with stories etched deep in their crevices. The dark grey buildings matched the pavement. Polished floors reflected sunlight, heating the square. There was a fountain in the middle with four running waterspouts and a large, circular bowl. A church to one side. Soaring wooden doors, like wings. A clocktower and archways for the horse carriages. Church bells chimed. The bells seemed to be telling me that God was watching, and, more importantly, that Ella should arrive any minute. At 10, my mind whispered under the hands of the stone Virgin.

The bells rang once, which meant half past ten. No sign of Ella.

"Be patient. Enjoy the wine. She's Italian," I thought. "She's probably just closing the cafe. People here didn't view

20

time the same as a northerner," I rationalized. By 11, my faith sank. My pasta was finished, and I had drunk a quarter of the wine. Then, I remembered. Ella had given me a business card with the phone number of her café. I noticed two women and a man sitting on the church steps. I approached them, determined.

"I'm sorry," I paused before continuing, "but I'm in Italy…Wait, do you guys understand English?"

"So and so."

"Ok, so, I'm here, walking to Istanbul, I have no phone and gotta call this number here – I flashed the card towards them." After baffled looks, one of the girls agreed to call.

No answer. Again. No answer. After three times, I had to accept failure.

"Hey man," the bloke started, "my English not so good, but where you sleep?"

"To be honest, I'm not sure," I conceded. My idea of staying up all night with Ella on a hilltop had collapsed.

"I have studio. Small mattress. You want? Here too cold late notte."

"Is there a shower?"

"Yes, well, something as."

His front door was at the bottom of a small, narrow set of stone stairs. It was a basement studio, part of a long corridor of townhouses. Entering the flat was like crawling into a tunnel. The shower had a mop and bucket and empty paint cans inside.

"I use for work," he apologized. Before he left, I shook his hand, thanking him.

I paced, thinking of Ella. "What if she came very late?" I couldn't stop thinking about her. "What if she was there now?" Mosquitoes attacked from the screen-less window. "Fuck it." I set back out to the square.

I saw at first glance the man, my new friend, and the two girls he was with earlier, but I ignored them. Off the low, long set of church stairs, Ella bounced to her feet, rushed toward me with a big smile and kissed my cheeks.

"Sorry, sorry, I late," she said soothingly.

"You want a drink?" I offered from my bottle.

She replied with excitement, grinning, "Per che, non!"

The half-moon brightened for us. As we sat on the rim of the fountain everyone disappeared. I gazed at this wildflower,

21

grateful for my persistent nature in not giving up on her. I was paranoid of the repulsive, sour, musky odour of my hair and socks. I hadn't showered in three days. Salt and dirt had created a body cast. I reeked worse than a tattered street dog from the slums of Manila. Silence. Fucking silence. The haunting wounds left from the isolation I regularly imposed on myself had unlearned decades of social interaction. While my leg muscles strengthened, alone on The Way, my communications skills with women deteriorated. The allure of rugged wilderness, the history of human migration, brought me a mesmerizing love for life. I led this lifestyle with determination and in defiance of fear. My social circle was almost non-existent. Farewells became daily chores. I tried to avoid seclusion through curiosity for other people. But that required me to speak about myself. It felt narcissistic. Getting other people to share seemed to necessitate that I do it first. I hated this about the road life. Before I left Canada, I asked a lot of questions. My imagination was entranced by people who ignored limits imposed on them by cultural guardrails. My thirst for experience was emancipated by heroic tales of detachment. Protagonists on the hunt for more than a bachelor's degree. But I heard stories of those coming out successfully on the other side, stronger and more stable because of it. It was they who drew my envy. I never thought that this Way could create an antisocial person. Yet, being alone for long periods of time had done that to me.

On the Camino de Santiago pilgrimage in Spain, I'd met numerous old, lost men who wandered without purpose. They used the stamps they'd collected in their pilgrim passports from churches along the Way over the years they'd been walking as collateral for donations, so they could buy cheap wine. It scared me. My own Way, to break from monoculture and understand diversity, had led me to shelter within myself. Communication became irrelevant. With Ella, in a matter of time, we would have to part ways and never see each other again. This was a harmful, repetitious habit that I had to own. But if I didn't reach out to others, my heart would harden. This contradiction was my biggest vice.

"I made dinner for us but ate it when you were late. I am sorry."

"Oh no, you make dinner? Oh, I want for try your pasta," she purred with a luminescent smile.

"Come along," I suggested. We got up from the fountain, her shoes echoing off the tight walls as we exited the old town. We happened upon a stone fence about a meter high. It was the same woolly grey colour as everything else. We sat down. I passed her the wine. Her hair toppled back as the wine swished down the back of her throat. After she swallowed, she exhaled in delight. She had one hand on the fence and the other, gangster, around the neck of our bottle. Her olive skin was stunning in the dim light cast by the overhead lamps.

"Very beautiful, quiet, so peaceful. Nice to enjoy. I work too much," she sighed as she looked out into the darkness.

"Well, it's only midnight, so there's plenty of night left to enjoy," I wanted to grab her hand and her face and beg her to run away with me for a few days, or a week even.

"Freddi," she looked at me, very serious. "Don't you miss your family, your friends?" She exhaled something heavy. "Don't you desire a little how, what is," she paused a second. "Oh, my English so bad, sorry for this."

"Stability?" I suggested.

"Si. Stab eee liltee, si. It must get lonely?" She spoke as though imagining herself out on the Way, unable to grasp it because it was so different from everything she knew. Her fascination with traveling revealed excitement mixed with genuine fear. My life was prone to the chaos caused by that contradiction. Torn between the desire for time alone and the need for community and love. The same paradox that ended Kerouac's life as he'd confessed in *Big Sur*. The cold air of my past raised as an only child. I spent much of my time secluded. I became desperate for friends – and attention. At the same time, I also became accustomed to the luxury of my own space. I had my own room and a dog. I could have friends sleep over on a weekend, but never had to share space with a brother or sister. When I left home and rented my first apartment, it brimmed with people all the time. I liked it that way. I hadn't the faintest idea what to do with myself. Over time, I became caught between worlds, a duality of desires. Torn between someone who wanted an isolated cabin, overlooking a quiet lake on a mountain side, and a person nuzzled into a flatshare in an urban quarter with

23

cheap candlelit bars and Turkish kebab stands.

I gazed at this unselfish, approachable woman. Unmistakable subtlety with lust in her eyes. A panther tied in the back room on a loose chain, waiting for an antelope to pounce on. This happened once a month on the traveler's circuit. And once a month, I had to say goodbye to yet another potential perfect match or close friend. Accepting the Loneliness and Isolation package wasn't as effortless as I had hoped. Those old, tired men on the Camino frightened me. Accepting the life of an eternal loner looked pathetic. I fought to stop my heart from hardening, to feed it compassion and gratitude and keep my head above water.

"It gets lonely sometimes – but then I meet you," I blurted out.

"Well, it is interesting that lifestyle."

"You might be right darling. It is definitely different." Silence. Change the subject. Quickly. Say something clever, or profound, "Ella, tell me about your dreams."

"Pfft." She sighed heavier than when she spoke about working too much. "My dreams not important in my family. I quit school. Wanted change. No school, they said, oh, ok, you quit school, now you work for café!" She sat in silence for a moment, drained. "That wasn't why I quit school – you know?"

I felt sorry for her. Family pressure was unfamiliar to me. It seemed unfair that she never had any real choice or any chance for personal growth. Then it got worse. She spoke about financial crisis, the troubles that ensued. I had to wonder, though, after eating her sandwich and tasting her milkshake, if her culinary skills had anything to do with the crisis. I imagined her café's menu blowing in the wind, embracing the wild, floating the entire length of the pilgrim's trail. I envisioned us grinding under the sun together, then unwinding under a large night sky, breathing against each other's necks.

"Our bottle is done here. Think we need some hydrating before we dry out."

"I invite you!" she celebrated. With her hand in mine, we returned to the fountain. It was quieter than before, but I could still hear the barrio's clave echoing through the midnight streets.

"Chin-chin," she exclaimed.

Her hopes and dreams may have been ripped from her heart before she could figure out what they were, but the wine she drank was pure. She wasn't a victim. Her heart wasn't fragmented by the ugliness of depression. The edges of her eyes were unwrinkled, she entrusted that everything would work out. She had self-confidence. In front of me sat a woman unafraid to be bashful or to wail in the streets at the top of her lungs, even while sober.

"And what do you think about us taking the rest of this bottle to my little room?"

She responded in bewilderment. "You have a room?"

"Well, my dear, while you were running late, I was replacing you," I teased as I gave her a mischievous smirk and kissed her cheek.

"Is that right?" She played along.

I looked to the sky and swung my hands together as a triangle, waving them forward as any Italian would at this point. She took my hand, and I led her through the archway to my new basement flat. In the little studio, I opened the futon and sleeping bag. We could see the stars from outside the screen-less window. The mosquitoes had died off.

"Do you think, Freddi..."

"Sometimes," I joked before she could finish.

"No, non, listen cazzo, please," she squeezed my thigh.

"Yes, ma'am."

"You think you are romantic?"

I loved how she fumbled with her words as she tried to persuade me to confess how wrong we were to be on that futon.

"There have been a few stunts pulled off over the years," I stopped and glanced down. "I guess it depends on your idea of romance. Ella?" She was gazing at me, anxiously expecting me to explain further. "Like rolling this sleeping bag out or cooking dinner – which you missed – or bringing the wine and waiting an extra hour for my new friend." Her eyes rolled down her crimsoned face. When her eyes came back up to meet mine, I continued. "See, I wasn't trying to be romantic, but one could say these things were romantic, no?"

"So, this. Me and you. This is kind of your chance, the pilgrim, to be romantic?"

"I suppose you can see it like that. Love is almost always

accompanied by pain and regret; it gets mixed together with long-term commitments, and then it becomes a stifling prison. Yet… With nothing to love, time can become a chore. Without love, we are crippled," I declared before my brain caught up to my mouth and I could gather my thoughts enough to continue my disclosure.

"I want to feel. Don't you?"

I was ready to embark on unprecedented and wondrous journeys with her. But the truth was that Ella, like everyone else, could admire and even fantasize about a gypsy-lover but couldn't fathom being devoted to the lifestyle necessary for loving one.

"So, you've been in love?"

"Every day is ripped up by love. Love torments me every day. Probably because I'm not ready for it. The compromise of being in love. Or," I paused dramatically. "Maybe I'm just afraid of being conventional."

"What is conventional?"

"Doing things the normal way. The way everyone expects you to."

"Well, you certainly don't go normal road, cazzo! But some of women, we have expectation, you know?" I nodded in agreement, and she continued. "Are you a liar, Freddi?" She made eye contact as she said it; her gaze, penetrating, piercing as she waited for my confession of all the filthy skeletons in my closet.

I finally replied, "In fear of speaking the truth, yes, I have lied."

"Only in fear, huh?" she retorted.

"This is it, the inability to trust and communicate and believe in unconditional love, these are all very complicated things, no? And they take time. So, instead of that, I take increments of love. I shine small beams of romance from skint pockets when I can, and I do my best to embrace the moment. Squeeze it onto my pores to melt into your skin, so the smell will remind you of me. Like this. Like right now. Here. When I am lonely and all by myself, I can remember you and this place, and what we are doing, and what we shared. Experiences can be meaningful and profound even if they are brief."

"That sounds exhausting. You should try and let it come more naturally."

"Didn't I?" I looked at her with a witty seriousness.
"When?"

"You. Did I approach you?"

"Well," she blushed, and for the first time I saw real vulnerability in her. I put my hand on her cheek to kiss her. She pulled back.

"Freddi, I am not like you, it is not my way, sorry."

"Which way am I?" My heart spun like a whiffle ball.

"Loving hard and fast, then walking away. This is too much for me."

I nodded, again. She was right. It was too much.

"You could come with me for a while?" I suggested as I looked straight into her eyes. I could hardly believe I got it out.

"Maybe another time."

Another time? Something like, "maybe if it was another time, we could..."

Time doesn't exist!

I laughed at her comment cynically, offended, but still prepared to backtrack in hopes of saving the moment. "Look, I love that you wrote that piece and gave it to me. That took courage. Nothing like that has happened to me. I'm impressed that you weren't afraid to be yourself." I thought some more, "I'm grateful you chose to share your poem with me. I'm honoured that you trust me enough to..."

She interrupted me, "Never happened!"

"Never. If I could stay here and make love to you for the next five years, so that you could consider it reasonable, I probably would. But you wouldn't have me stay here. So now what?" I paused and then continued, "Right now, you're fucking hot. You're staring at me with those sultry eyes. It makes me want to experience you. To have you, even if it's only for tonight. All I can think about is my teeth sinking into your beautiful, round ass cheek."

She cut my rambling off again, "You wanna bite my ass?" She whispered, "A biter, huh?"

I lifted my eyebrows and smiled before carrying on with my rant.

"I'm hopelessly full of sexual tension and a long history of lost loves I can't friggin' escape," I blabbed. Let this not be one, I thought, as I took her hips in my hands. She stroked my beard. When she kissed me, it confirmed what I was sure I saw in her eyes. Her upper teeth bit lightly at my lip, like I wanted, then

27

her tongue moved slowly into my mouth. Her hands remained on my face, holding it with her paws. The panther in her moved in. I moaned.

"You are full of passion," she whispered, "and you're lucky I like the beards." She lifted my shirt and kissed my chest through the dark hair. Her lips were hot. I went silent as I fell into the pillow.

"But what about…" Her hand covered my mouth before I could finish.

"You were very honest. You're tired of lying, playing games. Your sincere-ity," she stopped. "And my body is hot, too!"

"I guess you still won't come with me tomorrow, though, will you?" I lamented as I pulled back to gaze deeply into her eyes.

"No, I won't."

In the morning, I woke up in a panic. My eyes snapped open, but the room was so bright, I had to close my eyes again. For a moment, I couldn't even remember where I was. It hit me. I stretched out my arms to feel for Ella. My right hand found a blanket.

"It can't be!" I shouted. My arms pulled the blanket into my chest as my hands groped over the bed, searching in desperation. I clutched the blanket in my arms, pretending it was her. She looked so happy, felt so real and right. I held the blanket as close as I could. The dream was so lucid. The deflation of our night cleft my spirit with two iron hooks. That it was nothing more than a fantasy wilted my heart. There was nothing left but the unabating road and that she stood me up. But it wasn't a time for lamenting; many footsteps lay ahead.

Ep. 3
The Winds of Change

Innumerable times, people asked the same question, and the pity was tangible, "Why? WHY would you walk to Istanbul?"

It shocked them. Many thought I was insane. And to each one, I offered an answer. A scenario related to our moment

28

together. "Runnin' from the law," I would say. Or, "Escapin' the Schengen."

In truth, I had multiple reasons. A chance meeting had initiated this ridiculous idea before winter began. When I arrived at the Vatican Plaza, it was empty. Long, metal corridors for the Pope's morning speech. Behind one of them, blocking the Obelisk, quite a way down, I noticed the end of a stick, pointing to the sky. The closer I approached, the more my hunch crystallized. A man held that stick. He gripped the wood with his hand every step he took. When I neared him, his grizzly beard suggested he was older than reality. His gear was minimalistic, but he looked ready for anything. His face, darkened by the road, his feet looked like mine, like leather. Hair tied in a ponytail, blond like his face and eyebrows, he might have been Scandinavian. There were many Danes on the Santiago Way, I recalled. He even had the blue eyes. My face brightened when I reached him.

My spine tingled. I was blunt, "Did you walk here all the way from Santiago?"

"Nah, mate," he spoke softly. In proper Queen's English, he introduced himself as James. He looked like a replica of myself a couple months back, except for the hair and accent.

"I walked a couple of parts in Spain – too busy for me, though. Have you been that way?" he asked, as though he were on a cloud far away from the Vatican square, on a permanent psychedelic excursion.

"Yea, just came from there. And you're right. Too busy." I sat down.

"Well, I walked from Genoa," he explained in his calm, inviting tone. "On the Via Francigena through Tuscany. I'm headed for Istanbul." His speech was so quiet and unassuming, I nearly missed it. My ears became possessed. His last words engulfed my attention. My eyes widened. Could he be serious?

"Really?" I asked.

"Sure. What a wonderful Way to live, isn't it? So much time – and space." I swear he noticed the spark his words had ignited inside of me.

The Way he used the words "space" and "busy" assured me that we spoke a common language. He felt like a brother. Whatever he was doing, I understood it. I wanted to be a part of

29

it. I wanted to join him. I wanted the mysteries that lay ahead. The adventure. I was jealous. It gave me purpose. I knew what I had to do. Except there was no money left, and my future was already in motion: hitching north to Bratislava to teach English.

James gave me a hug and went on his Way. He left behind an idea, like lighter fluid for a fire in my future, and a shadow of a man.

Seven months of teaching and a few weeks of hitchhiking later, I arrived again at the Vatican obelisk. This time, James wasn't there. I had a straw hat, my own walking stick – which I would ditch a couple hours later – and a cardboard sheet inscribed: *Help the pilgrim walk to Istanbul.*

I handed out small poetry books I made, written along the Camino. The cover was a small image of a pilgrim inside the trademark seashell symbolizing the Santiago Way. The donations would help with my trip. My plan was to keep selling poetry books along the Way, but I didn't consider how few people would be able to speak English, let alone read it. So, they became gifts for anyone who offered help to me. Selling my first piece of literature at that Obelisk felt great until the Vatican police arrived. The journey began there.

* * *

That first day out on the Camino Way in Spain, it was grand how we all fell together. In Roncesvalles, the albergue was filled to the rafters with pilgrims until our bodies fell from the windows. The three lads and I sat in the sun celebrating our unified harmony with bottles of Estrella. Outfits were notable for being unremarkable. People packed light. Throngs of people in unidentifiable clothes. In these we would get to know each other. Clothes off the communist shelf at the travel shop. Matching, cheap Quechua mats, dangling seashells from walking sticks. Women in tights, everyone in quick-dry t-shirts made of polyester and rayon. Only the hats were unique. We were many. We were quickly becoming a circle of friends united by a common pursuit.

Shell out cash on a hotel or walk to the next town? I had a tent with me. The forested riverside down the road was perfect. Many glared with surprise, the women first. Even my Italian mates scowled at the idea. Only my fellow Canadian, Amos, didn't hesitate. I realized then that none of them were weathered travelers. It would be me that popped the cherry of those who accepted the challenge. I would be their chaperone into the world of wild camping. With everyone ready to sleep in the albergue, I found it strange and disappointing. I expected everyone to sleep outside, or in churches huddled together. The conversation I had with the volunteers at the registration office scribbling our names down sounded in my ears.

"This year, forty thousand pilgrims will walk to Compostella." My eyes inflamed like a hemorrhoid.

While Dani and Cosimo were reluctant, Amos, like many Canadians, had experienced plenty of family camping trips in the woods. The three of them slept with me in the forested area half a kilometre from the barracks. Another pilgrim joined us at the suggestion. A large and boisterous Spanish man with few English words; he walked with a beach umbrella strapped to his pack.

They all had sleeping mats and sleeping bags. I chose a tent instead of a sleeping sack. We crowded a small fire, and I made rice with tomato frito, onion and garlic, some tuna, and a pack of cheap olives. The night was cold. The Italians suffered in thin, two-season bags. My teeth chattered through the hours before sunrise.

I was shocked that everyone would sleep in dormitories, countless stinking stocks hanging everywhere. The snoring and farting and coughing. People accepted it as part of the endurance required for this journey. Some dorms accommodated more than a hundred. Outside, there was space in every direction, and quiet. Silence except for the river. I was the only one with camping gas. They needed the stove or had to eat in restaurants. And the nights were colder than expected.

I tried only staying in donation albergues along the Way. Otherwise, after that first night, I borrowed blankets from little bars. Everyone gathered at the albergues before heading to a river, and everyone ate together in the common house. I felt sequestered many times, alienated, so I paid for a bunk. It tore a piece of the joy from me. But I also didn't want to camp alone while everyone sang and laughed and showered back at the house. Many pilgrims became agitated at the mere mention of

31

"camping."

"Sleep outside? Are you crazy? And get robbed or killed or worse!"

We passed through old villages. Criminals didn't lurk in those bushes. They crept only in the shrubs of the mind. That part of the Camino bothered me. Many refused the unknown, their small adventures were spoken only in vanity, in groups. I tried everything to motivate them.

"Just do it!" I wanted to shout many times. That was what brought them on the Way, after all. A kind of unknown risk in the face of a preposterous obstacle.

The dainty ones were afraid of everything that moved and full of excuses. Unprepared to try anything more than walking 20 kilometres a day. Plenty struggled with that, even after a nice shower and a bed. Walking after a restless night in a tent on hard ground after waking to shit in the forest. That was the challenge.

A few rituals began the second morning. People who passed us, we knew them now, and they all shared the same compassionate words.

"Buen camino," they all said, waving their hands or commercial seashells and walking sticks, as they exited the albergue, following the yellow arrows. These words became part of our momentum each morning. Acknowledgements of familial support. Encouragement that brought assurance of a good day lay ahead.

Our small crew, we all had sleep in our eyes. We shared our breakfast supplies. Our Spanish friend talked animatedly, making us laugh even though it was early morning. I had a litre of Gazpacho, he had little else but his morning energy. Besides the Tortilla de Patatas in cafes, Gazpacho became one of our rituals. It saved carrying extra kilos of muesli and yogurt. My muscles ached. My feet even more. I massaged them at the picnic table in hopes of some relief. My feet were getting worn in. My body was adapting to the pilgrim's Way. Putting my pack on that second day, for another 20 kilometres, took a moment's strength. Each one of us had our own ritual for loading ourselves up like beasts of burden. We huffed our own heavy breaths. Once the treads hit dirt, everything subsided, and the Way took over.

* * *

Huge, wrapped bales of hay like massive snowballs outside Ceprano followed rolling valleys of olives through medieval villages. There was no lack of visual splendour in these unaltered towns. Remarkable, transfixed and maintained, yet forgotten. Along the Istanbul Way through Italy, however, on the bloody roadways, it was busy, noisy, full of litter, reeking of sewage. An industrial wasteland threatening to crush my spirit.

The villagers from Artena danced in my heart and memory. More than that, the aneurysms of bass echoed through my bones thinking of Ella's missing, fictional touch. I'd had enough of the bitumen. There was no telling when a driver might swerve and hit me. If this was all the Francigena had to offer, shouldering cars, I needed to find another route. Online resources were dead ends, offering no solutions. At Mignano, a quaint, cliffside village, I was finished losing myself and destroying my knees on cement. I hoped to find the Padre at a small church for a little floor space that night. Maybe I could get directions or even inspiration from a higher power. The large, wooden entry was locked, but right next door was the town hall. Instead of the Padre, I found Elvira.

She was busy mopping when I swung the door open. Her eyes burned furiously at the sight of me. She waved her arms and threw down her mop. I looked back at her, confused – she launched as a matador in my direction, speaking in rapid Italian. I gave her a sharp response.

"Scusa io sono Canadese, non Italiano."

She stopped talking and brought me down the hall. She pointed to a small bench against the wall across from the toilet and spoke again, "Pelegrino a cua." She followed that up with the name James, pointing to my beard.

"No fucking chance," were the first three words that sprung into my bewildered mind.

James had slept there for a night. I was on his trail. It had been ten months since we last met. He should have been in India by this time. She said it was just four nights ago. I thanked Elvira and said good-bye. Outside, I looked for a supermarket and a place for my tent. There was a group of post-grads around a picnic table.

33

"You looking for a place to put your tent?" asked a young man in perfect English. He glared at me with that same southern suspicion despite breaking the ice. "Where did you come from?"

I spouted a quick answer. The whole gang warmed immediately and invited me for a beer right afterwards.

"It's the best around, and trust me, I live in Napoli," said my new friend, inviting me to share in their Friday night pizza ritual in the next town. He was eccentric, loud, jubilant, and happy to fit me in his car. He worked at a big hotel as a front desk clerk. He spoke multiple languages with a flamboyant enunciation. The pizza was great. Everyone chipped in a couple bucks for my share. The hotel clerk walked me down to the bottom of town once we returned to Mignano, to an unexpectedly tranquil park.

"I would let you stay, but I am at my mom's place," he said apologetically.

I found a comfortable cave overgrown with green, fuzzy moss. Below it, the clear river would be perfect for my morning bath. It had a flat area for my tent just under the cave wall. The ancient stairs led to old Roman baths. An ancient site, forgotten and transcendent. I was glad the hotel clerk lived with his mom.

"Frederico! Ciao Bello! Pelegrino!" Elvira exclaimed when she found me packing in the morning. She announced her discovery like an archaeologist who had just unearthed an important artifact. She was with her friend Donatella, who had also met James. They brought two huge sandwiches: prosciutto, sliced provolone, and fresh tomatoes. I could have kissed them both.

"Grazie mille!" I repeated to the ladies, "pero..." The ladies talked, Donatella a little in English, both motoring. Their faces saddened when I mentioned leaving.

"Not without an espresso." I had a lot to do this morning. They insisted.

My friends from the pizza party had opened a new corridor of thought, "You want to see Pompei? But you are going the wrong way. You must visit Napoli and try the pizza!" They also mentioned the nearest beach, Formia, was only forty kilometers away. That was my answer to the crowded tarmac roads. They swore the place was magical. A paradise. And I was foolishly going the opposite direction.

"Shit... that could be done in a day if I walked steadily," I proposed to myself and to them. It would be a long day, but it was possible. They laughed at my suggestion. The hotel clerk offered me a lift if I waited two days. Did they think I was exaggerating or boasting?

I left Elvira and her adorable friend and started for Baia Domezia, down the coast from Formia. Not far out of town, on my descent from a mountainside village, a strange mirage appeared. Like a towering ship on the horizon. A device appeared, as if gliding on sails, like nothing I had ever seen before. So peculiar. I froze in disbelief. I rubbed my eyes. It was clouded in a summer haze. Maybe I was wrong. NO way I was going to let it pass me on the road. But all strange curiosities were demystified when I heard a man's voice from high up on a double decker bicycle.

"Yea man! Ciao Bello! No oil! No oil!" he shouted enthusiastically, fist in the air. This guy was unreal. He turned the pedals of two bikes stacked atop each other. He was the man on a flying carpet passing me on a metaphysical escapade. He was here to remind me of the righteousness in what we were doing. He was, no doubt, on his own personal crusade, which in this case, right now, was to boost my spirit and assure me I had chosen the right direction through these winds of change.

Ep. 4
Mignano's Paradise

Days lacerated by unwanted strain. Landscape panoramas intercepted by asphalt. Discouragement replayed itself in two busy lanes. This daily drudgery had lasted over a week. Soon, though, I would reach the coast. I had visions of immersing my body into the cool, brisk sea. Break the heat. Beat the habits. Throw my body in and just let it float around under the sun, engulfed by underwater sounds. A sandy pilgrim ready to be cleansed. Hours of accumulated excitement forged on the Way. After mounting a small dune, though, I was stupefied. The image below was demoralizing. I was crestfallen. There were thousands, maybe millions of people cluttered onto every square inch of sand. An entire coastline saturated with chairs, towels, and umbrellas.

Middle Italians had me in unanticipated astonishment. The Mediterranean coast was a repulsive manifestation of ugliness. Deckchairs brought out every morning. Patches of sand used like front lawns. Other patches as landfills.

"These people pay for these fucking rigs?" was my initial, horrified thought. I couldn't let myself believe it. So many cronies flocking to these narrow strips, only to defile them like seagulls. But there *were* so many who wanted it.

70 kilometres of these generic stations until Napoli. All the way, thousands of deck chairs and tanning beds covered with corpses holding mirrors to blacken their already bronzed skin. The excess fat of modern Western culture. The words of my friends in Mignano came back to me, "It's so beautiful, you must go!"

What the hell were they talking about? This was far from beautiful. The south of Italy was poor, people said. Yet, these beach clans were overweight. They weren't ashamed of their cellulite wobbling from a turkey's beak. I was prepared for beaches with big crowds, but not half of Napoli. Bewildered, still in shock, I couldn't believe it. They came at breakfast and stayed until after sunset, bringing enough food to satisfy a small town for a week, under an awning and covered in shade. Everything from lasagna and arancini to long sandwiches, cutlets, eggplant parmigiana, and large bottles of Coke and Fanta. While I rinsed the perspiration from my body, the locals battled food sweats.

I stomped my Crocs into the damp, compact portions of the beach's never-ending sandy lane. One thing brought a fresh, more optimistic outlook in the face of this ongoing atrocity. In North America, boys were bullied for being overweight. Girls battled depression stemming from images in magazines and ostracization by schoolmates. They were outcasts for their weight. On these beaches, four hundred pounds didn't matter. Every person was a human, side by side. Old mate wanted to traipse around the beach with his junk squeezed into a pair of underwear. Let his belly hang way down. He felt liberated enough to exhibit himself to the world. I admired his confidence and freedom. Awful for the eye but refreshing to one's perspective.

Judgement existed in every corner back home. First, I was weak, targeted as a fairy with a high-pitched voice and long

36

hair. Then, shamed for being small, bony, and passive. Transferring schools, I rose to six feet and turned to punk rock and dirty hip-hop. Every turn brought new, abject opinions. Non-stop ridicule and antipathy from one set of ears to another. About everything. The ball-cap. How I wore the ball-cap. The clothing. The slang. The weed. The skateboarding. People labelled me a hellion and deadbeat, left to wither in urban alleys as a beggar or addict or both. Adults held an astonishing lack of discernment for the hormones and idle hands of teenage boredom. A kid who fantasized about more than his street and school. A kid that rushed from disconnection to explore whatever might exist beyond the banalities of normalcy. Running to escape judgement and its biases. Countless hours dodging policemen, raisings fists to superficiality. Stuck in a blue-collar cesspool of mediocrity. It was my sacred duty to make Dad proud by securing a comfortable life. Even if that meant abandoning dreams and any hope of self-expression. Throughout my adolescence, I sympathized with Kafka's characters and the judgements they faced. Nonetheless, everything I despised before my days on this trail arrived in Europe.

"But you speak English," they would say. "You have nothing to worry about. Your life must be so easy." Rage stirred in me. I couldn't resist rebuking them for their ignorant spiels. Admonishing them for their own poor choices. I craved the absence of judgement. Yet I was quick to condemn the actions of others. It was hard to admit and harder to change. I didn't want to pontificate about right and wrong. On this walk, humbling myself went hand in hand with letting go. Let go of everything. The body acceptance on these beaches impressed and inspired my heart.

* * *

Europe was where Greeks created Democracy. Socrates gave lectures. It was, for a time, the pinnacle of human achievement. The vestiges of Roman Imperialism were the envy of the world for more than a millennium until Michelangelo broke the mould. The foundations of civilization were under my feet. Roadworks from Alexandria and Tehran to London and Paris, Cadiz and Lisbon. These roads led to an exchange of ideas and eventually an age of enlightenment, then, the revolts of 1848. Centuries of education, equality, and politeness gave this place an unmistakable identity. Character formed through blood, struggle, and death. One either adapted, as a chameleon, or faced the consequences.

It was my third day on the Camino Way, and we had arrived in Zubiri. I hurried to the little supermarket for food, knowing I might get a donation bunk at the albergue if I was early enough. We'd been told by other pilgrims that along the Way, in some places, there were albergues where we could give donations instead of flat rates. This meant I didn't have to camp. This meant I could afford a night in a bed. What I didn't expect was the welcoming committee waiting beside the donation box.

"Hey, how much did you give?" someone demanded a nanosecond after my coins clanged together inside the large, wooden box. Amos and Cosimo stood behind me. Both dropped their coins in the box like I did.

"Sorry?" I asked, confused.

"The minimum donation is seven euros," the man replied contemptuously.

"Is that right? Seven euros, huh?" I retorted with equal disdain, a touch graver. He readied himself for a fight, but I wasn't going to let it pass. In all my years travelling, even if I was on this spiritual trail, I had never been shy speaking out against misguided ignorance. "Can't really say how much there was. I donated everything I could," I paused before adding, "It was all I could afford."

"You need to put seven euros inside," he said sternly. He stared at me and scoffed, "If you can afford to get drunk on the street and goof around, you can afford seven euros."

"Sorry, I am not exactly sure what you mean by that. If I get drunk?"

"I know you guys. I see you all the time. You come here, you give nothing, then you go outside and buy beers and wine and get drunk and cause problems." Amos and Cosimo stood a couple of feet behind. They must have felt my wings spread and talons tighten because each of them grabbed one of my shoulders.

"Listen, bro, I don't know who you think you are judging me, but I gave what I could. That's what it says, DONATION!

38

Read the fucking box."

"You Americans are all the same, you come in acting like you are better than the rest of us." He just crossed the barrier. First, I was a drunk. Then he used my accent to assume I was from the States.

"How the fuck you like it if I call you Mexican, or Portuguese, or Turkish, huh?"

"Yea, big, bad American attitude, you don't want to call me Mexican, okay. Trust me," he taunted, as his cheeks flushed with blood. Mine weren't far behind. He was a bull, ready to blow smoke for the next hour. I refused to back off.

"Listen, buddy, I'm not American, okay? I am Canadian. You don't get to throw your assumptions around like this. You wanna tell me I've got all the money because I'm not a poor Spaniard like you? That I'm a lucky, rich American tourist? You don't know me. Look around: I'm the only one here carrying my tent." I pulled it out and threw it on the ground. "See that! That's dirt on the tent, because I use it! I slept next to a hobo in a bunch of bushes in Montpellier a week ago on my way to the Camino. How many times have you slept in a bush, huh?"

"You Americans don't know what it is to be poor."

"I told you, I'm friggin' Canadian. How arrogant can you be? I don't know poor? Man, I've been traveling for six years now. Six! And the only way I can earn money is in shit jobs on fuckin' minimum wage. You got no idea about me, Chico!" Dani came running when he heard the commotion.

"Come on, Freddi, it's okay," he coaxed.

"No! No. It is not okay. This bully wants to go around making all kinds of assumptions, calling people all kinds of shit. This guy has no right to be here. I wanna talk to someone, a fucking manager or something."

"Oh yea, is that right, you wanna talk to a manager! I'm the only manager you get to talk with, okay?"

"Freddi, back off, come on, grab your bag," Amos tried to calm me. Dani nodded pleadingly.

"I can't believe you, Amos. Come on, he just called me an American, he called us Americans! The guy is clearly a prejudicing dick."

"Yea, but whatever, leave it alone," is the last thing I heard before all three of them surrounded me and tried to restrain me. I reached for my pack, heaved it onto my shoulders like so many times before, spun, and then stormed out the double doors while passing other pilgrims trying to enter the building. I bought a liter of San Miguel and took a seat on a cement wheelchair ramp. Halfway through the bottle and 30 minutes later, Amos and Dani arrived.

"Hey man, you okay?"

I shrugged and took a sip.

"I spoke to the guy, in Spanish," Dani said. "And you can go in and sleep there if you want."

"Yea, whatever, thanks." My face couldn't have been more austere.

"It wasn't worth it, he doesn't understand. And who cares, man, why bother fighting?"

"Because he had no right to ask us for a minimum donation. That's bullshit. If they want seven bucks, they should ask for seven bucks. They wanna push us around. You don't understand how many times I faced this kind of thing travelling in Asia and Africa. They do it because they can get away with it, because nobody stands up to them."

* * *

It took two days to walk the sandy Way into Napoli. First thing was a pizza. Not so incredible that it changed my life, but it was good. My concierge friend from Mignano agreed to host me for a night. Showering at the clerk's flat did to my body what Technetronic had back in grade school. The girls busting their bodies against each other to the music, bent over like bridges. I noticed for the first time their gyrating movements, their crotches bouncing in my face. The wild expulsion of negativity. I lost myself when C and C Music Factory shouted for us to sweat. Excited dancing. So intense we forgot where we were. Some of us even tried to forget who we were.

The next day, clothes hung everywhere on tiny, metal balconies. High, ancient buildings dusted in charcoal and graffiti. Sculptures burned brightly with pink spray paint. The rustic neglect inspired adoration. This was my kind of city. But after numerous attempts, the many churches refused to host me. The nefarious reputation of this city had me frazzled about sleeping outdoors. Around eleven at night, I walked as far as I could from the center. Hours before sunrise, I crashed in the bushes of a closed elementary school.

Walking on these trails, life became imagination on the move. At thirty-three, I was around the same age as Jesus when he left on his pilgrimage. He fasted but walked less. Getting older robbed travelling of its beauty for me. Everywhere, youthful bodies running around. Some, like Amos and Cosimo, were fresh out of high school. Comparatively, I was headed for the nursing home. It wasn't just the idea of reaching sixty and having no money to retire. My body wouldn't be able to handle sleeping in a tent, hidden by some bushes every night, for too many more years. If I wanted to travel, I would need enough financial support for a decent bed.

My whole system began rejecting the hardships. Wild nights of endless pint glasses consumed on the road, in parks, and inside hundred-meter gorges. Sporadic cities. Too many to count; so many chances to say hello, and why wouldn't I? Walking on the Way, I felt constancy for a change. The only important decision I had was taking the next step. Every morning, I was obligated to wake up and walk. Then, choose to reflect or write or dream. Strenuous and conflicting at many corners. Loneliness that seemed too tough to bear. But all parts of my own objective. The Way was important. An accomplishment I'd set for myself. The world was far away. Before this journey, a normal life was getting old, getting married, having kids, paying off a mortgage. Preparing for the golden years of a proletarian. I was light years behind. But out here, on the road, I was at the top of my game. The kind of traveller few locals had ever met. My comrades were more likely to meet unexpected and early retirements in a wooden box than to be successfully settled in suburbia. Unceremonious. Dropped in the ground and gone. Easily forgotten.

When I was younger, history, civilizations, geography, migratory patterns, our past relative to our present, the classic myths and novels speculating purpose, the philosophical treatises—I ignored all these things because I was fixated on being a chaotic fucker. Like the Pappas brothers who left Australia to become professional vert skaters in America. I wanted to push myself into the darkness, past fear. I spent too much time idolizing the wrong people, focusing on shopping cart races, ollying over bodies, and leaping from buildings on the run from sirens. I spent my early twenties apprenticing as a chef, chasing drug-induced fantasies, hip-hop concerts, and catchy rhymes. Since getting on the road, more and more I wanted to drink history. The European continent was a vast, unlimited background, and I was stupid and ignorant. One of my best friends in high school called me that once because I couldn't spell. She was right. But I didn't give a fuck then. Somehow, hanging olives brought harmony. The chime of church bells carried my thoughts to a time before watches. Soaking in ancient baths helped me register how lucky, privileged, and entitled I was. I had wasted so much of my life chasing false idols and the wrong dreams.

I stared at the line for one small Napolese pizzeria, astounded by the number of sheep waiting for their pie. Everyone says the best pizza comes from Napoli. And once upon a time, someone made the first pizza in these very streets, topped with the world's first mozzarella. These narrow alleys for horse carts and donkey trains forged pizza's fame. It made sense. It was like prosciutto. Impossible to imagine this cured ham could be better somewhere else. Those guys in Parma had been doing that shit for centuries. Everyone tried to copy them, but the intelligent knew that the best came from the heartland.

When I learned that a city had been ruined by a pyroclastic flow in Italy, I had to investigate further. Bodies encapsulated, covered in ash, preserved like mummified corpses. Protected from air and greasy hands. Safeguarded for almost two thousand years. I wondered if I could manage to get there. I didn't want to break my walk and hitch a ride. I would walk the entire Way, or I wouldn't go. Once that team in Mignano had tempted me with a beautiful beach, Pompeii became part of the Istanbul Way. Only an hour from the elementary school where I was camping. Months of history classes could be absorbed walking through its old city.

"Hey, you want a lift?" someone shouted in a British accent. The offer came from a stunning Italian woman as I climbed a long, roller coaster mountain road. Two other beguiling women rode with her, all in their late twenties.

"I'm walking." I avoided looking at them. I feared they would notice my exhaustion.

She persisted, "We can see that, but do you want a lift?"

"Well, to be honest, if you had a shower," I chuckled uncomfortably. "Well, now you probably don't want me in the car."

The driver leaned across her friend's lap and spoke while blocking traffic, "We don't mind, really." She seemed so mellow. They were all so fit. Tanned and on vacation. A story awaited me in that car. She said again, "If the shower was ours, we would." They were likely staying at a glamorous beach house with a resident DJ, some Grey Goose, Laphroaig 18, and a rooftop pool.

"Thanks anyway, I'll keep walkin'." The hollow, pointless integrity left me lamenting to myself.

"OK, suit yourself, ciao." They drove off, honked twice, and waved out the windows.

Numerous times, people demanded I stop in Amalfi. A rest at the top of the long cathedral stairs for lunch, then a quick bath in the sea off the pier – with a picturesque backdrop – was enough. On the coast, the typical male was barely knee deep in water, wearing a pair of undies, sporting a large, shiny watch, dark sunglasses, and a gold chain dangling a crucified Jesus. And there was the *pelegrini*, or pilgrim, who everyone took a long moment to notice. Crumpled straw hat, matted, unmanaged beard, white button-down stained with the dirt and sweat of four long, intensely hot days. Board shorts worn along the Camino de Santiago, a year before, horribly stained and faded. A pair of dirty, once-white socks in cheap, plastic shoes. Then, hanging like a limp body from my filthy pack, a smelly, bug-infested, earth-soiled pillow. Drenched in sweat, crumbs in my beard from lunch, a litre-and-a-half bottle of water in my hand. I received daunting, abrasive stares from captivated crowds of women adjusting their tube tops and men pulling on their junk bare chested, glistening from tanning oil, behind crucified Jesus. I fled Amalfi and its decadent image of paradise.

Ep. 5
Combing Maiori

The road ran along the contour of the peninsula's hip. More bitumen. Another vertical ascent. I noticed the sea distancing itself from me. This bothered me, so I stopped. There was a small speck of shade on the public beach. I recalled a recent quote from a pamphlet or billboard: *It all starts at Maiori.* Looking down at the beach, I questioned myself, "Why do I have to keep moving – what's the worst that could happen if I stopped?" Every now and again, a pilgrim had to slow down and remind himself to absorb his surroundings.

It was hard to ignore the dozens of dark, oiled, voluptuous women sunbathing in revealing bikinis. These beaches had more curves than the alphabet in cursive. And more celluloid than an American buffet on a Saturday night. The busy beaches of Italy struck a different tone for me than other parts of the world. Maybe it was a South Italian thing. An unparalleled energy of sex, wafting its odor in all directions. Guys proudly grabbed their cocks in their skin-tight undies, squeezing them while they talked with friends. The women, with legs wide open, squeezed and adjusted their tits while swinging and tying their hair. The famous Italian body language became more primitive and unfettered at the beach. The weather was stinking hot. Appealing people. Lubed bodies. Half naked. Those around me appeared so happy in their cliques. Confronting this urge to belong was conflicting. And invasive. And distracting. In truth, I wasn't even that interested in *belonging*. Yet, I tormented myself with doubt and inadequacy. Situated in a small corner of shade, I made a panino and escaped into my book. A vivid tale of Huck Finn on the Mississippi. A book that Amos passed to me as he left our Camino Way behind. After falling into that childhood adventure, detached from my self-deprecation, only a few pages in, a man interrupted me.

"Scusami, tu sei Italiano?"

"Canadese."

"Ah, well, I must ask you to move. Sorry for that."

"Of course, you do. Why wouldn't you?" I relented,

annoyed. I pulled the zen pilgrim from within and slipped into a calm, pensive state, "Capito, capito," as I packed my things.

"Only two meters that way, my friend." He had no idea how many hours I had searched for this space. He needed the area for his beach equipment. I got that. It wasn't about him. Even at a secluded beach way back before Amalfi, the sun was so hot I couldn't relax. I had to sit on a rock against a ridge wall. And soon after, I became hungry. It was always something. A restlessness I couldn't break.

"Dove sei a Canada?"

"L'approssimo di Toronto."

"Bene, bene, and why are you here?" he asked, noticing that I didn't fit in.

"Io pelegrini di camino, Roma a Istanbul."

"Really?! No bus, no trano, no auto-stop?"

"A piedi."

"Well, I commemorate you for walking this peninsula. It's nothing like the Santiago de Compostella!"

We talked shit until the sun slid behind the massive mountain summit that cornered Maiori's cove. He gathered his gear and carried on with me in broken intervals. The kayaks and deck chairs were his life's marrow. I was both impressed and disgusted. For him, I applauded his entrepreneurial perceptiveness. Find a means, and the masses would drop stacks on needless shit.

"So, I want to invite you to a fiesta tonight. It's August tenth," he suggested. I stared back at him blankly. "And it's full moon."

"Do you think I can," I pointed to the rock face and sand, and before I could finish, he interrupted.

"Put your tent?"

"Si."

"Yea, per che non; for one night anyway."

"Si. But police – problema cone polizia?"

"Non, non, no problem as long as *you* are no problem."

"Ciaro. And dove sei la fiesta?" I imagined it was back in town at his place.

"Here! Cui!" His ability to own the beach was impressive.

"Ah, so maybe I won't be sleeping after all," I laughed.

"Not late – 1am maybe. I am Francis by the way, Francesco in Italian, but on the beach, I am called Chico."

"I'm Freddi Woomba! But on the beach, they call me 'out of place'."

After he left, two girls locked eyes and ran toward one another in the sand. They shouted words back and forth, kissing and hugging. One was dark and dangerous, the other paler, with big, curly afro hair. Afro Curls introduced her friend to everyone else. I resisted gawking at them. Chico's fest was at 9:30, he said. The sun was descending. At the same time, I noticed the very dark, Sicilian-looking woman with a confident presence – like everyone in a 400-kilometer radius – taking snaps of the mountain hiding our sun, inches away from me. With my poor and intimidated Italian, I attempted communication.

"Tu tienes la ora?" I asked. She told me the time in her broken English. "Is my Italian that bad – is it that obvious I'm not from Italy?"

She laughed and nodded without hesitation, "Oh, my English, yes, yes, no good."

Trying to re-word for her I repeated myself, "So can you tell I am not Italian?"

"Spanish maybe?" she responded. My twenty Spanish words would fix that. "You spoke in Spaneeshh, so maybe, non?"

"I did?"

"Tu tienes."

"Ah, so como sidiche in Italia?"

"Tu tieni."

"Ah ha! I can see why you thought that, yea."

She appeared open to the possibility of pitfalls, and I wanted to dig in with some dialogue. Her energy attracted me. I glanced through her friends, about my age. As they moved further down the beach, away from me, I sank back into Huck Finn. She reminded me of someone. I couldn't relax until I unravelled the mystery. Two couples nearby rubbed each other, dry humping. It was then I remembered. It was my Hungarian friend from back in India who had introduced me to that word, *pilgrim,* and the Camino de Santiago. The Camino was never far away, I thought. My mind raced away from Huck's river raft toward our contrasting skin colours. The idea excited me, pressed up against each other, just like the dry humpers, as I had been with that

Hungarian back in India. I would do nothing less than beg for this woman to dance over me with her bikini bottom as close to my teeth as possible, just out of reach. My arms pinned by her knees. Me with a coltish grin. Her vagina's scent in my nostrils. She would peck at my face as I tried to bite at her tongue.

I approached this jungalist and her friends. I avoided her eyes, afraid of revealing my own, the naughty desires within them.

"I guess you speak pretty decent English." It wasn't a question, though it sounded like one.

"No, I don't, it's quite bad."

"Okay, yea, sorry, well this doesn't have to be too complicated," I joked. The whole group laughed. Ah, great, a stroke of luck. They all spoke sarcasm. I explained my predicament. I needed some vino rosso like any sensible bloke. My pack was an unnecessary weight. I needed a break from it.

"Could you please, I mean, do you guys mind watchin' it for a bit?" I asked.

Jungalist responded with unimpressed hostility, "Well, I don't think, we still going to meet more friend, sorry. We will have a..." She refused my pathetic attempt at making friends.

One of the lads interrupted her, "It's no problem."

"Quindicci minuti."

"It's no issue for me," he proclaimed. This guy was unscathed, impetuous. Dark and Intoxicating, on the other hand— I assumed she saw something else. A horny imposter, perhaps, which wasn't wrong. I grabbed the cash from my pack and dropped the fucker like a sack of potatoes, relieved. On my way up the stairs and away from the beach, Chico approached me.

"Hey pilgrim, dove vei?"

Level-headed with a melodious voice, Chico was sharper than many I had met since Rome. He knew I was no beach bum at first glance. He paid attention, read me well; he was a weathered traveller himself. Men in this region spoke in a language of confrontation, in my face with loud and predictable words. The people of Southern Europe had a reputation for being chill, laid back, and slow moving. Their boisterousness must have come from espresso. Chico spent his summers working Maiori, he told me, accommodating tourists. After the busy season, he went to Spain for winter. He lived by the season, moving at his own pace.

His character reflected that. He was surrounded by men like race car drivers. Vehicles passed narrow cliff sides like bullet trains hanging on two wheels, gliding over death. Hands swinging everywhere, including the handlebars of Vespas, lit like dynamite sticks. And the people spoke constantly at every opportunity. It was exhausting, albeit entertaining. Having a conversation with a Southern Italian man resembled the small aftershocks of an earthquake, tremors rumbling through my head and shaking my brain. Chico was an outsider. I saw some of myself in him. When he invited me to his fest, I had to go.

An older woman had joined the group when I returned from the bottle shop. She was no different, snarling at me. All the women snarled at me. A protective mechanism against their bold-faced men. Or else they had gelato-sharing boyfriends, to visit the cinema with and share Sunday dinners.

"No one had to sacrifice their life to save mi borsa?" I approached the team with my new bottle of wine and thanked them. They laughed and introduced themselves, but for the older woman and the jungalist, who remained silent, suspicious.

Then, "Gia," said the jungalist – Gia, like the famous model, I repeated in my head.

The older woman stared at me. She hadn't said a word. It was either stare or not look at all around here. She spoke at me, not to me.

"So, YOU are the pilgrim?" she queried. The conversation between everyone stopped dead the instant she said the word, *pilgrim.* Everyone noticed. Curiosity sparked like lightning. This pilgrimage concept was popular in Italy. I had met many Italians on the Camino Way aside from Dani and Cosimo. The same questions came that had flooded my route thus far. One typical question that killed me every time.

"You walked from Canada?" the older woman asked.

"No, I rode a dolphin!" Her eyes nearly popped out of their sockets when I told her how many years it had been since I left Canada for the road.

"What about your family?" she gasped. Pain had erupted in her voice. Once she started, I wondered when she would stop. In Italy *everyone* asked about family. Did I have any? Did they

48

love me? Did I love them? After waiting an eternity, dark and thin, jungalist Gia, who paid little attention, broke the silence.

"We are going to dinner now – will you come?" she offered. I had eaten a couple sandwiches, terrified of the menu card prices.

"No, I'm alright, thanks anyway."

"So, I guess, we see you later." Her voice softened, "My friend said there is party here tonight."

"Si," I replied. So, she *was* coming. Fantastic news! "Un piacere concetera a tutti, ciao."

One by one, a group of people formed near the shore. All in their fifties and sixties. Bumming the odd cigarette that walked by, I stayed in the shadows and sipped my wine. I decided to admire the stars, sea breeze, and sand between my fingers until I was sure Chico had arrived. Four men joined a circle of old-school beachcombers. They brought drums and a guitar. A circle of percussionists began booming and banging, rhythmically.

"Pilgrim! Hello!" Chico took a drum and sat beside one of the other men to make room for me. The guy's face beside him was polished by the wind. After I sat down, he pulled a tambourine from under the box they sat on. A third man began drumming, and a fourth as well. Chico stole the lead, riding slightly off-beat, through a door the others had opened. He revelled in his role as the leader. With the help of his crew, they created a steady flow of unrelenting, irresistible trance music. The melodies unfolded like ribbons from a mandrel, working their way through my ears until I fell into the nod. When the music stopped, I bolted back upright like a spring. The tambourine man grinned widely at me.

"So, where you from?" His English was brilliant, like Chico's. Between their accents and their music choice, I became more and more convinced I wasn't with a typical community. My first guess was eastern European, maybe Romanian.

"Canada, but what about *you*?" I asked, puzzled and intrigued, expecting something uncommon from his band of gypsies. Maybe Moldova.

"I'm from here, nearby."

"Really? And why you speakin' such decent English, bro?"

"I lived in America a long time ago, and England too." He was a painter. As we spoke, I noticed the woman with the big head of beautiful curls. And then her sinister friend, the jungalist, just behind. The defiant ardour of her shadow sank into the night air. She was barely visible, but for her sparkling lips. Her movements scolded my inhibitions, my hormones heightened by the afternoon's constant sex party. I watched her from my right eye while speaking to my new friend. In gallant steps down the sandy, red carpet, she approached us. Everyone kept to themselves as Afro Curls opened a conversation with me. She told me she once lived in Montreal as a performer. She wasn't the only performer, either. She got up on the stage and got busy, and their friend, Gia, got busy on it as well, dancing beside her.

Wine dripped its way through the corridors of my body. Words fell through time and in a perfect parabolic oval of communal fire. The drums batted and banged behind us. Chico and Afro Curls spoke in Italian. I noticed Gia, pensive and alone, peering at the sky. My moment. My window had arrived.

"Ah, and where you from then, now that you know my life story."

"Roma, we are all Roman except Alana – Afro Curls."

"Right." The word escaped my throat into the air and stretched as a giraffe. "And you guys are here for vacation, I guess?"

"Si, for a week." Two of those days could be well spent walking with me to Salerno, but I fought it off and listened to her instead. Her English accent was enchanting. I loved how she stumbled for words, sliding her lips along with her mind, mixing Spanish, Italian, and English all together.

She spoke about reading and the value of reading. I could have listened through constant rainfall without distraction. When we arrived at the Americans, she bowed her hands exactly the way Dani did back on the Camino. Said the same things as well.

"For me, the Americans start, of course," she bowed her hands again before carrying on, "with Charles Bukowski." That was it. I was lovestruck.

"You're wrong." Her voice was shrill. Her stoic words slapped me like a blunt object. I froze. "You need to go home." I looked at her with the dumbfounded face of a kangaroo staring into a set of flood lights. She continued, "I listened while the

50

others asked you things. You have so many experiences, all those years and on the Camino also. You need to go home. Stop moving – process. Let the years soothe and find their space." I was speechless, pining for a counterargument. "From there you can find your voice. Only from there. You're lost until then."

This Way to Istanbul *was* finding my voice. A long period of time to rehash past years and find the Way for my future. She was unsympathetic, telling me to return home. My mom would have loved her. I questioned myself: was this pilgrimage what I needed to bring me resolution? Again, she looked me dead in the face and read my future from the scroll of a page she saw beyond my eyes.

Silence. Awkward silence.

"You won't find anything until you go home. I'm sorry," she advised with genuine empathy and concern. She pulled out a spill of hash to soften the blow. I poured her some more wine. We smiled at each other. Her first registration of my looks. Her body language flirted with me. It was too dark to see her, but my attraction to her was impossible to miss. I avoided her eyes, but my eyes frequented her face. To occupy myself, I rubbed my head, pulled at my beard and moustache. The hash hit me when I started explaining my thoughts on *The Old Man and the Sea*, how it was about a survivalist winding down for a long rest. My immediate thoughts were interrupted by a memory of a young, British woman telling me that I was an open book.

"Of course, you like Hemingway – he's macho and sexist. And you probably love *On the Road*, too, every pubescent boy's favourite tale." She persecuted me further before settling it up, "Old Man and the Sea is different."

Maybe I was shedding my boyhood fantasies. To me, Hemingway was a grandfather. He provided all the advice anyone could need. And Kerouac, a deadbeat father who popped in now and then, passing me an inheritance no one would want. Competing desires. Wanting both isolation and community. A battle I fought often.

Gia's friends called her, anxious to leave.

"You could stay," I looked her in the eyes then away quickly.

"Yes, yes, good, good." As if she forgot English. Her friends pulled her away like a piece of their vanity.

"We can chill here, talk a while longer," I protested.

She nodded and kissed both my cheeks. She didn't want to admit something. Or she was hiding something. Maybe it was that she'd been waiting to finally be rid of me. Chico came to say goodbye. My shoulders slouched. My acuteness dulled. We talked a moment, or two, or three, with his drumming gypsy friend.

"Pilgrim, I am in south Spain all winter. You are welcome anytime."

"Gotta contact me first," I quipped as I put my poetry book in his hands with my email. "Then we'll see. I'll leave it in your hands." I knew he wouldn't. The beach became silent, but for the couples kissing. I knew I wouldn't hear from him. I knew I wouldn't hear from Gia either. I was alone on this course. I knew that well, though I tried to ignore it with everything. Tried to believe that things could be unpredictable.

The only thing left to do was set my tent and slug back the last of the wine. The hash had me mellow, glowing like a Halloween pumpkin. A couple in blankets, on the sand, not far away. An old parody by NOFX trickled into my mind. The lyrics leaped vividly into my head. Their fantastic humour. It was Fat Mike's perception of middle America that encouraged and corrupted me when I was young, insulting all the pretentious behaviours of life's most pompous deceitful bastards.

Once the tent was up, I popped some wine down my throat. Wine Chico had left with me. I lip synced:

Together in the sand,
We walked hand and hand,
On the beach fronts,
She smiled at me, as she tightly held my hand;
I had my fingers up her...

And I began to nod off, off with the sound of swells striking the sandy shore. A smiling face appeared, blocking the stars.

"Hey! You're blocking the view, buddy! Either move or slide down here with me," I said, loud enough to send vibrations through all the neighbouring sweethearts.

She got down beside me and kissed my cheek.

"I miss anything?"

Ep. 6
A Comedian

If that termagant had returned, it could have been the two of us walking from Maiori. But she left without turning her head.

"And why the fuck did I care," I prodded myself as I bundled my gear. "Better than that, did I?" It was the touch. A moment of war, excitement, and dopamine. The eruption on that first kiss. Hotter than kettle steam. Our heads spinning with exhilaration. Hands ready to rip into each other's swimming bottoms.

"Now, pay no mind to this shit, Freddi," I told myself. If I walked a good, solid day, I could make it to the outskirts of Salerno. But I couldn't stop my thoughts from fixating on Gia and my lascivious compulsions. Testosterone peaked in the morning. And the beach filled with nearly naked, pleasure-seeking people again. A speed bike and a glittering, neon cyclist passed by.

"Buen Camino!" I shouted. The squealing rubber told me he had slammed his brakes.

"Ciao man, come va?" He asked me where I was from and greeted me a second time in broken English. "I go that way in Istanbul couple years finished, bellissimo! But, you go by foot, no?"

"Yea, three months I guess."

He tipped his neon beanie. "You cannot. It must be so hard. I could not walk," he grimaced.

I shrugged, "I'd say the same about cycling, hombre." My legs could handle hours of walking, but one full day of pedalling uphill curtailed any capricious ideas of cycling. Some were destined to traverse the Way on wheels, others by foot.

"Where do you stay, this night?" he asked me with compassion in his voice.

"In my tent. I mean, that's the status quo." I shrugged.

"State of what?" he asked me in confusion.

"Never mind. I'll probably sleep in a park on the outside of Salerno. Do you know of one?"

He got on his phone right away. I heard the classic word, *pronto,* from the other end. My cyclist friend spoke in excited fury. His words were unintelligible. Cars ripped passed us. A few honked. The sea sparkled under the sun. I glanced at it and back to him with a broad smile. I sat down before he finished.

"I have some place for *you*!" He put his hand on my shoulder. "You can have shower. Good, no?" He beamed with a proud grin. I thanked him for his selfless act and shook his hand.

"How do we meet up? Unless you want to double me on that thing?" I laughed jovially. We chuckled together looking at his skinny racing tires. I took his phone number.

"You call 7pm, I pick you up."

* * *

Mornings enriched by walking. Dani's voice said, "Leave it in the past." He was right, just keep walking. The thing that donation box guy missed, though, was that without the pilgrims, there would be no them. Our community forced collaboration. People made mistakes and lost their cool, but the coolest knew when to walk. Or, hard as it was to accept, nod and smile. Each day marshalled enough excitement to warrant positivity. The unified power of countless pilgrims, despite diverse backgrounds, offered an opportunity for profound learning. We had limitless time on the Way. All it took was hearing the name of someone's home country, asking about their feelings on colonialism, and a good hour of enlightening discussion awaited us. My favourite times were shared with the lads I made snow angels with in Roncesvalles. We caught up to one another, dropping back or forging ahead to meet others, then reported back. This was how our family circle grew.

We arrived early at the outer brick paths of Pamplona. I'd heard a great deal about this city. And what greater way to explore it than high on a communal buzz, in the best of moods, with my favourite people? A sunny day as the early morning clouds dissipated. A united band of wanderers, full of laughter, grateful for life. We wanted nothing more than to exist in this moment, one step at a time. The Way life was lived.

Pamplona expanded fast from the outskirts. From quaint dwellings in the countryside to long lanes of three-story apartment complexes with ground cafes. Pilgrims exited small bars with white plates. They sat on cheap, metallic chairs on the red-bricked street, tasting portions of food. I hungered for years to try Pamplona's authentic *pintxo*. One- or two-bite wonders. It was the Basque word for tapas. The previous villages were too small for anything more than tortilla de patatas. These pintxos sat neatly stacked in display fridges. No better time for this than before siesta. A colourful mosaic of exquisite mouthfuls danced before my eyes, tantalizing my taste buds. Along with a pintxo, one had to drink a *cana* – a half-pint of beer. I walked under a colourful awning and into a lively little bar. Near my outdoor table, where I took a *croqueta de bacalao*, sat two girls I had met along the Way. A little Dane with freckles and her friend, an Italian kindergarten teacher. Dani arrived behind me and put his hands on my shoulders.

"Cana!" he shouted. I turned with my dish and beer, nearly losing them. I pulled my chair next to the Dane.

"Been waiting for this baby!"

"Waiting for what?"

"Pintxo!" as I bit into the breaded roll of cod and potato. It was magnificent. I carried on, telling them about the time I worked in a restaurant called, 'Pintxo,' a Spanish restaurant run by a crew of Mexicans using Montreal standards. "It won an award in Montreal."

Quail egg on toast with roasted pepper and pesto. Jamon, manchego, and free olives with the beer. Our table had grown. Cosimo arrived with Amos and others who crossed our paths. A tasting frenzy erupted once the others saw what I was doing. They raced for pintxos. Our pilgrim dynamic was clear after three full days of the Way. It was a social uprising every afternoon. With Dani and Cosimo, I broke off to the centre of Pamplona for a few bottles of San Miguel from a *tienda* – local market.

"We should drop our bags before getting another bottle, Freddi," Dani paused to look around. "Where the cazzo is Cosimo?"

I grabbed more bottles, "We don't have to finish them now. I mean, might as well have them close by," I smirked.

He grabbed a bottle from my hands, smirking back. "Where is Cosimo?" We stood a few feet from a *mirador* – viewpoint – looking over the surrounding city below us. This old town was built high up, and we elevated ourselves on the edge of a brick wall looking out over the entire region.

"Che Palle!" he exclaimed when he saw Cosimo in a motley group. Cosimo had a guitar in his hands, singing in Italian. Every time his fingers caught the strings, my heart throbbed. And every nearby girl felt the same. Dani and I looked at each other, because Cosi, the beauty of this lad was, he didn't give a holy hell about any of it. He played. He played for everyone. He played from his own agonizing soul. But, unlike some, he didn't do it to grab ass. He was an eighteen-year-old more aware of his distress than any adult I'd met. I'd sat beside him on the Way more than once with tears in his eyes, guitar or no.

"Hey guys, I find guitar!" His smile was jubilant. Infectious. The kid was on fire, emanating a mammoth wave of positivity.

"Come on, man," Dani said in my direction. "We gotta find the albergue. I want to drop this fucking bag and take the sun!" He tugged on Cosimo's arm, grinning at the distinctly odd cast of characters around us. Cosi spoke to Dani in Italian as he handed the guitar back to a man against a brick wall. Dani turned to me.

"He says they can get some coke for us," he spoke with a doubtful air. "But for sure it will be shit. What you think, Freddi?" He looked at me as if he were being pulled into something, somewhat desperate for me to intervene.

"I say, I'd rather not snort talc. We're foreigners, maybe pilgrims, but still tourists, and tourists get ripped off. That's the way it is."

Dani agreed as I passed my beer to Cosi, "Beer is enough, no?"

In the old city centre, where the road dropped and a circle of bricks spun into a topographic spiral, Cosimo dropped my bottle. Broken glass echoed everywhere. I glanced back from the noise, then lowered my head and laughed.

"Gonna be a long one, eh, Dani?" He sighed.

A long row of beds, like a chicken battery. A vaulted ceiling with colourless, dirty walls. High slabs of parchment paper to divide the space enough to cram in the maximum number of bodies. The lighting was low, which gave it the sense of a bunker. No windows starved the room of any natural light. The only things with any character at all were the backpacks, wooden staves, boots, and all the hanging, sweat-perfumed socks.

"You won't stay?" Dani asked ironically.

"Oh yea, for sure," I replied ironically. "I ain't payin for this shit, brotha. I'll find a park for my tent." Cosimo asked Dani to translate.

Dani sighed, "I can't do this forever, cazzo, translating…"

I put my hand on Dani's shoulder, "You're a better man than I. But can you ask him to hurry the fuck up with unpacking so we can get back outside, out of this god-forsaken death hall they call an albergue?"

The young woman behind the main desk said goodbye to us all. She didn't mention anything about me leaving my pack behind without paying. Cosimo turned to reply and smacked his shoulder into the door frame. The lot of us laughed as we piled into the street. People walked in rows. A perfect, azure sky above us. The hottest hours had passed. Locals had finished their siestas. A cathedral tower rang five times. A waft of garlic hit my nose. Not a car to distract us. It was a traffic-free zone but for loading vehicles. We had our trusted San Miguel; the three of us were loose.

"When do the bulls run, is it soon?" Dani wondered in July.

"It's only a couple of weeks away. Wanna finish the Camino and come back?"

Cosimo said something in Italian, Dani translated. "He says he is ready to fuck a bull. That the bull is in trouble if Cosimo comes back here." A bronze statue, high on a pedestal appeared.

"Guys, what are we going to do now?"

Cosi spoke, pulling on Dani's shirt sleeve, rambling like a puppy needing a shit. "Guys?" he said in English.

I made a suggestion, "Think we should go meet some of these pilgrim ladies. Maybe that kindergarten teacher and Dane?"

Dani's head was up to the sky, breathing with an air of impatience, "Che palle! Cosimo what do you want?"

"Look. Is Hemingway!" Cosimo proclaimed. We all finally turned to the statue. We sat without a word between us, down at the feet of it, full of respect and deference.

"Pretty decent spot for a drink, I'd say. *To the written word, lads*!"

"To the written word!" the boys shouted, lifting their bottles with approval. Cosimo's face was childlike. His eyes glossed. He wobbled as though if trying to stand, he'd just fall back down with us. He tried anyway. I was right.

"You sure you wanna light that, Cosi?"

"What he say, Dani?" I asked after Cosi lifted his arm with his spliff in hand. Poor Dani. It had been three days of translation. Cosi could wail some gorgeous harmonies on his guitar and shower emotion with his Italian voice. But the kid was no linguist. And neither was I.

"Never mind," replied Dani. "He's a big boy. Besides, Freddi, if he pukes in the albergue, it will be very funny."

We sat under Hemingway, trying to channel even a bit of the strength and wisdom from his time in Pampolona.

"God, he really picked a spot here. Can you imagine how simple it must have been ninety years ago, Heyzeus!"

Dani looked up at him, "A lot of farm animals, I bet. Did you speak with the kindergarten teacher, Freddi?"

"Bro, you wanna talk girls while sitting here, under this great man? Speak about *A Farewell to Arms*, or Paris, or your bloody time in London, or Orwell and his bloody time in London. But girls?"

"Hey man, Hemingway was always talking about fucking the girls, no?"

Dani had a point.

"Yea, I spoke with her. She's got some serious cans, huh?" I laughed looking at Cosimo as he sang to a group of passing girls.

"Nevermind him," Dani replied to get my attention, "I think she is pretty cool. Maybe more than the others. What you think?"

"I think you like her boobs, and I think Cosimo isn't even using real words anymore." Dani assured me I was right.

We stumbled into the albergue late.

"I'll put my tent in the fucking toilet here, these guys won't mind. Donativo!" We entered the kitchen. After making spaghetti from kitchen leftovers, it was time to see the cute little

58

Dane lass.

"Don't do it!" Dani warned in a high whisper.

I wanted to share the spaghetti with her. I had to win her over with the spaghetti. Win a kiss with her, as well. End up in her single bed spooning the last couple hours before everyone arose. Once the place emptied, we could have it to ourselves, or so I imagined. She didn't share the idea and turned away from me to carry on sleeping. I returned to the kitchen and passed out beside my plate of half-eaten spaghetti.

She woke me up, "Hey Freddi? You alright?"

She had showered. She was excited and ready to walk. This was absurd, and a bit lame. Shortly after six, the room was ready to flood the trail. When I opened my eyes and saw her face, I felt a pang of guilt for making moves on her, for being a creep a few hours earlier.

"Come on, Freddi, it's no big deal. You were drunk. Why don't you get some more sleep?"

"Ah, yea, I should, but I didn't pay for a bunk last night." I sulked, groggy, dizzy, and embarrassed. "What time is it?"

"It's 6am. Go to my bed then, I'll bring you – even though you know where it is," she laughed. "You've probably forgotten already, huh?" She pulled my hand toward her. "Come on, Freddi."

I rose as she led me to her bunk. Her gear was packed beside her bed.

"Just let me put my boots on, okay?"

I collapsed in her bed while she finished her laces. I mumbled, "Thanks so much. I'm sorry, really, I was…"

"It's alright, just sleep now. See you later."

* * *

The cyclist brought me to somebody's two-bedroom flat. Inside, at the kitchen table, were two men, a woman, and her child. None of them acknowledged me. One man in his mid-forties stood and greeted my new cyclist friend after I had closed the door. The man brought a chair to the table. He invited me to sit by pointing towards the seat as he carried on speaking in Italian.

"*Lui parla Inglese* – he speaks English," the man told the others. They all smiled but continued speaking in Italian. At the same time, he asked if I wanted coffee. My cyclist friend remained standing near the door.

"Per che, non?" I acknowledged graciously. I seldom drank coffee, but in Italy it was an obligation. It was the first step in breaking bread with a host.

I thought this was my cyclist friend's flat that he shared with the coffee man. There were two bedrooms, the large dining area, and kitchen. There was no couch, so I wondered where I would sleep. The cyclist then suddenly said goodbye and ended that mystery. He mentioned he'd speak to me soon. I didn't see how. He said he'd come by in the morning.

"Oh, it's okay, I am leaving very early. No problem. Thanks so much. Buon viaggio."

He waved to the others and left. This encouraged the others to stand and walk toward the door. The woman smiled encouragingly, brought her child beside her, then gave her phone to the man who'd made me coffee. He stood in front of her, the child, and the second, mysterious man who hadn't spoken a word since I entered the flat. Coffee man took a photo of them all. And another. She hugged the mystery man and kissed his cheeks, then the same to the coffee man. She left as the cyclist did. It was no more than a minute before another knock came at the door. This time, two women and three children. Mystery man stood again. He greeted the new guests with big smiles and spoke for a few minutes in Italian. And, like before, the coffee man took photos of them while everyone hugged. Then they, too, exited.

I sipped my coffee bewildered and fatigued, watching, wanting nothing more than to fall asleep and rest before another day of walking. It was a revolving door. As soon as one set of women and children left, another knock arrived. I still had no names, no idea who owned the house nor what the hell was happening.

"Sorry," I sighed to the coffee man, begging him for help. "*Pero, aqui tuo casa* – is this your house?"

He nodded and smiled. He brought me to one room. The door was open. A bed had been made. There was a dresser, mirror, and lamp. Very tidy.

"For you, put bag. Okay?" he offered with a broad smile.

60

Coffee man invited another guy inside. He was older than the other two and shook our hands ferociously before sitting with us. Another group of women and children were right behind him. Coffee man turned them away and closed the door. Once he had sat down, the three remaining spoke in detail. All in good humour, all laughing.

"Are you tired?" the coffee man asked curiously.

"I'm okay. No problem. But I'm walking again tomorrow." He nodded, then looked to the others. I assumed he was explaining what I said.

"So, you come with us, okay?"

I finished my coffee first. Coffee man locked the door as we descended the stairs. We weaved through narrow streets. It was dark. As we turned a corner, a floodlight glow shone from a large square into this narrow crevice of a street. The coffee man put his hand on my shoulder. His smile was so uplifting, so pronounced with anticipation. But for what?

"I am Padre here, so no problems for you, no problem. Only enjoy," he promised. We were a crew. The pilgrim and the priest walking behind… a wrestler? The mystery man who gave the ultra-magnetic smile to everyone. The permanent fixture, with random people hugging him and snapping photos. The closer to the light we got, the louder the commotion became. The crowd rustled and rumbled. It grew to a roar, a stampede of energy, enthusiasm. The square was packed. Hundreds of bodies had been squeezed into a half-moon around a stage, which we approached. Most of them held half-litre cups of beer. My host, the priest, now turned to me.

"If you want, take beer, I must go. You stay here, by stage. Talk soon. *Bene* – all good?"

"Sure, bene, no problem," I replied.

He passed me beer money from his pocket.

I waved it off.

"Si, si, enjoy."

The priest paying for my beer, Christo! I was shocked to see him get up on the stage. The priest rivalled mystery man with his luminescent smile as he stepped out. He stood at a microphone beside a doll sitting on a chair. The crowd went wild, clapping and hollering. He spoke in a strong, soothing voice. He remained calm despite the hundreds of people screaming and cheering. He said something loudly, and the lights got brighter. Then, one of the spotlights stopped on us. The crowd around me parted as the ultra-magnetic, mystery man jostled up the stage's stairs. He stepped onto the stage. The crowd roared. He stood beside the priest, and they shook hands; the crowd roared again. The priest repeated himself again into the microphone. I couldn't understand a thing. The noise was incredible. Deafening. The crowd was in a frenzy. The priest left down the stairs again.

"Okay? You okay?"
"Yes, I go for beer now, thank you."
"Nothing."

Toward the beer stand, I turned back to check the stage every few seconds. The crowd thickened, so I used my hands to navigate through the bodies. The man on stage had taken the doll in his hand. He spoke to the crowd. Everyone laughed. He spoke to the doll. Everyone laughed. Hysterically. He stopped trying to talk because the clapping and cheering was too much. He blushed and tried again, but they continued hollering. The people refused to quit. Refusing to let him speak, incredible. After four attempts to stop them, they settled. The act was a kind of ventriloquist comedy set, but I understood nothing, not even the man's name. People laughed, they chuckled, they clapped, they screamed. Children were everywhere.

With the beer in my hand, I made my way back to the foot of the stairs. No one spoke English. The priest was busy engaging with his many admirers. The lights flickered as the man and his doll shook and rattled. Whoever he was, he was funny, and for some reason, they loved his doll. This was no ventriloquist dummy. This was a stuffed toy. Something Jim Henson could've created for the Muppets a century before. But the people loved it.

250 kilometres remained until Bari and the Adriatic Sea. A stretch of infinite silence. The high, mountainside townships of Campagna were finished. The flattest, least populated part of Italy stood before me. A miniature version of the Canadian prairies. Arid, dry, treeless. A barren threshold. Not a lake nor river. It would be a week before I felt the Adriatic and its breeze. This

monster needed a mantra.

"One foot in front of the other," I told myself as I made the bed in the priest's guestroom. I could stop walking at any time. "I've chosen to walk and keep walking each day," I told myself, as I clamped my backpack closed. It was my choice how long I dragged this on. The best choice was to walk and keep walking each day until I couldn't. Whether that meant forty or fifty or even sixty kilometres a day.

Ep. 7
Puglia Plains

Before transforming into a pilgrim on the Camino de Santiago, I was a glutton. The world was a smorgasbord of pleasures for me to feast upon. A thrill seeker. Always hungry. In the past, my body would have pressed against my partner as we strolled along a beach. Smelling our honeymoon fragrance. We'd climb on a moped, her legs around my buttocks, through hills and tea plantations. Hike to a waterfall deep in equatorial jungle and swim behind it spooning while we treaded water to a secluded cave. Her red sarong would come off. Our love would last until the moon disappeared.

Thrill seeking for months and years, through murky groves and sanguine mountain passes; new pleasures were the presumptive reason for travelling. That's what I thought before becoming a pilgrim. Enriched by this continuum of cultural acquisition, nothing mattered until they all stopped. When the highs stopped, the curtains fell, and the room darkened. When the curtains opened again, they revealed familiarity. Landscape colours bereft of vivacity. Anything less than sensational had become unsatisfying. On this pilgrimage, I went from one city to the next on a motorway. I never expected such monotony. I wanted to run from the monotony. Everything was still. Life without creativity or change. I was myopic, hardheaded. Instead of working on love with a partner, I chose this Way. Eventually, this partner lost her trust in me, as I was always searching. She abandoned the road to go back home for Christmas with her mom and brother. That's what she wanted. She was tired of my ambiguity. I was still bent on sensationalising life, pushing limitations and exploring anything but our relationship. She took refuge in her social normality. Above that, she was excited. The road life for her was finished. It developed within her a satisfying result. Now, she was ready to start her own family. What she really needed was a man prepared for the same. The ravenous, irrational bond we shared, strung together by fantastic highs and sexual encompassment, was behind her.

My solution was a lot different than hers. Striving for nomadism, I wanted to get as far out there as possible. My failure to be the guy she needed had become a burdensome weight I couldn't shed before I joined the Camino de Santiago. I was unearthing new, virtuous struggles that justified my unwillingness to commit to anything. That trail, with all the other pilgrims, showed me I didn't need to conform to her perception. I was okay with my lifestyle choice. But it wasn't far enough out for me. I unravelled what had manifested from our deconstruction on that Way to Santiago. I faced my t-boned ego with a lifestyle that fit on a path that felt great, surrounded by others struggling with crossroads anxiety on an avenue unlike any other I had experienced before. But it was not mine. It lacked the exclusivity a journeyman sought. I couldn't calcify my integrity there. I needed the vivid illuminations of colour in my life, a pilgrimage of my own choosing. Meeting uncouth characters with unique, indigenous hearts in forgotten parts of the civilized European world. Landscapes that offered a chance to walk the Way as others had two thousand years before. People of commerce, soldiers, and refugees of the Roman Empire. Humble, calm, timeless. To tackle it all with one simple, fitting line: "One foot in front of the other, no matter what."

As this adventure carried on and the hamada in Puglia widened, this mantra became more important; the sun suggested retreat. I could curse no one, only remind myself it would end. It wasn't the Sahara or Great Sandy, and there were life and coastline awaiting me.

"And James, my friend James, did he think like me?" I wondered. "Did he also push himself for inner nobility? Did he struggle through his fucking lonely heart while he walked on this God-forsaken plain?"

"No, he probably stayed on the Via Francigena and stuck to townships like any sensible person. He wasn't unsettled by expectations or disjointed by the roads he walked." I paused and looked up from my lanky straw hat. "He probably had a fucking map to guide him and also found the friggin' foot paths too, so he wasn't almost getting hit by fucking cars every day and stared at by street hookers on motorway shoulders before every town."

Mere drops remained in my water bottle. Just enough to lubricate my lips every ten or twenty minutes so they didn't stick together.

"I wonder where James is now."

"He's gotta be well ahead, because I'm a slow fuck. Probably cruising along, that bastard, fargin' on easy street skipping along and passing all kinds of fresh fruit and spring water in Albania. Maybe he's even made it to Macedonia," I murmured back to myself, staring at my feet.

"I'm right here, bro." I leapt up quickly at the sound of his voice.

"Finally! Thank fuck!" I said with my arms raised to the sky. Even his voice in my head was enough to provide me with some companionship.

A car stopped dead in the middle of the road and brought me back to reality. The driver exited his car. I went toward him.

"Per favora tienas agua?" Dust blew across the roof and into our eyes. He walked to the trunk with his keys in hand, opened it, and lifted out a large, beautiful bottle of water.

I was so happy and relieved, I fumbled for words. "Merci, danke, I mean shit, grazie, grazie mille. Thank you so much."

The man looked at me calmly. He put his hand out and I shook it.

"It's nothing."

He said no more and climbed back into his car. As he drove away his family turned to wave goodbye. There she was, my ex-partner in her red sarong and her happy family she'd made. She was happy and so was he. And with this water, so was I.

My hat saved my nose, but the sun had rifled into my knee pits. Bending my knees caused my jaw to clench. Tension strained my jowls. Anyone who embraced the idea of curiosity, accepted the challenge of the Way, had to crave the unbound vastness of the desert. Infinite space and intoxicating quiet besides the wind. Away from inhabited land plagued by disappointment, prejudice, hatred, and, more than anything, death. In the unending immensity, I could be ageless. This plain wasn't a desert, but it sure as fuck was empty. And felt infinite. On the Way, events took shape, the clock moved forward, but time felt like it was standing still. There was no connection between me, this Way, and the real-life events unfolding for everyone and anyone else. Everything was irrelevant, for the road itself was timeless. On the Way, time was measured with an occasional glance in the mirror. Age's connectivity to time was only found in the photographs of others. That partner in her red sarong, holding hands with her boy on a pebbled beach on the Baltic coast. A high school buddy beside his teenage daughter on her birthday. Besides these hints, neither time nor age was measured but through scraggly grey beard hairs and cavitation bubbles cracking in early morning joints.

This woman in the red sarong believed I was so spellbound by this lifestyle because it negated obligation. That I was warding off reality, details, payments, and retirement savings. Some agreed with her that I was ensnared by that concept of freedom. Little more than ruin awaited me on the other side. Others praised the freedom of such an unhindered lifestyle. I was an example of real, unrestrained living in peer networks where most people feared risk and social disapproval. They believed safety and conformity were the main objectives. Few contemplated that the most important thing in life was happiness. Real happiness. Internal happiness that came from self-worth. The most radical of things could be achieved, but self-love was the Holy Grail. No one could deserve love without first loving themselves. On the road, weeks and months would elapse in a flash. I remembered a gap-year student I met. His comments on my generational chasm. But on this Way, on the road less travelled by foot, nobody cared. Everyone was the same age. We treated each other with the same respect. We unfastened ourselves, attaching to one another as friends on an even plane. A respect I wouldn't have gotten in different circumstances. The estranged, wandering pilgrim in a search for *answers* was the farthest thing from a threat. A phenomenon, on an unfathomable quest. I celebrated each person as much as they celebrated me.

My appearance was no greater surprise than theirs to me. We valued each other quickly on this unconventional path. My longing for friends, family, lovers all fell into the fold. I walked in a parallel universe where time didn't exist. Anything further than arm's length was inconsequential.

Shadows grew where I walked alone, absent treasured meetings with strangers. The darkness rose, a wrinkling, worrisome presence monitoring me. Something hovering like a vulture, waiting to pick my bones. Not quite evil, nor dangerous. The threat of becoming obsolete, a failure. The odd car that stopped on that stretch slowed down to look at me with concern.

"Do you need a ride?" Did I ever. All I could do was repeat my mantra and say no thank you. The shadow appeared as the striking blood orange seeped across the sky. It faded into the arid horizon behind a long line of wind generators rotating with the breeze. Small, centrifugal micro-vibrations pulsed through the land—a swooning, meditative, unbroken hum. It was one long road. The shadow grew. This wasn't a plain of a thousand scorpions. Old, abandoned stone houses, cluttered with debris and broken glass. If I had more time, I could have swept one to check for rodents, then slept there. I didn't need a modern permutation of Black Death. Then I would really have to quit this thing. As the shadows became more than outcrops of my body, darkness stole everything. The likelihood of meeting a giant, rabid rat intensified. Without a single streetlamp, I had serious reservations about putting my tent anywhere visible to the road. Too easy for someone to stop. What kind of freak would be driving a hundred-kilometre plain in the middle of nowhere at midnight? I couldn't see a fuckin' thing, and I still had 40 kilometres to the nearest town. I reminded myself that this wasn't the United States, but still, the possibility of encountering a psychotic agitated me.

"Fuck this, this is bad. Fuck. All it takes is one car! One drunk fool that couldn't keep his eyes open. I gotta stop. Gotta set up camp."

The personalities above me became louder. "You're not exactly glowing, now, are you Freddi! Might as well be covered in a fucking Burqa!"

The voices in my head, they spoke in rotation.

"How many hours of walking have you done? Think about it, how many hours already?"

"Just keep walking, that's all I have to do is just keep pushing. Fuck it, keep going, come on, pussy."

The villages were gone, not even the remotest cluster of light.

"You're going to be very hungry soon. Especially tomorrow morning."

The taunting voices quieted as a light appeared in the distance. My nervousness subsided with this glowing bulb. I wanted nothing more than to reach it. Ploughed land stood between myself and the light. My feet sank into the soft, corrugated lumps. Whatever was planted was about to show its hairs.

When I finally reached the lamplight, I let my pack collapse. This was a sensation better than any drink of ice-cold water, even on the hottest, driest day of the year in the African savannah. But it wasn't as good as lying down after camp was set. The outer tarp off. A billion, trillion stars sparkling overhead. A cool breeze brushing my naked skin.

A parked caravan had grown roots over a small football pitch. An old pizza oven, discarded patio furniture, everything was covered in leaves and dirt. There was a house. Not a single light, but for that single bulb facing the road. Post-apocalyptic, except the grass had been mowed. And though the clothesline was bare, wooden clips hung everywhere. Windmills, abandoned houses, and now this. I could see a castle in the far distance to the northeast. Nothing else. It made sense for this to be a farmhouse, but for the pizza oven. Even if it was Italy. Disbandment was possible given the recent economic crisis. Maybe it was a failed restaurant. A stupid idea from someone with too much money. No one would drive 50 or more kilometres from either end to eat at a restaurant.

The grassy area was the perfect solution for my tent. Nonetheless, I remained low without moving. If that camper was occupied, I didn't want to appear a thief. I recalled as a teenager, one night like many others. We had hopped a fence, me and three of my friends. We wanted to have a swim. The back door swung open, and a woman cried into the house. "Robert, get the gun!" We ran laughing down the road.

The fourth or fifth step I took triggered a motion sensor, and a flood light brightened the whole yard.

"Shit," I whispered, and froze.

When no one came out, I moved slowly toward the pizza oven. I could see inside the house. There was a light on at the end of a narrow corridor. Closer to me, I could see a wooden table with a few chairs and fresh cherry tomatoes in a thatch basket. A man passed. He passed a second time with plates in his hands. He had a white dress shirt on, black pants, a black apron, black shoes, and a long, dark, pointed beard down to his sternum. A waiter. He crossed the corridor again. Then a fourth time. And looked at me. We both gave each other the same puzzled look. Exhausted, drained, on my last ounce of strength, I wanted nothing more than my tent, three minutes of stargazing from my floor mat, and my head sunk into my pillow.

Two days without human contact, except the family that had donated their water. At the door, he grinned, and I smirked, shrugging my shoulders. I was as haggard as the plateau. Filthy with dust and white residue from dried sweat.

He opened the door, "Dove vei?" The waiter's expression didn't change, his mouth hid behind his moustache and beard. "Auto-Stop?"

The way he said it, pitched at the end, indicated his uncertainty.

"A piedi," I said dejectedly, absent strength. He went inside and closed the door. I reached for him after he turned, but he was too fast. I wanted to set my tent. And fill my water bottle. What I didn't want was a group session. A string of questions and answers and a trivial situation where everyone became confused. The young Beard-O returned with a metal salad bowl in one hand and a plate of toasted, thick bread slices drizzled with olive oil and chopped parsley in the other. He placed them on the table.

"Sit, please, enjoy your meal."

Inside the bowl, a couple handfuls of chopped, cherry tomatoes coated in olive oil, chopped garlic, and torn basil. He brought me a stunning, rustic, fresh entree of bruschetta. And perfect seasoning, with healthy flaked salt and fresh pepper. The tomatoes tasted exquisite. They came from the basket in front of me. Garden fresh, traditional. Brought to me in a local way from local hands. Bloody Christ on a bike this was a breakthrough in my luck. An hour before, I was suffering, pondering another day full of walking without much food. Suddenly, I was eating at the top of a social ladder, served by a waiter.

What Germans did with symphony to the ears, Italians did with food to the mouth. It took centuries to build and many long hours to prepare. Irresistible mouthfuls of juicy, organic, sweet bulbs of cherry tomato crushed by hand. That was it. He returned with a simple, white bowl. Pasta I'd never seen in my life. I studied culinary in school, worked in Italian restaurants, read books, travelled across Italy three times, but this pasta was unique. Before the man turned to leave, I called to him.

"What is this place?"

"It's agri-touristo."

"That bruschetta was incredible, thank you."

"Nothing."

This original pasta was fresh. It resembled fusilli, but not as tight. I bit into one. It was perfect. Perfectly seasoned and perfectly cooked. Tossed with a parsley pesto and some extra oil, pepper, and shaved parmesan. The oil, richer and darker than any commercial oil from a store. It came closer to the colour of an olive. It tasted like the olives had just been squeezed. Again, the man exited the restaurant onto the patio to my table and dropped another plate. This time with a dessert.

"Sorry, what kind of pasta was that?"

"Sagne cannulate."

"Sagre what? Perdona, che?"

"It is Puglia specialty, fresh, rolled pasta."

I went inside after licking the pastry cream from my plate. I thanked the kitchen staff from the doorway, the servers afterwards, and then, I gave vigorous praise to the owner when I met him.

"He says you can put your tent wherever you like. In the morning, you come for coffee if you want, after nine."

With my back on my floor mat, the outer shell of my tent off, I finally got to stare up at those stars. My first breaths were heavy. I sat for a moment and took a long drink of water. Lying down again, back to the stars, I exhaled a few more heavy breaths.

"Unbelievable. Cazzo!" I said loudly, looking at Orion's belt.

I tracked my eyes to the red giant, Betelgeuse, and remembered vividly Amos beside me.

Ep. 8
The Boat

My new family gathered at an empty, grassy slope on a riverside near the albergue in Puente La Reina. The treeline created shade. Plenty of sun everywhere else for sarongs and Quechua mats. A swim in the cool, fast-moving water rinsed our walking sweat. Being together and talking, we created a harmony together, a sense of belonging. The chatter generated thirst. Only a few minutes remained until siesta chimed and shut the markets. They nominated Amos and me to fetch aperitifs. Finding the nearest shop, we discussed the current chances of our Vancouver Canucks winning the Stanley Cup final.

"Never again will I put my faith in that team, goddammit. My heart can't bear any more pain," I declared somberly. "They're doomed to choke." I mentioned the '94 New York Rangers, who'd beat them by one goal in game seven. "We were so damned close. But, on the positive side, I did win sixty bucks from my stepdad because of it." I lifted three bottles from the fridge.

"How's that? You bet against the 'Nucks?" Amos looked back at me indignantly as he pulled more bottles from the fridge. "You gettin' beers for Dani and Cosi then, guy?"

I put mine on the counter. "Nah, fuck them," I said in jest. "Yea. Okay, but they said I get a blowjob from one of 'em. They were gonna draw straws." I glanced towards the clerk, "Quando questa, porfa?"

Searching for my money, I turned to Amos. "The bet was actually brilliant, bro. I bet my Brett Hull rookie card against sixty bucks that the final that year would be Vancouver and the Rangers. My two favourite teams. And that shit happened! Thirteen years old, and I had sixty bucks to blow—shit was real." I stepped back so Amos could reach the counter. The door sounded. We both looked. There she was. She strolled over to the

71

counter beside me. So confident. She waited for Amos to finish. I looked over one more time.

"Buenas," I said, smiling toward her. She replied with the same. She had this incredible, adumbral skin. She wore a loose-fitting tank top with knee-high, black leggings and lightweight hiking boots. She won on all accounts but for the overcompensating footwear. There was a tattoo on her rib cage where her tank top slouched. My heart skipped when I saw the exposed curvature of her breast. She goaded my adolescent lasciviousness. She was a Venus flytrap. A gorgeous, rough, jaded, two-faced predator posing as a housecat. I invited her to join our party. She agreed, then bought a pack of smokes.

"You guys are drinking down there?"

"Yea, some mid-day shenanigans, how could we resist in this weather?"

She grabbed her beer from the counter. The three of us left, introducing ourselves, bottles clanking in plastic bags.

Most had disbanded for dinner when we returned. I cooked some garlic and tomato rice. By dark, it was just Leah, Amos, and me. "Beetlejuice! Beetlejuice! Beetlejuice!" Amos shrieked. We stared at the stars, our backs on the grassy hillside.

I turned and laughed. "What was that for, bro? I mean, funny movie, sure. I don't think you could speak when it was released though, guy."

He chuckled the way he always did. Up and down, jolty. "I wasn't born! But it's a classic. Come on, yo."

"So, what gives?" I asked again, jeeringly. He sat up. He looked over at us.

"See that red star?" he asked, pointing upwards. "Just there, see it?"

"Nope." We both replied unanimously, laughing.

"Guys, come on, okay, look for Orion's Belt. Go to the middle star, okay, then go straight up."

Both of us again replied in synchrony, "Ah-ha."

"Yea, so that star is called Betelgeuse!"

"Fuck off," I sneered.

"Seriously, Betelgeuse is the right shoulder of Orion."

I didn't know Orion was anything more than a belt. Amos pointed to the lower body, the upper body, and the sword. "A Greek hunter needs his sword," he said sarcastically.

"Amos, you're such a nerd!"

"Knowledge is power, guys!" The three of us cackled.

Amos stood up from our sloped little knoll. "Well, gotta get some sleep so we can do this walking all over again. Wine fountain tomorrow!"

"Absurd, right?" I blurted as he left.

"Incredible," he retorted with his back to us.

I turned to Leah, "Looks like we're the last of the Mohicans, huh?"

* * *

Sweat covered my face and left my pillow sodden. This heat meant it was closer to noon than sunrise. I slept late. Another lesson for me to learn on that Way to Santiago. When others woke early to beat the heat, they were conditioning themselves. And here I was - unfit and flabby, a sloth of a pilgrim.

This strip across Puglia was no different than the Spanish Meseta. Many pilgrims skipped the plain on their way to Santiago. It was a flat, dry line with few trees. Anyone with time constraints had an easy excuse. The toughest battles came from within. If I was going to walk the Way, then I was going to walk it all. A commitment to my personal goals, and brash follow-through. There was too much at stake to skip over the hard parts. One could succeed in love or basketball, but the resolve *was* to succeed.

Back on the Meseta in Spain, I romanticized the wheat plain. It was a time to relish. While many omitted this one part that required endurance, I celebrated it. It was the best environment for reflection. On this route toward Bari, after all the coastal days in Sorrento, I resented time alone. I longed for the company of others, not to be divided from them. Plus, the Meseta was in mid-June, before the big heat wave. Here in August, the Puglia heat was sweltering.

"And when the sun rises tomorrow, I'm gonna do it all over again," I said to myself. "One foot in front of the other." My pillow was damp. I wanted to read, and then a half-hour of stretching and another for meditation. I didn't want to walk. Of course, it was my choice to walk fifty kilometres or five. There was nothing between me and the coastal townships. The

73

restaurant wasn't a place for squatters. They shared a nice meal with me in passing, but it wasn't an open invitation for meditation.

A tree would have been the perfect excuse to stop. Better than that, a small forest beside a small market. But it would be a long few months before greener pastures. Most of the trees here had died long before the Holocene. Any that remained were cleared for agriculture and olive or wheat production. The few oak trees left, which once reached central Europe, grew only in small copses. Too far north, Castel Del Monte was replete with birch and oak. And two days to Gargano National Park. A massive woodland for hunters and gatherers.

With the Adriatic and Ionian seas tied to the Aegean and Eastern Mediterranean, plenty arrived before Hellenization spread from the Balkans and Asia Minor. During the Mesolithic and Neolithic transition, advancement spread from the Levant and reached the British Isles. In the region of Puglia, tradespeople and pasture seekers arrived by boat with new ways to form pottery and tools. In the south of Italy, where I had walked, people would have moved toward development. The islands of Lipari and Sardinia by word of mouth, in search of obsidian. While some travelled by sea, others came along the Danube, changing the whole face of Europe with their new technologies.

Illiryans, named by Greeks who first crossed paths with them in the Copper Age, colonized Puglia as they followed the Adriatic coast from Albania through Venice. Before Romans crossed the only donkey trail from Benevento to Brindisi, Illyrians had mixed with the natives. They formed three separate yet similar tribes who spoke Messapia. Between the north, centre, and south, they divided Puglia. In the central part, where I walked now, Peucetians lived and paid no mind to Bari. It was an ignored territory before Romans built a port, whereas Bitonto was their capital. They built megalithic walls around villages and towns between the fifth and third centuries B.C. to protect the inhabitants from offshore colonists, pirates, and feuds with neighbours. Illyrians painted their *trullis*—Small, circular, stone houses with conical rooves—white and built them thick to keep their homes cool during summer and warm in the dead of winter.

And the olive trees still covered this road along both sides. They thrived in dry heat, loved rocky earth and would grow on sloped land. All terrible conditions for a camp. At ten in the evening, it was like a runway. Two lanes of pavement. Lightless and empty, giving the impression that the seaside would arrive any time. But the road continued. A week without the sea, and I was wilted like a sunburnt spinach leaf. A dried shiitake mushroom. And I missed summer life. The road I'd chosen from Ruvo di Puglia to Molfetta was motionless. It was a side road that missed the principal highways. Eventually, I would hit a small coastal road and turn south into Bari. Imagining this would happen before evening, I continued. The closer I got to the port and ferries into the Balkans, the nearer I was to confronting a customs agent with my passport. I had overstayed in Schengen Europe by two years. For me, it made this walk a little more sensible. The best way to exit Schengen Europe undetected was to get out in a way no one else would, so I would leave from a coastal port, on a ferry. I just needed to buy a ferry ticket and show them my Camino "passport"—a collection of stamps I had gathered on my Way to Santiago—and then the stamp I received in Rome a month prior to this to prove I was walking to Istanbul. I hoped for a discount on the ferry, but it was only my cover story. They would ignore the entry stamp in my real passport, from Spain, at Algeciras two years and three months before, mystified by my bells and whistles. My plan was solid, success assured. I felt anxious, but most of all ready to get drunk on local wine.

August 7th, 1991, a large cargo ship left Durres, Albania. The name of the ship was *Vlora*. After the collapse of Communism and the USSR, an unprecedented number of people fled Eastern Europe. And in Albania, many starving remained. People stormed embassies in the hopes of being saved and taken away. Some were lured by Italian television commercials. The few channels allowed under communist rule convinced them the outside world was full of prosperity. Few thought twice before leaving on the *Vlora*. A better life awaited them. But even before arriving at port in Brindisi, they'd been refused acceptance by local authorities, so the captain switched his course and made for Bari. Giving no notice to authorities this time, they arrived at the bay and anchored. People swung from ropes, jumping into the Adriatic. They were promised planes and buses to other cities in Italy where food and help awaited. A catastrophe without warning. Nothing awaited them. Those who failed to escape the boat were held in a stadium for deportation.

I had decided to skip the Peucetian capital, Bitonto, to avoid the main road. I traded the beautiful township for quietude in the countryside. A coastal road promised charm. When I reached the seaside, I crumbled. A solid 40-kilometer day. Five days of walking 40-60 kilometres. I was back in the salty air, with a blue horizon and a swimming pool in my front yard. Many times, I'd swam the coast in my mind. Instead, I set my tent and fell asleep. It was nothing but rocks and rubbish in the morning. The motivation to swim was lost to my rumbling stomach. I was parched, my water bottle empty. In Giovinazzo, the siesta period had begun. Bari, scarce of happenings, was quiet. The whitewashed streets reflected light like my fondest memories of La Rochelle, France. La Rochelle's seaside town centre was a spectacular, unpigmented gloss in the sun. It was a port town with immense historic value; Giovinazzo was a suburb. In search of food and water, I noticed a young man ahead of me in the square.

"Perdona?"

"Dimmi." In Italy everyone started with the same greeting. In English, it would be presumptuous or bizarre, but here, it was the polite standard. "Tell me." So direct, so clear.

"*Sa dove e' il bagno, per favore* – could you tell me where the nearest toilet is, please?" My face was desperate. He laughed and congratulated my Italian.

"I know a cafe nearby, there's a WC there. Please, tell me, where are you from."

"Canadese." He walked and I followed, holding my nuts between my legs.

"And how did you come to Giovinazzo of all places?" His English was good.

"It's a long story, but I walked from Roma." His eyes bulged, he looked at me and paused.

"By foot, really?"

"By foot." We arrived at the cafe as he expressed his passion for art. An artist, a painter with aspiration. "No life experience," he declared solemnly. He had finished studying fine arts in Bari. He hoped to leave and challenge life, too. "But I don't think by foot," he crowed heartily.

"Yea, I don't blame you. I have to hit the toilet, I'll be back."

"Please, what you want to drink?"

"Oh, nothing."

"No, please, I invite you."

"One beer would be incredible – and a glass of water, a big glass."

I returned from the toilet and my new friend was at the table with our drinks. Before I could settle in, he spoke. "The bar owner, I told him you came from Rome by foot."

"Oh yea," I sipped the beer, a cool waterfall.

"He wants to speak with you." I turned toward the bar. His arm high, the bar owner smiled. I put the glass down, huffed, and stood.

"Sorry, I hope you don't mind?"

"All good, man. Normal shit, I guess."

At the bar, the man was excited to shake my hand, "Please, have another beer, I invite you!" Couldn't argue with that. He spoke loudly, cackling until he came to his point.

"I telephone friend, she is report in radio, she wants interview you, non?"

"Huh?"

She arrived with a bit of paper, a pen, and a tape recorder. A teenager. Her face unscathed and unwrinkled, her existence yet to be paralyzed by the fickleness of life. Her English was weak, but she managed to ask a few basic questions. None about my pilgrimage to Istanbul. She wanted to know where my favourite country was, where I was from, how old I was, my favourite local food… It was like a short audition for a dating site. My visions of local infamy deflated with her lack of vigour and talent. Or maybe it was me. I didn't have the improvisation required of the moment.

Back in Rome, I'd stayed in pilgrims' accommodations for three days. Bari had another one affiliated with the church. It had been a solid five days since I stayed with that priest, entertained and mystified by his decorous, comedian friend. A shower, a bed, a few days of undisturbed sleep. I repeated these in my head until I reached city traffic. A collection of foreigners from Africa and Central Asia surrounding benches. A park teeming with hustlers, illegal immigrants, slaves to the dream of shiny coins and eclectic life on a long, paved strip between shrubs. Disbanded from Italy in an instant, I was transported to another world inside this park. I could hear a multitude of languages, a colourful rainbow of intonation. Most of them were men, all of them on the cusp of making it and heading straight back home. All it would take was a quick raid by the police and half of them would be credentialed and deported, including me. Only, it was painfully obvious I would blend in a little better with the local Italians if I kept my mouth shut. And the police would be anything but colourblind. Opposite the park, the old centre unfolded. A Norman fortress guarded their colony's eastern port. It stood beside a humble Basilica, where I hoped to find information on the pilgrim accommodation I sought. At the small marina, beside the fort, sailboats bobbed in the subtle current. I stared across the Adriatic and tossed my pack from my shoulders. It hit the ground and shook the masonry.

"Nearly there, bro. You're nearly there. This church is gonna help you out. In a few minutes, you'll have a bed. Come on, son!" Sweat trickled from my wrinkled forehead. I snarled at myself, exhausted, and took my pack up again. I had to crouch to slide my arms into the shoulder straps.

"What a fucking shit show." I collapsed to my knees. I lifted myself, swearing the whole way. People watched as they walked past. The door of the Basilica opened with a push I barely mustered. The inside was dark and cool. The kaleidoscopic windows and wall paintings were irrelevant in my exhaustion. I scanned the room looking for a priest, past the rows of wooden benches and bible shelving.

"Please, do you speak English?" A man pointed to a door. It led down a hall and then to another door. Inside sat another man.

"Please," I said with my hands gripping my knees. "Do you speak English?"

"Tell me?"

"Oh, thank you, okay, please, I have walked the past month from Roma. I am very tired. And I heard there is a place for… Pelegrinos?" I had my pack open and shuffled my arm inside.

He made a call. "Please sit," he said, waiting for an answer on the other end.

Forcing a desperate smile, I removed a Ziploc and placed my Camino passport on the bureau.

"Wait here, okay?"

"Sure," my vision dizzied, curved, slanted. I hit the metaphysical wall.

A man walked in and they spoke Italian before the priest pointed with an open hand to his subordinate. "He will show you, okay?"

I rose from my seat and turned to him in his long, black robe.

"Freddi, do you know James? He is from England?" My face lit up. "He left here one week ago for Brindisi, sorry."

I followed him as he walked in silence through the streets. When we arrived at the building where pilgrims could stay, we had to climb stairs. He opened the door. Two single beds surrounded by sordid walls, a lamp in between, and some sheets folded at the foot of each. A fan on the ceiling and another in the corner. A little classroom across the hall plus an unfinished cement corridor.

"Grazie mille, my brother," I beamed while shaking his hand. "This is perfect!" I hugged him before he closed the door.

"Oh, fuck yea!" I said, slamming my pack down and toppling onto the mattress.

Ol' James the Blond had been in the same room. Back at the obelisk in Vatican City he was so calm and clear. "South Europe has always made me feel at home." He would take short pauses, not to reflect or think but maintain his pace. "There's something I connect with more than in the U.K." He sat poised and radiant, "I'm in no hurry. I guess that's what I love about walking. We can take our time and really enjoy the process." I spoke about my issues at home and how long I had been away.

"Sure, my relationship could be better with my dad. He's no reason to hit the road. I am full of love for him even if we butt heads. Something that rings true, you know, of my dad within me, I guess, is that I have no problem discontinuing relationships with

79

others who have burned that bridge. Guilt is such a useless emotion – a drain."

"Freddi, we're out here to live, aren't we? Enjoy the ride, count stars, and meditate when we can. I don't know, but I think we got it pretty good out here. Don't let useless baggage weigh you down. Your pack has all you need." He smiled extravagantly and passed me a paper with his email and blog information. The bastard spoke great Spanish and Italian on top of his charisma. It would have been the icing on the cake to share this room with him. Someone to process the last month's experiences and liquefy it all. Let it all roll off before this next leg of the journey through the Balkans. The average person couldn't identify, relate, nor offer support or guidance. Even more simply, to have a bit of banter as I had every morning with Dani or Amos. James was a one-off, like them, but not getting any closer.

Ep. 9
Transitions

The layers of sweat had been soaped away. My clothes were as clean as I could get them. A barber snipped the long hairs of my tousled moustache. At nightfall, a breeze stroked these long, bristly, whiskers, but they no longer tickled my lips. I hit the dusty trail feeling and looking better. Rested and showered thanks to that church. A fresh, Adriatic transition. A clean break from Italy. Still anxious over my passport controversy, I kept asking myself the same tired questions. Reason enough to feel reckless and detached. The only way I knew. Noise of all kinds swept the laneways, but like all of Italy's city centres, little belonged to vehicles. The jostling feet of locals and tourists hunting gelato and pizza. On stairs, through alleys, and at small tables, drinking glasses of wine or espresso from ceramic cups. Like always, I walked through it all, smelling the toasted garlic and stewing tomatoes. Glaring through restaurant windows. Poking my eyes through outdoor menus. Sniffing at what I missed. Antique lanterns hung from walls once illuminated by whale fat and sparked by a lone, reliable man. He promised everyone enough light to get home after their big dishes of orecchiette and rapini.

Unlike the postman doing his morning tour, the lamplighter did his rounds before sunset.

At the fort, the docks glimmered like a small airport runway, sparkling against oily water. The causeway reminded me of a boardwalk in Mumbai, only cleaner. A short brick wall with couples sat with an open view of the harbour. Locals and foreigners divided. The travellers were easy to spot. From France to Iran, Korea, Japan, the United States, Poland, U.K., Saudi Arabia, and Russia. Mumbai was a port city of incandescence, and the tourist area, Colaba, was small enough to host them all. But here in Bari, I wouldn't find backpackers chancing the night. And despite my slurred words and stuttering Italian, I received encouraging responses from locals. Only, they weren't half as drunk as I.

"Vu, vuoi, vuoi del vino rosso? Per favora ooooune cigarette per oi," after motioning to my lips like I had a smoke. A few offered tobacco. Fewer shared my wine.

"It's only a matter of time before someone invites me to their home," I thought to myself with disillusionment. "Who could resist me with my dedicated Italian?" Unyoked eyes and marooned teeth. There was no turning back from that second bottle of wine.

In a frenzy, I rose in my tent. My head was a stack of metal sheets sliding against one another in the back of a pick-up. Sweat covered my face. It was daylight. Quick, sharp chatter from outside thrust me out of my hung over state. Two workers stood beside my tent, displeased. I apologized in English, bagging my stuff in haste. I had propped up my tent at the crack of daylight after climbing a locked fence to a small Botanical Garden.

"Che ora? Che ora?" I begged.

Before they could grab a hold of me, I ran for an open gate.

These workers saved me by startling me awake. The ferry to Dubrovnik was leaving in an hour. I felt like a bag of shit, but I knew how to walk. Looked like a bag of shit, too. At least I had already bought my ferry ticket. My mouth felt full of marshmallows that refused to dissolve. "Water," I thought. "What does a man have to do to get some goddamn water?"

The woman held my passport. Disengaged by the hangover and focused on finding water for my bottle, I didn't even flinch. She opened the book to an empty page and stamped inside.

"Ariva-mutha-fuckin-derchi, yess!" I found a shaded area on the ship's outer deck to lay my floor mat and snoozed nine hours to the Croatian coast.

Crossing that pier, the first step on a free bridge where I was no longer illegal took an anvil of weight from my overstrained shoulders. Of course, others bore far heavier chains. While caged birds sang, my nerves loosened, and my tunnel vision vanished. I could now roam free without an eye over my shoulder. It wasn't necessary to rely on anyone else. No customs agent could stand in my way. Every step from here would be my own.

Putting an end to two years of paranoia ended one battle but started a new war. No more excuses. The following 1000 kilometres would conclude once I landed on Turkish soil or else once I threw in the towel, bearing the truth of my own lack of piousness.

While sailing for Croatia, thousands of refugees and migrant workers climbed into illegal smuggling vessels. Some of them lost their lives on small boats without the faintest idea how to swim. Capsized from carrying too many people. Others were crammed into trucks carrying frozen meat. Without oxygen for hours, many never woke up. Or maybe it was on the street, met and beaten by racist thugs or robbed of the little money they had. Starved, exhausted, or sick, Death had many faces. And if death wasn't a deterrent, nothing could be. So many caught and held in camps. With idle hands, youth, and vigour, many were a decision away from a jail cell. After tens of thousands arrived in Budapest, the fascist right-wing, quiet for decades, would begin to mobilize in opposition to these foreigners. And they would rally votes, too.

Before arriving in Roma, I'd hitched with a man running a truck from Hungary to England. He was English with a Hungarian father. I met him at a petrol station with my little sign in hand and headed across Austria from Slovakia, where I had worked. We discussed migration during a refugee crisis. For years to come, these people would likely be moving toward Europe.

And as a European, he knew he would have to choose between hospitality and xenophobia.

"At least, in Hungary, if these so-called refugees get caught, they're goin' straight to prison," he said implacably.

This driver, dreaming of improving upon Richard Nixon's efficiency, wanted to gather up the fun-loving hippies, those trying to make a better life during the clusterfuck of war, and ensure they were sternly punished for their attempts at freedom. And not only the hippies fighting against the war in Vietnam, or the refugees now fleeing Syria, but their families and future families, too.

In a few months' time, the border between Greece and Macedonia would become clogged by a tent city filled with thousands of stuck Afghans and Syrians. Bodies suffering adverse weather awaiting passage to Germany, France, Scandinavia, Holland, England. They would be seeking a chance at residency and work. The work was much scarcer in the Balkans, Greece, or Turkey, where the economies weren't as stable. The sea port of Calais, between England and France, would grow astronomically once I settled in Istanbul and began my work. By the time I disembarked the boat from Bari, crossed the Adriatic, and stamped my passport at Dubrovnik's border control, the number of Syrians in Istanbul had already reached a million.

The irony of it all was that the same people scurrying for a better quality of life after the fall of the USSR would stand like that truck driver, appalled by the influx of these particular refugees. Muslim refugees. They would demand stronger borders, police controls, and drastic consequences. It would only get worse, too. Some of these post-communist countries, like Hungary, were in rough shape, but they were safe and relatively stable. And few of Schengen Europe's residents went hungry, so long as they put the bottle down long enough to take hold of a garden hoe.

Dark skin, unrecognizable languages, and foreign religion weren't welcome in the former communist bloc, even though most people here found their stability thanks to their own immigration, illegal or otherwise, in the nineties. They gathered cash on foreign soil to build stability back home. They would now undoubtedly create a righteous uproar, demanding the imprisonment of Arabs and the Central Asians and Africans following suit. Most remarkable was how indifferent one could become after finding comfort and sustainable wages. Once accused and alienated for stealing jobs, they would now raise their fists against others doing the same as they had done. People, broken by their struggle against corrupt and authoritarian governments.

As the sun set above the shoreline behind Dubrovnik and I took those first few steps of freedom, it had been twenty-four hours since I last ate. My stomach knew it. I had to find a supermarket. First, I had to exchange some euros for Croatian kuna.

The sun was going down, my stomach was angry, so of course the disembarkment had to be delayed. Tourists waved their selfie sticks high. I had to get off this dock! Hours stood ahead. Chores. Things I wanted nothing to do with. After the money exchange and supermarket, I still needed to beg a restaurant for cooking oil, then find a spot to cook and camp for the night. At least beer was cheaper in Croatia than Italy. Thank fuck the beer was cheap in Croatia.

All non-Croatians huddled in a line. Two guards cleared our entry. A gorgeous blonde woman in a thick vest and tight cap took my passport. She looked at me suspiciously. Back and forth between my ID and face. I resisted nervous fidgeting. If she noticed the gap of time between my Schengen entry and exit stamps, she could do nothing. She called another guard. Another contemptuous glare. He took the passport.

"I am walking to…"

He raised his hand. "Please, one moment." He showed me the passport after that. "What is this?" There was a scratch on my photo, a small one across my face.

"Oh shit, I don't know. It's news to me, must have just happened." He stared at me. "Sorry, I've been walking for a month, very long days. The passport must have scratched something. I will replace it. I promise. So sorry."

He looked at me again, then passed the ID back to his blonde co-worker before saying something in Croatian. She scanned it. Lifted the large, metallic stamp I'd been waiting to hear.

"Welcome, enjoy your stay."

Sliding doors opened. I was out. I dropped my pack on the other side. A large sigh. There was something missing, though. I scanned my pack, looking it over a few times. There was something off. Something was not right.

"Fuck," I gasped loudly. My durable, reliable, German-made, black sleeping mat. I'd been carrying it around my whole time in Europe. Not a speck of damage on it, now gone. I ran inside, my stomach grumbling.

"I'm sorry," I pleaded to the woman.

"You'll have to wait until the boat is unloaded. Then until it is cleaned."

"Can I just go to the boat quick, now, please?"

"Nope."

I pleaded with two more agents before I got through. On the boat, I called the nearest crewman. I explained where I was and how I had slept through the boat journey.

"Maybe someone put it behind the bar or a food counter inside," I shouted to him. His English was rough. We both understood he wouldn't give his search a solid effort. He came back shaking his head. Others refused to let me investigate. My back twitched at the thought of sleeping the coming nights on hard Mediterranean floors. I swore to myself over and over as I exited the customs office. I still had to find cooking oil and food for dinner.

With my little chipped bottle in hand, I walked into the first restaurant I saw. A manager brought it back full and offered me bread. I squinted, then smiled. The oil was olive, too. The mat was gone, but the Way provided.

* * *

Drunk as a sailor, I had put my tent on a slope. Leah became annoyed with the slant and left for the albergue. As I walked from town in the morning, she snuck behind me and slid her hand into mine.

"Hey," she said in a bubbly voice. I cringed, noticing our hands together. Dani glared at me with a winking eye. I looked at him like a caged animal.

I turned to Leah afterwards, "So, last night I was a bit too drunk, obviously, but today I'm full strength," I grinned at her energetically. "What do you say we climb into the next little forested area?"

"We should stay with the group." Her words were earnest. They annihilated my ambition. Oddly, her hand was still holding mine.

We walked the first kilometres of the day exchanging small talk. She had a bachelor's in business that she didn't care for.

"They wanted me to, so I did it, you know."

"So, is that why you joined the Camino Way? Looking for answers, the next step?" I asked her inquisitively.

"No, not really. My friend asked me along, he wanted to do it, but not alone. I joined him." She then carried on about the social drama she had back home with her four best friends. "My God! It's so good to be away from it." A handful of teen movies ran through my memory as the frivolities continued forth from her mouth. "My Spanish isn't good. I don't use it. My mom is from Guatemala, but she never thought it was useful."

"Fuck, if I had any Spanish right now, it would be bloody useful. That's how you get respect in this part of the world."

"I should practice," she said vaguely.

The ancient Monastery of Irache was formed sometime in the late 11th century. By the 12th, the Monastery was growing quality grapes and made wine for Spanish royals. The Bodegas Irache winery was built at the end of the 19th century. It produced quality wine in great quantities, whose commercial value became much more important than any monastic value the temple once had. Two kilometres from my river camp in Puente La Reina, in 1991, this winery built a fountain that flowed with both water and wine. Bronze, Camino seashells behind each one. A Templar Cross between them. And with the turn of a valve, a thick stream of blood-red liquid poured into my empty, two-litre bottle. Most of the pilgrims turned right. I noticed a path to the left. A forested one. I tugged on Leah's arm.

"Here's our chance," I whispered, "Let's take the Robert Frost road."

"We can't leave the group. Why would you want to leave them?"

"Why wouldn't we?" I thought to myself. Why not sneak into the little forest beside the trail? Giggle, cuddle, laugh, and embrace each other before getting lost and falling onto some grass. Instead of the small talk, taste a bit of fountain wine and feel each other's naked bodies. I wasn't the kind for sticking with the line. No unnecessary conformity. Sure, I loved my pilgrim family, but we had common degrees of separation each day. The more time I spent with them, the more I thought about alone time. And alone time with this deviant and her rattlesnake eyes, sucking at each other's erogenous zones, was better.

The whole science of mounting her body the night before was to share affection, intimacy, and throw our wild hormones into this unique escapade we were on. She appeared like a fantasy player to me. A kind of sex fiend. But the more I looked, the more I saw that her face may have been more grumpy than insatiable. It began morphing into a face that was voluntarily sucking lemons, not one that depended on orgasms and pleasure. And I bought the whole illusion on one, naked, hanging tit. She wanted the line. She needed the line. She was frightened and insecure without the line. The strangest part – I introduced her to the line she now depended on. I needed time to think.

Amos went left, so I walked behind him, alone, content to sip wine from my large, plastic bottle. The path followed a meandering trackway, parallel to another headed for Los Arcos. It gave me a distant view of a fort as everyone passed by it. The weather wasn't yet hot. It was perfect, alone. It felt necessary. After a couple more sips of wine, I started to sing. The surging reward of freedom. The words of Shannon Hoon struck my mind, so I bellowed them.

> *When you feel your life ain't worth living*
> *You've got to stand up*
> *And take a look around and look way up to the sky*
> *Yeah, and when your deepest thoughts are broken*
> *Keep on dreaming boy, 'cause when you stop dreamin' it's*
> *time to die.*

When I arrived at Los Arcos, I shelled for cans of *albondigas* – meatballs. I fried onions and bell peppers to make sandwiches for my family. While most pilgrims would stay in Los

Arcos, I planned to carry on with Amos. Once the rest of us arrived, they agreed, including Leah. The trail was a long, narrow, winding stretch of hillside cut between fresh green and rough patches of dried grass. A transition on the horizon, chopped into cubicles of farmland. We could see for an eternity. Small brick rooves topped the Way. A village no bigger than a supermarket in Madrid. The church had a bench where we unloaded our gear to rest. I diced vegetables for dinner. The others discussed sleeping outside. Leah and the Italians weren't keen. A man walked past. I put down my knife and walked toward him.

"Sorry, hablas ingles?"

"Yea, how are you? Are you walking to Santiago?" We all nodded.

"Do you have an extra blanket, a sleeping bag, anything I could use to sleep outside tonight?" I asked.

He considered my question. "I do, yes. No problem."

"Esta un albergue aqui?" asked Dani.

"There are four beds," he pointed down the road and to the left. "My house is on the right."

"Oh, that's great, so cool. Can I come and get what blankets you can spare?"

"Sure. You guys need a shower?" Eyes flared and hands too. It had been a couple of days for me.

"Well, maybe after we cook here, we'll come down?"

"You guys, I would host you all, but I don't have space."

"We're happy to sleep out here," I assured him.

"Says you," replied Leah sharply.

When the man left, Leah and the Italians insisted on checking into the albergue. Amos was happy as I was to sleep outside on the concrete for a night. We had our mats, he had his sack, and with the help of our friend, I had a sleeping bag. After we ate, the Italians turned in. I took a shower at the young man's house, then shared a few beers with him, Leah, and Amos. We left and stopped beside a metal guardrail near one side of the church. The three of us stood there in the night air. It was quiet and peaceful. The town below was only a kilometre or two away. It seemed within arm's reach, its lights as large embers ignited by light wind. Amos sparked a spliff he'd been carrying.

A voice interrupted the silence from above us. "Hey, you guys pilgrims?"

We turned to engage. A man leaned from his second-story window. We confirmed we were pilgrims. He asked us where we were from.

"Canada," we said, excluding Leah, before turning to her and explaining. "Look, we wanna make friends, not enemies."

The two of us laughed a moment.

"Is that right?" the man said in jest. He went inside for a moment and, next thing, a woman was peering from the window.

"I'm from Prince George," she said.

Amos and I looked at each other stunned. He asked first, "Prince George, British Columbia, Canada?"

"Same one," her voice replied in a calm and friendly tone. The man appeared in the window again.

"You smoke hash?" Our faces glittered like the town below. The two of them disappeared, but the man returned to the window. "You want beer, or wine? It's good local wine." They came down with a bottle of wine, a few chairs, and enough glasses for everyone.

"Please, sit down."

Our new friend was a lumberjack. He lost his job in the 70s to giant industrial machines. He moved to Canada to chop trees in the Pacific Northwest. They got married, had kids, and retired to this little village in Basquo for a quieter, simpler, cheaper way of life.

"So, where are you guys staying?"

We explained that aside from Amos and I, our friends checked into the tiny albergue.

"It's so nice outdoors, the stars and all," Amos said.

"Do you have blankets?" the Basquo asked. We mentioned our new village friend who had given us some.

"Nico?" he asked. We nodded. "That's my nephew."

We drank his wine and smoked his incredible hash. He told us of his plight as a lumberjack. Of Basque country and all the changes caused by the influx of so many pilgrims.

"If your town isn't directly on the trail, like here, it suffers, it's that simple." He was proud of his family's roots in the village. And the hospitality of Canada. "It was world class. People were so nice and helpful. Every chance I get, I will give it back."

Two nights later, we weren't so lucky. Instead of staying in town at the albergue, instead of quiet, slow, dispassionate sex on a tiny bottom bunk, Leah agreed to join Amos and I outside.

"As long as you don't put the tent on a slope, Freddi," she scolded me.

We walked a while more, like we did from Los Arcos, ahead of the others, until we hit a large, clear, field. Amos unrolled his sleeping bag a few meters from my tent.

"Should we collect some firewood?" Leah asked.

"Well, I gotta set the tent and cook our food, so you could if you want?"

She shrugged her shoulders and rolled her head side to side. We climbed into the tent, and I pulled at her leggings.

She rolled away from me.

"Hey, come on, I'm sorry, alright. But here we are, let's make the best of our own private space that we have right now, no?"

She rolled back over, facing me and gave me a half smile. "You're not wrong, Freddi."

She kissed me with the same vigour as the evening we'd sat on the riverside in Puente La Reina. She bent her tongue into my mouth and around my lower teeth the same way she responded to my caresses the other night in our bunk bed surrounded by other pilgrims. I felt her reservations ease with every second. I became optimistic, thinking that we could get more intimate from now on. We were out on a Way of free thinking, to release emotional dams and sedateness. We were out here to feel, explore, learn, and grow. The two of us had bonded more intensely, through our eyes and touch. It was not the time to be reserved. But we both had to be on the same page.

As Leah removed her panties and her mouth neared my waistline, raindrops hit the tent. I had my hand wrapped around the inner part of her legs rubbing up and down. I ignored the speckling taps. They gained momentum.

"Shit," Amos said gently from outside.

"Yea, shit is right. This is a one-man tent. Gonna have to get in here anyway, ya lil bastardo," I chuckled while pulling on my boxers. Then I opened the zipper door. We had to secure all three of our bags into their weather resistant covers and then tuck them under the tarp of the tent.

"Where's your pack cover, Leah?"

"Don't have one," she grumbled.

I sighed, "And your money and passport?" She didn't respond. "Leah, come on, it's going to pour down any second, where are they?"

"Who cares?"

"You will if they end up wet."

I dug into her pockets one after the other looking until I found them. A little wallet with her stuff. I tossed it into the tent. "Thanks for the guidance, eh."

With everything safe and sound, we piled into the tent together. I was crammed in the middle. It took an hour before my frustration dissipated and I could fall asleep with my lap against Leah's backside. None of us slept well. We all woke stiff and miserable. The rain didn't subside. Leah ran with her pack to the nearest café straight away. I had to pack the wet tent with a haze sprinkling from the dreadful, grey sky. When Amos and I arrived, we were drenched.

She had a hot coffee in front of her.

"I can't believe this shit. I should never have listened to you about sleeping outside. Everyone else probably had a great time in the hostel last night. Nice showers, warm, dry, everything."

Grumpy, sulky, and irritated, I'd had enough. I cooked for her, set up that tent she resented. Our group took her in and shared our hearts with her. Some start on this trek with no idea about "travel." The constant shuffle between sunny hours, wine-soaked afternoons, *and* the times that took more patience, sympathy, and devotion. Any desire to create intimacy with Leah was gone. Amos was grumpy, too, but neither of us dared complain about anything beyond our power. I decided to break away from her – and my lovely family. At Burgos, instead of stopping with everyone else, I walked another few hours until I spotted accommodation. It was a small donativo albergue with two other pilgrims inside. One of them spoke English. When I woke in the morning and stretched, it was my first day being on my own. It had been two weeks.

91

Ep. 10
Long Nights

Humble, yet abrasively loud. Hospitable, but skeptical and wary. Crass objectivity. An insufferable dedication to presentation, respect, and appearance. Mindless obedience to tradition. Willing to accept both the narrow and wide, I was trapped between lines of hellfire. More laughter in their welcome than tomatoes in their sauce. A group who truly knew how to win over hearts through hungry stomachs and satisfied palates. No strangers to subservience, necessitated by a downward economy. Trapped in a land of blood and limoncello with only history to sell and style to pride themselves in. The best of cultivation to plate. Extroverts who had dinner until midnight, sipping conservative drinks. Masters of malleability.

I was ready for change.

The wine hangover from Bari kept my condition on the bow of ruin. My mind thumped. A drink would help. The firewater begged for company. Stuck in the day-after syndrome. My mind was untethered. But my lips weren't yet out of petrol. Anxious for scattered banter. A new country to defile. Ready to ascend into curiosity. As on most nights the past five weeks, I needed to pitch my tent away from the common eye. Or find a church. Then read a few pages of fiction after a small pot of pasta and hope something or someone manifested, modifying my night into a memorable one. It was late when a local directed me to the nearest park. I passed a few drunken youths and glanced enviously at their beers and communal joy. A content, elderly couple passed by. Next a tall, thin blonde woman walking her tiny dog. A shiver of middle class fluttered up my spine to my neck hairs. Then, a large clearing that overlooked Dubrovnik's old town. I went straight to a young couple under overhead lamps. Half-wasted excitement engrossed me. A sensation to stir new connections. Perhaps a pair of drinking buddies. I had so many questions. This was once friggin' Yugoslavia.

"I was young, but I remember a lot of bombs. They come from sea and land. They fly from all directions. They block roads, so we can't get out. They keep us within the walls of the city.

Bombed us for a long time. I spent many of time below street, you know in flats, piled with others. They destroyed parts of the city. They stole things when they come in."

"But I can hardly tell!"

"Union and UNESCO. But, not same as before. Still, you see tourism here?"

"Yea its fargin' full, mate. Jesus, I never saw so many tourists outside of Barcelona and the Eiffel Tower."

"So, you can understand the importance of authen… hmm…"

"Authenticity? Not an easy word. Yea, I do."

"Right, sorry, my English not so great."

"Your English is fantastic, never mind. Go on."

"Right, the authenticity to bring in the tourists. Our economy is stronger than others in old Yugoslavia now. We got the coast. Well, most of it. Probably because Tito was a Croat."

"Was he?" I asked with surprise.

"Yea, so with Tito gone, the Serbs wanted Dubrovnik coast badly, or at least the JNA. Our history is very complicated. Many problems. Dubrovnik was once a country, you know?"

"No, for real? I didn't. Jesus, this continent is bloody complicated. Canada is one nation across 10,000 kilometres. You have more than seven countries in 1000. Fuck, its mind-numbing. Gives a man a headache."

He laughed and nodded. "It is funny, but look around. That is why we have such beautiful women in the Balkans," as he lifted his eyelids. His girlfriend shook her head in sardonic disappointment and pursed her lips.

"What? It's true," he turned to her and carried on. "We have so much history. Thousands of years ago, many tribes from different civilizations far away, they all come to Central Europe. Canada is made of old Empires. People were bloody tired of all the fighting. That's why they left places like this. Canada brought promise of land, new life, and most important, peace."

Just then, I thought about the First Nations of Canada. If not for Europeans, perhaps Canada would still be cut into many different slices, divided by tribes.

That coastal tourism that brought prosperity to Croatian Dalmatia was guaranteed by borderlines. Borderlines drawn once Tito and his Partisan army "reformed" Yugoslavia after World War II. One small, awkward piece of that coast was divided on maps. This went back to the end of the seventeenth century. Ottomans were forced to relinquish land to the Habsburg Empire and Venice. A treaty between Empires was signed. Their war was over. Dubrovnik, however, like my friend said, was a sovereign state. They feared attack from the Venetians and gave a portion of their land to the Ottoman Empire. With Ottoman lines redrawn, Dubrovnik had a protectorate between themselves and their enemies. A shrewd strategy to shield themselves from any attempts by the Venetians or Habsburgs to control more of the Adriatic and its pearl, Dubrovnik. That decision gave two Ottoman-ruled provinces a tiny slice of the coast. Two provinces known as Bosnia and Herzegovina. When Tito stopped all the fighting between the Ustasa and Chetnik militias and became President, he insisted that the Bosnia-Herzegovina district be drawn to respect the old, Ottoman lines. This was something the first Serbian-led, Royalist Yugoslav government failed to do, intentionally. They lost support because of it.

"Here, people never get tired of fighting. Freddi, we lived months without water or electricity. When the JNA attacked, they went for electricity lines, or, wait, what is the fucking name? Ah, grid! Months without power, I remember that."

"What's the JNA?" I asked.

"It's complicated, but JNA was the Yugoslavia army. The thing is, it was mostly Serbian fighters at the end, you see. Everyone else was pushing for independence. When Tito died, everything fell apart. Not right away, but disaster started. When Yugoslavia fell, Slovenia wins their independence quickly. Then, everyone wants independence."

"So, Slovenia was the first. But I never heard of any war there?"

"It happened. Ten days. Many problems came from that."

"Ten days? Deezam, that was quick."

The Yugoslavia People's Army, or JNA, was a Serbian army. After Tito's death, it took some time, but in 1989 a President was named in the Socialist Republic of Serbia. Slovenia held a referendum, declaring independence in 1991. The Yugoslav People's Army responded. Tito's General People's Defence became the Central Defence, with its Headquarters in Belgrade. All districts were ordered to disarm. Slovenians resisted and repositioned their artillery. They had foreseen a reaction from the JNA. This led to numerous catastrophes. Of course, the cunning of Slovenians, and their internal government, saved them from any of it after many Slovenes changed sides during the Ten Day War and the JNA's failed attempt to seize the country.

None of the Croats I met mentioned Ustasa—including this young, educated couple. Ustasa was a different people's army. Croatia was a Nazi puppet state during the lead-up to World War II, guaranteed autonomy from the first Yugoslavian Federation by Germany if they agreed to the alliance. This Ustasa Army was created to defend newly independent Croatia. Instead of protecting the people of Croatia, the Army was used to murder hundreds of thousands of Serbs, tens of thousands of Jews and Roma, to create a "pure" Croatia. The Serbs were orthodox Christians. And the backbone of Ustasa was a Catholic pride dating back to the Holy Roman Empire, the Habsburg Empire, and finally, the Austro-Hungarian Empire.

When Germany invaded Bosnia in WWII, it became part of the Axis along with Austria, Hungary, Italy, and Croatia. Croatians agreed that Bosnians were a part of their historical lifeline despite their Muslim lineage. Together, Catholic and Muslim became allies with the common goal of exterminating the Orthodox Serbs. Ustasa built concentration camps similar to those in Poland and Czechoslovakia. They brought large numbers of Serbians to the camps for a massacre that is rarely mentioned. Some say seven hundred thousand Serbians died in those camps, or en route. Others say fewer. Some refused to admit they existed at all.

The deeper one delved into the "Land of South Slavs," or Yugoslavia, the easier it was to understand how Bosnia, Croatia, and Serbia-Montenegro were drawn into internecine wars. So many Empires and histories and traditions and cultures. All of them proud of their identities and dedicated to nationalistic aspirations. Diverse political movements gathered enough support to form their own guerrilla armies. Tito banned any talk of fascism or the atrocities that were committed before his Yugoslavia. Violators were punished. He held it together, cut clean from Stalin's Federation, yet remained allies with both Russia and the West. He became a self-ruling dictator respected by the global community. But once he died, the lid came off, and the "Habsburg Dilemma" erupted in a violent climax.

Everyone disapproved of the conservative Habsburg family and the Austro-Hungarian Empire. Movements in the nineteenth century popularized ideas of democracy and free speech. Dreams of liberty and autonomy spread across Europe. The Habsburgs ruled an enormous chunk of the continent for centuries, and once they agreed to a mutual denomination of Austria and Hungary in the "Compromise," the terrain was set for this long-standing consolidation of power. Bohemia and southern Slavs were rejected, ignored in this compromise. But Germans and Russians grew stronger, independently, and sought constituencies. Perhaps the Habsburgs weren't so awful after two World Wars and the seismic catastrophe that detonated after Yugoslavia's second disintegration. If the Habsburg family could have held on and become a union of states, like the European Union today, or the British Commonwealth, maybe the divided nation states wouldn't have been dissolved, or paralyzed by Hitler. That could have saved multitudes of Serbs, Roma, and Jewish from genocide. Many thought it would be greener pastures after the Habsburgs collapse; instead, an indescribable number of people died throughout Central Europe.

The young man assured me it would be fine to camp on the hill. He apologized for being unable to host me. "Our economy is not that good. We are both studying and live with our parents. But we can afford to buy you a beer if you like?" He looked at his girlfriend, and she nodded happily. "We're going to meet friends at our local pub."

I followed them with my gear through one of the prettiest cities I had ever seen. The fortified walls emanated a dazzling glimmer from the nightlight. A real castle city. One of the world's best success stories. Truly majestic. The Serbs had every reason to want it. This city-state had a fleet of two hundred ships as early as the 1500s. In the late eighteenth century, Dubrovnik boats sailed to America. A city for merchants, traders, politicians, and investors between the Near East and Colonial West. It flourished with artists, travellers, and even tourists. At the beginning of the 19th century, Napoleon realized its value and dispatched a man named Marmont. After two years, the French Army ruled. Marmont was made Duke of Ragusa (the city's name before Dubrovnik) for fighting off Russian invaders. He brought unfamiliar infrastructure and remained another ten years until the Congress of Vienna—a gathering of Great Powers after the defeat of Napoleon. Bonaparte's Empire was divided and returned. They claimed it was a mission for peace. Aside from the Crimean War, it worked until World War I. Then, Ragusa, or Dubrovnik as it was called after World War I, was handed to the Habsburgs during the Vienna Congress.

A heap of nonsensical hogwash erupted as my Croatian friend opened the bar door for his girlfriend and me. I hadn't felt this type of energy, the drunk camaraderie, since that day shortly after walking out of Rome, in Artena. Everyone crowded in from town for their last drinks. Two empty seats beside a group seemed the best chance for champagne-like release.

"Mind if we sit here?" I asked for a seat from another table. A young man acknowledged me and obliged. He responded in an obvious German-English accent. When he told me he was from Berlin, my words raced. "I lived in Berlin, crazy, yea, I lived in Prenzlauerberg. Man, what a place. Insanity! So many good times. But geezus, it was dangerous as well. I told a friend whose couch I crashed on, just before I left, I told him basically, 'I gotta get out of this city, it's killing me.'

"Ah, yes, ze nights de-ah kan get very late, ja? We gahzer in bars to forget ze horrible vinter veatha, oder?"

"Yea, the weather was shit. So grey. It might be cold in Canada, but fuck me, at least we get some sun. But man, I def had so much fun." We shared stories about parties, the street food, and cheap, fat, tasty Turkish kebabs. "And it was a place where international people go," I celebrated. "Something like here, but full-time, you know. People go to stay and there is art and music everywhere. Beautiful." In between tales, I was interrupted.

"Freddi," my Croatian friend called. "We're tired. We will go home. Are you okay here?" I looked at him with a frown.

"Come on, it's only starting here, my brother! You sure you need to leave?"

"Yes, it was great to meet you my friend and discuss many things. Good luck on the walking ahead. Maybe we see you all in Berlin!"

We hugged and I kissed his girlfriend on the cheek before sinking back into conversation with the Berliners. They had a caravan and a holiday apartment between them for the weekend.

"De-ah is a fridge with bee-ah in it and ve have some wodka? Maybe you like to come, Freddi?" I peered at a few girls across from us, at another table. One of them had made eye contact with me a few times. My pack was hard to ignore. Maybe my smell, as well.

"But of course, my friends! I would love to! But wait," I turned toward the girls. "Hi, how are you guys tonight? You wanna join our tables together?"

Before they responded, I moved our table and introduced myself. Surrounded by people who had the bug of travellers' ideology. A space where I could speak my passion and feel compassion from those around me. A space where I belonged, and was, more than anything, worth something. They were younger, but we sang similar songs and loved each other's company. We set out into the unknown world for these experiences. People came to Dubrovnik from many distant lands, just as they had before Napoleon. And the city wouldn't disappoint.

The city's cream-tiled bricks were a house of mirrors, or a white chocolate fantasy. Not a chip nor dent could be seen. Hundreds of people walked the main foyers. Voices deflected off the high, narrow walls. It was a maze of corridors and alleys filled with little Mediterranean restaurants. It was Santorini on the Adriatic. The sound of shoe soles echoed. I thought I could still hear a faint murmur of the suffering of those who'd faced the gallows, questioning Christendom. There was a jostle in the air. Bodies flowed through every inch of space. The congestion made it hard to think. Still, the walls, towers, and huge Renaissance

98

fountain captivated me. A gorgeous feature carved into an Ottoman bath house. Ferocious grins protruded everywhere, disgorging streams of water. Designed in the light of a new age and a growing city in need of river water. Impractical, questionable aesthetic, ugly, but wonderfully Baroque. Endless domes and palaces. Church ceilings made valiant and convincing attempts at expressing eternity. Spectral shapes offered heavenly order. A new order where a middle class had the chance to be a part of the show. A cosmic realignment. Something other than the wealth amassed by one's family. There was salvation for all, and art became a part of a civilized and cultured society. The architect's grandiose designs provided the illusion of pomp and circumstance for the Monarch, but it also gave the lower classes a taste of the beautiful and sublime.

It might have been harder to peel away from all of this if I hadn't gotten lost after a chaotic night of beers and spirits. My host had bowed out. Work in the morning. I waved him off, surrounded by men and women whose energy enchanted me. It wasn't that he left, but that I had only been to his house once. The one time I left my pack somewhere, with all the money I had in the world, and my goddamn passport. I didn't even get his address. Everything I owned was at his house. There was a thick blanket on the ground and my trusted pillow. How the hell would I find my stuff? The stairs leading to his studio flat looked exactly like at least a half-dozen others. They all led up steep hills. All identical. I thought maybe I should start yelling his name as loud as I could. Tempting. Instead, I walked and walked and walked, inspecting every door frame and comparing it to memory. There was always a small chance. Each time I thought I knew, or believed I would finally get lucky, I tried the door... and it was locked.

"I'll put the key under the mat," I remembered him saying. I had to find the door mat, only I couldn't remember how it differed from any other. Did he have plants out front? Of course not! Exhausted, I passed out on some stairs around seven. My best chance was to go back to his restaurant, find him and get the keys.

I remembered him saying, "My shift is pretty early, I gotta go."

"What's early?" I snickered.

"Okay, well, not that early, but early enough. Ten o'clock."

He would be at work after ten. All I had to do was ask around. "Do you know a restaurant where you can jump from the rocks into the sea?"

I walked into many little pizza shops and corner stores until one clicked.

I found my host running plates up and down the stairs. "Bro, you will not believe my night," I moaned.

He looked at me. He laughed at the state I was in. "I'll take a break in a few. Take a seat on the rocks and wait for me."

After a swim, I slept that whole day.

Ep. 11
Meditations

My uncle would say, "If this were Dodge City, you'd be dusted in flour and chased out of town in your britches." My time to get the hell out of Dodge was now. With the Bosnian frontier only a short, tough stretch, it made the challenge conceivable. An hour or two's walk would put distance between me and Dodge. Used my few Croatian Kunas to buy some food. More like sustenance than food. Booze sweat steamed off me even as I rested. Days of hiking with no shower made me feel dirty, but not as dirty as the liquor sweats. Loathing. I needed to hydrate. I hoped the border guards wouldn't be able to see, or smell, what a sorry state I was in.

I got lucky: the border-crossing was so busy, the guards seemed content to quickly process everyone to avoid delays or unpaid overtime. The land was barren. A full day of winding, rocky, mountainous roadways. All the traffic veered north. Cars heading for Mostar in Bosnia, before turning towards Split and the Dalmatians. Mostar's bridge attracted many. A bridge designed by Istanbul's builders and a young architectural apprentice of the Ottoman in the 1600s. Croatian troops destroyed it in late '93. Then, because they needed it for the war, they rebuilt it as a cable bridge to cross the canyon. Afterwards, Croats remained on one side. The Bosniaks stayed on the other. Reconstructed with the same regional limestone as before; too many scars lingered for forgiveness. A city once highlighted by integration, now divided by Stari Most.

The Way was full of lush forest until Trebinje. A full day of walking through gorgeous woodland. Ahead would be a grind. 30 kilometres of shimmying through a gauntlet of a trail. The people of Trebinje struck me as odd. Very tall. I thought of a Bosnian girls' volleyball team I'd seen on TV during the last Olympics. Tall, thin, bronzed, smiling women in the streets. Food prices were so cheap. People could afford to go out for a meal. Like in Italy, lots of people spent their time after dinner meandering through streets following the streetlamps. I wanted nothing more than to speak with the locals. Meet some random Bosnians. Take advantage of the cheap beers. But my tent ended up, by itself, between some bushes near the river. I couldn't resist lying down after I ate. Another long day. I awaited the Montenegrin border.

A roadhouse appeared.

Everything on the menu was affordable. A hamburger and chips for a couple euros. Wood-finished benches surrounded by dense forest. The scent of pine and lavender filled my nose. A stream was close enough to hear, especially when I closed my eyes and focused. The server greeted me like an alien. A strange foreign entity arrived from Timbuktu. They howled in laughter after I explained my pilgrimage. Keep moving.

The winding highway straightened a few hours after lunch. A stunning auburn dawn covered the landscape. I climbed to the border. Tall, strong trees stood off in the distance. I watched the flat valley change colours. The fire in the sky diminished. A shanty with bar stools tempted me. The massive, undisturbed field offered ample space. I ignored the signs and pushed for the crossing. Montenegro's border, 1500 meters. The night deepened.

My tent was bitter. The late, Mediterranean summer remained warm, but in the mountain night, cold scratched my bones. Hostile air dripped fear into my eyes as my breath appeared. In a field of high, wet, and later frosty grass, I could only fantasize about sleep. A fear of freezing every single, sleepless night until Istanbul haunted my imagination. It played tricks on me. It tore at me as I ground my teeth. Shivering in the only clothes I had and a thin, summer linen sack. Alone with a headlamp and two dead batteries against the frozen earth. I thought of my floor mat, rolled up on the Adriatic ferry deck.

"Why, why couldn't someone have just friggin' asked me if it was mine? I was the only one around that it would have fit anyhow. Most of the others had rollie suitcases, for fuck sakes! I mean, one look and you woulda realized," I vented, curled inside my cotton liner.

"Why didn't I just turn and notice the fucking thing. I'm such an idiot. Fucking idiot!" At sunrise, I drifted off to sleep once the earth stopped pushing cold against my skeleton.

The Way continued down a long, steep hill. Hours ahead for my knees to endure. The idea of clear, refulgent seawater suffused my tendons, muscles, and nerves with excitement. I knew how the water felt. I relished the scent of the air. On the road to one side was a bunch of boarded up country homes. One grabbed my attention like an areole on Mount Mashu. Built like a cairn, intermittent layers of clay and marble-coloured stone. Fences so short they spoke of life preceding the many nations who'd won and lost Montenegro in defeat. An expression of free reign, a time exempt from fear. A perfect, unobstructed view of birds flitting, neighbours gardening, and the intoxicating deep, blue sea. I pictured myself in this stone cabin, hacking away, digging for words to display my disillusionments clearly enough, then jumping on my moped and heading to the Bay of Kotor for a swim. Only a two-hour walk uphill from the tranquil, exotic coast, it rested in mid-air, catching summer breezes and morning clouds. A church further along exhibited the same subdued abandonment. I found a market to get lunch.

Afterward, I squatted with my thin liner on flat, sandy ground. With my legs crossed, I breathed. Five seconds. Air filled my lungs. "One, two..." I counted the simple mantra in my head and let the air release. A full month of walking to rest and meditate. A place, inside of me and outside, inviting serenity. The defining moments on the Camino de Santiago. I chased this idea, but failed time and again to sit and release until now. Torn by the desire to continue walking longer in search of the right tree. Interactions with others, or distractions on full beaches. The desire to read a while or sleep early or splash a few nights away with wine and beer. I had now settled into calm. Nothing more than breathing. The breathing exercises released my shoulders from their hinges. I went from feeling like an Indonesian labourer, carrying 70-kilogram baskets of sulphur from Mt. Ijen, to a hawk gusting over the Camino Meseta in Spain, where something quite peculiar had once taken place.

* * *

The wind was still, the heat coiled along the skin of my temples. Many people skipped this part of the Camino, calling it boring. I called them cowards. This tedious, unfurling prairie brought silence. Days before this, I left my Camino family and walked ahead to clear the air. The crowds of people thinned as the land transitioned into a plain. Sensationalizing freedom meant appreciating wide open spaces. I strolled out, alone, from the last village, knowing the notoriety of the coming trail. Eighteen kilometres of nothing, including shade. I stood at the foot, looking down at the pebbled country under the last tree. Beside me, a man sold overpriced drinks from his food truck.

"Bro, you've given me the wrong change."

He apologized for his mindless error. The long plain wasn't the only reputable thing on this Meseta. I sipped my crisp drink ignoring his static, which I was also warned about. The icy liquid froze my overheated face.

"Eighteen kilometres," I repeated to myself.

"Long way, my friend, maybe you buy a water, no?" I shrugged and looked at the Coke, now half-full and tepid.

"Why is it only those first and second gulps?" I murmured, shaking my head. "It never carries to the last mouthful." I put the empty can on his truck counter, waved goodbye, and pressed my plastic shoes against the shattered stones.

"Buen Camino!" He shouted supportively.

Fitted, tawny grains at the spear-tips of dry, wheat strands reflected speckling amber light across the long prairie. The whirr of a single tractor. The only sound but my footsteps. I could see it trolling through high, straight, golden hairs building haycocks. My mind, rather than the heat, enslaved me. My memory shuffled through recent encounters.

"The other day, Freddi, I was walking alone," Amos had

103

said, walking beside me. He sounded confessional. "The landscape, nothing around but hills. Nobody around. I decided," he paused.

"Decided what, yo?"

"I just stopped there, out in the open, and pulled it out. I started masturbating, staring out at the nature around me. The wind doing the work."

The idea percolated through my mind. I carefully looked around. Only running flatlands, solitude, quiet. Pristine air. I was rattled. Paranoid. A second, curious combine driver had appeared. I shuffled my feet and continued walking. One foot in front of the other. I breathed in, stepped forward, and breathed out again. I watched my shadow on the ground and followed the fringe of land from the stony road. My mind wandered, again.

"Freddi, dear, I want you home for supper, okay?" My mom spoke with a tempered finish to instil seriousness. I had my Tonka trucks on huge, upright mounds of sand and stone. A stagnant bulldozer was parked beside. The city was doing road construction near our house. The weather was fresh. A perfect, 27 degrees Celsius with a gentle, refreshing breeze, playing in the dirt with my workman's face. Eight years of age, ready to be the caretaker for my single mommy. From one end of the street, two boys stormed past me on bikes. Older boys from my block.

"Little Freddi! What's up, buddy?" A voice interrupted my silent play. I rose to dispute his claim of being little and took chase. He was too quick for my ambitious but short, undeveloped legs. The two of them turned the corner at the stop sign long before me. I reached it panting, with my hands on my knees. There was another older neighbourhood boy leaning on the rear of his family's station wagon.

"Freddi! Get over here, waddaya doin', buddy?" In between breaths, I explained.

"I was moving the dirt for the road workers tomorrow when Mitch stormed passed and called me little. What a punk."

"Did you really think you'd catch him?" His look suggested I was delusional, but I paid no attention. It only strengthened my resolve.

"I will. Next time." As a resilient sportsman at school, races were my moments to show off and prove myself. Crowning moments. Then the boy mentioned that *The Monkeys* were on TV. My mom didn't have cable, so I ran enthusiastically with him to his basement. His rotund mother stomped down the stairs.

"Hello, Freddi. Good to see you. You guys head up and get some Tang when you want, it's waiting for you."

"Thanks mom! Listen, Freddi. I got this thing I want to show you. It's real fun, wanna see?"

My head nodded, excited for everything.

"We have to get in the back of my wagon. It'll be way better there."

"After the show!"

The Monkeys finished. We ran out the swinging, metal door singing the theme music. It bounced closed in repetitive jaunts.

"Me first!" I announced cheerfully, peering into the long station wagon's back hatch.

"Okay buddy, check this out!" My friend pulled a can of whipped cream from a pile of clothes and sprayed it in his hand. My face brightened.

"Try some." I didn't know what to do at first, so he took it back. "Look here, silly." His face inflated as the cloud of sugar and gas expanded into his mouth. I grabbed it from him and packed my mouth.

"Oh, it's so good!" I proclaimed. Before another mouthful, my friend took the can again and claimed he had something even better.

"Is it cherries? I love cherries!"

"Better," he replied.

He unbuttoned his pants and pulled his hardened penis out and sprayed it with whipped cream. "Now try it from here, Freddi. It's even better, I promise!"

A supersonic train, carrying nothing but hyper-nervousness and anxiety ran right over and through me. A sudden realization: I was not meant to be in the car with this boy. The space became small and suffocating. I looked at the door, the windows, and the carpeted floor. I glanced everywhere, except at the whipped cream.

"It's okay, relax. It's fine, it's only fun, that's all. Here let me show you, it's nice, trust me." The boy offered a conciliatory smile. I froze. He took a button from my shorts. He pulled them

105

down with my underwear. I had only ever touched this thing to go pee and wondered why he was touching it.

"Now, I am going to put the cream on. It's funny!" He covered it and stopped. "Not bad, right?"

"It's cold," I trembled. "Why don't we just eat it?" I asked nervously.

"Freddi, we will. Let me try yours." He bent over and put his mouth around the foam to swallow it. I shuddered, my teeth grinding. My body felt strange. He lifted his head.

"Wow, that was great! Wasn't it?" My face contorted in discomfort. He carried on consoling me. "Just try it, buddy. It really is better this way, I promise." He took the back of my head and moved it toward his waist. "Taste it now. It's so good, go ahead."

I had my mouth open when his hand squeezed my skull and hair. Just as the white cream hit my lips, I backed away. "Oh, no, I gotta go, sorry, thanks." I spun for the door, wiggling the handle.

"Freddi, it's okay, buddy. Relax, what's wrong with you?"

"Yea, nothing, just that my mommy said I had to be home for supper. I forgot. I'm gonna be in trouble." I got the door ajar and swung from the confined space feeling first the open air. I landed on the pavement, on my feet. I ran to my house.

The screen door was closed. When I hit it, the sound reverberated throughout the entire duplex. My hand vibrated, trying the door.

"Freddi, Freddi, what's going on with you? What's wrong?" My mom's voice held a tension that seemed unusual but appropriate. She reached for me and wrapped me into her chest. I wailed into her shirt.

I exited this trance stunned. This distant, forgotten memory. Now so lucid, vivid, colourful, even fragrant. My feet moved, one in front of the other on the long and stony road as before. The wheat was to my right, a buzzing tractor far off and dead, burnt shrubs to my left. I stood atop a hill, shaking and confused. The sun waned; the dead air cooled. At the end of the descent, about a kilometre further, I could see a building, more behind it, and a paved road.

"I can't believe I just went there," I said loudly, looking up. "All of it, like that?" I shook my head in disbelief. "Some kind of meditative walking. It's like I was transported away, into the friggin' past. But I didn't even stop walking, what the fuck?"

Ep. 12
Harbour's Thunders

Under bulging, sparse white clouds, I paddled softly enough to stay afloat. My first Montenegrin sky revealed itself. A mellifluous song played each time the wake rolled in gently from distant motorboats. Steady, underwater, hummingbird vibrations. They soothed my nerves. The buoyant rhythm of the sea shook me from my morning slumber. Out of the water, I reached for my light, cotton liner to dry myself.

"Hey! You going Istanbul?"

I squinted. "Hah, uh, yea," I said, confused. "How did you…"

"I'm from border," he explained, laughing from his truck window. "I saw you. Remember me?" His face widened, his lips cleared his teeth, eyes wide.

"Um, yea, sure," I muttered, even though I didn't. I did remember two border guards who laughed in my face. Alone, at the edge of their light, surrounded by black mountains, at the edge of a foreign country where I'd never been. They not only laughed in my face, they also gave me inaccurate advice.

"Go back to Bosnia *or* 23 kilometres walk to Herceg Novi, that is *all*." It was a 90-minute walk back to Bosnia's last town. "Oh," they carried on, "watch for wolves, plenty in the area."

Herceg Novi wasn't the first village. Their tasteless humour reflected weak minds. The old church was five kilometres from the border. It was only two kilometres from the border where I found houses and a field for my tent.

This border guard now greeted me as if nothing had happened and continued with his courtesies. "It's impossible to camp in park."

He said there was a public beach about three kilometres ahead. All the *beaches,* as he called them, were cement walkways. I paced onwards until a patch of grass with three benches and one large tree covering the area. Ideal for one night. A supermarket a few meters away. In the market, I scanned prices on bar code stickers, trying to match them with beers in a large, industrial fridge. I looked for the cheapest. I wasn't the only one.

"Grab that one," a scruffy guy suggested from over my shoulder. I pointed to 65 cents.

"Yes, yes, same, grab one for me too!" He pointed at my beard, "What's with that? I mean, I guess my beard is no better." He chuckled to himself through tobacco stained, untreated teeth. We found a place to sit at a picnic bench across from an 80-year-old man. I stared at another old man, in the sea, washing his catch from the day. The scene before me assuaged my soul. It suggested a healthy, long, uncomplicated life. My new friend passed me a cigarette.

"Probably best place. If you camp anywhere, I guess it can be."

I complimented the beer, "Is it Montenegrin?"

He responded swiftly. "No, no, Serbia." He grinned wearily and looked at me with despair. "At least they are not complete fuck-ups." I tapped his can with the heel of mine.

"It's not bad at all, brotha."

"This is my tenth one – and still sober," he replied. A shellfish diver and dealer to hotels. He worked thirteen-hour days during the warmer seasons.

The old man beside us spoke. "Where are you from?" as he passed me a cigarette.

"Shit, you speak English?" He had been a worldly sailor, the diver told me. After a second round, my new mate stood from our picnic table.

"Have to go, you know? Or else I get trapped here. Take care, man. Have a great trip," he finished empathetically. "Get back to that park for tonight, don't worry about stupid border guards."

I bade the archaic sailor goodbye and took to a bench in the park to cook another dinner of pasta. Afterwards, I opened my book under a streetlight, under the big tree, looking at the glowing skylight of stars and moon. A grand surprise, as I turned the page of my book. Hemingway wrote of Roncesvalles in Basque Country. He had gone there to fish before meeting with his friends at the bull races, in Pamplona. He mentioned a man in Roncesvalles who'd walked there from St-Jean-Pied-de-Port. 100 years later, I walked the Camino from the same place. Completing these grand endeavours had more of a gritty veneer of bravery then, when the average person would never consider such an expedition. But pilgrims had been walking the Camino Frances for five hundred years or more. Before automobiles, people had their feet, or horses.

Two young women approached. One flicked onion with her fingers onto the grass. I tried to concentrate on reading until one of them left. The one that stayed lit a cigarette. My book cover closed.

"Hey, sorry to bother you, but do you have a smoke?"

"Why not?"

"Per che, non! I'm Freddi – and incredibly thankful."

"I'm Anya," she announced, then paused for a moment. "Are you from Italia, Freddi?" Her voice resonated crimeless lyrics written by a patient hand in cursive letters.

"That's all my Italian, I'm actually Canadian. And you?"

"I'm Serbian."

"Shit! That's funny, I met a Serbian girl swimming this afternoon. So, you're really everywhere in this hood. Where did your friend go?"

"She went to pay somebody something. She's my sister."

"I guess she likes warm beer?" There was a sack of cans by Anya's feet. She giggled playfully.

"She drinks cider. I'm the beer drinker." The bullshit poured between us from a burst dam once we'd pushed past the surface material. She was energetic. She showed no signs of being self-conscious. She was a student of life, an eccentric. She was a bookworm, in love with illustrative and insightful words. She was talking about her last year of university when her sister arrived.

"Well, sorry for interrupting *you guys*," her sister emphasized her irony with bulging eyes, "and your little party."

"Did you pay off the debt collector?" Anya redirected.

"You guys are sisters?" I asked, changing the subject.

"Well, we are cousins," Anya corrected herself, "but we call each other sisters. Don't we?"

Her cousin nodded.

"So, the whole family is here then?"

"We come every year."

"I'm Freddi. Nice to meet you."

"I'm Mila," she introduced herself, "when I had blonde hair, people here thought we were Germans. Blonde hair, dark eyebrows. Especially, Anya's unibrow!"

"Don't worry, Anya, some people like unibrows, don't let Mila fuck with you." I gave Mila a deserving fist pound.

"So, are you gonna come with us to the bar, Freddi? We are meeting Mila's boyfriend."

I had an ignorant opinion of Serbs before crossing the Adriatic. It was ugly. It came from speculations about awful historical backlash and hatred. The Balkans gained a stigma of violence during the political disorder that followed the dissolution of Yugoslavia. Media in the West convinced most people that Serbs were the evil villains of the conflict. Feudal violence should be left to its territories for its tribes to resolve. American napalm in Southeast Asia made that clear thirty years earlier. The enemy was easy to demonize as sub-human: savage Indians, communist Russians bent on world domination, Muslims who hated freedom and wanted jihad. This conflict in the Balkans had so many moving parts. It was difficult to ignore what had happened in the Yugoslav Wars when President Tito died. But that was only one portion of the overarching narrative. The collapse of Yugoslavia in '92 led to Serb offensives and encumbering genocide against Muslims, especially in Bosnia. Few Bosniaks survived. Where it became complicated, and what media ignored, was that Serbs were also the target of genocide by Croat Ustasa, who had fought alongside Nazi Germany forty years earlier. I began to appreciate what my friend in Dubrovnik meant when he said, "It's all very confusing." Before seeing things for myself, before getting here and meeting people, whenever I heard Serb, or Serbian, I imagined a militant, bloodthirsty, jagged-toothed soldier. They were reckless, uncompassionate, trained killers. I never had similar thoughts about Croatians or Bosnians.

And then I crossed a mountain pass from Bosnia into Serbian-allied Montenegro. The last group of people, fewer than a million, to gain their independence from Yugoslavia. The gorgeous, mountainous coast was filled with Serbs.

"We're here," said Mila and Anya unanimously.

"Already?"

We had taken 30 paces from our bench to a medium-sized tiki-hut with a roof of dry palm leaves. The minute we breached the straw door frame, Mila ran to her man. The bar area was packed, shoulder to shoulder, with blonde-haired men in matching buzz-cuts. Tight fisted, with unimpressed faces, they squeezed their pint glasses instead of drinking from them. I was about to smile and nod, but Anya pulled me aside.

"Freddi, come get a table with me, okay?"

I scanned the list, looking for the word Pivo between all the mixed cocktails from Cuba, Mexico, and Thailand. "I'll have …"

"Yea, that's the same as me," Anya confirmed my order.

I looked down at my nearly finished beer, then at Mila. The portrait of a fool, she stood beside six guys. Each of them had an arm on the bar, holding it down, grunting. All of them were seated. I couldn't tell if she'd gotten in a single word or if her wonderful man had even acknowledged her to his friends. He didn't present as a guy she should run toward. She was a sensational young lady, with the gift of gab. He was a closing vice grip on social progression.

"Hey Freddi! Never mind her. She is a big girl," Anya interrupted my thoughts, noticing my attention. Somehow, I doubted what she said. We got a second round. Anya loved to read, even in English from time to time. She called her boyfriend in Belgrade a hermit because he "didn't like people."

"Or people don't like him, I'm not sure. Mila says people don't like him. And that he's too tall, bony, and pale."

He sounded like a dream.

"So, with all these great qualities, what is it you guys find in common?"

"We both love to read."

"Right, okay. So, he's a Peter North in the sack?"

"Who's Peter North?"

I grinned comically, "A Canadian porn star with a huge cock."

Before long, we were talking about McCarthy's, *The Road* and how darkness and truth brought about human despair.

Mila returned. She looked morbid, embalmed in bitterness. She fumed from her ears. She was either going to kill someone with her beating eyes or break down crying. I felt horrible for the poor girl, but shit, I could tell the guy was bad news when he sat with that lazy ass bartender. Her "boyfriend" sauntered over in confident, paced steps, grinning. He introduced himself calmly, to Anya and then to Mila, who replied with aggravation.

"I'm Karolina," she responded.

Pulling at my beard, I was frazzled. "Maybe it's not the guy?" I thought to myself.

I kept silent and turned my attention back to Anya, uninterested in their summer drama. As soon as we got to talking about *Cloud Atlas*, Anya spoke with enthusiasm.

"It brings real life out of fantasy. I love this kind of thing. A fantasy in real life." She froze a moment and looked at her glass before smiling again. "It makes everything seem possible, know what I mean?"

I did, but for Mila's sake, I hoped that the relationship she had in her mind was more than the fantasy it plainly appeared to be. A couple side glances across the table, and Mila was sulking with her arms crossed. Part of me felt parental and protective, but I thought at the same time something else.

"She's finally realized. He fucked her in his car, then, like other seasonal hook-ups, he was ready to move on."

Self-pity and disillusionment became evident in her building tears. Worse than everything, he sat smiling and unscathed through the awkward silence between them. He looked at her, then at us smiling, then back at her again, smiling some more. Anyone could see it made her feel smaller and smaller every time he looked over and grinned. She was his big punchline. This summer's joke for his friends. Only she didn't get it until this moment. He backed into his place at the trough with his mate where he'd left his beer, chuckling intentionally. She was marooned with embarrassment and shame. Tears accumulated in her eyes.

"Mila, Mila, come on." The guy was a prick and not worth her tears. "You don't have to. I mean, hey. Look, come on, it's summer and, unfortunately, speaking as a traveller, very well-versed in this game, this guy knows you're leaving and he's taking care of number one. That's the long and short of it, I'm afraid."

112

Her shoulders relaxed and her face calmed, momentarily. I carried on rambling about something that might help her overcome his arrogance. I reminded her that he would make ugly babies and even uglier grandkids.

"Men are insensitive, especially him," I added. We were, after all, only humans, and most of us prick men were selfish before we had children, some of us even afterwards. We got ourselves glued into a narcissistic way of life, ignorant to it as well. We fell too far into the rabbit hole to ever surface. "I'm sorry. Plus, you're far too intelligent for this guy."

A few moments passed of silence, Anya and I sipping our beers while Mila trembled in front of her cider. Her despondent stare was ready to shatter the thick mug. Then, she erupted.

"I'm going home!"

"Well, you don't have to go, finish your drink at least?"

She stormed away in a fury like a small tornado. I took care of her drink.

"Another round, Anya?" I hoped she wouldn't race off with the teen queen.

"Yea, one more sounds good. Problem is," she relinquished in a guilty tone. "After a couple, I don't wanna stop, you know?"

I wanted to push the table aside and dive in for a big hug. She was preaching to the choir. I loved the words falling from her lips. I no longer needed to hide my insatiable lust for debauchery. Thunder broke in the sky like a shattering wall of concrete. Rain started to fall.

"Now where the fuck am I gonna sleep? Anything but rain, come on!"

She assented compassionately, "I'd let you sleep in our little shack, but my dad wouldn't be a fan."

"Plus, with Mila the drama princess and her gang, where the hell would I fit anyhow?"

Her phone rang after a booming crack of thunder, "Mila is back at the house." It was beer o'clock, and Anya had me on my heels waiting for her next dialogue. "I should go," as she flicked off her phone. "Told my dad it would be about an hour."

"I guess now that Mila is there, you are alone in the wild night; lucky he doesn't know you're with a derelict beard-o!" I stroked my beard with a suggestive smile. Out from the shanty bar and away from the dry palm leaves, we walked toward her place, away from my park.

"I think I know a place where you can stay the night."

"Oh yea?"

Two cars in a very large, wooden, over-the-water garage once used for boats. It was dark inside, very dark but for the night sky. I spun around as she prepared to speak. I knocked my hat from her head and kissed her with both of my hands wrapped behind her ears. She jolted her head back. As quick as she moved back, she fell into me again. Her mouth busied and her tongue coursed through my lips and against my tongue like a rod trying to clean a pipe. She kissed me like it might have been her last, ever. Like morning would never come and this was her last embrace. It left me startled and lascivious. Rain slapped the roof. She trembled excitedly. My hands raced along her body, groping first her long, gorgeous neck as I'd wanted to do for hours. And then through her thin, short dark hair.

"Oh, hi!" I said comically, "Is this, okay?" Not a word was spoken. She went right back into my face with animal confidence. Wanton and uninhibited, she took my cock into her hand. We passed words without sound, without more than faint cries of salvation. I slid my hand into her undone pants – she backed off.

Sweat poured from our bodies, our moisture mixed. I unhooked her bra strap before lifting her onto some wood panelling. I grabbed her left breast like a cup and twisted her little nipple. My heart smashed with the storm above. This wasn't a time to be cantering along, I alerted myself. Bereft of patience, she spoke.

"My dad is gonna worry."

I twisted her nipple gently. I looked at my open shorts, then a second time with my eyebrow up inquisitively.

"Well, I mean, what's a little while longer? Really, you wanna stop?"

"No, I really don't wanna stop." I pulled her by the tight, little shorts that had been taunting me, covering the upper part of her long, slender legs. Before she contemplated changing her mind, I squeezed her waistline and pulled at her shorts until she helped me slip them all the way to the ground. Her arms rose to the wood frame above her head. In a gazebo, with short and quick

114

breaths, a series of panting echoes fell into our chamber. Legs tight and stiff, her thighs squeezed my cheeks. A force of dawn-like light, her horizon exploded. Intensity needled her nerves, and she fingered my hair, pulling like she was out in a garden, uprooting weeds.

"Oh, fuck," she hollered. I glanced around, thinking there was someone, or worse—her dad.

"What, what, wha?" I looked up at her, frantically, then out and around again.

"Nothing, nothing, fuck! Don't you fucking stop!" I approached her by wrapping my body against her back and torso and out leapt a throaty, harrowing call of excitement. Over the banister, across the sea being pattered by rain and lit up by strokes of lightning, a huge relief of unending curiosity. A chiropractic disassembly of a dozen knots tied into her shoulder blades. I forced one hand down on her neck and the other against one ass cheek. Her teeth clamped into the wood banister.

When I panted that my moment had come, she swung around 180 degrees to face me, hit the ground, and forced me straight into her mouth. She might have stopped breathing for a full minute. My legs convulsed and knees gave out on top of her. At the brink of consciousness, two voices erupted.

"Hey! Hey!" Flashlights sparked like cameras snapping. Both of us naked with clothes everywhere, half drunk and smelling of sex, startled, bitter, but laughing.

"You go! You go!"

"Shit, yo, this has got to be awkward," I responded facetiously. We left the garage, apologizing. "Guess I won't be sleeping there. And what about tomorrow?" I asked confidently. "Let's meet for breakfast and a swim, or?"

"Well, I tried to mention it before you ripped my pants off," she paused with a smile.

"Yea, okay, and?"

"I'm leaving back to Serbia in like three hours."

"Really?"

"I'm sorry. I have to go."

A single, final embrace under the awning of a shuttered restaurant. The rain quit. On the boardwalk, feeling defeated, a church's little steeple, bumping into the clouds. It was close enough to the sea that I could still hear the mild ripples. Before

115

making a move for the church, I noticed a small boat bobbing up and down. The shadow of a rod perched over the steel trim. Dark shadows that would dance until sunrise. The clouds receded. Soon, the stars would dominate the sky again. The world propagated fear in barrel loads. We were, most of us, so afraid of one another, we became consumed by self-loathing or self-indulgence. No one was safe from rejection.

The sea moved like silicone, jiggling slowly as I touched it. I noticed a fisherman off the side of his boat, his feet kicking in the water. He was on the bow of a metal dingy packed with a single-horse engine. It was barely big enough for one person. It could have been the Old Man and his Sea. He sharpened his boning knife on a piece of hide hooked to the anchoring rope attached to the pier. That whetting sound from the blade, from skin and steel, rocked me gently, like the boat did for the fisherman as he chased dusk every morning. He belonged nowhere other than in his little boat. Smooth winds against thread-like vibrations, the same oscillating rhythm brought me to a drowsy stillness. The crashing symbols in my brain ceased, and I nearly drifted far enough away to shake off Anya. I could still try. No better way to wash the beer glaze off for good than to dive into the cold abyss. The slow waves hypnotized me with their emerald chimes along the chimneys of my lobes.

"Forget her," I said to myself. "You know how it is. Focus on peace and calm, Freddi. That is all there is."

Ep. 13
Projectile, Hard Times

Cars appeared like micro-machines, hovering as they whisked around on the other side of the water. I noticed a ferry darting quickly back and forth from each end of the bay. Here, on the Way toward Tivat, the spotless sky was light blue ink. Flawless reflections of the mountains splashed across the sea. A group of kids played volleyball knee-deep in seawater. The season was nearly finished. The rich, bare-chested Russians had returned to Moscow. The only people left were trying to savour the final moments of holiday before re-integrating with society back in Serbia. Tivat's cobblestone lanes hosted swarms of couples and families over white tablecloths. A conspicuous pilgrim cast a long shadow over their exorbitance and vanity.

After gathering lunch from a supermarket, I spent the second half of my day meandering toward a small peninsula past Tivat's airport. The only sign of life was a glowing bar sign, shaking from the music inside. I still needed to find a decent camp, but I needed a beer even more. The place was a massive, overhanging open terrace with a stunning view. All of it centred around a small pool, beige leather couches, and a huge, glistening dance floor. Despite all it offered, there were only two people inside. The doorman and bartender, sitting together.

Minimal imagination was necessary to visualize the money that floated around this place in the busy season. Ice buckets of champagne, premium Russian vodka, skinny blondes in tiny shorts and lifted tank tops, and egos worthy of a mighty king. Dress shirts, dark sunglasses, neck tattoos, and black, polished shoes. After my beer, the young man behind the bar filled my wrinkled, plastic water bottle. He assured me that along the bay, there would be space for a tent. His enclave was no more than a pile of stones and a lawn chair. An incline in the road was something to follow. A lay-in of dirt appeared with a log across its width. It took no more than a few minutes to set camp.

* * *

Separated from my family on the Camino, I met many new pilgrims, one at a time. New people and the hunt for a different future triggered verbal diarrhoea, stories of past struggles and self-doubt. Most of the other pilgrims were on their version of the Way for a particular desire or objective. They believed it would bring them a conclusive answer or resolution. For some, it was therapy. For one woman, it was a challenge she promised herself long before life took a turn for the worse.

In a small courtyard across from a cafe, a Colombian sat on a fake-metal Chinese-made chair. Shaded by high, golden brick walls, she sat alone. A book between her hands. As I walked by exiting town, I noticed a beautiful sketch of a Gothic church. Her round cheeks widened from her lips as she acknowledged my compliments. Between sips of coffee, she explained why she had titanium crutches. Sticks that looked quite different from anything others used. I leafed through her accurate drawings. Her work was impressive—remarkably detailed and realistic, yet still aesthetically pleasing.

"I was an architect back in Colombia," she looked at the images, then to the steeple above us. "I was on a site, monitoring with the head builder. There was a deep, unnecessary hole. I fell inside." My hands pulled away from the pages and covered my eyes. They slid down my cheeks then came together under my bearded chin. Such devastation deserved great sympathy. But I had no words.

"It was a long time ago. I've moved on." She spoke calmly after my expression of empathy. She was paralysed for years after that fall. She had to learn how to walk again. It took years to learn how to use the crutches.

"It took patience," she assured me.

"And strength," I replied.

She was a different type of pilgrim.

"I got good compensation." The worksite paid her comfortably, so she didn't worry about money. When she could roam with confidence, she took her crutches to Thailand and became a diving instructor. "I always wanted to do that, so I went to Koh Tao. It was wonderful because I didn't need my legs as much."

Her English was incredible. The woman had studied, worked hard, and was a survivor. And the architect inside insisted she explore the world.

"I went to India afterwards. It was very tough."

She was pale enough to be foreign, but she had dark skin. She had a noticeable body. I knew how it was for foreign women in India. I heard the stories of misguided men without control.

"I could hardly walk, and they were grabbing my breasts on the train and in the streets." But she was not bitter. She was defiant. "It was hard to enjoy my time there. At one guesthouse, I was in the outdoor shower. A few minutes of washing off, and I noticed two sets of eyes overhead, looking in. I screamed." The guest-house owner had sold tickets to men for a peep show. Unfortunately, these kinds of events weren't uncommon. Tour groups went with their guides on paid excursions to beaches south of Mumbai. In Goa and Gokarna, the men walked beaches scanning free-spirited Europeans in bikinis, some, if lucky, topless.

"I didn't let it stop me. Saw a few of the great halls and enjoyed what I could. And then came to Europe. I promised myself three things if I ever walked again: I would scuba dive, visit the Taj, and walk the Camino de Santiago."

It took 55 days, but she did it. Nobody carried her pack, and unlike many lazy punks, she walked the first day out of St. Jean and the whole Meseta. She faced only one minor blister. She was forced to move with patience. That became an advantage. She had to form a special romance with the Way. Others took the bus at Santiago, but she continued walking to Fisterra's lighthouse, at the very edge of Spain. She stumbled upon Mar De Fora beach. She was the last of the pilgrims I met on that beach. When she arrived, I had already been living on that beach in my tent for a few weeks.

From the courtyard where we sipped coffees and discussed her life, we decided to walk together. She was a blazing candle in anyone's dark room. She was a beacon of motivation and inspiration. Life dealt her a cruel blow that would have destroyed many people. She found her Way to overcome all the obstacles. She was also charming to the point where I wanted to be around her just to soak in the positive energy. Barely older than me, years of gruelling rehabilitation had sculpted her into a paragon of humility and effort. But most of all, she had forgiveness. Even for that guesthouse dirtbag in India. She could have been angry and frustrated. She could have demanded revenge, or even fair legal consequences. Anyone who took the time to slow down and engage with her would confirm that the world needed more people like her.

* * *

Morning routines were mechanical. Get in motion. One foot after the other. Do it again. Every task, completed in sequence. Each item went back into my pack in the same place. Mental checklists prevented mistakes. Packing a rucksack day after day, it became easy to leave behind items like socks and tent pegs. A mundane rhythm with a surprisingly spirited choreography. A daily, ritualistic dance. A peaceful meditation before my first footsteps. On a solitary log, overlooking the tranquil Bay of Kotor, I used my last few drops of water to brush my teeth.

The first house I encountered, I approached the door and asked, "Please, water?" as I pointed to my bottle with pleading eyes. The man filled it for me and shut his door.

The hot sun remained tolerable, unlike near Rome. Still, sweat poured, and I became increasingly weaker. My body felt as soggy as a wet carpet. The Camino taught me to put my back foot to front, no matter how sore or tired I was. The road descended and split in two directions. The nearest town, Rose, was down a long, paved switchback. My stamina faded on every turn. And my face wrinkled with every irritating car horn. I couldn't wait to bite into a sandwich. A layer or two of salami oiling my fingers. A few, well-salted tomato slices on a baguette with mustard.

Rose was nothing but a few summer rental apartments, a classy restaurant, and a simple Inn. My stomach growled at the menu prices. I was so tired, I couldn't think, never mind decide what to be overcharged for.

There was a pebbled beach in a half-moon bay a few minutes' walk from the cafe. One other man lay in a shaded area. I unrolled my cotton liner, put down my pillow, book, and notepad, and closed my eyes. One after another, flies stormed my face. Infiltrating my ears, nose, and mouth. A constant stream of buzzing from invisible pests. I swatted at the air in vain. The motion only encouraged the flies. I rolled to my side. They attacked my ankles, knee pits, stomach, and elbows. I turned and turned again, throwing my arms and legs around until I was so tired, I had to concede defeat. The flies won. Back at Rose's hamlet, I sat on a large, cement flowerpot under a tall bushy tree to escape the three o'clock sun. The only way out was back up the huge hill to the top road leading to the next village. A grim, five-kilometre climb. Then, another two hours of walking from the hilltop. And finally, another fucking hill, back down again, no doubt the same as this one. My body trembled. I was scared. I felt nauseous. My patience was almost gone. My condition deteriorated. I was getting dizzy. Every smug, drinking, giggling tourist made me clench my teeth in disgust, or anger, or maybe envy. In the cafe, I asked the server to fill my water bottle. I threw my pack on, shook it noisily up and down before it fell into its sweet spot. Time to go. Nothing left but an arduous uphill hike.

As soon as I topped the hill, my body failed. I shed my pack and fell to the ground, eyes closed, fingertips on my temples. I tried to regulate my breathing, but I couldn't stop panting and gasping for breath. Asthmatic. My heart raced, and a headache grew with intensity. Sensing my weakness and inability to fight, the flies arrived again.

"Fuck my life."

Restless and exhausted, I was melancholic for reasons I didn't fully understand. Being unable to identify the source of the pain was frustrating. Then it made me angry. "What the fuck did I do?" I yelled at the sky. I wished for a god to believe in so I could curse them. Fuck everything. Fuck everybody.

It felt good to release all that negative energy. But soon, there wasn't much to do but start walking again. It took everything I had, and I soon realized I wasn't going to make it very far on my own. This battle had lasted hours. Our bodies communicated, if we listened. The power in my legs failed. Someone needed to step in and help me to the next village. There was a man standing at a signpost. The road went straight to him. I staggered in his direction, trying to get his attention, but I fell to my knees.

"Help!" The word breached my mouth in a high-pitched whisper. On my hands and knees, I crawled towards him. "Please!" He was busy reading a map. As he turned back to his car, he noticed me, and froze in confusion. "I need a supermarket. I need food and water.'

"Oh, I don't know," he replied in a strong Russian accent, unable to hide his disdain. His face scrunched and contorted as he struggled to understand the situation. "You know where the next village is?"

I nodded. He didn't believe me. "Fuck, dude. I need food. Please, man. I've been walking for days, and…"

He capitulated. I sat in the back. Agony stirred with every bend. Breathing took energy. This guy wanted to speak about Mother Russia. He was the right age for the old Soviet Union. He knew his history well. He spoke of his Cold War and the USA with enthusiasm. My eyes rolled. Then we finally came to a stop.

Zanjic's market was at capacity. I grew tired of dodging bodies to get a glimpse of things I couldn't afford, so I settled on a bottle of water and a coke. Sprawled out on a picnic table, I watched tourists walk through the parking lot to the beach. I sipped the water. Cold. Refreshing. The hydration instantly alleviated some of my headache. Drink more. Drink more. It is life. Then I took one sip of Coca-Cola.

Vomit, projectile puke as long as an elephant's tusk exploded from my mouth like a broken water valve. Instead of worrying for my well-being, tourists pretended not to notice and continued walking. My stomach was emptying itself involuntarily. Every time it came out, it burned like battery acid. My eyes watered. Everything was blurry. My hands trembled. Fear seized my thoughts. My body erupted a dozen more times before I regained control and my breathing relaxed.

"What the fuck is wrong with me?"

I sat with my face in my hands trying not to look at, or smell, the massive puddle at my feet. My muscles ached, limbs trembled. I was afraid to look up and see how many people were staring at me in horror. Were mothers pointing at me to remind their children what bad people do?

I noticed a woman and man around the corner, seated on a bench.

"Excuse me. I'm sorry, do you speak English?"

They both looked at me askance.

"I just puked like crazy. I have no idea what's wrong. I just… I think I need a bit of help. I feel like I'm dying."

The looks on their faces went from suspicious to perplexed.

"I feel like, I think I need some ginger and lemon tea. I have a lemon."

"My house is clos', but I don't have ginger, sorry," the man said. My resolve took another punishing blow. I was hoping for a bit more than ginger.

"Do you guys have any idea what's happening to me? Should I go to the hospital?"

"Not sure if you should or not, but ginger won't help you." Before I could start to reply, he shoved a shot of Rakia in my face. "Drink this, you feel better."

I had no desire to drink, but I wanted to believe him. "Are you sure it will help?"

"No." He walked to his car and opened the trunk. He handed me a roll of toilet paper. Both of them laughed. "You'll

122

need this, too."

I still needed sleep. Way too tired to carry my pack much further. There were a few stony parking lots around the store where I found bread and tuna. Locals explained that camping was prohibited, but the police probably wouldn't do anything. I could see a grassy area at the back of a house.

I secured the outer layer of the tent in case of rain, flopped down, and smothered my head in my pillow. My angry stomach roused me from my peaceful slumber. The tent zipper stuck. I had the toilet paper in one hand and had to drop it to get the little deviant moving again. I couldn't remove my pants fast enough. The explosion had changed its origin. But it burned my throat all the same. The weight of my body shook my legs. Not a light, not a soul around but for one single house down a small hill across a gully. Above the fence, I could see a set of bodies inside, dancing and warm, me squatting a few metres from my tent launching bile and tuna out of my ass. The night was long. The pain continued. I wanted to leave the tent cover off for air, and of course, it rained. I was outside, now without pants. The house was dark and silent this time as I crouched between bowel movements, head, knees, and feet taking the rain.

I listened to the raindrops, grinding my fingers into my palms as my gut turned and convulsed. Every time the pain subsided enough for me to drift off, I had to make another run outside to evacuate my bowels.

A tall, thick man towered over me. At six feet, I rarely had this experience. He stepped from a camp with two upright tents as I passed. They had small tables centred by a fire pit. I was envious.

"Hey, bro, you guys pay to camp here?"

"It's wild here, man. Just gotta find a spot and claim it." My face lit up until I recalled bitter sentiments. Better advice from the locals, and I could have had a patch of grass to myself. My tent pegs wouldn't have been ruined. Worst of all, there was even a fucking toilet. The young man was from Bosnia.

"It's our second year. We liked it so much we came back."

"I ask because last night I puked about a dozen times then pissed out of my ass all night. I still feel rough, zero appetite, couldn't be food poisoning and, well, I'm wondering if you have any idea what the fuck is going on?" He grinned and shook his head pitifully.

"You got *it*. I'm sorry."

"It?" I responded with confusion.

"Yea, *it*. I got *it* last year too. It comes from the tap water around here. It's horrible. But at least it passes quickly."

"So, all the people from the club, the bartender, cafe owners, and workers all knew about… *it*?"

He nodded.

Everywhere else in Montenegro, the tap water was fine. Yet not one hint from a local. Everyone laughed behind my back as I tramped away with a bottle full of their poison. Expressionless communication, full of indifference—a gut-wrenching reminder of the border guards my first night.

Not far away was an island jail called Mamula.   At the time of Austro-Hungarian rule in the late nineteenth century, a man with the last name Mamula built this fortress on the tiny island. It covered most of the island's surface. On the shore not far from my beach was a castle turret. I put my back to its cylindrical wall and sat on my liner to stare at this funny little offshore citadel. Positioned strategically on the Adriatic, Mamula was the first line of defence against incoming threats. Lost in thought about the history, a woman startled me as I opened my eyes. We greeted each other. She was Serbian. And terribly agreeable.

"That island. Yea, it was a fort, I guess, but it was also a concentration camp." I looked at her curiously as she carried on. "It was World War Two, I'm pretty sure."

"Well, not exactly a light discussion for two strangers, eh?"

"Around here, this kind of reality is too common. War and death were normal for a long time. Thankfully, we have peace. For now, at least."

"Yea, and you can enjoy the summers, relish the coast, and eat what you like."

"There's still a long way to go. But yes, things are much better. Where are you from?"

"Canada."

124

"I would love to visit Canada. It sounds like such a peaceful place."

"Depends on who you ask." She looked at me unconvinced, so I carried on. "What I mean is, we also have problems there between the First Nations people and the colonial government. We fucked them over. Colonialism affected most of the globe, but some got it worse than others. Europeans arrived and took land, brought religion, disease, new types of warfare, and alcohol. It ruined millions of lives. Many tribes lost more than 80 percent of their population in just over a hundred years. Again, real light banter between strangers."

The young lady left me with a twinkling smile, "Maybe I'll see you around?" she said as she walked off. All I wanted to know was if she cared to walk a bit of the coast with me. Maybe jump in the sea and swim. Instead, I traipsed coastal boulders, away from Mamula and the mainland turret sparkling in the sun's glow. My strength trickled back. My power resurfaced with bottled water in hand.

Returning to the busy campsite brought my headache back immediately. I noticed a guy loading his car. His space was large and grassy.

"Are you leaving or setting up?" I asked, to be sure.

"Leaving."

I bundled my tent and crossed the gravel lane. I told him about *IT*. I detailed my sickness, the two months of walking ahead of me, and the dreadful seven-kilometre hill from the foot of our wild lot.

"I'm driving to Albania," he explained. "I'm going to explore the country for a few weeks. It's nice here, but I want to see more."

"Don't we all."

He drove a station wagon from Germany, with all the gear he would need inside.

"I can sleep in the car if I don't feel like putting up a tent."

"Yea, I understand. A few days ago, I nearly froze at the Bosnian border. The car should be warmer."

He looked strangely at me.

"You're walking to Istanbul with no sleeping bag?"

"I'm an idiot. See, I crossed Italy in July. It was so hot, I

125

only brought a little sleeping bag liner. Figured it would be enough until September. I imagined Greece with warm weather. Didn't consider the mountainous roads. Taking this route, my Way through the Balkans, was actually a last-minute decision."

"It adds a few weeks to your trip, no?"

"Exactly. Bad organization on my part!"

"One moment, please."

"Sorry?" I looked at him tentatively and confused. "What's up?"

"I think I have something." He put his head in the rear door, turning things over. He removed this black, synthetic ball and placed it in my hands. "What do you think, or?"

"I think you are my absolute hero!" I looked down at the sleeping bag and back up at him again. "But are you sure you don't need it?"

"I am sure. It is old, and I have another. Germans always come prepared, ja," he motioned sarcastically. "It was just in case," he paused. "And, well, I think you can use it much more directly."

"Man, what can I give you?" I asked excitedly while hugging him.

"Eh, come on, naathing. Just keep walking. What you are doing is something unique and you've come a long way already. Don't give up!"

Random acts of kindness.

"What about giving me a lift to the top of the hill?"

"Yea, for sure. I can drive you as far as Albania as you want."

"Nah, just to the top of the hill. I will be fine from there." My stomach wasn't yet ready for hours of uphill drudgery. At the top, there was a huge parking area, a flat one. I made the two of us some pasta there with lemon and wild mint, garlic, onion, and peppers. We ate on the ground. It reminded me of so many moments. Great ones, together with friends on roadsides, camping, no exact destination. My strength needed to rise again, but this chance meeting had given much-needed grit into my tendons and muscles, and the road ahead felt optimistic.

"I can't thank you enough, Aaron!" I hollered as he drove off in the midnight hour.

126

Ep. 14
Sri Lankan Kottu

My sentiments spiralled as Albania neared. Nervousness and regret wreaked such havoc, I felt feverish. Waves of uncomfortable emotions and a relentless barrage of questions arose. I set camp and woke each day on an unpopulated coast. Refreshing dips in the sea. The forgotten stone cabin I saw myself in, overlooking Kotor Bay. The hint of peace it offered. A refuge where time moved slow with enduring calm. Weather was agreeable. Life was affordable. Locals kept to themselves. I was irritated by the apathy of meatheads like Mila's so-called boyfriend. When I became ill, people ignored me without offering help. Water poisoning, a ripple that passed. My dear, old uncle would have said, "Don't look a gift horse straight in the mouth when in Dodge City."

After a month of people staring and shouting in Italy, it should have been a blessing to be left alone in silence. Maybe I just wanted something I could never have. Trapped in negativity. Enslaved by doubts and fear. On the Camino Way, battles with ambivalence were frequent. There were also many times, sharing with others in mutual reflection, listening, seeking to understand, that provided me with perspectives that enriched my own life. Trust. Everyone was given the time and space to work out whatever personal issues brought them on their Way. It was effective group therapy for anyone willing to listen and be honest. Relief and strength through temporary friendships.

There were other times on the Way when I had to digest, adjudicate, and solve every tribulation on my own. Forced to accept whatever my own logic could deduce. And so, I distressed about the new country ahead, despite no previous experience to justify it. Fears and doubt strewn together on a clothesline of gossip.

"You should be wary," people said.

"Don't trust them," they warned. Albanians were always a potential danger. That was what people told me. Worst reputation in Europe. A sense of ominous foreboding engulfed me

127

as I walked alone toward the border.

People on this planet lived under a veil of wilful ignorance, feeding on propaganda that suited their worldview. Most warnings based on stereotypes were easy to ignore. These warnings were different. Unavoidable discomfort.

"This time, something could happen," I reflected to myself. Alone and vulnerable in a country full of *predators* and *criminals*.

On the Way, it was late evening. I pushed further than my body wanted, like I had on the flatlands of Puglia. Arriving shy of the border, I could do an early crossing without traffic. Large, dark patches in the sky and city lights a long way down from the very steep roadside. Little could be seen of my mountain region. The air was cool, and I smiled, reflecting on Aaron and the sleeping sack he gave me. I was surrounded by huge, black, towering mountains, above and around me in every direction. Black cut-outs in the sky, below millions of blinking, glowing stars. Clear, brisk, calm.

Inside the Albanian border, I stumbled into a village called Bushat. Most of Western Europe had changed, but this little town still had an internet café. I had to check the online map to plan my Way south to Durres and the Egnatia Way to Istanbul. A quick look at the map, and I realized that I had already walked as far as that whole flat, mountainless Camino de Santiago.

The air was staunch and humid. I crossed the road to grab lunch. I sighed and sat on a staircase outside the market. Rain covered the gravel road. People watched as I sliced tomato and cucumber with my lightweight Henkel knife on my little, fluorescent green chopping board. I needed rest. I bit into my sandwich. I noticed an African man in a long robe—a shiny, blue-grey clergyman's robe. Bible tucked under his arm. He looked more out of place than I did. He went through a large, metal gate. The gate had a buzzer. I hit it. It took some time, but the Holy man appeared.

"I'm very sorry to bother you," I explained myself to him. He stood in the metallic doorway frame. I begged him for a hot shower. He disappeared, closing the huge, metal doors behind him.

"Freddi, accept what is in front of you," I told myself.
Another man arrived. He spoke far less English. The local

doctor. This wasn't Montenegro; people were curious again. Like everyone who could pull a few English words together, he asked the same questions. I rolled my eyes as discreetly as I could, took a deep breath, and then, before I could recite my origin story, the priest returned.

"Come with me, please," he said with an American accent. I waved goodbye to the doctor. This priest sounded like he grew up speaking English. But his words were too neat, too clean. He took me to the back of the house directly across the street, inside another huge set of gated doors with a buzzer.

"Hey, sorry man, but what's your name by the way?"

"I am Brother Avery," he said in his perfect pronunciation and well-educated accent. "I am from Ghana." He was brief in reply and only asked that I show him my passport to sign me in. When I couldn't find it, buried in the bottom of my pack, he deftly manoeuvred around that. It was hard to tell if he was displeased with my presence or anxious to escape my stench.

"So, it's okay if I take a shower here, then?" I enquired as he led me up a small set of stairs. He removed a set of keys from his robe pocket without answering. He jiggled one of them into the keyhole. He jiggled it a couple more times.

"It is meant to be the right key," he muttered. Again, the jiggling continued, "Finally." We stepped into the dining area of a small apartment with a kitchen, toilet, and two separate bedrooms. "Okay, you can stay here. I will bring you some lunch." I wallowed in self-pity, dirty and tired. A shower was what I needed, and maybe my clothes washed. But I resisted asking for anything more.

"Well, uh," I stuttered.

"Yes, I will bring you some lunch. Please, feel at home here, okay? Relax."

When the word *relax* exited his mouth calmly, my pack fell to the ground. I sighed in relief and grabbed him by the hand, shaking it. "Thank you so much, really, you don't know what this means."

"If you would like to prepare your clothes, I will have them washed."

There was a knock at the door as I exited my steamed toilet. It was a soft knock, so I assumed it was Brother Avery again. Instead, two young men stood in the entryway with the same robes as my host and the same rosaries around their necks. They both had large smiles shining across their faces.

"Hello, we brought you lunch," one of them said. "It may not be up to your standard. We are poor around here, but it is food." When he said this, his head wobbled from side to side.

"Oh, I am sure it will meet my standards." I was excited for some home cooking. "It could be just about anything, bull's balls or chicken feet, I would eat it. I'm easy. You guys from India?" The smaller of them stood quietly, smiling, his arms crossed like a V in the sleeves of his robe.

"We are from Sri Lanka. Do you know Sri Lanka?"

"Oh, yes. I know it quite well. Was there a few years ago with my ex-girlfriend. It was brilliant. Not as cheap as India. But it was great. We spent a long time on a moped cruising around the island in sarongs."

"Wow. You've been to Sri Lanka?" They both looked at me in disbelief, "Where did you visit?"

"We went everywhere except the north. We went to as many hidden corners as we could find. Are you going to make Kottu for dinner?" I asked ironically. They both laughed. A white man had just asked them for Kottu in Albania. That had to be a first. The food they brought *was* simple, but it was good. There was meat, rice, vegetables, and even soup. I ate in luxury. I didn't need to crouch on a piece of lumber or bench, using my lap to support my cooking pot. I ate at a dining room table, not perched on my heels, hovering over wet grass. Normal, daily activities had become foreign. The apartment provided a safe, brief escape from my pilgrim's Way. It was time to relish it. It was mid-afternoon, and this was Southern Europe. All signs led to a siesta. I washed the dishes, organized my clothes, then emptied the dirt and sticks and bark from my pack. Just as I reached my old hospital bed for a rest, someone tapped at my door again. The two men from Sri Lanka were waiting there to take the empty tray *and* my dirty laundry.

"How is your time in Albania?" in enunciated English. "We don't want to bother you, but if you don't mind us asking, why you come to here, from Sri Lanka?" he asked while he shook his head from side to side.

"Well, from Sri Lanka, that's a very long story, but how

130

my trip in Albania has been, a slightly shorter one. Maybe you wanna sit down?"

"Oh, no thank you, brother, we should stand." Both of their heads wobbled while smiling. Their arms remained in their confident, unilineal shapes.

"Do you guys want some tea? I saw some tea in that kitchen, might be Ceylon," I winked at them before looking back towards it.

"Oh, no thank you, brother," they both replied in uniform.

So, I guess I can start at the border, or just before it, around Sukobin, where I camped the night before crossing the frontier.

The rain started after breakfast. I retreated to the doorway of an abandoned house. I'd managed two kilometres. It poured in splashing buckets. Huge puddles formed on the broken pavement of the cross-border road. With no real timeframe to live by, the hour was immaterial. The little doorway was mine for as long as I needed it. The house blocked the wind. As I lay across the cement porch, using my pack as a pillow and with a book in my hands, a man arrived on his bike.

"Hey, how are ya?" he asked in English, rain falling on him. I folded my book closed.

"Not bad, considering. Better than you, I guess."

He laughed, looked at himself before replying. "Yea, it's raining pretty hard."

He rode an old, beaten bicycle. He was completely drenched, soaked through. A shovel ran across the mid-frame of his bike, wheel to wheel. I felt bad for the guy, but happy to be on a little porch. His accent wasn't Montenegrin. It lacked the chilly, Slav-Russian twang. His was softer and less resolute.

"Where you from? How did you learn to speak English so well?"

"I'm from Al-bah-nya. I'm like you, a traveller. I've worked in England and America and Germany and Italy."

My face morphed with the impression. His missing teeth echoed the words of others. "They are not to be trusted!" But we were no different, except I was the fool judging him.

"I came back to Albania, to live simple and enjoy my country. But there is no money. The fucking government.

Corrupt. The whole country is broke." He was ambitious as fuck with his bicycle and his shovel, crossing the border, pedalling through the rain. He was the first Albanian I'd ever met, anywhere. And he was the first person to talk to me in a long time. Montenegrins were expressionless. The gaps in his teeth gaped as he smiled and laughed. He was animated. The gaiety of his smile was inviting. His glare sparkled through his disfigured teeth as he awaited his fate in torrential rain. He spoke Italian, German, and English. His character embodied the centuries of cultural influences that had passed through Albania, creating something unique in its people. My first encounter with an Albanian, and I already doubted all the derogatory stories I'd heard about this undeveloped country.

The rain persisted for hours as I scribbled and read. The man passed again on his way back to Albania. Shovel between tires under his water-logged jeans. He smiled radiantly through his few, broken teeth. His eyes sparkled because he knew the game too well. He was born and raised in the Albanian shuffle. More than one car offered me a lift into Albania. The buzz was undeniable. The area itself, bare of life minus a border, yet everyone who passed wanted to know me.

One of my Sri Lankan friends interrupted. "So, in Montenegro, people are not so friendly?"

"Well," I paused a second to gather my opinion on the matter. "It's not that they aren't friendly. It's that they are reserved and private and self-contained. They were helpful when I asked for help. But no one offered me a single thing nor rarely even gave me a look edgewise. In Italy, people offered rides without my thumb out. But, in the couple weeks I was in Montenegro, I didn't receive one offer. Not one. It didn't matter, because I didn't want one. But just the actions of the people, they were simply so very different."

"So, you like Albania?"
You could say that.

When the rain eased, the morning had passed. I made my move, as night would arrive soon enough. I wanted to get in as many kilometres as I could before dark. No reason to go fewer than 30 kilometres. Sometimes, it took hours of walking before I found a decent camp. Somewhere that didn't have droves of cars wheeling by my tent flaps. After crossing Montenegrin security checks, something strange happened. There was no border to pass through on the Albanian side, no security, no passport stamp. Changes took place. Garbage and refuse everywhere. Discarded land. People passed on oxcarts with donkeys. Chickens scurried in the street. One side of the road was lined with aluminium shanties. Clotheslines hanging laundry. On the other side, an open field with cows and goats plucking grass. Everyone smiled. Everyone acknowledged me as I walked past, startling them. Many said hello. Some even talked to me. It all resembled many parts of Asian countryside, which felt so right.

On my way toward Shkoder, a car stopped and unrolled the window. The man inside said something in Albanian, recognized I didn't understand, asked where I was headed and if I needed a lift.

"Hey man! I'm goin' to Istanbul!" I said with pride and excitement. "Buen Camino!" Before I could finish my sentence, he tossed a small package from his window and into my hands.

"Good luck!" he shouted as his beat-up Mercedes left. A chocolate croissant. I'd only been in Albania an hour or two, and I was in love.

One of the boys interrupted. "Do you think A-zee-ah is like this, Freddi?"

"Not everywhere in Asia is like this. But in a lot of places, it was still countryside filled with people just trying to survive off the land. It was very humbling for a Westerner like me. It was the same in many countries. Once you got away from the cities, you found honest, hard-working people full of hospitality," I replied enthusiastically. "Albania feels so comfortable to me. First-world issues evaporated so quickly."

"Freddi! We love your story. Thank you for sharing. But we must go prepare for prayers."

"Please come if you want to join," the other one said. "Feel welcome to rest, of course. You had a long journey."

I woke up after a long nap. It was dark outside when I walked into the dining area. The pair of brothers rapped on the door again. This time with a new tray of food, organized in the same way.

"Freddi, here's some dinner for you. Must get strong for walking!" The smaller one, the shier of the two, asked me quietly if I could finish my story about arriving in Bushat—and about my feelings of Albania.

Of course, why not.

Tractors sped through the streets. Bristly-bearded old guys on horse carts waved me along. Vintage cars. People who looked "poor" because they lacked the conveniences of modern technology. They were self-sustaining and uncorrupted by the chimaera of Western media, still content with basic survival. It was perfect.

Toward Shkoder, a castle sat on a high hill. Rozafa castle, first built somewhere around the 3rd century B.C. by Illyrians. This castle in Shkoder withstood the purge of the Ottoman Empire in the 15th century, and recently, the fight for the Albanian Empire in the siege by Montenegrins in 1912. A wide and metallic bridge was the only access for cars to continue north. The sky darkened as I crossed the bridge and noticed a large, cozy patch of grass on the Bojana river. Under the pale moonlight, I could set my camp. At the roundabout after the bridge, I found a corporate gas station and my only supply of food for dinner. Chimes rang when I opened the door. Two women greeted me with looks of surprise. They wore Jihabs. I asked the younger one for directions. She spoke English. The distance, she said, to Durres, was a hell of a lot more than I'd thought. Demoralizing. Exhaustion washed over me.

"You have to be kidding? No. You're wrong." I only got arrogant when I was excessively tired, run down, and stressed out, or when someone breached my personal space. I felt bad for being reactive but said nothing about it. My shoulders sank three inches into my chest.

"Urghh. And what about the nearest town?" At first, she mentioned Durres—almost 100 kilometres away.

"How's it possible that there are no towns between here and Durres?" My face was about to leap out of my skull. "I mean, what's between us, then? Corn? Enough corn to compete with Canada?" The sarcasm was thick. She remained nice—and certain.

"Yea, there is nothing in between."

"Are you sure? Do you have a smartphone, maybe?"

"Yes, you can look. But I'm telling you."

She showed me the map. There was a small city in between.

"Can you zoom into that place," as I pointed at the map. She complied. "And what is that, then?" I commented rudely and unnecessarily, again feeling guilty.

"That's Lezhe." She checked the distance. "It's 35 kilometres from here."

This reminded me of the guards back at the border in Montenegro. I wasn't even convinced that Lezhe was the closest.

"Can I look, please, again?"

"Certainly," she said politely. As the map zoomed, it revealed a small side road leading to Bushat—eight kilometres.

"Thanks so much." Afterward, I explained my journey from Rome. She said her mother wanted to help me along. She must have missed my sarcasm and nastiness. They gave me a large bottle of water and a can of tuna. Guilt again.

My friends interrupted. "Wow! They were so nice. Giving you water. Very nice. We don't go around Albania. We simply stay here, in Bushat. It's very nice to hear these stories."

The Albanians' casual energy, free of the anxiety so common in the West, was what impressed me most.

At the riverside, as I set up my tent, everything went black. I stood in the moonlight on a small, flat brick with my gas cooker going. The bridge had disappeared. Pasta boiled away while the sounds of the constant, squirting flame caught my ears. The butane pushed through a slow boil, struggling to cook my salted penne. I mixed it together with a couple smashed garlic cloves, a chopped tomato, the gifted can of tuna, and a bit of soft cheese with olives. I savoured every bite of it in my tired, gratified state. The surrounding lights danced on and off, time and again, generators pumping. I'd stepped into Asia, and it felt outstanding.

On the grass, the river ran a few metres down from my feet. Stars shimmered. Something was happening on the bridge. Two dark figures stood at the guardrail halfway across with fishing lines down fifteen metres. A party boat came along. Vivid, soft dreams of travel winds and their spontaneity. I crawled into my tent. Gentle visions of adventure filled my tired mind. It would take strength, perhaps more than I had. But I was ready.

I woke up to the sound of something against my tent walls on both sides. Startled, then foggy, and finally alert. Just outside my tent, sheep were pulling at grass everywhere. A fog covered the river and the road. A farmer came strolling out of the mist. We didn't speak. We exchanged smiles. He made eye contact with me and nodded. He approved. He wanted me to know that he condoned and respected my lifestyle.

The main highway was less evocative, and the sooner I could get off it, the better I'd feel. Wind blew hard. My straw hat flipped and flopped and flapped in my face. Wait. Up ahead, on the side of the highway, a man was selling street food. He sold Burek. And it was cheap. About thirty euro-cents. Oily, filled with home-made cheese. I had two.

"And then I arrived here, in this fantastic situation. So, as you can see, it has been a great road in Albania so far."

"Freddi! You tell a story very well! We must go for prayer time."

"Well, thanks so much for the dinner. I will come down and thank the others after prayer time."

"You do not want to join us?"

"I don't think so. Not today, at least," I responded with a grin.

The next morning, I woke refreshed. Homestays were few. Rare nights of undisturbed, safe, regenerative sleep. Sleeping outside made it almost certain that some random noise would jolt me from my slumber. Freight trains, cargo trucks, storms, insects, scavenging animals, or sheep, something would disrupt my sleep. If it wasn't something real, it was something in my head. Spasms of paranoia frequently erupted throughout the night, startling me ajar before sunrise. Or a dream would be too lucid. Worse than the mental afflictions were the physical realities that couldn't be overcome by willpower or mental fortitude: a small pebble under my hip, or an overlooked chunk of rock.

Comfortable and present, I exited the shower thinking to stay another two nights. A tap against the door again. The timing couldn't have been more convenient. It was Brother Avery, food tray in hand, his smile radiating kindness.

"Good morning. How are you, Brother Avery?" Like his smile, I was relaxed.

"You seem rested. You slept well?"

My body was loose from the shower. I'd done a few stretches. I felt great.

"Oh yea, I slept better than I have in a long time. It was subatomic. And I guess I will…" I paused for a moment. "I suppose I will start going pretty soon, if my clothes are ready? Once my clothes are ready, I will take off, don't worry."

"Oh, Freddi, you can stay here tonight. Take your time. Take your rest. You have come a long way, and you still have a long way to go." The little sonofabitch did care, bless his heart.

Ep. 15
A Mother's Hand

The Brothers huddled around me in their blue-grey robes as I ventured to the main hall. Two came from Nigeria, another from India, and the two from Sri Lanka. Avery was their headmaster, but he was missing.

"Guys, you all speak English so well. Can you read English as well?" They nodded. "The thing is, I just finished my last book. Any chance one of you has an English book you're finished with and could pass on?" I was sure to get scripture. There was a moment of reflection from the lot of them before I continued. "I have nothing to read now, and I really don't know when the next place will come," I circled the group of eyes. "Where I might be able to even find a single book in English, let alone anything worth reading," I hesitated. "Maybe you guys have an extra bible laying around?"

"Oh, yes, we have some things, I think. Let me look." The smallest of them, from Sri Lanka, went with the Nigerian man. I glanced at the other Sri Lankan. "Is there a bookstore in town? Maybe somewhere you find things to read?"

"Oh," he said, shaking his head, giggling. "I wouldn't know."

137

The Nigerian man came back with a piece of reading, like a pamphlet, but larger. It was an animated folklore story about Mother Teresa. I ogled it, sighed, and rubbed my temples. "It's not quite, I mean…" I didn't want to be rude, but thought at the same time, is this really the best we can do here guys, couldn't I, at least, get a Bible. I mean, shit, come on, I'm surrounded by bloody priests. 33 years on the planet and I hadn't read the Bible. Maybe it was time. Just as I finished my thought, the little brother from Sri Lanka entered.

"Here you go, Brother Freddi," he spoke in his soft, boyish voice. "I have this for you." From his hands to mine, I glanced at the title and then pulled it closer to my face. The official autobiography of Mother Teresa.

"Perfect! This is exactly what I'm talking about! Thank you, guys, you are legends and lifesavers!" Excited, I almost didn't think it through, but I looked back at the lads. "Are you all sure you don't want this?" They all shied their faces.

"No, it is a gift for you. Please enjoy."

I shook their hands and thanked them all again for the meals and peace. I wanted to slide into my bed, back in my little apartment to read the story of this woman I knew so little about.

The book was based on the life of Mother Teresa and the Missions she established. Her reach went far, through the houses she built for the poor, sick, and disabled. She started with one little school in Kolkata, but before her death, she helped start missions in over a hundred different countries. The missions survived on donations alone. She made sure of that until her last days. Collections from the workers themselves—and from Mother Teresa, right down to the day she died. "The Missionaries of Charity," they were called. This inspiring woman was born near the border of Macedonia in Albania. In the autobiography, it didn't say which town exactly, for even she didn't know.

The Missions were divided by gender, and everyone wore the same, simple uniforms. There was something familiar about all of it. Before complete confirmation, before I could be certain, I ran outside to the front gate. It all seemed surreal and strange to me.

"But why would they decide to put one of her homes in this little town so far away from Tirana?" I ran to the gate and spun around to look for a sign or symbol. A plaque had been screwed into one of the house gate's red brick pillars, at the front of each house. The plaques both read, *Missionaries of Charity*.

"Wow. What are the odds?" The Brothers from Sri Lanka, the night before, had told me about their work in this place. They weren't simply clergy. They worked in the other building, the first I visited, which hosted people with special needs from all over Albania. People who couldn't afford medical treatment. The Brothers in their matching robes were priests and caretakers for these people, but also physiotherapists. Both the Sri Lankans had studied at university. Their mission was to help those with muscular dystrophy and similar conditions. Necessary and expensive treatment that no one else would provide.

Mother Teresa fought for the chance to be an independent missionary. A pilgrim on her own Way, instead of blindly following what the Church had always done. She knew there was much more that could be done to help people. Her solitary pilgrimage led her to the streets of Kolkata, where she gave lessons to street kids under a tree. The community responded, and soon she had a classroom. One led to two, and her vision of Missions slowly materialized. A selfless life driven by God. Imperfect as other human beings, she forever espoused the conservative dogma of the Catholic Church. The use of condoms was forbidden in her eyes, as was birth control. But the amount of good she did was outstanding. I had no idea.

Kolkata was a city of extreme poverty in the 70s, especially after the civil war granting Bangladesh independence, which sent millions of refugees through Kolkata at the border. The government's disregard for the sanctity of life seemed like a natural consequence of the turmoil caused by a billion people around the subcontinent fighting for independence from Britain and each other. The government was young, disorganized, and corrupt. Multitudes were left to die on the streets all over India. Mother Teresa acted. She put pressure on the Vatican and worked the streets for donations. She came from modest and humble beginnings, where most people accepted their fate, however bleak. This woman went into the world on a pilgrimage and changed the lives of thousands of strangers. Her Missions never turned a profit. She lived the simple, spartan life of a pilgrim. Emotions poured from me without control. And I couldn't put the book down.

Tears flowed as I read of how she intrepidly accomplished so many of her goals. Her life was one long story of relentless effort overcoming what appeared to be insurmountable obstacles. She brought out the goodness in people. She was a paragon of unconditional love. One person at a time, she changed lives. So much self-sacrifice. As I contemplated this woman's selflessness, the envy and self-loathing welled up inside me. I felt sorry for all the people I had crossed paths with who were suffering. People were suffering everywhere I had been. Suffering didn't belong to the afflicted alone. Emotion ran through my veins, thankful that others followed her path, a truly righteous pilgrim's life.

She loved everyone. Anti-abortion, anti-condom campaigns made it challenging to see her as flawless. But her vows were too strong to tolerate any deviation from her Way. She was absolute. Devoted to the charity of love. She had so much love and shared it with everyone: the forgotten, the discarded, those who society had zero use for, left to wither and die on the curbs of Kolkata, Mumbai, and Delhi. She wouldn't let that continue. What began in India spread everywhere. She worked to create more and more Missions until her death in 1997.

A layer of apathetic self-loathing mixed with my sadness. She had done so much for people who had nowhere to die. No one to hold their hand on their way out. I admitted to myself that I feared this most, being left destitute, alone, withering away in some filthy hovel. I did abandon family life, and I was socially deprived. I had no one and nowhere to go. In it for myself until the end, a lonesome, tormented, wandering pilgrim. I thought of one man. Dave. Poor, lost, foolish, unlucky David. I met him a few times along the Santiago Way.

* * *

Dave's tent. It drew my attention. The first tent I came across on the Way to Santiago. Compelled to meet the person inside. Hundreds of pilgrims walked to Santiago. None of them were prepared for camping. Few even bothered with sleeping bags. Startled and intrigued, I was tempted to introduce myself. Resisting my curiosity, I continued forward to Los Arcos with Dani beside me. That was just before I broke ahead of my family.

140

Eight of us grouped around a circular, metal table. It wobbled to one side. I jammed a folded napkin under one leg. The medieval square had many uneven tables. The boys from the first day at St. Jean-Pied-de-Port collected at the table. Dani sat beside me. Cosimo and an Italian kindergarten teacher named Sandra sat down afterwards. Amos arrived last with Leah and her friend from home. We gathered like this every day. Los Arcos was meant to be the day's end.

"I think it's hot enough for Sangria, no?"

Most of us nodded sweat from our heavy brows. The first jug hit the table, and everyone piled on, filling glasses with haste like dehydrated hippos at the beginning of a Burkina Faso wet season. Not long after that, Dani ordered a second pitcher.

"You are my fucking hero, Ginzy!" I gazed at him, smiling like a six-year-old holding his first bike. His dense beard and thick, plastic-rimmed glasses deserved the nickname. After catching him writing a few times, I called him, "Ginzy—the Italian Ginsberg."

"It's only 'cause I wanted to beat you to it, Chenaski—Bukowski's pen name in his novels!" His lavish grin matched our fruit-filled Sangria. We discussed our Way forward after lunch. I offered to cook. Everyone agreed.

"We can save the lunch money for Sangria!"

While waiting on my suggestion, Amos spilled his drink on the table. Some guy had shouldered him while dragging his chair to our table. Then he sat down and made no acknowledgement of it.

"Alright everyone? God bless you," he blurted while simultaneously reaching for the Sangria jug and pouring some into a cup of his own. "My name is David, and I walked here from Rome. God bless. I am not going to do what you think I am, though." Two surprises already. Everyone sat quietly, puzzled by what would happen next. The slow pour of the Sangria certainly had shock value. He shouted for the closest staff member. The man was serving espresso at another table.

"I don't need your money. I'll order Sangria, too. God bless you!" His voice boomed, filling the entire mediaeval square. His leather skin wore a deep tan. This was no fake-n'-bake; his came from the sun. His eyes bulged, veins like streams inside full of blood. He had very short hair and walked with a thick, wooden

141

staff, seashell, plus his dangling rosary. He wore a poncho with cargo shorts and thick, heavy, all-weather boots. When he pulled at the jug to fill his glass, his hands shook. Amos poured him his second to prevent an accident. He explained that he was serving God, working in churches along the Way. He spoke louder than the three Italians combined. The barman put his jug down in the centre of the table like the last. Sandra reached for it.

"Hey!" he barked ferociously. "That's mine! You can't go drinking from that like you own it!" He howled as a rabid dog, with ravenous teeth bared in Sandra's direction. She was mortified. His eyes looked everywhere, at everyone, as he pulled the jug into his arms like a golden elephant. "It's mine!"

I left the table so I wouldn't cause a scene. I bought two cans of meatballs, some onion, garlic, and tomato, plus enough bread for our group. Beside the church, I ignited my little cooker, got out the cutting board, and went to work. The others left David alone and gathered around the cement block with me. These Chinese, five-dollar cooking pots got red hot the moment they touched the flame, so I had to be ready to sweat the chopped onions. The tomatoes went in to make a paste and a few pinches of cumin from my pack's little spice bag, then the can of albondigas. I had spoken to Dani off and on for a few days about meatball sandwiches. I mounted them into baguettes for everyone, and then David arrived.

"Do you think you could help me with some spare change? Some money to help me arrive in Santiago? It's God's work, and God bless you."

We all stayed silent. He walked off.

I had just passed the Meseta, so it was still a two-day walk to Leon. I had been looking for a dear friend from earlier in the pilgrimage who'd skipped ahead after horrible blisters foiled her walking plans. We shared intoxicating discussions. I missed her ginger curls and freckles and jovial attitude. I adored her. She reminded me of a friend back in my hometown. Only, back then I made the mistake of fucking that friend, along with a couple of her mates. That ruined our relationship. I refrained from succumbing to my urges this time. We had a bond from the first day, like the Italians and Amos. I cherished our time together. We shared open and honest discussions about everything. We spoke candidly about sex, which of course made the whole thing provocative. We discussed our expectations from our partners, sexually. Too much of my narrative focused on sexual compatibility. Sex. Fucking. Orgasms. My heart swelled interacting in community. But once my heart swelled, so did my cock. When she disappeared, I was sad to lose such an engaging friend. We still had weeks of discussions ahead of us when she climbed aboard her bus and vanished. Once I'd walked ahead of my crew, I started asking around for her. In Sahagun, I asked the right person. They took me to the albergue, and I snuck up on her.

"*Freddi!* Oh, wow, how the hell!"

Few hugs in my life were as memorable. A dissolved blood clot, my veins could flow freely again. It didn't take long before we were engaged in deep conversation. She was, however, running out of time. She had to skip ahead another step, on another bus, in the morning. I made us a big dish of gnocchi to share. In the morning, we had coffee across the road before I watched her walk away again. It was still early, around nine, and I wasn't pressed to walk. I wanted to jump on the bus and spend more time with little Elena. But as this silly idea fumbled in my mind, David appeared.

"Hey pilgrim, God bless! I've walked here from Rome. But I'm not gonna do what you think I am."

He sat beside me on the patio with two small beers from inside. He gave one of them to me.

"Ser fuck it like!" I declared, despite the hour. I thanked him and took a sip after tapping his glass.

After the second round, he started to fill me in on his life. "I lived in Canada. In Oshawa." He enunciated every word carefully. I thought immediately that nothing good ever came from Oshawa. He continued, "I had a girlfriend, and my job was pretty good. I liked it there. Life was easy."

I nodded, "Except places like Oshawa. The outer suburbs of Toronto are so ersatz and mundane."

"It wasn't bad, I tell 'ya. It was good. I woke up in the morning and," he cleared his throat, his Adam's apple jiggled as his eyebrows tightened. "My girlfriend didn't..."

My face contorted in confusion. I put my beer down and looked at him. "Waddya mean? She didn't wake up?"

His crystal-blue eyes got glossy, then emptied. "She never woke up." Silence. My brain was trying to process this tragedy and connect it to the human sitting in front of me.

"Holy shit, what did you…" I was stunned, unsure how to carry on. Life had certainly scarred him. "So, what then? Fuck me, I can't even imagine."

"I got up and walked 500 kilometres to Montreal. After that, my family in England called me home. Before long, I started walking again, that time from Canterbury."

"How long ago was all that?"

He finished the last of his beer and rose from his seat. "Seven years ago."

I rose quicker and insisted on buying the next round. He spoke. I listened.

"I'm going to walk to Jerusalem after this." My eyes widened doubtfully. The sentence was as overwhelming as the thought of a dead girlfriend lying beside me. The idea of passing through the Middle East bordered on absurdity. This guy was a lost soul. As I listened to him tell his story, a few times, when he talked about his compulsion to just walk and get away, I saw myself, and it worried me. It scared me. It wasn't the first time I was forced to reflect on my life and the vagabond style I had adopted seven years ago. We left Canada at the same time, and we both left our girl behind. Except my girl simply didn't want to go travelling. Speaking with David gave me this explicit image of what my lifestyle could lead to when I was 55 years old. All I had to do was look at David, and I had my answer.

"I got some kilometres to do today, quite a few," I said, and thanked him for his honesty. "Good to meet 'ya, though, brother."

"Don't rush it, Freddi. And take this." His hand covered mine, so I turned my palm over. He did the same. Four euros fell into my hand.

"Nah mate, nah, nah," I shook my head insistently. He closed his hand and stood back.

"I told you I got some money from England. And you'll need it, I am sure."

I stopped my refusals and hugged him, then turned away.

I didn't meet David again until the very end of the Camino on the isolated beach of Mar Da Fora. I had been squatting in my tent a couple weeks when he and three other men around his age walked down the cliff path and into our tent camp. When he arrived, he had on new clothes and looked as if he had bathed and eaten a few solid meals. He looked healthy. He wore a straw-coloured sombrero and a new poncho. It was like he had stepped off a plane from Mexico. He was dark as well. All four of them looked older than they were, beaten by the sun. Blood pressure surging in their cheeks.

The four of them brought chaos to our beach. Battles with a few of the younger pilgrims that got in their Way. The whole fiasco lasted a few days before they ran out of money. One of them left, and things settled back down. A month after I left the beach, I heard that David hadn't left peacefully. He'd occupied a stack of wooden shelves on the beach for some time where he made coffees for all of us throughout the day. "Dave's Coffee Bar." A sign, and a pile of empty wine boxes. His coffee bar gave him some direction and purpose, distracting him from the constant binge drinking.

One night, he had a mental breakdown. He became hysterical, screaming and ranting. His face was surely flush with that same evil we'd seen back in Los Arcos. He burned down the whole area, including the coffee bar he built. He burned it all to the ground, dancing and hollering like a madman. The fire trucks arrived and, with that, the beach community disintegrated. People migrated to Santiago for their mission back to the world, and a few, not yet ready to part with the simplicity, turned to the nearby forest. David followed a few to Santiago and stood in the square collecting money from other pilgrims as he displayed his Camino Passport full of stamps.

"God bless you. God bless you," I heard him saying as coins fell into his sombrero. This was of course meant to be his start for Jerusalem, as he'd told everyone on the beach a hundred times before. He got drunk instead. During the night, his backpack, tent, sleeping bag, everything he had collected and relied on, was stolen. He went straight for the church, hands open asking for forgiveness—and help. That was the last I heard of Dave. But I think of him often enough. Sometimes when I'm looking in the mirror.

Ep. 16
Albanian Hospitality

Avery had a brusque veneer that rattled me. A motionless command of everything around him. He delivered curt debriefings, yet with softly spoken words. As we said goodbye, I realized he was uncontaminated by outside life and his judgments were few. His devotion and love were irrefutable. His meditative state, which I mistook for irritability, was everything I couldn't be, and therefore it puzzled me. I couldn't recognize relative peace. I feared judgement because I was always ready to judge. The first day, he left me feeling unwanted and foolish. I mistook his calm for tension.

He didn't want or need anything from me. No reason to criticize me. It was simple for him. God and faith in God's plan. He was doing God's work and didn't need to explain or beguile anyone. As we parted, he shook my right hand by covering it with both of his, as did the priest my first day in Marino. I mentioned Ghana and my desire to teach English there. Only then did I see any alteration in his otherwise calm and collected disposition.

"It is neither simple nor easy in my country," he said sharply. "The Government makes everything very difficult," he finished with a saddened face. "We wish you well and good luck."

I walked out of town reflecting on Mother Teresa's devotion, absolved of any life other than being a Missionary. She had absolute love and kept the flame burning through blind faith. A disciple who worked hard to share the love she found with everyone, every single day. Her work was not done to gratify her ego. She was far from vain. Nor was Avery. He didn't live to amass praise. His work was done out of love. The kind of love a mother felt for her child. Unconditional, like my mother was in her devotion to my safety and health.

It had been years since I saw my mom or hugged her, and I knew that so many of those days she suffered. This emotional bond of hers, I couldn't fathom it. It was something only a mother could understand. I started to realize that she must miss me more than I comprehended, yet I stormed away still. This was where Mother Teresa's strength lay. She was a mother to humanity. My ego drove me to my own Way, away from love. The partner I shared a scooter with, and lived with in sarongs around Asia, she allowed herself to bond with me, even devoted herself to my feelings. She mothered me when my mom was 10 000 kilometres away. She was there through the hardships and supported my needs as I supported hers. But I had the yearning of a pilgrim within me who needed to sharpen his sword in the world and eschew comfort. To shake off materialism and prove he could simply live. He wanted nothing more than to connect with the earth and live under the stars, appreciating the earth and wilderness, like Thoreau.

I missed my mother. Growing up as an only child, I got all the attention. And in a country with little traditional culture, I thrashed for more. We learned little in history class other than Canada's role in WWI. There was a whole bloody globe, full of life and death and struggle, hardship, adventure. I rubbed my plastic shoe sole against the gravel and looked to the ground. Overcome by shame for my mother's selflessness and that of Mother Teresa and Avery and the Sri Lankans. The world was an endless miasma, full of desperation and temptation. I rarely abstained from anything. Chasing self-gratification at every chance without focus. While Mother Teresa's disapproval of contraceptives and abortion were extraordinarily out of place in today's world, and wrong in my eyes, she was still everything I wasn't, and it depressed the fuck out of me. Her book shot all these thoughts out like a broken valve, discharging an abundance of pressurised sentiment. Tremulous from my neglected heart, I wanted love and to be surrounded by it. But most times I was an ugly, stray dog who saw my home as a frosty marble prison. The world I was born into was a superficial fraud. A social atmosphere dominated by ignorant, opinionated philistines. There were social obligations and requirements to be upheld. Out on the Way, alone so much, there wasn't any need to act out a role for social acceptance. One only had to be social in brief intervals. I tried to fill the gaps with community love. The engagement I abandoned for the Way, I filled with temporary lovers. Success measured in moments. But I was becoming colder with time as the ties dwindled. I gave myself to anyone who would open themselves. No lover was willing to endure this nomadic lifestyle. When a lover accompanied me, lustfully connected on this undecorated path, I soon had an all-encompassing fear of impending doom. And few were as perceptive as I concerning the approaching train wreck. I wasn't frigid. I was boiling hot until suddenly cooling down to avoid the ineluctable rejection. It was my lifestyle choice that made it inevitable. A lifestyle I needed to carry on growing along my Way.

My soul had been hollowed out by an ongoing series of torn hearts and lost communities. I had to accept that I lived for myself and be okay with that. I remembered one of my favourite films. I cried the first time I saw it. Ben Kingsley stood over his son as the boy died from an accidental gunshot. He prayed over him, calling out time and again, "I live only for my son! Please, I will let the beaks of a million crows peck out my eyeballs if only you save my son! Please, Almighty, I live only for my son!" That unconditional and limitless love. It left me regretting many of my decisions. It was a universal, inescapable obligation every parent owed to their offspring. My mother's filial connection was a duty imposed by nature. Was that duty of love a burden? Was it a gift? I would never know, because I didn't have kids. I felt pangs of guilt for never surrendering myself to my family, a woman, a job, a movement. My mother deserved better. I was a reprehensible ingrate. Surely Avery's Christlike devotion to his fellow man made it easy for him to see the selfishness that drove my hedonism. He probably sensed it, smelled it the moment I entered the guesthouse before he even talked to me. I hoped that people like Avery, Mother Teresa, and my mom didn't waste their goodness trying to help people like me. The incorrigibles. They should help people who deserve it. All I could do was be honest about my lack of worthiness. Redemption wasn't even something I believed in. Atonement was logistically impossible. I couldn't join a movement or donate (even my time) to a praiseworthy cause. Maybe penance. Maybe my penance for my privileged upbringing was refusing to accept the comfort of western materialism. Exchanging it for pilgrimage, never enjoying any comfort, let alone luxuries. I hoped that Avery, Mother Teresa, and my own mom would understand, could one day even appreciate and respect, why I chose this path.

There was nothing to be done but carry on walking. After all, I was created by the wind and soil and fire and sea, and going back to it would bring my ultimate transformation. Mother

148

Teresa, Avery, my mom: all of them wanted nothing more than for me to be the sun. To carry on moving forward, shining brightly, positive rays, inspiring others to step out of their wormholes to reach seemingly unachievable goals.

"Hey! Come join us, friend!" a man called out as he waved me over. I was on a footpath that led to where they were sitting in the shade. A shot glass waited for me. Filled to the brim. They sat at a table in front of a dilapidated mudbrick house.

"I live in England. Been coming back and forth many years. When this is done, I'm gonna retire back here," he said with equal parts pride and satisfaction. He was happy and comfortable with his life in Albania. He was secure. "It's too hard here. There's no work. No money. Government does nothing. They keep it all for themselves." He looked at me seriously, "What are you doing here anyway? Isn't everyone rich in Canada?"

I laughed, and replied, "Sometimes life is not about money or material comfort." I stopped trying to explain; he seemed genuinely perplexed and puzzled.

"Really?"

"Well, I'm not walkin' to Istanbul from Rome for the pay or luxurious accommodations," I joked, motioning to my rucksack and tent.

Silence. Was it disbelief? Disgust? He looked at his friends. Rapid talking amongst them, back and forth in Albanian. Then more silence. "By foot?" he managed to ask.

I grinned. They all stared in disbelief. He laughed. Then they all had a good-natured belly laugh.

"Are you crazy?"

I smiled at the boys and finally took my shot. Wow. It felt like my face had been dunked in ice-cold water. My eyes bulged. I swore I could feel my skin peeling back. They appeared to enjoy my facial contortions. Someone refilled my shot glass. I pushed it away, refusing politely. After a few days of relaxation, I was physically and mentally ready to do some serious walking. A couple shots of Raki would lead to a half-litre, and that wasn't what I needed.

"No thanks. I've got a lot of walkin' ahead of me today."

"Okay. At least have an Albanian coffee with us. You're a guest in our country, and we must treat you like one." One of the men disappeared, returning with a few small, porcelain cups and saucers. He brought out some cheese and olives.

"Oh, it's not..." before I could finish waving off the food, the man insisted.

"Who knows when you will eat again?"

The coffee was thick, glossy, dark brown sewage water. It looked thick enough to stand on. It was dreadful, but I bit my lip and swallowed another mouthful. This foul-tasting concoction they called "coffee" would be more appropriate for enemies, not guests.

"Maybe he made a mistake," I thought. "Or maybe his wife is the one who normally makes coffee?" I didn't want to insult anyone, so I remained silent. I took another sip. It was smoother, less grainy. The grounds had settled to the bottom. There was a nutty flavour, but far from an Italian espresso.

We chatted about his life in England and his struggles as a migrant worker there. In 2004, the Schengen of Europe accepted Poland into their club. The economy was still thriving in Ireland, the Celtic Tiger flaring up in the mid-1990s. The Poles flooded into Ireland as unemployment at home rose, not unlike the Irish immigrants who'd landed in Canada in 1847. After 2006, hundreds of thousands of Poles had settled in the UK. He asked why people in the UK were so accepting of the Poles, yet so hostile toward him and other Albanians.

"I prefer Albania; this is my home. My family's here. This is where I want to die. I'm happy about that, ready for it once my house is finished. My children have given me grandchildren. There's simply no money here." He continued, "People are good here, Freddi. They will be very hospitable. But Tirana is different. It's like London or any other big city. You don't have to pass there, right?"

"No, I'm headed to Durres for the Via Egnatia to Macedonia."

"Ah," his face lit up. "The new highway!"

My face dropped in horror. "New highway? What do you mean? It's the old Roman one from 2000 years ago, right? Wait a second, hang on. They called the new highway to Macedonia, 'Via Egnatia'?"

He nodded.

The worst news since the water poisoning. This was going to sting more than it burned, though. And cause great anxiety.

Shenjin was five kilometres north of Lehze on the coast. My plan was to navigate the coastline and avoid the busy, stinky, main road into Durres. A two-day journey.

In town, I had to hit a market stand. "Never shop for food on an empty stomach," I thought to myself. Inside, "Thank fuck this Burek is so damn cheap." I wolfed down the baked, filo pastry stuffed with bits of meat and cheese. A sensational young woman in her early twenties was sorting vegetables as I finished my snack. The washed-out burgundy of her polo shirt complemented her tanned skin. I tried to avoid staring. I thought she was leaving, but then she turned around and looked directly at me. I asked her, in English, about the cost of the tomatoes she had in her hand. She was unwilling to communicate in English. Instead, she passed the supplies to the man working the counter so he could weigh them. She looked at me again, grinning this time. We smiled at one another a few times before I left the store. I adored her. She was the loveliest woman in town. Her worn-out clothes somehow made her even more attractive. She was like me, a simple pilgrim, waiting for her journey to forever. She was beautiful, but lacking courage. I waved as I left the store. I looked back one last time. She looked directly into my eyes. I wanted to expose her to the Way and get lost with her while traversing the Adriatic.

On the crowded street, under derelict, crumbling buildings, dark clouds settled. I looked around and saw the bridge I needed to escape the suffocating traffic. No one understood English when I asked directions to the beach. I continued asking people regardless. A young man approached me.

"Can I help you, please?" he offered.

"Yea, you can tell that girl to join me for dinner at the beach tonight," I replied with a laugh.

"What? Please repeat, my English is not good."

"Oh, never mind, only a dream anyhow."

He looked confused.

"My friend, I am trying to reach the coast, can you show me the Way?" I asked.

"Of course, my English not good, sorry. I am Marcus. Your country please?"

I barely said, "Canad…" before he interjected.

"Wow, Canada, how can I go Canada? You can help me go Canada?"

Marcus wanted nothing more than to get to Western Europe or the USA or Canada, believing that merely arriving there would be sufficient for him to acquire a Mercedes and the newest smartphone. A world where money fell from trees. He seemed to think that simply getting "in" to Canada was like winning a lottery.

Like every other time I'd heard this, I chuckled and tried to explain that unless I worked at immigration handling their specific papers, I couldn't be much help. We were standing under a corrugated metal roof, attacked by machine gun pellets of rain. The noise was so loud we could hardly hear each other speak. Once the sun went down, it got darker than a basement cellar. Marcus suggested his family would be happy to host me. We walked to the outer township.

"Canada so good. Why you leave? So many jobs. Are you a criminal?" My new friend laughed and patted my shoulder. He continued facetiously, "Albanians are criminals, no?"

"You guys are the best in Europe!"

"Here is nothing." Marcus seemed sombre all of a sudden.

"Here is compassion," I retorted, grinning and patting him on the shoulder. "And Raki!"

"Oh, Freddi! You like Albanian Raki?" The sombreness was replaced by exhilaration.

"Of course!" I declared.

"Well, we will have Raki at my house then, before dinner."

There was a large garden in front of his house. It was mostly open space with a few vague hints at a fence line. A simple square made from cinderblocks covered by a tin roof. He did have chickens, goats, and even a cow. He said he had nothing, but by the look of his house, in my world, he had everything. Pillars of wood held the porch together and a dim, yellow light lit

152

the doorway area. He opened the door and invited me in. The family was all in the living area. I felt the coolness of the cement on my feet as I took a seat on a weathered couch.

"My uncle's cousins," was Marcus' way of explaining the full house. They all came from nearby houses. They all worked together as a community to keep all the families functioning. There were four rooms. Two of them were small bedrooms, one for his parents, the other housing three younger siblings, two brothers and a sister. Marcus slept in the living room. The living space consisted of a couple old, shaggy couches around a small, ancient television with rabbit-ear antennae. There was a kitchen; the toilet was outside, smelling of methane.

"My sister away at school in Tirana. You sleep in bedroom."

"Where will you sleep, then?"

He pointed at the couches and floor.

"No, no, no way. I have my tent. I can put it outside. I will be fine. I do it all the time.

He laughed, then translated to his father, who shook his head in disagreement while pouring us all shots of Raki.

"Okay, fine. I'll sleep on the couch. It's the only way."

Marcus was 22, but he didn't have good grades like his sister. He was no pilgrim, either. Marcus thought freedom meant making the endurance race towards England or Canada. But the gent was already so free. He could be swimming in the Adriatic within an hour. He had seasonal vegetables on rotation. There was fresh cheese being made from his goats. He had organic eggs and milk. He was genetically programmed to be a bricklayer, carpenter, or builder of some kind. He was the son of a craftsman and farmer. He had every right to want more than to share his space with his three siblings. Another simple house could be built if he invested. But, like so many others who fall prey to the allure of luxury and glamour in this era of globalization, he wanted to race to the city for riches. He couldn't see that the farm was the best place for him. He would need to leave before he could see that. He needed to learn so much more to be competitive in that world. I didn't discourage him, only pitied his choices, fuelled as they were by the fantastic propaganda of capitalism.

Mom appeared abruptly at one point, from the kitchen. She said something to her children. I tried to stand up, but

153

Marcus' father put his hand on my shoulder. The kids set up the dining table. This was no simple, poor man's dinner. It was an incredible feast. Marcus had a mother like most traditional, European mamas of the south. She had a knack for simple roasting, and everything was seasoned perfectly. Lamb chops, stuffed peppers, mashed potato, rice, fresh bread, large blocks of hard, salty cheese, olives, marinated tomatoes, and peeled cucumbers. After dinner finished, the ladies brought out that dreadful Albanian coffee.

"You want more? You have so much walking to do," Marcus asked me as his mom looked on, insistently.

"Please, tell your mom it was amazing, but I am absolutely finished. Well, okay, I'll have one more piece of cheese, but that's it!" I smiled at her gratefully. I started to collect and stack the plates, but the men at the table reached for me. "I can at least help with the dishes, please."

The lot of them laughed, nearly into an uproar. It was Marcus that responded, but all the guys said the same thing. "That's women's work, Freddi." He spoke as though it were a universal and self-evident truth. I was startled. His little sister was right then crouched outside washing dishes. I wanted to object, but it was their house, their food, and their country. If I were to stand up and rush outside to push the young lady aside, it would do nothing but anger the men and cause a huge disruption. It wasn't my place to criticize or condemn or even try to educate. Their progression was, in all seriousness, up to them. Western development can also be judgmental and often binary: right or wrong, good and bad, moral and immoral, the sacred and the profane. I wasn't here to start an Albanian women's movement.

Marcus' deepest desire was to jump headfirst into what I was trying to escape. His misogyny and acceptance of patriarchy were merely a product of his frame of reference—including generations of cultural, social, and religious confirmation of traditional male-female roles. His thoughts on life in Canada were even more delusional. He saw himself micromanaging knuckleheads who would be delighted to bring him coffee. He would use his four weeks paid holidays to head back to Albania, and then he would have a retirement package, so he could float on his back at the ranch until death. He would shuffle into the local

154

watering hole each night, counting the hours every day, so that he could sign his bi-weekly pay cheque, cash out, and run home to his overpriced condo, exhausted and bored. He would inevitably be stuck on busy streets, surrounded by enough carbon dioxide to choke out a seagull. The noise and the air, the continually rising costs. The pressure would throttle him like gale force winds. The struggles, the tooth-grinding anxiety, and the ultimate con: that his work mattered. All to earn a banana at the end of each week.

Without a fuck on dial, a job that depreciated annually and a ballooning mortgage payment for some back-alley shack, it was enough to leap off the nearest bridge. The whole fucking routine was revolting. A constant pukefest of bile and mucus from the disease-ridden oxygen we inhaled, surrounded by the thousands of other debaucherous fiends that filled every city. It was all too obvious from the crow's nest of my social perspective. I didn't fit well into socks. Sandals were enough for me on any given day. I wasn't cool enough, didn't fit in, so why force it? I was made for skid row, only I was too overprotected as a kid to know how to drive a motorbike. The only way I seemed fit to go out was like the biker Country Beamer in Hunter S. Thompson's *Hell's Angels.*

> *"Country had died in the best of outlaw traditions: homeless, stone broke and owning nothing in this world but the clothes on his back and a big, bright Harley."*

Marcus had a large family all around him. Life was cheap in Albania, and he didn't need to work. He was surrounded by love and siblings who needed him. A functioning, self-sufficient farm with a father who could use his young, strong muscles to take a break himself. The boy could backstroke the clear, blue Adriatic all summer and pick up that hot chick from the market every Friday night. She didn't care about his haircut or shoes. But instead, he wanted to dine with the vultures at McDick's staring down tall, underweight blondes with tightened faces and expense accounts big enough to feed a small country in the sub-Sahara. The energy inside of me wanted to shake him a little and explain that the road was a long one. That if he walked it, instead of running, he might just taste a little bit of the good life.

155

Ep. 17
Walnut, Banana Pancakes

Long streaks of white ran down the coast in lagoon-style concaves. The coastline had one gap, but it appeared manageable. A gravel road with a swampy marsh on both sides led me to the Way. The gravel finished with a guest house tucked into the forest. Nestled into shade, and behind it, a strip of grey-white sandy beach. If it wasn't the start of my day, I would have set my tent here without hesitation. A dynamite, friendly, forty-year-old woman ran the show. The type one would sell the ranch for. This was a paradise. Had she invited me to stay a while, I would have obliged and slipped my crocs off.

"You won't make it," she remarked bluntly about the broken portion a few kilometres away. She didn't know my resilience or strength of mind. Still, the depth of a river mouth was uncertain. In times like these, I had to listen to local advice. That's why I decided to hit the beach and try anyway. Walking back up the dirt road to the highway, at least I could have a swim. Swamps dotted a bird reservation. I recalled Chitwan National Park in Nepal, where my friends encouraged me to go after hiking to the base camp of Mount Everest. I had just gotten over a hard case of pissin' out of my ass, so the ten-hour bus ride sounded grotesque, but they were a great crew of laughs. My first experience with the jungle. Wild, intense humidity at night. Sweat more than I imagined possible. Candles were my only light. A mosquito net kept away unwanted pests. An experience I'd craved for so long, but short-lived. Sounds flared like firecrackers all night. Luminous insects buzzed, and unseen animals screeched and sang through the darkest hours.

I hit the beach and followed it downwind. I came to a gap where seawater trickled through. It was easily crossed.

"I knew it," I shouted.

Groomed sections of beach with deck chairs and kayaks stacked together reminded me of Chico back in Maiori. A line of empty market stands. One remained open. At the end of this abandoned tourist beach, I found the cougar's warning to me. The

156

break in my Way. A rather large breach that required a boat. After cursing and swearing, I decided to put down my pack, cool off, order a beer, then smoke a cigarette like a hippo, blowing smoke instead of water from my nostrils. The sun made its way down. This detour was a stint of gout in my foot, but a great place for a tent.

At the main road, after ten kilometres of diversion through side lanes and dirt paths and goat trails around swamp waters, I walked another solid ten kilometres and traversed a huge mountaintop. People told me I had to find a town called Ishem. From there, I could reach the coast again. It was a huge climb up switchback roads. Revolted, I kicked and whined and wanted to punch everything in sight. I struggled to find a way to focus on anything positive or uplifting. I felt weak. It was dark by the time I began the ascent. People kept pointing uphill. My face covered in dirt from the highway, my shirt soiled and wet. My shorts were in a disastrous state. It had only been two days since the priests washed my gear. My feet ached and shoulder blades stiffened. Starved, running on chocolate bars and cookies, I wanted to stop and eat but needed to reach Ishem. It soon became evident that Ishem rested at the peak of this horrendous mountain. In the morning, it would all be downhill, if I could get the fuck up there.

A group of men sat in a small shop, lights bright with a porch reaching the pavement. My stomach longed for buttered omelette.

"Just reach Ishem, Freddi, keep going," I told myself, head down, feet dragging. My shoulders sank. I pulled myself up. Worst of all, I needed a place for my tent on a bloody mountaintop.

There was a fine chance someone spoke Italian in groups around Albania. Since leaving Italy, I had lost some of my Italian, and the fact I was utterly beaten down by all the hiking made me want to puke instead. I found a few words.

"Pardona, Ishem per favora?" I ventured.

"Si, a cua," someone replied.

"A cua?" My face became a candlelit jack-o-lantern. I smelt the food lingering in my nose and envisioned Coca-Cola drifting coolly down my throat.

An old man stood from his chair as the others offered tea. He waved them off.

"Come. Come," he said, as he put his hand on my bicep. I followed, confused and hungry. A few of them spoke Albanian, the others in Italian.

"Please, I am Canadian, I speak English."

"He wants to take you to his house," one man called out. My face sparkled again, this time like a Christmas tree.

His small living room had upholstered furniture with plastic covers. He slid out a bed from one sofa. His wife brought water, and she fetched me a cold Coke. She also brought food, lots of food. The old man brought a bottle of Raki. Neither of them spoke a word of English. He had a handful of words, but he also didn't give a damn. He was happy to host. I could see it in his eyes.

With the mention of Istanbul, bodies leapt, alerted to the vagabond who needed their help. He was up before I could pronounce the first letter of my name. He was a stout fella, no taller than a clothing rack. His wife was adorable and sweet. They had kids, away in other parts of the country. Ishem was a place to retire, not begin.

It took a full day to get around that 300-metre gap in the coast. Hours of unnecessary exhaustion and spoiled seaside calm. Every switchback that bent left or right, I rinsed out words of resentment. I was tired. The Way's completion was only a matter of time. A few months invested and money spent, eventually the end would be met. The process of life and the battles with myself were additional obstacles along my Way. These self-imposed tests were to determine whether I was a pilgrim seeking a deeper understanding of my potential and strength and patience, or just another character on another road challenging myself and documenting the results. These interferences, these obstacles, made it more difficult to keep going. When these stumbling blocks appeared, I treated them as monumental injustices. If only someone would help me along. And they did, just not with a boat to cross a coastline gap. These unexpected tasks were the integral labours of the Way. This path was my own path. There were no trails to follow. And so, I created my own Way. That was one portion of a pilgrim's plight, or delight, depending on perspective. This Way needed to be different from the Camino de Santiago.

The morning came like any other. When I stepped outside after sharing goodbyes, I saw a big, white sign with black lettering: *ISHEM*.

Huge bales of hay sat along the roadside, and beyond them, a long way down, countryside. I walked with the main road. Not a cloudy day, but the sky was milky. Spectacular, vast, wide open, the green pasture ran everywhere below me. Not a speck of development. For all the times I begged to find an area free of tourists, here I was, spoiled with fresh air and solitude. The road went back down behind my homestay in a slow descent. A mosque stood above small houses, and a young man who had perched himself sideways on a donkey followed the narrow, dirt road. A few kids watched over a collection of sheep. The dusted, yellow gravel road, surrounded by rich forest, twisted and turned in dizzying degrees. Tiny village homes and shanties, cool air compared to further down on the main road. As I came to a bend heading downhill, a lake appeared on my right. A wide one that stretched all the way to the horizon. Behind this unspoiled lake, covered in forest trail, the Adriatic ran to the Atlantic. Donkeys carried wood and feed. Sheep sounded in the late morning breeze. The lads chased me and laughed at my appearance. People everywhere waved and sent good vibrations. And less than 24 hours before this, I'd cursed my obstacles on the Way. The sweat on my brow would remind me for a lifetime: this feat had to be endured. And the process would carry on reoccurring, until I accepted the lesson. For every unfortunate turn, something cosmic awaited further along the Way. Only with patience and understanding could I hope to achieve this without stress. For every hurdle cleared, a light came down the mountainside. I had looked down from Ishem's signpost as I began today. I felt proud for not giving in. Priceless, unsullied oxygen and a sweet silence, free from the incessant honking horns of antique cars. Few voices could sing the harmony of this mountain.

Flax and vanilla shoreline ran behind a lane of small, thatch houses beside dense forest. The houses were empty. They were vendor shops or bars, but the season was over. Everyone had packed and gone. Bamboo frames waved in the wind, interrupted by bleating sheep. The herders spoke in the distance, their voices nothing more than faint echoes. The sea communicated as well. Dozens of sheep shared the beach with me and this ghost town of tourism. The sandy foreshore was separated by fencing and huge, overturned, concrete bunkers. They'd been placed in a diagonal line to form two separate beaches. On the latter, a pair of bulldozers pushing back sand and dirt, creating a high dune. The beach ran its course as I stared back in amazement. The large machines worked on the shore.

Although the sea was rough and murky, it still appealed to me. The current seemed unpredictable and mighty. Powerful. Dangerous. The land turned to mangroves. Dark brown compressed dirt. It reached a wingtip where large trees bent over from their long, strenuous lives. A two-story, decrepit brick house stood there, with the same ghostly aura as the abandoned encampments. Again, a great place to squat, but too early yet.

"The beach is mine, though. How often does one get such a spread? I could go back and take up a lawn chair and chill." My thoughts were interrupted by the fact that I had little water and no food. As I stood on a rock looking over the Adriatic, the neglected house spoke.

"Hey! Hey!" shouted two men standing on the balcony of the second floor, one spoke immediately in Italian.

"Dove?"

"Durres!" I hollered at them.

They shook their heads vehemently in disagreement. I used my hand to point down the coastline and then gestured to my feet. Again, they gesticulated in protest.

"What were these guys on about?" I thought to myself. They waved for me to join them upstairs. "Gotta keep going! Adesso! Now! Go Durres, thank you, though!"

They laughed and put their waving hands over their heads. The coastline remained shallow. The men were sure I couldn't pass.

"Birra?" The larger man waved a bottle in his hand. "Ten kilometre," he called in English as he pointed through the tough, resilient bush. "Auto-strada."

I knew very well how far back I had to go, "Why the fuck you think I am here?" I said under my breath.   "No Auto-strada!" I shouted in irritation as I turned to leave.

The water covered my feet and pushed against a metre-high platform of hard, compact sand. The area was covered with industrious shrubs, making it impossible to walk on the solid ground. The water slammed in hard from the sea. A current pulled the water back, along with my feet. I took my Crocs off and tied them to my pack. The water rose as the sea came in. The Way deepened until I was forced to lift my pack over my head and carry it. Large stones underwater became constant. They were covered in a slippery film and nearly impossible to balance upon with 12 kilograms over my head. I forced my feet and toes to grip the best they could. My determination and grit kicked in. "Fuck it, Fred, you got this!"

All my money, my camera, everything I had was in that 12-kilogram pack. If that fell in, all my notebooks, all the ongoing stories, pictures, my passport… everything would be destroyed. The stones kept coming, slimier and slipperier. My frustration grew, and I wanted to cry out, but I had to concentrate on every step. Time nearly froze. This nightmare was going to last forever. But it couldn't. This would end. It had to end.

"Fred, keep concentrating!" My bare feet were struggling to wrap around each boulder. The sea level reached my breast. I was in deep shit if it rose any higher.

"Come on, son!" The force of the incoming current wanted to push me over. Everything wanted to bring me down and end this pilgrimage right in its tracks. My heart raced, my muscles hardened, shoulders tightened, and arms ached. Step after enduring step, and then it broke.

A group of fishermen appeared on both sides of yet another river mouth. They turned their attention. Pack over my head, half covered in water, pushing toward them. They were all blindsided. One man with a rod in hand stood on a patch of sand further out than my deep water.

"I can reach him," I thought. As I took another step, I pushed down on something sharp. Something like a tube of bamboo under the murky water pierced the middle of my bare foot. I wobbled and yelped and cursed to the sky. The mass of land was so close, I was almost there.

"Just keep pushing ya' muthafuckin' bastard, come on." The men waved at me as I approached them on the dry patch. They waved me off, told me not to proceed. I ignored them, as I ignored everyone. I couldn't go back now, as I couldn't go back before, as I wouldn't go back ever again in my life. I had to get across the river mouth; it was the only choice. The closer I got to the men, the more resistant they became until I stopped. My foot throbbed, my arms limp. I had little left in me before the pack and I both collapsed.

"Keep going, Freddi!" I screamed inside to keep myself from quitting. One of the men came to me in his huge, forest-green fishing pants and long, yellow rubber boots. He grabbed me, making me stop. It was then I noticed a small rowboat coming towards me. The bag went in first. I pulled myself up after that. My body convulsed with exhaustion. On the other side, I could see a clearing of jasmine-bleached sand. I lay under the sun, breathing heavily with my pack close, under my head, safe. I asked for a cigarette and pulled at it while my fingers and hand shook. Before carrying on, I checked my foot. A bloody hole glared at me.

I pushed onward, and the coast transformed into a miniature desert. Piles of rubbish stood to my waist, cars drove along the plain, spinning donuts. There was a small township a kilometre or two's walk. A stream divided the township from my beach area that cut off into an impassable lagoon. I had to cross a bridge to carry on. There was a dirt trail that went uphill and between two large hills, like a saddle. The sun descended and glowed like a florescent, mackintosh apple. The Way led around a seaside, and the sun's colours spread across the entire landscape. City lights emanated as the sun faded. I thought I was on the Durres harbourfront, but I couldn't be sure. I arrived at a ferry terminal and a small restaurant. I rushed in to beg for water. He obliged happily. The food was too expensive, though I was starving and could think of nothing better than the calamari he wanted to prepare for me. I was famished and ready to collapse. He offered me space on the little restaurant's property for my tent, but I insisted on carrying forward to the city for something affordable, like fresh Burek. The Way was dark, but streetlamps neared. Houses and short buildings appeared, then the noise of people and cars. When I saw this young lady in a chair with a pint glass in front of her, I knew she spoke English. She was the first woman I'd seen in Albania with a drink in her hand. She knew how to live life on a dime, so I hoped she could point me to a nice, cheap meal or a market for some food.

* * *

The Camino de Santiago had a knack for demonstrating life's recurring lessons over its four-to-six-week journey. Sadly, many didn't catch them before it was over. We had to slow down, enjoy, embrace, and interact with our immediate surroundings. In this world riddled by distraction, one also had to unplug. As the challenge of unplugging increased, the pilgrimage only became more relevant and necessary.

Buildings rose, clouds intensified, and rivers became milk, with people racing through it all, breathing in their own early demise. Chasing platinum dreams, running from death in the rear view, one couldn't fathom why. The more people departed from undeveloped environments across the globe, the more this absurdity intensified. People suffocated in overpopulated, urban prisons with more anxiety than a trumpeter on a 19th-century battleground. The more people searched out this "strange road to Santiago," as Paulo Coelho coined it, so would the accommodations need to increase along the Way. This threatened villages and their peace. Demanded pilgrims search out personal, immaculate side-quests. From time to time, a pilgrim needed to veer off the Way a little. A wrong turn at any point in life could be a blessing in one's heart for a long time.

Inside the fantastic castle gate of Carrion de Los Condes, a stone plaque read, 'Los Hospital Para Del Alma'. Once fortified against Moors and other pillagers, the turrets remained. My Colombian friend and I were walking, about to keep going, but we simultaneously stepped back. We enjoyed each other's company so much we nearly missed it.

"Should we have a look?" I suggested.

"Hospital for the soul," she translated. We looked at each other with matching grins.

"Hells yes!"

Inside, black and white photos hung on the walls. Stills of both the Way and off-trail nature. The shots all had one common element. They centred on a poised man with a long, white beard and bald head. The photos captivated me. Unlike poor, wandering

Dave, whose suffering was immense, this man had a mixture of melancholic sentiment and humble love in his eyes. He existed in the scenery, blended, bound by the dry earth beneath him. A man who connected with the nature around him. He needed little and asked little in return, for he was on his own righteous path, solely out of love. He may have been old, but he didn't walk with darkness like Dave. The quality of the shots was undeniable. Laid in front of me as a scroll of the Dead Sea, it became clear my struggles would perish once I slowed down. The man sat on arid land, with his back to a thick-trunked evergreen, bent over him in cosmic union. I wanted exactly that. The whole, filthy embodiment I had sought for myself on this planet could only be attained by rubbing naked against a woman's free-flowing body, speaking to me with her sensual desires and passionate release. Only after that could I, or we, lay for an hour or three beside a tree, pecking away at cheap olives and tomato salad. This photographer's love for nature was undeniable, but also her love for this bearded man. Each frame existed as a collection of emotions from their unified souls. Together, they helped heal mine, even if only for a few days.

The photographer's name was Nia, and her life partner was the pilgrim muse. She stood silently, preparing food in a little kitchen. We carried on without knowing she was the photographer. When she finished and put a lid on her food, she greeted us. I had been absorbed by the photos, while my friend and her spoke at length. The man was a great, weathered traveller on a never-ending pilgrimage. They met along the Way and settled at Carrion de Los Condes a while so that Nia could share her incredible work.

"This guy is amazing."

Nia pointed through windowpane doors to a garden lit by the afternoon, "He is out there if you want to say so, but his English is not great," she said as she smiled. He had walked great lengths on three continents. The two of them fell in love. They created a home within each other and felt the Camino was right where they needed to be. They explored each other instead of the outside world. They gave and created this organic space, nurturing each other and sharing it all, asking for little back from the pilgrims.

164

After leaving the Colombian in the morning, I came to a sign that said, "Art Gallery – 2 km." An arrow pointed off the Way. I reflected on Los Hospital Para Del Alma, and I turned. A small, brick house surrounded by beautiful vegetation. Everything glowed and vibrated around it. I approached slowly and stuck my head inside. The interior had a few rooms with framed works of art on the walls. The first that caught me was the Camino's famous seashell in an abstract made from what looked like rock dust. It had a charcoal-like rub, layered and rich in mineral illumination. Almost as if it were inside a shallow stream, reflected by the sun.

Noise came from the kitchen, so I entered. The artist shuffled across the room, and a familiar young pilgrim sat and chatted with him.

Our artist-host spent years in South America, mostly in Peru. He offered me tea. The leaves were beautiful, Peruvian mixed with quality green. The man spoke little English. My young friend had a good grasp on Spanish. He had walked the Camino and, like Nia and her lover, settled on the Way. He based his works on this Way and used stones and other pebbles, river pellets, minerals, and salts he could find along the trail. He mixed them with collected items from Peru, smashed them, and bound them into his paint. Colours originally came from minerals, so he created them all himself.

The house was aromatic. I could smell ginger, jasmine, and cloves. A light sound of traditional, American music. The tea coursed through me like magic cactus juice. It lightened my head and quieted my mind. My pulse eased. He placed a crepe in front of me. It was as beautiful as everything else in this house, full of its own kind of magic. They tasted incredible, so light and savoury, made with the same slow, compassionate love as his paint and designs. I was entranced. His banana crepes had walnuts and the nuts were toasted evenly. Time slowed all the way to a Roy Orbison love song, with dark shades and heavy anaesthesia. The man was at least a decade wiser than me, but a millennium closer to a mountaintop prophet. In one room, a dim, melon-clay light reflected a large triangle. Soft carpet and cushions covered the floor, surrounded by dark walls. It was a meditation room. I left two hours later, like my face had been sandblasted and my body had been sitting in a sauna for the afternoon.

Ep 18
Pussy Whipped

Salt stained my shirt's sweatier parts and my shorts were long ago torn. My face glowed like a GMO bell pepper. Enough liquid for a fishbowl could have been wrung from my straw hat. Prickling needles jabbed at my left shoulder blade. My hands lifted my pack straps to ease the weight from my strained collar. Hair burnt stiff by the sun. I looked like complete shit. Still, I managed to ignore all of that.

"Sorry to interrupt," I looked down at this young lady sitting across from her friends. "Do you speak English?"

She was the most Western-looking woman I had seen up to that point in Albania. She nodded with large, pearl eyes.

"Do you know where I can find something cheap to eat right now?"

She turned to her friends and spoke in Albanian. "We're not sure, but you can sit here with us and have a beer."

The two lads stood and frantically moved some chairs around to make space before I could respond. Everyone introduced themselves and shook my hand excitedly.

"The kitchen is closed, the girl told me."

I sighed and faced the floor.

"But they are bringing you a beer."

The pint glass arrived frosted, the chair was comfortable, and my hunger could be ignored after a couple more cheap beers. My nerves eased once I let my Godawful pack down to sit. "Thanks so much, guys," I said as I looked at the round-eyed girl.

"It's nothing. This is Albania."

She spoke gently and clearly in English. She was the first person in the country, aside from the brothers in Bushat, who could speak fluently. While her friends wanted to know about me, I wanted to speak with her for hours about everything else.

"So, what the hell are you doing in Durres? Travellers don't pass through here like this."

166

I explained how I had been travelling in Europe for a couple of years, walked the Camino de Santiago, and then decided to walk a pilgrimage from Rome to Istanbul.

"How do you afford all of this?" she asked, translating for her friends, who were much more curious than her. I looked at the two young men, because I was sure it was they who wanted to know.

"It's not how much you earn, really, or have. It's how much you spend. You can imagine walking from Rome wasn't too expensive."

The girl became excited and put her glass down. "Wait, you walked here? All the way?"

My eyes keyed and the thrill sparkled through them. "Yes, well, I took a ferry from Bari to Dubrovnik."

"So, you walked here, from Dubrovnik?"

Again, I smiled and shrugged my shoulders. "I came here from a small town called Ishem today, on a mountain halfway to Lezhe. It has been a long-ass day. And this beer tastes really fucking good."

The boys' faces maddened, and the girls grinned with shock. One of the lads bought me another round plus a round of Raki shots. He put a shot glass in front of me before speaking.

"You tried Raki? Long walk, crazy man you. You need." He glared at me, impressed.

"Oh yea, I know a little bit of Raki," I beamed back and took the glass in my hand to cheer with them. "Gezuar!" I announced to them, "Faleminderit!"

"Wait, you speak Albanian?" The sweet young lady enquired. I shook my head in disappointment.

"Those are my only words, sorry."

We had a second round in front of us nearly before the first empty glass hit the table. "They are from another table," the waitress told my new translator. We saluted the other table and drank with them from across the room. Music crackled from under-insulated speakers. Rock ballads from the mid-eighties whined throughout the room. Our table got larger, people joined, drinks arrived, beer glasses were pounded, laughs got louder, and people swayed.

"You can stay at my house. The city is still a pretty far walk," she paused and laughed to herself. "I mean for most

167

people." She looked at me kindly with her intense, globular eyes. Her expressions radiated constantly, emanating fervour and zeal. She could drink like a Slav, too. It shouldn't have surprised me, of course, and I guess it didn't. But most girls I knew back home would have been trollied from the continuum of shots.

"You don't mind sleeping on the couch, do you?"

I insisted on the couch. "Hell, most days I'm in my tent. Well, except in Albania. Honestly, happy to sleep on the floor, whatever."

"You got the couch, so don't worry."

I turned from the dancing commotion and flying beer foam to learn a bit more about this wild, westernized woman. She lived in Belgium, got nailed for overstaying, and was sent back to Albania.

"They banned me for five years from the Schengen." It was the first time her lips subsided a little and lost their supple cheer. "I love my family and friends, I like Albania, but there is nothing to do here. There are no chances, no jobs, it's kinda shit."

I nodded in agreement, understanding as I could be, though I still believed that in the countryside, self-sustainability was easily achieved. And without demoralizing corporations everywhere, life was much calmer, land much cheaper. She, however, had been tainted by the consumer's lifestyle.

"Not to mention the division between men and women," I said, trying to move into another direction. I told her about the men who laughed at me when I tried to wash dishes after dinner. "Economic hardship is one thing, but this enormous chasm between the sexes here is awful for a woman who wants to roam free and make her own mistakes." I slapped my hand on her thigh and then waved it around the room pointing it at all the men. "Too many pseudo-Muslim men who want a housewife or something, a piece of property to clean house and raise children while he gallivants about. I can hear them now: 'I pay the bills here, so I can stay out late, got it, woman?'"

She nodded along and drank the last of her beer. I pointed to the empty glass and spun my hand around to the server.

"Yea, Freddi, I'm young, I wanna have some fun. These guys, they all want the housewife, or worse, a slave. It was so different in Belgium. This is the only place I can drink around this part of the city. For sure, it's different in Tirana. But here, and deeper in the countryside, the women don't go out. It's bullshit. I'm lucky to have my girl!" She threw her arm around her girlfriend, the only other woman in the bar besides the waitress. They hugged and kissed each other's cheeks.

"I missed this sexy bitch while I was gone!" her friend blurted as the two of them smiled together. "We're young, Freddi, this is not the place for us!"

"Especially when you like that five-letter word that rhymes with cleanest and meanest," I laughed. She looked at me dumbfounded, waiting for an explanation. "It's a quote from a rap song, by Naughty by Nature. It means penis. A five-letter word that rhymes with cleanest and meanest, he's talkin' 'bout penis."

She laughed and looked at me straight. "Yea, when I like penis." She continued, "I almost married a guy to stay in Belgium. He turned out to be such an asshole. He turned out jealous, possessive, controlling. I'm only twenty-three!"

"Twenty-three is old in some Muslim countries," I chuckled and finished my drink.

"Let's get going, okay?'

I agreed. We reached the street and a small alleyway. I pulled this little darling into it and kissed her. She didn't resist. We groped each other's bodies under our clothes and the rage was pure and the fire was honest and it was clearly a night to remember. I stopped into the next shop to buy a few beers. At the house, I met her parents, and the two of them joined us, opening the cans I bought.

"I should have bought a few more," I said, as her father finished his first. Her girlfriend joined us. Her mother brought stuffed peppers and bread and cheese. The house was small, on the ground floor of an old, two-story building like those lining the streets of any city in Europe. The difference was, most of them, especially in the West, had been re-finished.

Her girlfriend left after her parents went to bed, and the two of us remained in the living area on the old, red, worn-out couch. We jumped on each other instantly. I ripped her clothes off and grabbed for her like stairs on a ladder, reaching for a wonderful, rooftop view. My mouth fell into her and she ached with joy. She squeezed my head into her pelvis and pushed her thighs into my cheeks. I felt her freedom; she wanted to surge within me.

169

I had one hand on her left breast, rubbing her nipple, and the other grabbing her right cheek when the noise happened. We both paused, but I carried on. I pulled my pants and undershorts down. My dick was throbbing and went straight for her. The noise happened again, only this time it was much louder. The door had opened and shut. My friend's whole body froze, and my sex bounced off hers. She had on her a look of fright I'd never witnessed before. We scrambled for blankets and clothing as the shouting began.

A thick cloud of awkwardness covered everything. It became sticky, tension oozing from the walls. The ceiling and floor closed in and shook. Her eyes glossed over as the shouting stopped. We were both silent—and clothed. I didn't know what to say or do.

"Should I go?" I finally whispered.

She shook her head. "No, no, Freddi, please. It's not your problem; don't worry."

I opened the last beer can, still somewhat cold, and passed it to her. There was another already opened on the table which I drank from. Her can shook in her hand.

"What did he say?" I stammered cautiously. She didn't answer me but sipped the beer instead.

"He is ashamed of me," she finally unloaded. "Says I have shamed the whole family. He is disgusted with me. Says I am dead to him." Her face was somehow paralyzed and white. The whole evening, she had been lit up like a city skyline at night. Everything was great, and even with her parents, we all laughed and giggled together. Suddenly, because of our moment of intimacy, my twenty-three-year-old, adult, female friend was colder than the Siberian steppe in November. My face dropped and my heart raced. I swallowed before apologizing and offering to leave again.

She grabbed my arm and leg. "Stop, please, you'll leave in the morning. There is nothing to do now, it's late and it's me that is sorry."

I squeezed her hand and insisted he would get over it. That it would all pass. She hardly acknowledged me. I squeezed her thigh and grabbed her face. "It'll be okay."

She barely looked at me. "I should have known better," and shook her head.

"Come on, we wanted this. We had been talking all night about something like this. It felt good. And you were enjoying yourself. It's his problem, not yours," I reasoned.

"Yes, but it's his house. And I should respect what he wants."

"He should want what's best for you at this stage and be a little bit more reasonable, especially after you were away in Belgium for so long. Please, don't beat yourself up. He is your father, he loves you."

I couldn't shake the image of an Arabic woman in a similar fate, that she might be stoned. The harsh penance she would have to suffer for defying their outdated notions of misogynistic morality. This woman in front of me was far from a Muslim. She may have acknowledged being one to avoid confrontation with her father, but she hadn't practiced any form of prayer nor observed Ramadan in a long time. Her parents didn't strike me as conformists, either. But her father's voice was coarse. I was glad he didn't leap down after me. Glad I didn't have to run from the house naked at 4 a.m. I'd thought that was my fate when I heard that door open and saw this poor girl's pale shock.

"Okay," she kissed me. "It's time for bed."

She slept beside me on the couch, in my lap. And in the morning, she woke me gently. "Hey, Freddi. Hi. You sleep okay?"

She gave me the time to get ready and stretch and flick my brain on. I could feel it was time to go from the moment my eyes opened. "I'm gonna call you, and we're gonna hang out, right? I can stay in the city for a few days at least. You can show me the town?"

"Let's see," she said, ready to turn away.

"Come on, I want to see you again. Please, don't... why you... hey," I grabbed her face and kissed her with both lips. Her mouth hardly widened. I pulled back. "Come meet me, okay? Or I'll find you, whatever."

"Okay, okay." Then she explained the directions to the commercial centre one more time before I left.

Albania cycled through every great power that conquered Europe, like a kidney stone between intestinal glands, from the Greeks to Germany. An illegitimate child that had to be fed from time to time. It was home to much of the Adriatic coast. From the Ottoman Empire's annexation, the country saw one year of independence before being swiped in the spoils of WWI. Between the two great wars, ongoing conflicts remained between Albanians and Italy and Yugoslavia. The Italians used Albania as a base for attack against Greece in the late 30s. Before 1944, they had little chance to adopt a national personality. They were a fragmented nation of tribes with different dialects, mostly farmers. When Enver Hoxha took over, like his mentor Stalin, he ruled with an iron grip. The country was far from united: some were Christian, some were Muslim, mostly they were awaiting guidance into modernity.

Hoxha had the perfect country to mould to his vision. Inspired by Marx and Lenin, he formed the Communist party in Albania. He brought Communism, but also a national identity. He prohibited all religious practice and killed anyone who protested. He supported a singular national language and put considerable effort into developing education. With no universities, it was a tall order. The national population was dwindling. Albania had been subjected to numerous colonialist encroachments, and Albanians had fled to other parts of Europe seeking a better life. Hoxha's plan was to keep everyone in this time.

In the wake of his inauguration, he tracked down some 400 of his opposition members and had them murdered. After that, he led the nation as Foreign Minister, Minister of Defence, Commander-in-Chief, and ultimately Prime Minister. He confiscated land and businesses and created collective farms. He nationalized banks and introduced modern industrialization. Anyone who rebelled was either put in a prison camp or executed. Once Enver Hoxha seized power, he stayed until his death in the mid-80s. The man put in a solid 40 years, a touch more than his big daddy in the Soviet Union. In the latter part of his term, the country went into great isolation. First, Stalin died, and Hoxha didn't tie in with Khrushchev during the mid-50s. He then formed his largest alliance with Mao of China, but when Mao died in the mid-70s, he had nowhere to go, no allies and no aid. It wasn't long after his death that Communism collapsed altogether.

With that, as all the former Soviet and Chinese alliances, Albania sank into chaos. Through the dissolution of Yugoslavia and the horrific Balkan Wars, Albanians continued to suffer. In the late 90s, several investment schemes went nationwide: half of Albania's GDP was made up of public contributions. Many people naively invested their life savings into what eventually amounted to elaborate pyramid schemes. When the whole thing imploded, more than a billion dollars of cash went up in flames. This financial nightmare caused people to demand government restitution. Riots ensued and threats were made. Civilians armed themselves, causing anarchy in the streets of every centre. They continued until the government was brought down. Shortly after this, the Kosovo Liberation Army, demanding independence for Kosovars, gained momentum. The five percent of Albanians who were Serbian-Kosovars disagreed and sided with the president of Serbia. Milosevi was a nationalist trying hard to keep Yugoslavia's last remnants together. While the ethnic, Muslim Albanians wanted an independent nation as a majority, Serbs insisted the land was rightfully theirs. Hundreds of thousands of ethnic Muslim Albanian Kosovars were displaced into struggling Albania while the Kosovo war was fought. In fact, 90 percent of the population, over a million people, were displaced or killed. NATO bombed Serbia until Serbia stopped fighting in Kosovo and accepted a peace treaty. Albania was left in ruins at the turn of the 21st century. That same year, I was snorting crushed up ecstasy and crystal while slamming 40-ouncers and spitting rooftop rhymes, becoming homeless by the end of summer.

As I walked through the streets here, it was easy to see how far behind the conflicts and political machinations had left the average, poor Albanian. They were not helpless. However, any kind of modern development from the mid-70s onward hadn't arrived. In 1920, Tirana became the temporary capital and then, became permanent. Durres took the backburner but remained the main port for goods coming into the country. Not much bigger than my hometown, it struggled to shake its scars from the past but had a lot of charm. As in other parts of the country I had seen, the people had a friendly nature, unscathed by the indifference inflicted on so many Europeans by social media and fast-paced, booming corporate economies. Fresh vegetable markets and street vendors lined busy lanes. Unpaved back roads used as dumping sites. Stained buildings, neglected into dystopia. All of this made for a great wander in the late afternoon.

The Missionaries of Charity refused me, as it was a female institution. This forced me to look for a church as I had in Italy. A priest opened the doors of his locked palace and reluctantly let me put my tent in a corner of the front lawn. His English was poor, and our communication wasn't great. He gestured to my backpack and hat. He pulled at his chin and pointed to my beard.

"James?" I blurted out.

He nodded, excitedly.

After unpacking and setting up, I sought out an internet cafe and called my lady friend. There was no reply. I called a second time. Online, I searched out messages and a map for this ancient Roman Via Egnatia. I found a vague outline and a few articles from the Way. But in my mailbox, there was also a message from James. He had left Durres after taking a boat from Brindisi, Italy and was on his Way to Istanbul. I had missed him.

Back at the church, I cooked dinner with the help of my headlamp. My thin cooking pot tipped over, and blazing hot oil spilled onto the skin above my ankle. Three more days passed with me calling this girl, hoping she would answer, that we could meet for a sunset on the beach. I wanted nothing more than some company, some loving, intimacy, and companionship, as any human being would. Silence after the shops closed. Few spoke more than a word of English. And I couldn't find anyone with any details about the Via Egnatia trailhead. After three days being pussy whipped and resting on the front lawn of the church, I made my move. I tried schools, churches, and the Mission of Charities. No one could understand what I was on about. They all acknowledged the Via Egnatia. They nodded and offered directions. But they spoke about the new highway to Macedonia.

I passed a bunch of shanty houses built under the new overpass of that highway. A dog ran after me barking, and a crowd of derelicts came to observe the commotion. I walked out of Durres and put my tent up after a gruelling 20 kilometres of pavement. One thing was for certain, Albanians loved to wash their cars. I passed several car washes. And everyone I met pointed to the road in front of me, every time I asked about the Via Egnatia. It was a flat, uneventful landscape and a long, unvarying, paved road. One side had plenty of village communities, and I wanted to venture through. I found a turnoff

174

across train tracks and followed crisscrossing dirt roads through shanties and past donkeys and open, garden farms. I decided to follow the tracks instead of the highway.

Ep. 19
The Canadian Note

My ambitions faltered. Nothing but shrugged shoulders and dead ends. The village roads led me to train tracks. A blog post kept me on them. A turtle appeared between lumber strips. His little paws moved across the stones.

"He has wandered so far from the river," I thought. "The years it must have taken the old boy. Where will his pilgrimage lead him?" Three months were nothing to a turtle; it must have taken it years to cross one valley.

A huge, deep, dark tunnel burrowed through the mountain's flesh. Instead of returning to the traffic, I reluctantly walked into darkness. If a train ploughed through, I had nowhere to go. It was a closed circuit. Unlike *Stand by Me*, where the boys could jump into a lake, I was trapped. The first tunnel carried on and my heart thumped like an alarm clock on a bedside table. Any moment, a huge spotlight would surround me. The metal gears would grind as the train tried to halt. It would be too late, though. The poor conductor haunted for years. Headlines across Albania and Europe would speak of one foolish pilgrim run down like a top-sided turtle. Inside the third tunnel, my anxiety boiled over. I couldn't handle it anymore.

Aside from the car washes, nothing but a wide river, the long road, traffic, and a mountain in the near distance with homes scattered over it. That mountain seemed better than this goddamn highway. My anxiety shifted to grief and self-loathing. What the fuck was the point of walking a fucking highway? The only option was to get indefatigably drunk. The sole chance I had at resolving my sheer disappointment was to wreck my head with Raki. As I approached my night's rest stop, a bar appeared on the side of the gravel road. A mirage in the Sahara? Its partially roofed, open terrace beckoned me. A few young men watched television from a couch. They leapt at the sight of me. Moments later, a beer and Raki rested on the table.

175

"Oh, hey! Ha!" They cheered and laughed, as I slammed the shot glass back and ordered a second. "No, wait, come on, I buy four! One for all of us! Nostrovia! Fuck Egnatia!"

Six or seven hours later, they gave me the sofa and I passed out.

Back on the road and many kilometres later, a small resto appeared. It sat on the riverside in a perfect spot with plenty of grass. Black, metallic framed tables with white tablecloths. A man in his 60s came over.

"Ca va?" he asked in French. He had lived in France. We could be civil in our communication. He had but a few items to offer, but there was food. We spoke while I waited. He explained that the Way was on the mountain top, as I imagined it must have been.

"Il faut passé la rivere." The man served me a brilliant omelette with a half dozen cubes of hard cheese, toasted flatbread, and roasted vegetable salad. There were a few rooms to be rented.

"The yard is free?" A massive, healthy meadowland ended at the riverside. The best place I had camped in a month.

"I know the Way you are after," he explained in French. "But from here it is far too difficult to find, it's all the way to the top, trust me." He noticed that I was unconvinced. "Listen, I grew up here. You can't get there from here. You must go to Elbasan. There is a river crossing. Even then it will be difficult, but you are determined. I can see that. It's the old road, nearly forgotten; few realize it's there."

Tell me about it, I thought. "But there are villages up there?"

"There won't be supermarkets, but there are a few villagers. Why do you do this, walking to Istanbul? You are religious? Why not take the bus?"

I put the tips of my fingers to my temples and then hands on my heart. "On the bus, I would have missed all this countryside and your omelette. Worst of all, I wouldn't have had the chance to share a Raki with you," I grinned emphatically.

He went inside and returned with glasses of milky water. "It's not Raki, it's Pastis."

The first few times I drank Pastis, it made me cringe. It reminded me of other malevolent-tasting, liquorice spirits. Mixed with water, it became a milky substance that inspired an awful soap-like appearance, shaken into a glass then boiled with star anise. Raki was made from seasonal fruit. Perfectly unregulated, it was stronger than Ricard or Pastis. And while Raki rocked the eye out of its socket at four in the morning, Pastis managed to do one better.

"Ah, trop bon," I thanked the man.

He put ice cubes in and as they melted, they thinned out the sharp anise. As the liquid hit my throat, it cooled my overheated muscles. A few sips later, my whole body loosened, my mind quieted, and I sank into the chair staring at a movie his son was watching in the dining area. I finished the first glass. He poured me another. I spoke of my time in Albania, praising it with my new friend.

"So many multi-linguists here. It's like fucking Switzerland. Incredible," I exclaimed. One could hardly believe that before ol' Hoxha came through, most of the country was illiterate. But a country constantly infiltrated and dominated by Royal Empires or colonial powers had to adapt to the presidential language, literate or no. Once my tent went up, the old man invited me inside.

"We have some pasta if you would like," he said in French. His wife brought a large porcelain bowl to the table. My eyes were red from exhaustion and Pastis, but they widened at the sight of this beautiful bowl of spaghetti Bolognese. He poured me a glass of red wine. After a few hundred grams of durum wheat and that glass of maroon-coloured Bordeaux, I had to peel myself from the chair where I stared at Schwarzenegger, in dubbed Albanian, hollering at some criminals. I walked to my tent with my chest leading the way until I plummeted headlong onto my pillow and woke a few hours after the sun.

* * *

A few people along the Way in Albania asked me if I was religious, including the Brothers in Bushat. But on the Way to Santiago in Spain, I was like most people, including my dear friend Dani: we couldn't give a fuck about despots and autocrats calling themselves organised religion. When Dani and I found a church host for our little family, it was for a bed in a small room with four bunks. The church aspect was just a novelty. This pilgrim's path wasn't about God, or pledging allegiance to St. James, or other apostolic figures who followed the so-called word of Christ. It was a trail that brought mind, body, and soul together, which ultimately, but only temporarily, unified the frayed wiring in my head for a harmonious life force. Little, ginger-haired, and fair-skinned with freckles, Elena was the only family I saw for the two weeks out on my solo path. She was the closest to a Holy Person I could imagine. A rabbi who was curious about religion in general. Of course, there was Dave, who often behaved like a Holy Man, but from my point of view, he used the church as his saviour on a regular basis and that was it.

Dani, I missed him a lot. He wasn't so far away. Only a day or two behind me. So many things that came to pass, I missed his point of view and perspective. He was a brother. Weeks of travel and connection side by side; if the bond was to survive, there needed to be relatability deeper than nation states or musical tastes. The two of us fought through dependencies, we were the same age, born at the cusp between the 70s and 80s. We both wrote to wash out our emotions. We both came to the Camino instead of the Dalmatian Islands, Algarve, or Thailand. We had both lived lives that included stories of death. Had friends who fucked up and died too early clinging onto self-destructive nights. We both processed the constant flux of life in the same way, or maybe we both just learned to survive in the same way.

"You never think it will be you that gets AIDS, then just like that, the whole world around you changes. The guy wanted to give up, Fred. He saw no reason to carry on living."

That was one of Dani's closest friends, who took the wrong shot in his vein. The difference between us and our peers was our survival in a gritty lifestyle. We made it out of circumstance, whether by luck, sheer will, or something more cosmic, like fate; we made it out. Now, we followed the sun, fleeing our internal darkness, like sunflowers reaching away from shadows of doubt.

In Bethlehem, so many lined up to grovel over the birthplace of Jesus at the basement of a huge church. It was Easter, and I arrived outside the church by fluke, so I followed

178

crowds inside. As I watched the people channel through the small, dark space, I felt pity and also misery for their dependency. They reached for hope from divine power instead of within themselves. Muslims, as well. I watched within the Sixty Dome Mosque in Bangladesh. They shared a similar ritual, but instead of kissing the floor where baby Jesus rocked back and forth, they wrapped their arms around ivory pillars inside the Jammi, kissing and praying for what they couldn't have. How could they believe that kissing an old stone would do anything except chance a little mouth herpes?

The Camino Way forged empowerment. Determination to keep walking, even when it became pointless. Empowered by meeting people who made sacrifices in life, real sacrifices to disrupt their current despair or mundanity. A life that often chiselled us down to hopelessness. With people like Amos, Cosimo, and Dani, I found a routine. We worked together to extirpate the symptoms of a fast-moving, capitalist world. We had group meals and group discussions. This Way broke free from dependencies. Out on my own, I met a German, 33 years old, who walked out of his financially secure job, tired of it and how it made him feel. He was a vulture, he confessed.

"I hovered over people, waiting for them to become weak, so I could dive in and swoop up their money. I felt horrible all the time, depressed from living a life of zero worth. A dwindling existence without purpose, spoiled."

He left Munich with zero dollars and walked the Way to Santiago. The man spent months approaching strangers on the streets and at their doorsteps. We were hell-bent on the concept that we needed so many things to survive. A buyer's economy, we were made to consume. He went out with nothing but his pack and sandals to see if the world could be different; how much love would there be? His heart told him that love surrounded him, so he walked out of Munich.

"Some people slammed their doors, others didn't," he told me in his acquired, patient tone. "I had to deal with a lot of rejection in a way I never had before. Some days, I ate very little and walked slowly. It was a discipline I needed away from a world where I could have everything."

His face was so bright with general content. And like my Colombian friend, his strength culminated in an inimitable presence. While some would say he was self-destructive, I listened to his every word. I listened because he had learned. When we met, he was on his Way back. He was heading back to Munich by foot with nothing more than his backpack and sandals. This man wasn't travel blogging or making videos for YouTube. He wasn't proving anything or trying to advise others. He was a pilgrim on his own spiritual quest. His sword was in each footstep. Finding food was a daily battle that he had to face. And the demons, he assured me, which haunted him before this Way, disappeared.

"I've never seen the world so vividly and healthily, Freddi. I took a lot for granted."

Like the German, I also had demons, persecuting and tormenting, feeding on times of low self-confidence. This timelessness and space, the interactions gave me an arena to face them. As an only child, I fought with loneliness my whole youth. Single parent home with a mom who worked 12-hour shifts. My days were often left playing alone. It bothered me and created great stress. I did everything to spend time with classmates and nearby friends. The older I got, the harder it became, until I had no friends. Surrounded by people I didn't know in my first year of high school, all my school friends were elsewhere or cliqued up in a world of post-pubescence. Competition rose in sports, and I couldn't keep up. I had the will to succeed but not the core strength. I was too soft. Things came around as I found a family through skateboarding, drugs, and booze. Slowly, years passed, and it was the same battle over and over, trying to fit in, surrounding myself with other like-minded people to avoid the fear of boredom and being alone. I had been travelling five years before The Way. Groups came and went. I met a woman who I fell in love with, but I couldn't commit. I had to keep going until the woman grew tired of me trying to find groups to encircle us. Scarred by abandonment and aware it was coming, I fucked other women to hurt us both. It wasn't until The Way that I felt a sense of belonging. Yet, I'd left the whole family because of one girl.

"Sounds like you need to find them again," commented a Danish man from across a metallic table. He listened to me pour out my past trying to paraphrase my current struggle. He wore a large, thatched bucket hat that covered him wholly with shade. He

180

had walked the Way to Santiago from St. Jean-Pied-de-Port six times.

He let me speak and vent about my struggles as a derelict in Europe without a visa or work permit. How my avid loneliness surrounded by others enriched and excited me to join albergues instead of my tent.

"I like camping; I just don't want to do it alone. I can't handle it, feeling left out."

"At some point, you'll have to face that head on to break through it, Freddi." He spoke to me earnestly, like other pilgrims, and he listened the same way. "I come back," he started as I ended a sentence. "Because it's a great way to remind myself of life's lessons. Freddi, the Way always provides, as long as you stay open with yourself."

He left me at the table with that, but I leapt up and shared a hug with him. He shook my hand before leaving to find a hotel.

"I'd let you stay with me, but I like my space and love my own company. Buen Camino, my pilgrim friend." He put a twenty into my hand, after paying our tab at lunch. "Suerte."

* * *

"You never walk alone," I stared at this for a long while. Cars passed as I locked onto the spray-painted slogan. Beyond the tunnel, a valley opened around the low, narrow, cloudy river. An ugly, obstructing city developed on the opposite side, cut off at both ends, a few buildings reaching five or six stories. Surrounded by forest, green mountainside, and patches of evergreens, it was once a landscape of small, self-sufficient settlements. Remnants of old, stone cabins, their orange, tiled roofs faded to black, overgrown and overtaken by coniferous branches. The reek of abandonment permeated everything.

Clouds gathered around far-off mountain peaks behind the obstinate city line and kept the sky perfectly blue. A bubbly woman smiled at the sight of me behind her tray of freshly baked, golden-brown Burek. I bit into one and lit up, acknowledging her efforts. Children waited on a set of stairs outside, passing their lunch hour. They paraded around me. Beyond them, I saw a small bridge, a narrow river running below it.

181

"Il faut passé par la rivere." The old man's words echoed as I noticed the trail beyond the bridge. The children glamorised me and laughed, one of them asking questions in English for the entire group. I answered as I glanced at the bridge. The pebbled road narrowed to a dark brown donkey trail and led to a house embanked in shade under bulky brush. Birds sang. A young woman smiled and greeted me from her porch before running inside. Her mother came out with her, and the ravishing young lady this time put a large bag of walnuts in my hand. I shook them away.

"Please," she said gently.

I pushed on with my new bag of walnuts and waved goodbye. The trail descended to sand and a quick-moving river. I climbed to look around and traversed steep rock faces to try to reach higher ground. Up one cliff then down another, the region was barren aside from river stones, beachside shrubs, impassable walls, and ascending hills. I resisted disenchantment. I crossed the river as he recommended. There were signs of life; surely there would be more, farther along. I was in nature. Whether I was communing with it or merely surviving, I was certainly "in it." I decided to follow the river. Water leads to good places, and following a river makes it difficult to get lost. I climbed and foraged and fell upon some trail that led steeply uphill. Voices interrupted the birds, screeching laughter. The brush covered everything and made the day seem quite late. A long, wooden footbridge hung across the expanded river. Teenagers carried books and backpacks across it. They were as shocked to see me as I was them. Homes and cabins scattered all around me, too sprawled out to be noticed from the mountainside.

"Via Egnatia?" I asked cautiously. It was the question I loathed, more than anything.

They grinned and nodded. The two of them pointed back across the wooden bridge.

I shook my head, trying to remain calm. "Old, ancia, antica Via Egnatia?" I asked, shrugging my shoulders with a desperate face.

The three of them discussed and argued, the tallest of them kissed his teeth and shrugged off the others. I looked to him and asked again. He pointed uphill. The Way was incredibly steep and densely forested. I was unsure but reflected on the old man's words again.

"C'est tout en haut de la montagne. Tu va te perdre. C'est très dangereux."

So, I walked. One glance from the gorgeous, wire and wood-panelled footbridge indicated I had already scaled a fair amount. Following his directions led through dense evergreens where there was no trail. I was becoming convinced that he had done me wrong. The path got steeper, my pack got heavier. Hands in the dirt, I ran uphill on my knees. A gate appeared. It led to a plateau. Dozens of PVC pipes ran perpendicular to the steep mountainside. They ran in multiple directions funnelling water to farmhouses. Stalks of corn appeared, and I sat under a cob ready to be detasseled, looking down at that infuriating highway, the Via Egnatia. So far down, it was a mucus trail left by an earthworm. One slip and I'd fall 100 metres before slapping my ribs against bark. Figs dangled from branches, acres of grapes, fences, and one distant farmhouse. Citrus fruit and walnuts grew enough to feed me through the following month. I gorged myself on the figs and pushed again, until I saw a man. He shuffled past a house until he saw me. His daughter and infant son were inside with his wife.

"One hundred and two," the man said as he introduced his mom.

Grandma looked at me with an evil grin that tightened my skin. She flashed the angriest eyes I'd ever seen outside of a movie. She moved slowly, like a set of biology class bones. She had only hatred in her eyes, like I was one of Hoxha's bagmen come to steal their farmhouse away.

Through a small hallway with a low-ceilinged living area and a kitchen behind it, his wife offered me a seat. I waved at Grandma and turned, but not before she clawed at me with her vicious stare. His wife brought out a porcelain cup of the swampy water they called coffee and some bits of food. I thanked her, repeatedly. I spoke with her husband in broken language and through his few sentences of English. He assured me that the dirt road above his house was the old, Roman Via Egnatia. While I wanted to sit and speak about nothing through hand signals, the excitement was too great. After stirring in my seat for another ten minutes, I rose and lunged out the door for my pack. Grandma was waiting there for me, staring me down with every ounce of vitriol she could muster.

Broken red and grey stones, clay tiles completely mulched and turned over. This was a road that had ushered travelling gypsies, merchants, and foot soldiers across the Empire. The Egnatia Way. Four days of desperation and I finally made it. The polished stones had been cemented into the ground by countless centuries of traffic. My feet suffered inside of my shitty, plastic shoes. From the road, I could look down as the Way cleared. The whole valley lay naked, with layers of green forest in front of me. The river, township, pollution, and noise. It must've been a good 500 meters down. Pockmarked houses, channels of rugged mountain crests, completely bare, exhilarating, wide open. The road split into two parts. One led downhill, the other up. A couple of young men walked ahead of me. When the young guys pointed to the road down, I shrugged it off. The Way wasn't getting lost again. I tried to ask patiently, but like usual, they pointed downhill, all the Way downhill to the highway.

"Roman, Romano, Egnatia." I went uphill as before, ignoring them. The lads followed me, chirping excitedly in Albanian like magpies in the morning. The road led into a village and the storefront of a small bar. I swung the loose, hinged door open and entered. It wasn't long before the one guy who could speak a handful of English sentences had me taking shots of Raki. I let my pack go and celebrated. The dust on the hard, cement floor rose when the pack fell. I sat down and sighed, knocked back the first Raki, and immediately took a second one for myself and my new friend. All the men, the whole village, came inside. One of them took a note out of a frame and brought it to me. I held it in my hand and squinted in disbelief.

A light blue Canadian five-dollar bill. Sir Wilfrid Laurier's bald head was still recognizable from afar.

The men bought rounds. We threw them back like sailors rescued from a cyclone.

"How the hell did you guys get this?" I looked at my translator and friend.

"The trucks, they come. They drive into mountain. They come back and give this."

He carried on about Australian trucks that also arrived there but apparently didn't leave a dollar bill behind. This village sat at the top of this wide mountain. There would be points slightly higher, but it wasn't slivered with alpine peaks. Whatever they searched for, the trucks left full. Five bucks for the villagers whose land rights merited a little school or hospital.

Then a man rushed into the bar. He appeared dirty, sweating. He carried a large plastic bag in his hand. The men celebrated and told me to look inside. Mushrooms longer than my hand. Their heads were black-spotted, yellow-skinned squid tubes. And the stem ran twice the length of my middle finger. One of the men chopped a few and fried them. It smelt damn good, the garlic in the air, the fruit Raki in my throat. I was drunk by the time the mushrooms arrived. I took one morsel in my hand.

"Holy shit!" I looked up frantically, everyone around me was chatting and smoking. The room was a hotbox, a cloud full of faces. I grabbed the thigh of my translator friend. "These are really good! Bueno! Muy Bien! Trop Bien!" I threw the pieces into my mouth, the liquid rich, the chunks incredibly moist. An explosion of earthy, umami flavour I had rarely tasted before. This was their annual harvest. Everyone waited for the season to forage these big, tasty fungi. My good friend, the translator, invited me to a house. An elderly man sat with us through all the commotion. He insisted I stay at his home. His wife had a bandana tied around her hair. Customarily, she brought food for us. An incredible assortment on a big, dense wooden table. A fresh, large baking tray of Burek. Stuffed peppers, hard cheese, bread, fried vegetables, potatoes, and omelette, all of them covered in baskets or bowls ready for her hubby. I filled my mouth as Chris McCandless would have if he had survived the Alaskan wild.

They ushered me to a small room with a single bed covered with colourful, thick bedding. The night-time temperature dropped. The padded blankets were for the hard winters. Their kids had gone away, and they offered the space to me. They were so happy; I think the wonderful woman was excited to be a mother again. I was happy to be her child for the night. At some point, very late, I was jolted from sleep and darted for the toilet. Everything was dark, completely dark, so I couldn't find my way to the toilet or front door. I looked frantically, grabbing at walls, looking for a hinge. I slammed into everything. When I got a door open, I fell into the toilet bowl. A furious waterfall of vomit shot from my throat. An old, Asian squat toilet, I curled my hands and knees around it as I poured my stomach into the porcelain's hollowed centre. My stomach tightened and suffered as it attempted to puke again and again. My body convulsed and my mouth widened like a mother bird feeding her infants. Nothing came out until again the fountain released and again sprayed into the porcelain squat. I crawled back to my new room and into the bed.

Ep. 20
New Jerusalem

The air smelled better, my feet were freewheeling, and my pack felt miraculously lighter. No cars, very little sound at all but for grazing sheep pushed on by a woman and her stick. Horse hooves, as they ran wild across huge meadows of grass, free at the top of Albania. A man invited me to share lunch with him. He called to me as he dug a hole. His purpose was somewhat of a mystery. There were multiple holes, and a lot of figs. We ate figs, cheese, and bread. Pinned with old stones, once symmetrical, the road was crumbling. The Romans built the road to be around six metres wide outside of cities, where it would then triple in width. The remains of ancient engineering were nothing but broken chunks of homemade concrete, smashed into pebbles.

The mountaintop village and the trail were part of Via Candavia, one section of the Egnatia Way. It led to the Candavia mountain pass, which in ancient times divided Illyria from Macedonia (Greece) at the city of Lychnidus, or as we know it now, Europe's Jerusalem, Ohrid. Soldiers once marched in golden armbands and steel helmets. They carried large, circular shields and spearheaded staves. They hustled from one end of the empire to the other, wherever needed. They must have sounded like a herd of giraffes stampeding to a savannah waterhole. Pompey rallied troops on this road to fight against the great military man, Julius Caesar. Rome's two greatest generals fought a civil war on the Candavian Way and on the coast at Dyrrachium (Durres) in 48 B.C. Pompey retreated to Egypt, where he was murdered by an ally who feared Caesar. As time wore on, the Romans pushed north to frontiers around the River Danube, and the Egnatia Way returned to its peaceful state.

No longer a military route, wheeled horse and mule carts filled the road. Pilgrims and monks walked the Way; even St. Paul walked this Way to Corinth to build a church via Thessaloniki. Paul was born in what would become the Syrian province of Rome. A Greek speaking Jew from Asia Minor who made tents, he could set up shop anywhere along the Way. He became a missionary for Jesus and took the road towards Lygos (Constantinople), then along the Egnatia Way. At times, he would travel by ship. Most of his journeys were done by foot with a mule beside him, carrying his tools and scrolls. He undoubtedly would have seen hard times in the cold and often relied on the generous hands of his converts. The Egnatia Way would see plenty of other pilgrims after he died in Rome. Many walked to reach his churches and follow his teachings. Slowly, a pilgrimage route began.

No faster than a turtle swam from its nesting beach at Ascension Island, I underwent my long and strenuous pilgrimage. The turtle relied only on her nose to guide her, as I had tried and struggled to do. By sniffing the air, and through steady paddling, she traversed 2000 kilometres of open sea to the sandy shores of Brazil. High above the river valley floor, I walked until the effulgent landscape descended. My soul was in nirvana, flooded by uncharted turf, jagged chimneys of earth covered by forest acorns, forgotten villages without electricity, nature at its divinest. Undisturbed old men smiled alongside their loyal soft- and swollen-cheeked wives. Generous hands poured lines of Raki and followed with cubes of hard cheese. The consistent breeze brought me high-grade oxygen and made harmonious wind chimes in the leaves. My nerves felt the climax of this whole escapade deep in my bones. Enmity poured from me as the Way descended back onto the motorway. I glanced around a dozen times asking myself why, for what reason, what was there to gain from that godawful modern road but suffering and torture? The Way dribbled to the road. My impulse was to avoid it. Clouds had been gathering overhead for a while. I had no idea where to go.

The sky darkened, and I took refuge in a little shanty with a tin roof. It had a broken sign, half lit with an Albanian name.

Inside, it was full of young men. Not one of them spoke a full sentence of English beyond "What's your name," and "Where are you from?" And they were all the barky types; guys that smashed things for a living and dug ditches. The men, despite being abrasive with their grunts and burps, forward and aggressive with their command of personal space, were friendly. I had no right to expect anything. This was their hangout, their routine. I was on their turf. Rain bucketed down on the tin roof, so I suddenly had another issue. The ground would be wet, and my floor mat was long gone back on that ferry to Dubrovnik. This made camping unbearable. Lightning erupted, and I remembered all the people who had helped me across Albania. Surely, someone would offer me a place to stay. But no one did. They only stared at me, spoke of me to one another, and looked on with grimaces. It was hard to find the gravity to stay calm. A burger I'd ordered landed in front of me. When I went hours without food, I could be easily agitated. I needed to eat and called for a Raki to bring the nerves down even further. The noise rumbled as I ordered the drink. The lads' staring eyes all shifted. I needed something to take the edge off. Not long and I had a second shot in front of me.

"You, come! Yes, you come," one short-haired young man with a round nose, olive skin, and narrow cheekbones called. He and two friends pulled at my chair and lifted my bag. They walked me through the rain on a narrow, dirt trail until the pebbled ground came to a set of stairs that led through a garden pathway, lined with small shrubs and short trees. Wooden fences in long rows covered with vine leaves and young grapes. The young man opened the door with his key. We entered a large, carpeted room with a small table, two spotless couches, an old TV, a fireplace, and a high, metal shelving unit housing an assortment of trinkets.

His mom came in and demanded my clothes. In return, they squeezed me into a lime-green, collared shirt and a pair of incredibly tight, mauve jeans. We all stared at my new outfit and laughed a good while. The young man reached to the bottom of the shelving unit. He picked up a huge, glass, balloon-shaped decanter with a spigot and ring handle. Inside, there was enough liquid to kill a man. It roiled, splashing with each of his steps. It sounded louder and more quaffable the closer he got. He set it on the table with a thud, then gleamed at me with a proud grin.

"Tonight, Freddi, we'll see if you can really drink," he said in Albanian.

I returned to him a pirate-like chin, up in the air, and a wink of the eye. We had enough Raki to get the whole Albanian army drunk for a night. He put down decorative, crystal sherry glasses for each of us. One of the lads waved it off, which earned him a few snarls. I pulled out a cigarette from a pack on the table, lit a match, sparked the tobacco stick, then rubbed my hands together, smiling. His mother entered with a plastic tray full of the usual foods for us to snack on. We may have had no common language, but each time he filled those pretentious shot glasses, the night intensified, and our communication improved.

We were best friends before long.

Morning came as an unpleasant surprise. I jolted up like a dolphin from a shallow pool for a bit of fresh air. I was the thirstiest I had been in a century or more. Dizzy, disoriented, and dumbfounded, after a few moments, I could make out the young man standing there. His very short hair sparkled in the light, and his face too. He put my clothes on the table. I stretched and widened my eyes. He gleamed, fresh as a daisy, glittering eyes and perky smile. My head felt something altogether different, like it had been struck by a lightning bolt. My clothes smelled fresh as a woman's body mist.

They brought that awful swamp water out again. By this point, I had become accustomed to what they called "coffee." His mother also had a glorious burek for me. They were so endearing, these moms. Every village had a mom to make sure I'd be able to start another day fresh and clean, with a bit of food in my stomach. These women were the heart and soul of this country. Every time one of them cleaned my clothes or brought me food, I tried to communicate my immense appreciation for their kindness and generosity. I hoped they understood how important they were, not just to me, but to keeping these communities happy places. The men may be unrefined and unenlightened by western standards, but they were also forced to go out and find work. They didn't have time to study or appreciate high culture in a civilized way. Without their sweat, there would be no shelter. Or food to prepare. I sometimes forgot that reality when I criticized young men for staring blankly.

I noticed the massive jug of piss was nearly empty as I left the room and house. I wandered to a shop front and ordered a single cigarette. With a couple drags, and a sip of cold Coke, I resisted the desire to vomit and tried to overcome my confusion enough to make sense of my situation. I struggled through blurred vision to assess the path. A gravel road, partially covered with grass, led upward to my new friend's little village. There it was, not 200 metres ahead of me. A beautiful Via Egnatia flag in horizontal orange and white stripes, spray painted on the tree.

The magnificent trail reached a plateau that overlooked a massive valley. Once again, I was free from highway roads and the bustle of noisy cars. The sky was clear. The scenic villages seemed frozen in time. Mediaeval time. I expected Willow to come running out of one of these thatched houses carrying a baby in his arms. The more I walked, the more the Raki resin washed out in my sweat. The spray-painted flags kept appearing on small rocks and trunks. They kept me on the right path. A lake appeared in the distance, off to one side. There was an old shanty, and a couple of kids bolted out at me as I neared their little township. The road was steep, leading to a high grassy knoll. A man and his mule were coming downhill at the same time. He let go of the mule's leash and took hold of my shoulder. He pointed straight up with his hand flat. Though my calves and shoulders flexed and ached, I took the shortest way between two points. Bitumen and busy traffic had to be crossed numerous times until I reached a borderless Macedonia.

* * *

Surrounded by strangers, I waited too long for Dani. It was time to listen to my heart and join my family again. And the only way to meet them was to slow it down. The first day, I walked a mere seven kilometres to the next village. There, I found a bench and waited for the hour when pilgrims would pile into town, one after the other. Unfamiliar faces passed me. None of them were a part of my original group. At the albergue, I got a bunk and went downstairs to ask around for Dani or Amos. No one recognized the names I mentioned. On the second day, I walked ten kilometres. I met a young man at a bench who ran the Way. Each day, he smashed 70 kilometres with nothing but a CamelBak and a change of clothes. His pace was three times mine and equal to a casual cyclist's. He didn't strike me as tired in the slightest. I felt exhausted for him. It was easy to feel inadequate or minuscule and lazy around this exceptional human being. I sat cross-legged in a park with a small group, waiting, hoping my family would come along. I then stood and walked slowly, following a yellow arrow through a narrow laneway. The pilgrims would all barrel through in droves quite soon or maybe they already had. It was a pedestrian street no wider than a horse cart. The yellow arrow pointed through it and into the little, ancient village area. I turned my shoulder to the sound of a pair of shuffling feet against the ground. I ran for the hairy bastard and squeezed him. I wrapped my arms around him and held on for more than a minute.

"Good to see you too, Fred." He smiled amicably with bits of his teeth showing through his savage beard. Shade covered us, yet the heat felt inescapable. I gained instant relief from his arrival. Cosimo passed through the laneway, rushing at me like an orphaned cub. I was excited to hear how his Way was developing, the young buck spreading his antlers.

"Freddi!" One after the other, familiar faces passed through the corridor. Cosimo had small sparkles of liquid in his eyes as he pulled away to look at me clearly. "What happen? Where you go?" He looked at me with his soft, freshly wiped eyes.

Before I could respond, Dani interrupted. "This sensitive bastard, every time he gets a guitar in his hands, the girls all go crazy for him. You should see it."

"Adda boy, Cosi," I tapped him on the shoulder. "I had to get away for a while and clear my head. Alone. Needed some space. Plus, Leah bored the fuck out of me."

Dani translated.

"Yea, some things have changed," explained Dani. He had a crush, a French girl we all walked with. A few new people had joined the family circle. "You'll meet them all."

I told them I had met Elena and we had a nice night cooking together. "She skipped ahead, bad blisters slowed her down early on. Oh, and I saw that madman Dave again!"

191

They both looked at me, confused.

"The guy with the Sangria. The mad cunt!"

"Oh no, that guy. Wow. He was something. Freddi, you honestly made the best pasta I've had from someone that wasn't Italian, my word to God. Let's make some food tonight, huh?"

"Tonight, we drink and eat and wait, your word to God?" I confirmed with a grin. "Which God? The pig God!?"

"Porcoddio Freddi, come on," he protested, waving his hands together up and down.

Cosimo grabbed me by the shoulder and put his other hand on Dani, smiling so brightly while he spoke in Italian. Dani looked at him disgruntled.

"Why I always gotta translate, cazzo, you can learn the fucking language too. Che palle, he breaks my balls this guy!"

"Alright, he says he is so happy to have you back with us and that things have not been the same since you left," he glanced at Cosimo. "Okay? There you go."

"Looks like we're back together," I said, as Dani translated.

"Yea, and I gotta be the fuckin' interpreter."

The three of us laughed.

"Think it is high time we grabbed a beer, no?" Cosimo pulled a spliff from his shirt pocket.

We entered one of the village albergues so the guys could drop their bags and grab a bed before they were full. I was putting my tent outside and avoided making any eye contact with Leah, who was also there. Dani introduced me as the pilgrims arrived. A group of Israelis appeared first. They drove the Way, some in the car while others walked sporadically. And with them, a Spanish girl. A puppy who followed them, in love with one. There was a French Canadian, a Latin Texan, a German girl who spent months in Ashrams with a famous Guru. And there was a young man who seemed to gravitate toward her that I recognized instantly.

"Ali!" His red hair couldn't be missed, but what I didn't get as we shared walnut pancakes and Peruvian tea was that he carried a big, huge flag with a set of hearts on it. The thing flapped in the wind from a large, wooden pole. He smiled and grimaced.

"I found it last year when I walked the Way. It was on the beach at Mar da Fora," he explained. I looked at him, waiting for more of an explanation. "It's the beach you're going to fall in love with, Freddi. Right near the end of this Way, three days after Santiago de Compostella, on the coast at Fisterra."

"Time we grab that beer, Dani boy," I insisted, smirking gallantly and slapping Cosimo's back. "You comin', Ali?"

A curly-haired man came around the corner looking joyful. "Alistair where are we going?" he asked in a high pitched, squeaky, but bubbly voice. Dani laughed and introduced him.

"This… This is Stan; he is one of a kind."

"Hey, come on Dahhni, we Polish are Al like this, okay? We are Al happy and cheery and full of love. Now, where we going to have this box of wine!"

I suggested the riverside. I grabbed some bottles of San Miguel and walked across the wooden bridge into an area of thin evergreens where a bench sat unoccupied. I lost my clothes, down to my boxers instantly, and sprinted into the shallow, wide, clear river.

"It's great to be back!" I exclaimed. At the same time, a large, bald, pale Irish lad we all knew well shuffled and danced across the bridge while playing his little flute. Then Stan ran into the river and the Israelis joined us. The Spanish girl followed them. I splashed water at everyone and did a backflip off the water's face.

"Fuck this feels great!"

It wasn't long before the bottles were replenished. We got as drunk as hooligans before a football match. We crammed into the town corridor, singing songs as people revealed their instruments. We were pilgrims in love with the world and the people around us. The wine went down so smoothly in such a space. We were close to heaven. When songs missed lyrics, the Latin Texan and I freestyled until we ran out of words and the moon disappeared. In the dark, I threw my tent up half blind. The river made noise, but nothing was needed on a night like this to rock me to sleep.

* * *

My eyes were struck by the spectacular, unexpected view. One of those moments when a journey justified itself. The work paid off: an unfolding natural canvas. The gorgeous lake of

Ohrid spread itself far, surrounded by fuzzy, green mountains. The lake's shade had a midnight colour, an incredible hole in the earth fringed by walnut trees. Far in the distance was a place where Greek Orthodox, Roman Catholics, Jewish people, and Muslims all shared a few narrow corridors of Ohrid's centre. It took a night and day to get there. Immediately, it had a different, cosmic energy. People jostled the streets, but not many were tourists. I approached a young man on a bench sitting at the lakeside.

"Hey man, good to see a familiar face," I said buoyantly.

"Hey bro, how you mean?"

"Well, your beard hasn't been trimmed in a while, and your clothes are pretty rough. I can see you're not the average tourist is what I mean. I can't really pinpoint your accent though?"

"Yea, nice, I hitched here from Portugal."

I carried on, praising his country, one that held my curiosity.

"So why the… how… what reason would you walk all the way to Istanbul, bro?" He asked, impressed but aloof. "Are you religious? Something tells me no."

I chuckled and nodded my head side to side. "I'm far from religious. Just wanted to try something different. Have hitched shitloads."

"But really, honestly, why?"

When a righteous traveller like this Portuguese lad asked me such things, I wanted to give him the deepest, most honest portion of me, so I unloaded: "It was about land rights and the sensationalism of being nomadic, genuinely, not cliché nomadic. We are losing everything that was sacred, just like aboriginals and First Nations peoples. The corporation is devouring everything in its path while feeding us fraudulent stability and imaginary security. Seeds have been modified, animals processed, food is mostly chemicals. We've become trapped between towering buildings. Cars starve us for oxygen; skyscrapers cut off the sun. People chase city lights and sparkling assets that have zero long-term value. It was time to connect with the land and slow down, to feel the earth below my feet before it is all paved and hollow and we're left with disease and debt, all for greater accumulation of wealth by the richest and most elite groups."

"Sensational!" he said, before explaining how he was studying to become a doctor. "I would really like to head out to a couple of places that need resources and help out. Like Doctors Without Borders. You're right about the way life is going. It's not looking good. I hope you make it to Istanbul, and hey, maybe keep going from there."

I suggested making lunch together. It had been a while since I'd eaten anything but figs and walnuts. "Is tuna okay?" My new friend agreed.

On our way back from the shops, a man walked alongside us, and I introduced myself. I had my pack with me, whereas my friend had checked into a hostel. The man asked if I had just arrived.

"Yea, I came from Albania," I responded respectfully. He nodded when I told him.

"I had a feeling when I saw you." He looked at me kindly.

"Yea, well thanks man. I walked here from Rome. Headed to Istanbul."

My Portuguese friend laughed a bit. "I still can't believe that."

"Me too," the new guy spoke of the Egnatia Way and the history of his people. "Where do you sleep?"

"Not sure, to be honest," I responded, glancing around the paved, pedestrian street. "Haven't got that far in my thinking."

My Portuguese friend cut in again, "You've been camping the whole way?"

"Most of it, other than homestays and that kind of thing. Zero hostels. It's too much money, I don't actually have it."

He agreed before replying, "Yea, I should camp more often, it's just meeting people."

"You can stay with me, at my place," our new friend suggested. I accepted instantly. "Both of you guys can come now if you like, have something to eat."

I looked at the Portuguese guy for a response. He agreed to join us.

Ep. 21
The Mud of Bulls

The man's flat was an archive. Pillars of paperbacks towered to the ceiling. He had a library he duly admired, justifying his linguistic versatility. The man studied. That's what he did with his time. He had devoted his life to research. The invigorated, professor type, he lusted to share, and despite his reclusion, learned to listen. Introverted, by the look of his flat, when the man's gums flapped, it was hard to slow him down. My Portuguese friend left, and then he really got into it.

"Symbols. You have to realize that everything has roots, Freddi," he said quietly, his eyes steely. "The Muslim religion's highest symbol, on top of all its temples," he spoke passionately, but froze as I nodded.

"The moon," I acknowledged.

"Exactly. An Animistic symbol for women, of femininity. A religion so patriarchal, yet," he emphasized, "a woman is right there standing above it all. They deny what's right there and live a lie. And the cross! A Pagan tool for torture, dating back as far as Egyptians. Paul even said it was a tree, in Greek, not a cross. This massive, holy symbol has no value. It's simply a tool to remind people of how HE suffered for us. To make us feel guilty. For what? I don't feel guilty." He carried on in this manner, while I sipped the last of beer, soaking in his words.

"Freddi, you are on a big quest, walking the Roman Via Egnatia! This, right here, where you are… This is the heart of civilization. We have everything one could need, an abundance of nutritious food right here for us, yet look around. It's full of poverty. The soil here is no better anywhere else, and the people of Mesopotamia knew it. You are standing at the centre of the world. There is a fault line underground. Those mountains out there," he pointed in the direction of Galichica, "are the dividing line that runs all the way north. Makedonia," he pronounced his country with a strong K instead of a soft C, "is a place of ancient tribes pre-dating Slavs and even the Greeks. People came a long way and settled here before any Greek set foot on this soil."

This was the debate. Greeks said this country had no right to use the name Macedonia, a province of the Greek Empire, important to them. This man's thesis argued that more existed than the Greek Empire. I also didn't realize that he was Slav. And I didn't know that Macedonia was part of Yugoslavia. This little country was an absolute mystery to me. They squeezed themselves out of Yugoslavia more discreetly than even Slovenia, avoiding war. I knew now that their forests remained pristine—corporate corruption had yet to ruin them. They had been protected, thankfully. Beautiful forests, as my new friend told me.

I asked about Mesopotamia. It was the first time I'd heard mention of this. He cleared his throat and waved his hands.

"Yes, Mesopotamia; these were the people of Babylon. The first modern civilization between two rivers. It is basically where modern Iraq and Syria are now. This is where symbols became words and writing was first developed. All this stuff in the Bible dates so far back, to this period with its story of Gilgamesh and Eden and flooding. During the Greek period, Dionysus, he was the son of Zeus, the son of God. Born on the 25th of December and placed in a manger. He was coupled to a tree, having been crucified there. I mean it's all there," he cried, motioning to his books. My eyes began to get heavy. He noticed.

"Freddi, I'm sorry, I've been talking like crazy, and you must be absolutely exhausted. Please, sleep in the spare room. The bed is made, everything is good, help yourself. Sleep well, pilgrim." It was wonderful how these things lifted his spirits. The following morning, we shared breakfast. I threw together a couple of omelettes. And he made coffee.

"This, Freddi, is Makedonian coffee."

It was exactly the same as Albanian coffee.

"Your omelette is good, you can cook. Maybe you want to stay a few more days," he laughed and ate simultaneously. I told him I trained as a chef before retiring for the road full-time and falling into pilgrim life.

"We need some good cooks here." He spoke to me about the Way and how the gas station at the top of town was just across the street from the trail leading over Galichica National Park. "You will find it easily, just go to the gas station and walk directly across the road. No problem. Then follow until Bitola."

When I arrived at the station, I got this feeling of regret. It would've been nice to stay on, listen to the madman ramble more about history and rest another day. I rarely took account of my surroundings when I was comfortable. I let my guard down a lot. I had no idea where he lived, so when I decided to turn around, it was too late. The urge to grab a few beers and find the

Portuguese lad was also on my mind. There was likely a hostel, a few more travellers. But then I would be sucked into paying for a bunk.

I turned back for the Way. And like he said, straight across the road, there it was on a banister, the little spray-painted flag of orange and white. This pilgrimage marker led me to the top of the long, Galichica mountain chain. Another awe-inspiring view of Lake Ohrid. I pushed hard anticipating it and at the same time heard the professor's voice.

"Everything is connected. And everything has a root!"

That lake embodied femininity. She characterised life in her pristine nakedness, vast and calm and glamourous. Not as dark this time, less mysterious than at the border of Albania. She was a mirror, uncloaking the nature of my existence. The sky hazed over distant Albania and the past. At 1000 metres, the long, empty, mountain bowl appeared lunar. The National Park's hiking routes fared well, but off-season now, the huts were locked. Not a soul around. I became startled as gnarly, dark clouds circled the sky above me. I pushed myself, in case of rain. A bench appeared before the trail went downhill. It was right above the large Lake Prespa. A vast, triangular, light-brown slice of land was in clear view, home to a village. The sun set behind the mountains; the sky cleared.

A stone cabin appeared first, before the township. It had a small, hand carved sign swinging outside. The heavy, wooden door opened to a smell of richness. The meat and onions caramelising couldn't be mistaken. Polished cutlery rested on clean, white tablecloths. My local host friend back in Ohrid had said Macedonia had everything. By far, one of the best meals I ate along the Way. For just over two euros, they served a hamburger patty, seasoned and fried, a pile of shaved cabbage, bread, and a large, scored pork sausage dripping fat all over the French fries. A glint of heaven. These guys had no idea how well the meal was received, by how many kilometres, how many hills, how many nooks and crannies.

"Do you, please, I mean this looks amazing, but do you have some Tabasco sauce?" I clenched my teeth, hoping. She hardly acknowledged me but left to the back. She placed the little bottle of genius red liquid beside my plate.

"Oh, thank you so much." I savoured every single bite,

and once it was finished, I wanted it again at breakfast with an egg on top, sunny as a Saharan Sunday afternoon.

I walked two kilometres past lines of gigantic, glistening red apples. The village encircled a huge beach, unoccupied except for a handful of small fishing boats. The perfect place for my tent. The sound of silence that Paul Simon told us to surround ourselves in. Prespas, like Ohrid, was profiled by mountains but empty of inhabitants.

Bitola was the modern city that replaced Heraclea after Slavs entered the region. It amounted to one big, long day, then a second, much shorter one. I stocked up in a small, desolate village with a roundabout, a market, and a few abandoned buildings. The dusty hole wasn't far from Resen. A beautiful, young woman worked the cash register. She smiled and her crystal blue eyes shimmered like platinum cufflinks. I wanted to know her story. What the hell was a girl like this doing in a stink-hole out of a Spaghetti Western? But like Tom Waits once recorded, *"Farewell to the girl with the sun in her eyes."*

Along the Way, my feet and legs became inebriated, heavier when food swelled my pack. The time alone achieved contemplation, but distress and fear mounted as I spoke to myself more often. It was the long stretches and still-life villages. The road passed through many hilled slopes of bulky pine forest. My mind was occupied in the trees, engorged by their aroma and consoled by their needled floors. But then, talking with myself would return.

"I should message James, maybe I've gained on him. Maybe he's in Bitola?" My voice was a loud whisper. "I've gotta get a new book in Bitola. Gotta get something to read. I've got nothing but time here."

A small, locked church appeared on a hill. The road became dark as the sun crouched behind walls of stalwart woods. I could hear a river pushing along. The cement road was almost tolerable, as I hadn't been disturbed by one car. Fruit trees lined the last hours into Bitola, plenty enough to satisfy breakfast. Again, I could hear my local host friend from Ohrid.

"Macedonia has it all."

I loved that the large, robust fig trees were a dime a dozen, until I shit their seeds. Tired of walnuts, I walked across them scattered on the ground. Ripe apricots became the new delicacy. This land flourished unlike anywhere I'd seen in Europe. Seeing all the fruit I bought in supermarkets out here growing wild. I passed a cemetery, small enough for a village of twenty, but no visible homes. And like Ohrid, a church and mosque nearly touched they were so close. Gurus from each holy place could see each other preaching from their podium windows. The mosque's temple had no kind of dome. It looked like the missile of a massive fighter plane.

Bitola had life the moment I entered. It had to be a student town. People filled outdoor tables everywhere. An art gallery and library awaited upon my entry. The library called to me, despite my tiredness. My mind rambled without interruption, wanting to erupt from my mouth. If I couldn't have the company of human beings, I could satisfy myself with an author's voice. My morning sounded perfect, grabbing the Albanian—that is, Macedonian— swamp water and a burek, then ducking into the library. I took my pack inside and a man led me through a long line of shelving units and doors before ending in the cellar, where English books were kept. Ancient, dusty books that needed a sweep. I opened *Exile and the Kingdom* by Albert Camus. Years had passed while I waited for Camus' translated work to fall into my lap. It didn't disappoint. It spoke true to my soul, describing a Christian missionary who lost his tongue for overstepping in an Algerian village. Sometimes I overstepped, and I wondered if the natives would take lashes out of my skin. But this short story spoke to me because of its detail and my distaste for organized religion. Some people thought something good for them meant something good for everyone. So high on the fumes of manipulation, they didn't stop to think that others might have the power to find righteous paths of their own. One could be suggestive, and one could be contemplative, but if one became bent on proselytizing, they were to be ignored. Despite my lofty thoughts on this topic, I needed to find a church before dark. I still needed a place to sleep and couldn't put my tent in the middle of a city, no matter how small it might be.

My disdain for religious hierarchy may seem inconsistent with the pilgrim lifestyle. Still, the overall truth remains: religious beliefs have been used to control people. This pilgrimage was for my soul. It didn't need an armful of scrolls, as St. Paul had. That was his choice, not mine. And the church was obligated not to squabble about who arrived at their door. God loved all his children. I had no quarrels with a priest who believed so strongly to share his own words or a house that brought people together. That existed around love. My problem lay with those who focused on making others live by their dogmatic rules. The ones who walked the streets ordained in their own ignorance telling others how to save themselves. I grew up down the road from a church, and my grandma went her whole life. I went with her often. I had no problem with any of it, except that it was boring. But their church didn't exist with the goal of filling donation trays. Her church organized community activities, developed programs to bring people together and help them, not convert them into Christians.

I strolled the cobbled streets and had my lunch in the park. The park was too open for my tent. There was a colourful squat of layered spray paint tags and smashed glass. After noticing some Neo-Nazi graffiti at a renaissance fountain, I didn't want to risk being too cavalier. The nearest church stood between a community of short buildings on one of the main streets. The church was closed. A tavern next door looked open, so I entered to speak with the bartender. A man in his 40s asked me why I was there.

"I walked here from Rome. I'm on my way to Istanbul." The man looked at the bartender astonished, then back at me. "Well, honestly, I was hoping I could sleep the night on the church floor?"

He made a call. The bartender told me to follow his friend, as both their English was quite poor. We walked for ten minutes, then he took me up a flight of stairs. He rapped on the door. A woman in a white cowl, black scapular, white tunic, and black veil opened the door. She spoke with my guide in their shared language, which sounded more and more Slavic to me.

"Tu parle Francais?" she asked. I nodded, though slightly stunned that I was looking at a nun. She asked why I had come to Bitola. I explained to her in French. We spoke for a few minutes. I tried to hide my exhaustion, but the beads stood frozen on my face. I wanted to get my pack off for the night. I needed sleep to recharge. Gentle with her words, she spoke in short phrases like Brother Avery back in Albania. I noticed that her yard had plenty of space for my tent. I suggested that, but she ignored it. When the questions finished, she made a phone call. She and the man spoke again after she turned the phone off.

"Allee avec lui et avec Dieu."

"Merci trop," I said, amicably as possible, and bowed, for lack of another way to respectfully show my gratitude and say goodbye. My legs were putty. A short walk brought us to a small building. Inside, a well-dressed man greeted us from behind a polished marble countertop. They spoke. My friend from the bar said goodbye. The well-dressed man asked me to follow him, in English. We climbed a few sets of narrow, sanded, wooden stairs. Each footprint echoed. We stopped at the top in a tight enclosure. Both sides had a door. We could hardly budge, shoulder to shoulder, because of my backpack. He turned and smiled at me, opened the door, and shimmied inside.

"Here you go, sir. Get comfortable, and when you are ready, we will order you some food. There are menus downstairs," I walked inside and asked about a supermarket, so I could buy some food instead.

"Oh, the food is already covered," he proclaimed, as he left me to the room. This place, that beautiful woman in the habit, the whole thing was surreal. The "room" was an enormous living area with leather couches and a corner bar. The liquor shelf was made of glass mounted to mirrors. I abused the television and movie channels for the entire night, other than the half hour I spent in a hot tub on the second floor. Everything, including the waterbed, replicated a cabin in the Rockies. Hardwood walls with a high, triangular roof. I opened my door again. *Penthouse suite.* The whole place was mine, and when the time came, like he said, he ordered me pizza and chicken wings from a place a few doors down. I devoured the food one impeccable mouthful at a time, watching television.

I was told about an archaeologist at Heraclea who could help me find the Egnatia Way, through the remote countryside into Greece at Florina and as far as Thessaloniki.

Philip II, the man who fathered Alexander the Great, established Heraclea. There are still some who debate whether Phillip was a Greek. This made Alexander, his son, quite the same, and that wasn't going to fly at all with the Greeks. Philip II of Macedon, in the mid-4th century BC, built his empire from Heraclea. It became an important city to Romans later, as it rested on the Egnatia Way. They built baths and a place for gladiators—until they were banned in the Empire. With the Christian insurgence, Basilicas were erected. In the sixth century, it all went sideways for Heraclea. The decline was precipitated by an earthquake. Things got worse for the city, as Slavic tribes ended the lifeline of Heraclea and left it for wind and time to decompose. Fourteen centuries passed, and now the theatre was running again.

It was my 70th day when I arrived at the old ruins to meet the archaeologist. He seemed a nice man, though vague, and after some names on a napkin, I left optimistically. Ten kilometres shy of Greece, I passed beautiful old houses, some crumbling like the churches, Catholic and Orthodox, both forgotten. Gorgeous pastures lined the hillside with nice country folk. Simple farmers waved me along. Cows milled around with sheep and horses. Chickens ran the narrow, dirt paths. I shifted off the Way onto a set of trails with horses and cows. I stopped to speak with a short, old man, his smile radiant, working in his field of apples, cutting away weeds. He gave me directions to the next little village where I could grab lunch. He suggested three kilometres. That meant a half-hour. After waving to the man, I noticed three young men. Two of them had large sticks. Behind them, about a kilometre away, I could see a farmhouse. And to my right, a hoard of cows. The wide path of muddy ground had puddles everywhere. And undoubtedly heaps of cow dung. When the three lads stood, I noticed all of them wore large, rubber boots.

"Hey! Hey, oh... Ah!"

"Speak English?" I asked. I was annoyed when people barked at me. It meant they were likely illiterate, and we would waste each other's time rambling about nothing. I was hungry. My body needed to eat before it became cranky or weak.

"No English; we Macedonia," one of them said, brazen and proud. His tone was strange and out of place in this countryside. Up until then, aside from the odd complaint regarding Greek and Macedonian heritage, I didn't feel a sense of deep Nationalism.

"Yea, Macedonia. Okay guys, have a nice day." I offered my cue to move on. I jumped puddles and teetered on the trims of dry mud, from the day's sun. My concentration focused into this ox-cart road of sludge and shit to avoid it. A clearing existed, though I couldn't yet see it.

"Hey! Where go!"

I responded without turning, "Greece, goodbye."

He whistled, but I didn't acknowledge him as I was concentrating on dodging the cow patties. I slipped into the gumbo, then the three of them circled me. I leapt from the grime and to the side where solid pastureland rolled downhill. I had to balance myself to avoid falling.

"Hey!" Again, the same boisterous punk squealed. "Show passport."

They closed in and I became defensive, feeling invaded.

"Huh?" I thought, "Passport?" Why the hell did this little shit care about my goddamned passport? The smallest of them stood in front of me and pushed me back with his thick, long, wooden stave.

"Hey! Show passport!"

I turned to look at the leader, feeling threatened. I connected with his blackened eyes and flat, intense expression. He held a gun a foot from my face. I looked at him incredulously and then at the gun. I was relieved when I noticed it was only a pellet gun. Still, a pellet in the forehead or temple, the hospital was a long way off. I would die by then.

"What the fuck is going on," I panicked in my mind. "Is this serious?"

"Serious as it gets," my conscience replied. He could easily slip and pull the trigger and accidently shoot me in the eye. A grating pain struck my shoulder blade from behind. I dropped to my knees in the thick mud, ankles and feet shaking. My confidence disappeared. The three lads were there, powerful as bulls, with wind coming from the largest one's nostrils. He stood above me, laughing as he put me to the ground with his big, wooden stave. All of them had their weapons in hand. There was nothing left in me but fear and the carnal necessity for escape toward the farmhouse. They built a triangle around me. They let me up after I showed my passport. Every time I moved to the left or right, a large stick hit my pack and threw me forward or backwards. The biggest one's voice demanded in a husky voice, "Money! Money!"

Looking intently to open pasture that went downhill, I put my arm out pointing, and shouted, "Holy fuck!"

Their heads turned, so I bolted through them with everything. A rabbit out of the mitts of a salivating dog to the farmhouse. The three of them got on their wheels in their boots, but I ran for something more, *and* I'd had a great sleep in Bitola. I reached the yard and kept hustling into the back area for a door to bang on. There was a man outside feeding his chickens. His wife was also there beside him, and another man across from them. All of them in a state of calm.

"Police! Police! Police!" I shouted.

The three lads paused, hitting one another to slow down, and when the two older men stood from their chairs in shock and came toward me, the punks fled the scene. The horror in my face told a story alright, but neither of them could speak a syllable of English. I was covered in mud, shaking, and pointing to the packet of cigarettes on their table. They passed me the packet and a lighter. The elderly woman grabbed a garden hose and pulled it out for me. My arms shook like I was entering cardiac arrest. Through a thick, dark beard and dark lips, one of the men spoke to me after I had washed off. He looked at me in the eyes, sympathetically.

"Whaz ist vong?"

The police arrived much later and got their car stuck in the mud, gave up chasing the lads, and brought me to their station. None of them could speak a single word of English. Instead, there was a man on a cell phone who spoke to me and riddled out all kinds of questions.

"What are you doing here?" he asked. "Why are you on this path?" he commanded. "What is wrong with Canada?"

It took so much back and forth, I was brutalized more by these police than the kids. I wanted an apology from the boys and a few bucks. A tiny bit of penance for breaking my fucking camera and ruining any chance I had to capture the last month of my journey.

"Yes, you must go to court. It will take weeks. Do you want to stay in Bitola for weeks?" asked the police officer indignantly.

I sat in the chair with my face in my hands, still vibrating. When they had finally finished with me, I was so mixed up and broken I could hardly walk. The sun collapsed on that old, beautiful countryside trail. A trail that was now long gone. It was a long drive downhill in the back of a police car.

"Why the fuck did I think the police would help me any time, ever?"

I didn't once consider crossing borders without a stamp because between Albania and Macedonia, there was no border. It slipped my mind, high on the Egnatia trail I didn't want to lose. They insisted, demanding I stay on the highway until Greece. I pulled my map of names from my pocket to double check the next rest town in Greece. Beside it, there was a number of kilometres left until Constantinople. It read 789. My swollen, red eyes were despondent. Anger and frustration forced them to close. My quivering lips stopped as I looked to the sky and took in a long breath. As I exhaled, I lowered my head to the ground, breathing in again. I lifted my head and wiped the dew from my eyes. I could see in the distance a border crossing. I breathed out again and took another step forward, the only thing I could do, or else my knees would buckle and force me to collapse into a nervous breakdown.

The border guard stared hard at my passport and back up at my sweating, hairy, dirty face. He had reason to send me back. Schengen's policy needed three months out of the zone before re-entering for another three months. And from Croatia to the border of Greece, it had been a lot less. My nerves were so rattled they were dead. It would only make sense if he sent me back. I looked on indifferently, awaiting his judgement. He took his big, metal plunger and hammered my passport. I walked into the first restaurant, famished. The pasta was awful, and my first meal in Greece disappointed everything I knew about the country's cuisine. But it was food. Somebody spoke to me from another table.

"Where are you from?" I turned, delighted to hear English. "I'm Canadian, too," he declared, as he ordered me a beer and ouzo. "Looks like you could use it, eh?"

Ep. 22
Twist of Fate

My tent packed swiftly as every morning. The open space around me kept me there. Centred on an enormous, vacant grassland, I recalled a black, soot-dusted hole back at the edge of Lake Prespas. I thought about how many times I'd bothered to have a fire camping the nights away. I never did. Most days, I was too tired or simply read in the tent with my headlamp. It took little to pass out, really. Other days, I didn't want to attract attention, or I lacked the energy to forage wood. But my biggest problem was my lack of a tribe.

The Way to Florina was contemporary and mundane. The Balkan East went by without a single wandering sheep or crumbling shanty. A world without views or pleasure, I was furious, agonized, discouraged, and a quarter inch from cracked. My countryside trail and camera were gone. Florina had nothing to offer but traffic and westernization. Thousands enjoyed the Aegean Sea in the south of Greece. The joke was on me. I went to the museum of archaeology, where the laughing continued. Drowsy as fuck, I received confused looks and apathetic gestures from a range of ages, but not a single positive offering. If I'd asked a question about Greek history, I am sure the scrolls would have rolled out and boils would have popped with excitement. The first few times I suggested an ancient road, in English (which also proved problematic), no one even acknowledged me. Once the word Egnatia came up, hands flared because the highway that passed through Florina, like in Albania, was named after the ancient trail. I hit the floor. My indignation burst from my eyes, furious. My patience ended.

How was it possible that in a room full of archaeology students and professors, not one of them knew anything about the location or even existence of an old road that ran from Rome to Istanbul? Genuinely considering my questions or attempting to understand my predicament was clearly too much to ask of these pseudo-intellectuals. Unsure of whether to laugh or cry, I raged instead. I stormed out of the museum, out of the city centre, out of the industrialized area that curdled milk with its toxicity. On and on, away from the city, until only the stench of its smugness remained.

"What the fuck am I doing? I can't walk any longer alone like this, hundreds of cars, toxic fumes, horns, and more fuckin' commotion and congestion.

"How the fuck did those cunts not know a goddamn thing! Nothing! University graduates bowing their heads to whatever bullshit their new-age professor spoon-fed them," I turned my head to the sky. "What the fuck? How much more suffering and bad luck?! Fuck everybody, and fuck everything you fuckers! What the hell did I do, huh?"

"Why are you pissed off?" a voice asked.

I answered truthfully. "The inability to communicate. It's too much. No one can communicate effectively, if communicating means genuine understanding. The disillusionment is killing me, destroying my soul, binding my stomach muscles, twisting them and turning them like New Delhi's most rotten chicken breast."

"Your angst is piling up," the voice replied.

"Can you blame me?" I responded quickly. "How many more turns for the worse are there, huh?"

"Didn't you just enjoy a luxurious hot tub, eating pizza and chicken, feeling like a King?"

"At what cost? My fucking camera, the only proof that I managed this, the only way I can show…"

"Only way you can show what to who?" the voice demanded

I said nothing.

The voice continued, "Is that why you are doing this? To show people? To show someone?"

I started to consciously question whether to continue this dialogue with the voice, or myself, whatever the fuck it was. It wouldn't shut up. It kept going.

"It's a journey, not a mission. The pilgrim wants to walk. All walks have to end."

The sun set. I dragged my feet into Vevi. I took a seat next to two girls.

"Hi," I said, noticing a small supermarket behind me. My first thought was beer. The girls smiled at me like I belonged there. Their faces said they had met me.

The village itself was nothing more than a square: one bar across the road from a market and a small prayer box in between. As other villages I passed through, this was a dead end. Thessaloniki's suburbs, a depressed countryside that gave up on

208

itself long ago in favour of western economics and "city life." Two more girls arrived. They were a bit older. The owner of the supermarket welcomed me, asking if I had eaten.

"I was hoping to buy something inside the market to cook. But I can't move," I laughed and wiped sweat from my head. "Right now, all I want is a cold beer."

"Do you want one gyro or two?" the man asked, like he was repeating himself.

"Oh, it's okay. I'm fine. I'm going to get a can of tuna or something," an ellipsis hung as I thought about the beer.

"I insist." He looked at me cheerfully, unshakable. These villages might be suffering from depression, but their hearts remained.

"One, I guess? Thanks."

He returned with two rolls, wrapped in foil, and passed them to me. He then pulled one of the older girls closer and wrapped his arm around her shoulder. "This is my daughter, Nikki. You know, our country is in ruin. There is nothing here for her. You guys can marry and go to Canada. She could have a good life there," he chuckled.

She looked at him in embarrassment then back at me, blushing. The Greek Canadian at the border spoke to me about pessimism in this country. I'd already heard countless people defend poor Greece: it was being starved by the evil empires of Germany and Schengen Europe. I said nothing, bit my lip. I mean, he was right. The town was shit. There had to be someone to blame. The town's people from 100 years before. The federal and rural governments that sold their constituents out. It definitely wasn't his fault.

"What, come on, Nikki! He's a good-looking man, and Canada is a great country." He turned to the girls on the bench after nudging me on the shoulder. "That is Nikki's younger sister." They spoke in Greek for a moment before he turned back to me. "You are most welcome in this village, please feel comfortable with us. Anything I can do, let me know."

He walked off with his youngest toward the supermarket.

These villagers had a high regard for me at first sight. They shared a unique respect and fondness for me without knowing me. Everyone treated me with a familiarity that I found unusual. This was my first real connection with Greeks. It was hard to accept. The grocer rushed from his market to feed me before I could ask the girls where I could camp the night. I hadn't even introduced myself. Only the red carpet was missing. The elder of these girls, a paler, blonder one, spoke confidently in English.

"There was another man, like you, he looked like you. He had a blond beard and blue eyes, and a long stick with a seashell on it," she explained, as she pointed at a small, steepled cabinet between two houses. "Instead of putting up your tent, you can sleep there. That is where he slept."

I shook my head.

"What's wrong?" Nikki asked.

"Nothing, I just can't believe you guys met him. I can't believe he was here."

James had paved the welcoming committee for me by leaving a good impression. In Mignano, back in Italy, the women who showered me with attention, applauded me because of James and his sincerity. In Bari as well, the caretakers welcomed me like a brother because of James. I would thank him, one day, I thought to myself. In fact, I was desperate for his company and had to wonder why he just didn't slow down for me.

"His name is James, yes?" They nodded in agreement. "How long ago was he here?' I asked, wondering as usual how far behind I was. They spoke in Greek, rolling their words together before the confident blonde responded.

"He came around the same time, late, like you, and tired. He was here some days ago, maybe a week," she said, smiling. The place they suggested for me to sleep appeared uninviting. The small chamber had no windows. The air, as I imagined it, was quite stiff and musky inside. My tent was more spacious, plus I could leave the cover off and stare at the stars for five minutes before passing out. I decided on a beer from the supermarket before making any rash decisions. The pale one introduced herself as Rena. I spoke with her at length. When my beer was empty, I convinced her to go to the bar. Nikki also came, and Rena's younger, very silent sister. It was a small bar with a larger patio area. I bought four shots of ouzo. They politely declined. I shrugged my shoulders.

"I can't drink them all by myself, come on," I pleaded, until Nikki first took one in her hand, ushering the way for Rena and her little sister. We cheered and threw them back. I bought another round. Nikki's little sister also joined us once the shop closed. Still, after a few shots, the only one to speak was Rena. Mostly, though, I spoke about the stories leading up to Vevi, and they listened. My urge to speak with someone else couldn't have been more obvious. They listened, absorbing some of my suffering. Closing time. I bought a bottle of wine. This was a night, one of those nights that wasn't meant to end early—or sober. The girls disagreed and turned in. Quiet, dark-skinned Nikki led me to my tiny palace. She flicked a switch, and Christmas lights decorated our fuzzy nest. The soft carpet was relieving. Only a dwarf could stand in the cube, so we sat face to face. The room was a padded shipping container, with the church's idols all lit up.

I finally got Nikki talking as we shared the wine. We passed it back and forth and moved in closer with each swig. She vented about her town being too small, while she was too big.

"I wish I was brave like you!" She lit a few of the candles. I rolled my sleeping bag out and yanked the pillow from my pack. "You want to sleep? I should go," she said softly. "I am speaking too much, you don't care."

"Please, don't stop, keep talking. I need it," I assured her. The attention, the companionship, her beautiful words in English with her wild, Greek accent. Her phone rang. She turned it off after looking at the flared screen. She grabbed one of my hands and called my long, slender fingers "feminine and attractive." I grinned. "Your hands are soft as well," she whispered as she looked down at my upward-facing palm. She looked up and spoke of my deep eyes and sanguine face.

"They say I have long eyelashes, too," I retorted, batting my eyes.

"Who says?" she queried, sarcastically.

"People, I guess," I stared at her. "I dunno. What can I say? Thank you, I guess," my face turned away again.

"You should shave your beard a little bit, so we can see your face," she suggested.

"Only after I arrive in Istanbul," I insisted. "Your English is very good, you have a hint of irony, humour I mean. Why have you been so quiet for so long?"

She took both my hands in hers and I moved in to kiss her. A knock hit against the little hollow's door before we could lock lips. She broke free of our trance, hastily, nervous.

"Hey, sorry," a voice muttered into our den. The door opened and Nikki's sister was there. They spoke in Greek for a few minutes then it all stopped and her sister left. She turned back to me.

"I am sorry, Freddi, but I must go. You are tired anyhow and you will walk a lot tomorrow. It is late."

I stuttered and reached out before replying, to stop her from getting to the door. "I don't care about all that, you don't have to leave," I pleaded. She shied away in disagreement, and I knew it was over. She gave me goose skin there with me, her dark, Asiatic eyes and words with rolled S'.

I stood at the two-story building behind the supermarket where she lived, very early in the morning. The store was yet to be opened. I contemplated knocking as my head drunkenly bobbed about. The idea of her dad answering restrained me.

"The gyros were not enough?" he would say. "I was joking about Canada," he'd continue, as he stared seriously with an unpleasant face. I orchestrated in fantasy a day spent walking with Nikki. She spoke in fascination with me about the idea. She could take a bus back 20 or 30 kilometres. Or knuckle up, walking her own Way beside me to Thessaloniki. The other two girls would arrive over the next couple of days to the city. Rena's little sister needed to pack up her flat and move to Florina. She had her first job after graduation. I hoped to meet them in the city and celebrate my arrival while they gave me a tour. I looked up at her house for a long minute, in great deliberation. Maybe it would be her that opened the door. We could at least hang for breakfast. She could explain what happened and why she ran off. Her father would stare me down in confusion from the little window of his red door. He would turn the cheap, Chinese-made doorknob and tell me to get off his porch. But all it took was a knock to find out.

Each time I left a group, the same misery soaked through me, reeking of gangrenous, callow adolescence. It took less than a couple of hours on the Way this time. A car of travellers pulled up to me and offered a lift.

"We're headed down to Kalamata, wanna come?"

212

There was an empty seat there waiting for me. Their group was neither young nor old, packed with enthusiasm. Their backpacks filled the trunk. And what stopped me, really? This ongoing suffering was persistent; I felt like a slug trying to advance through typhoon winds. A community invited me along, and of course, I turned them away. I sent a message to James the first chance I got. He told me of similar woes on his Way.

"The unceasing cement is running me down, too, brother, but I'm in Thessaloniki. It's a great city. I went north from Edessa to a hot spring. It will add a couple days, but it will get you off that main road."

* * *

Leon's albergue, an imposing brick edifice, resembled an asylum. A massive gate and parking area at the entrance. An enormous interior, the lights, walls, and beds all white and stainless steel. Like a hospital space, quickly organized during a pandemic to quarantine infectious patients. And once the socks were hung and bodies relaxed, it would smell like death's door.

"Fuck this, guys, this place is a trap. I can't stay here. I can't be a part of this. Look at these metal beds and all the tightened white sheets. Even the pillows scream 'surgical waiting area.'"

Cosimo responded delightfully, in Italian. He nodded in agreement until the effervescent Stan cut in between us.

"What's going on, guys?" he asked.

I told him about my idea for a night walk.

"Yea, let's do it, come on! I got wine!"

I gripped his arm and lifted my other, which held cold bottles of San Miguel. I looked at Dani, waiting for him to agree. "Let's just walk all night until we can't anymore, waddaya say Dani?" Dani lumbered hesitantly. "Fuck this place," I carried on, "we'll grab a few more beers on the Way, it'll be a laugh. Something different. No one else around, the moon, stars, fresh breeze."

Cosimo had his pack on as well as Stan, who waited at the doorway to escape the auditorium of deathbeds.

"And how are we gonna see the Way?" Dani queried.

213

I put my head torch on. Stan removed a flashlight from his pocket. Cosimo dropped his bag quickly and put his headlamp on Dani's head. By the time we got outside, the yellow, overhead light at the front door of the hospital was the only light. A few other pilgrims stood around us. I cracked the beers and put one in each of my brother's hands.

"This is not a hospital for the soul; we will relish our treads tonight!"

We tapped bottles.

"To the night walk!" Stan announced.

We walked through midnight, while Stan argued that we were headed in the wrong direction. None of us cared. It didn't matter; we were drunk.

"You guys don't know, you are wrong! We have to change, we are completely lost!" Stan kept on like this until it irritated me enough that I tuned him out. He demanded we stop. My two brothers and I turned to him with our headlamps as spotlights.

"And so, what if we are lost, Stan? What can we do now? Fuck it, no? We are in the general direction, there is a road. We are not headed back to Leon, for sure."

As we argued, another figure appeared from the darkness and startled us all. Alistair grinned as we jumped back. He looked like a ginger-moustached demon of the darkness, with a large poker stick.

"Hey guys, night walk, huh?"

Stan hugged him after the initial shock and pleaded to be saved from us. Cosimo had fallen over, so I had him on my shoulder. We laughed uncontrollably.

"Well, I'm headed this Way," he said. Stan lunged in his direction.

"Get me away from here, Ali! These guys are crazy!"

The two of them disappeared into the blackness. Our walking became wobbling until a park bench next to a bus stop. We rolled a spliff before scurrying over to the wooden bench of the bus stop and passing out. My brothers both chose portions of the park bench. At the crack of morning, a man opened the door to a cafe that rattled me awake. I brushed my face.

"Dani, let's get some coffee and see how lost we are." I shook him as he lay on the top of the bench while Cosimo had

214

fallen to the grass. The man brought us coffees and we took a seat on his cement steps. A few pilgrims passed, calling out the morning ritual.

"Buen Camino!"

"We can't be too lost."

* * *

At Edessa, I whirled up the mountains. It took two long, tough, drawn-out days to reach the hot spring. Steady little village stops every ten kilometres to share small bottles of white wine with kind locals. Grey and sullen towns mirrored the general energy of their people. I listened patiently to the continuing complaints of poor and miserable Greece. This was nothing like the Greece anyone had spoken about. Barren and lifeless landscapes. Uninspiring food. I ate only gyros, made with ketchup instead of tzatziki. I anticipated, wrongly, wonderful olive oil and cucumber sauce. I imagined Greek staples and historical little towns, but ended up with abandoned buildings, old, used, fryer oil, and crusty, overly baked spanakopita. I found only packaged taramasalata, in huge buckets, but, like all premade dips, the garlic was overpowering. Not even quality olives or cheese.

A guard closed the gate of the spring when I arrived. I pleaded with the caretaker, "But, I've walked the Egnatia Way from bloody Durres, come on man, just let me in for a little while."

In all honesty, I was so tired and run down when he refused, I retired pathetically. I saw my surroundings and cursed James for a moment. The spring had an entry fee, then huge sets of old tourists everywhere with camper vans and big families. At the first opportunity, I took a bottle of wine. I approached people for a cigarette in exchange for wine, as I had done in other parts of Europe. Most people ignored me with disgust. I approached a young couple at the outdoor table of a restaurant.

"Do you know where I can find a bar, with some music or something, some other people maybe?" I offered them wine, but they waved it off.

"There is a town, only place, it is ten kilometres from here," they explained, appearing anxious to get rid of me.

215

I walked from the town until only the lights of oncoming cars could be seen. I walked and swigged my wine as I did with the Italians back in Spain, this time reminiscing in drunken sadness with no one to laugh with or lean on. Two hours passed until I came upon any light. They were right, though. I entered a bar after midnight and ordered a beer, overenthusiastically. Again, people ignored me. I moved to the nightclub, where a bouncer put his arm out and refused me entry. He shook his head as I pleaded. I went back to the other bar and ordered another beer and sat alone. I tried to join a few of the groups but was shunned away.

The next morning, I was slow getting up and out of the tent. But like every morning, once the fog cleared, my instincts and habits kicked in until everything was done in its turn, methodically and unconsciously. Once I packed my little camp, I threw my bag on to search for a supermarket. No more than five steps toward the road, I stepped into a ditch. My foot lodged into the narrow space, grown over by long grass. My ankle torqued 180 degrees. It cracked and the sounds echoed for days afterwards, reminding me of my stupidity. The whole distorted sequence moved in slow motion. My foot stuck in the ditch, rotated away from my leg. With any more pressure, it may have popped. The feeling of these little bones in my foot twisting and turning, the tendons as well, it nauseated me. A man glanced towards me as I fell and disappeared into the ditch. On my way down, I managed a few words.

"No! Ah, fuck, no, stop!" I shouted in my mind before calling the man. I hit the grass, unable to use my foot. I called for help from the ground. He turned up his stairs and went into his house without hesitation. I used my arms to get up and onto my good foot.

"Come on, Freddi, you got this!" From there, I staggered to the road. I had to hobble along, biting my lower lip, grinding my teeth in pain. Every time my ankle hit the ground, a bolt vibrated up my leg and into my brain. A supermarket appeared. I limped like a desperate crackhead. People watched me. At the back of the market, I got deli meat and bread. I wobbled to the vegetables. At the fridge, I grabbed a coke. People offered me no more than discriminatory looks. Outside, I crossed the road to a barricaded storefront and collapsed.

With my cutting board and knife, I made sandwiches. People exited the market and stared before getting into their cars. I had to eat first. My stomach full and the coke alleviating some of my hangover, I got to my feet and tried to walk. It was impossible. I stumbled again, but this time up to cars in front of the supermarket, begging for help in English. My unkempt beard, dirty clothes, and ragged pack gave the appearance of a broken, homeless drunkard. And I probably reeked of booze. People scurried into their cars. Fear filled their eyes. They drove off quickly, without a word. I crossed the road again toward a few open shops. There, I found the owner of a scooter. He spoke English well. I first grabbed his shoulder, thanking him for a moment of explanation. I needed to get to the bus station. It was two kilometres away. The only way was on his scooter. He resisted a few times.

"You think if I walked all the way from Rome to here, I would be asking unless it was absolutely necessary?"

He caved after a bit more pleading.

At the bus station, I noticed a young, university-aged couple. They offered their phones so I could use the number Rena gave me for when I would arrive in Thessaloniki.

"I'm in big shit, Rena. I've twisted my ankle and can't walk. I really, really can't walk. I'm so sorry for this. I'm going to take a bus from here, it's about 50 kilometres. They say 90 minutes on the bus. The bus leaves in an hour. I'm so sorry. Can you meet me at the station in two and half hours?"

"Of course! Oh dear, okay, we will get to the bus station. You can stay with us, of course."

When I arrived at the bus station, the sisters were waiting to pick me up. Rena took me on her shoulder and her sister carried my pack.

"How the hell did you carry this from Rome!" Rena's sister exclaimed. I laughed and struggled at the same time.

"I love ya, the pack is heavy, eh. You know, this is the first time I have heard you speak?" I said, helpless and impoverished-looking.

They explained that the landlady wouldn't let me stay, "We found a guesthouse where you can stay. We are taking you there now, it is not far."

I trembled in pain and asked how much it would be. They were unsure. I didn't want to go. I didn't have money to stay in a guesthouse for days while I recovered. I panicked.

"Freddi, it is okay. It will all be okay."

I saw the end of my walk. In fact, it was already finished. They carried me into the office, where I negotiated the price and dug through my bag. The girls grabbed my arm.

"We will get the first night, okay?" Rena reassured me. They helped me up two stories of long, winding stairs. Rena's little sister dropped the bag immediately.

"Geez, Freddi, I can't believe you can carry this all day," the quiet one blurted.

Rena continued as a compassionate mother, "Can we do anything for you?"

I shook my head worthlessly, ashamed. "You've done so much already, I'm so thankful," I spoke powerlessly.

"Don't worry. Things happen," Rena said gently. "We will come take you for dinner tonight, okay?"

I had an empty tank and slept until they knocked around nine.

Ep. 23
Out of the Hazelbrook

Many times, crossing a village or valley, riverside or hamlet, I saw myself. Little, forgotten stone houses called out to me on the long stretches of road. I found abandoned homes alluring. It took five years, they said, of squatting in Greece without electricity or water, then the property was mine. But the country held the wrong fragrance, unlike that hillcrest village south of Montenegro's border where Anya and I would read books into old age. Thessaloniki, however, became one of my favourite cities once I could walk on both feet again.

A loud fist against the old, wooden door vibrated through the room and rattled me awake. This room, thanks to my dear mum, had been my home for two weeks of recovery. Gasping for air, I surfaced from an ocean. My head and hands cemented, mouth so thirsty, brain hollow. A bottle of water waited on the bedside table. I reached for it, feeling my hand crack as it widened.

"Who dat then?" I called in a raspy holler.

"C'est Benoit! Bon après midi!" I'd met French Benoit in a park, as I hobbled around Thessaloniki. I approached him because he sat beside his road bike, with all the gear, on a patch of grass. I figured we were on similar paths. He was shaded by the White Tower on the seaside. He needed a place to sleep for a couple of nights. I suggested my hotel. He had a remarkably porous attitude to any lethargic energy. I noticed that about him after we spoke for a while. Nothing could graze his positive momentum. I opened the door for him, coughed a little, rubbed my face, beard, and hair.

"You OK, Freddi? How was your night? What is happening?" His enriched spirit and well-behaved, well-educated personality still had the same veneer. He was bright on all sides, but hung over, I found it irritating.

"Come in, Ben, sit down, I got a story for ya," I said through foaming toothpaste.

"You're a bit pale, my friend," Ben observed.

I spat into the sink, rinsed, and turned to my compatriot seriously. "You should have been there. It was unbelievable." I sat across from Ben. An unopened beer lay between us. "What luck, leftovers!" My attitude flared like bell bottom jeans. I cracked the can.

"So, Freddi! Tell me, please? What happened with you?"

"Well... it all started when I was wobbling back here from the library and was hit with a beer can."

"You were hit with a can of beer?"

"Yea, from a car window. Fucked up thing was, I had this track in my head, as I waddled like a duck, down Egnatia road. A special track, *High and Low*, by Random Henchmen."

"Never heard."

"Not yet, Ben, not yet. They're from Vancity, pretty low-key so far."

"I do not understand, I am sorry."

"Vancouver, Canada. These guys are from Vancouver. The track has this hook, anyway, there's a female vocalist. The track is dead on. Cold lampin on a hot night and the top is down without a cloud in the sky my brotha from anotha mutha!"

"What? Ok, so what, this band... They are from Canada?"

"Low-budget indie hip-hop from Canada. You can tell they were raised in the nineties."

"Freddi, you're making no sense."

"To you, maybe, but I am speaking about Hip-Hop. These are the jams that pleased me. The shit that was raised on 70s funk, brought up on 50s soul, and inspired by early 80s synth. Kool Keith, Doug E Fresh, Slick Rick, Boogie Down, Gang Starr; a massive turn in the late 80s and early 90s. My generation was engrossed by it."

"I guess."

"You shouldn't guess; you should know, Ben. I'm getting side-tracked."

"Yea, and the beer can? How did this happen?"

"So, I get this tune in my head, from back home, as I'm peg-leggin' along slowly, then this can hits my hat and falls to the ground. I look at the can. It says *Kokanee*."

"And?"

"And? Ben! Kokanee is a west-coast Canadian beer, and I had some west-coast Canadian rap in my head at the exact same time."

I paused to give him a moment to absorb the coincidence. The severity and profundity of the matter was completely lost on him. "For fuck's sake, brotha, look around: we're in fuckin' Greece, Ben!"

"Oh, well, okay, calm down," he sputtered before gathering himself and continuing, "I guess that is a bit weird."

The point wasn't the rap song or getting dinged in the head with a beer can, it was the young lady who picked up that beer can.

"This yours?" she asked, full of sarcasm.

"Yea, thanks," I retorted with a sour face.

She laughed playfully and asked me if I was okay, in Greek. "You English?"

"Nah, I'm Canadian," I responded. "If that can were full, you might have gotten blood on your dope boots."

She laughed again. "Well, lucky me, I guess. What's dope?" She lit a cigarette.

I asked for one. She lit mine. Then this cat, Rayo Sunnup, passed us.

"It's like, I dunno, really cool. Hey, hang on a second," I turned. "Ray-O," I hollered. "What's up, guy?" He stopped and looked back then traipsed around the crowd. "I thought for sure you'd be outta here and on your way." He came over to us.

"Spent two days on the beach, camping with my girl, she split to Amsterdam. Thought I come back, chill another few here."

"Sick. Now what?"

"Play something in the park with a local guy I met."

"Mind if we tag along?" I looked at my new friend. "How 'bout it, you wanna hear some great music? This guy can play."

Ray-O grinned and shrugged. "That's his opinion, okay," he smiled awkwardly at her.

"Yea, sure," she agreed. We sauntered behind Ray-O, who led the way to a park. He also picked up a couple more strays along the downhill road.

"What's your name, anyway?" I asked her as we moved along and passed a large, old Turkish bath house.

"Elpida. It means *hope*," she replied. "What more can we have than that these days."

"That's a gorgeous name, Elpida. You know, Alexander Dumas wrote, *all human wisdom is summed up into two words: wait and hope.* Comforting stuff."

Tall with very dark, long, glistening hair, I wanted to dip my face in and smell it. Her tight, black jeans had the ass worked in. They were ripped a little under the cheeks, but not like she had been flirting with a barber. Her oversized T-shirt had an old, faded *G n R* logo on it with the sleeves cut off. It hung down off her waist, while the upper portion revealed her lacy bra. But that is not what first drew my attention.

"Look at those boots," I declared, "those boots are definitely my style. And they look damn good on you, too. But they can't be Timbs, right?"

"Timbs, my boots? Timberland, but they are fake. You like them anyways?"

"Shit yea. I'd steal em' from ya if I thought they'd fit me."

We both giggled. I nearly walked into someone's face as my eyes stared down at Elpida's feet.

She came from a good, wholesome, struggling family. Parents that raised her the best they could, bringing love into their house while providing her space. She wasn't spoiled and could rough it if necessary. She wouldn't complain about a 20-hour train journey or sulk about a stiff bed. This girl, Elpida—Hope— her eyes were fit for a Gemini, full of euphoric highs and agonizing lows. I could tell that her unfulfilled longings left her in a constant state of discontent. She thought she deserved more. Her dark skin, her native skin, her skin of African roots and olive soil drove me to a boiling point. She could have been Portuguese or even Peruvian if she were shorter. And the way she spoke English with her sexy, slithering S, I might have even thought she was from Spain. She was Southern European alright, with the core strength of a Sub-Saharan dancer. Her lower lip was fatter than the top, like a pillow where I could feel dozy and empathetic.

We made it to the park where Ray-O met his mate. The guy had a longneck, wooden guitar with a small, fat bowl. When I met Ray-O, he was playing a very short-neck guitar. Electric, yet portable, and he had a little mic and amp, equipped with a stand. There were three people lying around him at the White Tower Park. He leaned all the way back on his pack, caught between performance and sleep. He had a smooth, jazzy, R&B flavour. I dug it instantly. He reminded me of a young Raphael Saddiq. I waited until he finished the jam before introducing myself. What I loved most was his sense of humour. It reminded me so much of home. No one could keep up with his banter. He was witty, clever, and hilarious. We both grew up on a Chris Rock, Chris Tucker kind of style. He had this goofy, going everywhere humour, like Robin Williams or Richard Pryor. He sprayed it straight as it came to him. He had it. It reminded me so much of being home in the cipher circle.

On this day, however, he was detached because his lady had bolted on him to Amsterdam. He kicked in the sounds straight away with the first song I heard him play back at the White Tower. The song oozed originality; it felt like something freestyle. Like his humour. He amassed quite the following in

222

Thessaloniki. Charismatic people could do that. I kept pinching myself, feeling lucky that I was there with Hope. Everyone got lost in his music, throwing out whistles and hand claps. I was mostly whistling at Hope.

Ben interrupted my slumber, my dreaming about this woman. I took a sip of beer and passed it across to him. "Freddi, how is the ankle, anyhow, after this big night?"

"Good enough mate, good enough to head out to a cafe and finish telling you about the ruckus and shenanigans that went down."

We went to the same corner cafe I went to every day during my stay. They had big pizza pockets, full of cheese, and vegetables. They baked them instead of frying them. At a Euro and a half, they were great value.

"So, Ben, where was I?"

He asked with his usual zeal, "You were with Elpida, listening to Ray-O play music."

"So, do you like Thessaloniki, Freddi?" Elpida asked, with her big, wide eyes reading me for more.

"Well, I've spent most of my time in books, reading, because of my foot." As I filled her in on the whole story..

"I love Thessaloniki, and I'm sure you will fall in love with it too."

"I've already fallen in love with something here," I replied fleetingly.

"What's that then?"

"Your style!" I quipped.

"You calling me lovely, then?"

"Doesn't everyone?".

She switched the subject. "So, what are you doing out here, walking?"

"I wanted to confront loneliness. Experiment with silence and walking meditation."

"And?" she asked.

"Too much road, too much traffic, too much distraction constantly asking directions."

She sympathized. "So, it was hard to find that peace?"

"Sometimes. Mostly in Italy and here in Greece. Too much highway. And trail communication has been chaotic. I've made critical errors. It's brought me ruin. Testing my equanimity, and I've failed."

"But there have been some moments, come on. You haven't failed. You're here?"

I nodded and recalled a couple of scenarios, "I was stupid to think I would meet others like me. Many people treated me like a dancing monkey. A foreign object to ponder and stare at for a moment, like an atrocity exhibit. No one was willing to sign on for a day or two," I spoke sullenly.

"Sorry, I don't understand? There are many things you say I don't understand," she said, then paused and looked at me honestly. "But I would like to, what does it mean, 'dancing monkey,' and what does it have to do with anything?"

"It seems to me, and partly my fault, that when I meet people, they get curious and ask questions like, *why are you doing this*, or *what were you doing before*, *can you live a normal life?* Then, like a little monkey that dances with cymbals, I put on a show," I gestured for her with my hands, cymbals clapping together. "But there is no attachment between our worlds. They become bored. Finished with the monkey, it's back to reality for them."

"And you're wondering if I'm doing the same, I guess? Like, when am I going to get bored and leave?"

"You're very perceptive, Elpida. Your name takes too much effort. Can I call you Hope?"

"Well," she laughed. "Sure, you can and yea, I am curious, but it's not fake curiosity. It's not superficial. And for the time being, I am going nowhere. I am right where I want to be." She beamed until I smiled and acknowledged her. "But asking others to join you is a lot."

I knew she was right. "I can only hope,' I winced. "I'm troubled by this, to be honest." My eyes drew towards her shoulder and the music that Ray-O played in front of us. "It was too much; I took on too much. And I really thought, at least one or two friends were gonna come along for a couple parts of it. I don't know why I thought that. Life is a battlefield, alone most of the time, and that's what makes it remarkable."

"Not all the time, Freddi, but yea, sometimes we need to settle down a while. It's good to be around familiarity. Not a lot of people have the kind of courage you do. It must get lonesome all that way on your own. I understand you want company. I couldn't do it."

I didn't recognise this courage she mentioned.

"It is courage. You are willing to try things few would imagine."

"But I am struggling to cope. Well, I was, and then I twisted my ankle. And well, this city has been great, and probably the period of forced rest was the Way pushing me down a while." I kissed her gently as I moved closer with my words. My lips pushed against hers once and then pulled away slowly from her buxom lower lip. She widened her eyes and smiled. I was losing my ability to resist falling into her as we talked. It was so easy to imagine my hands caressing her long neck and dark chest. I cleared my throat.

"So, what are you doin' in this city, Hope? You must have finished your studies, or nearly, at least."

"I'm waiting for a call, actually." She spoke calmly, with indifference in her voice, like she had something else on her mind. She looked at her phone, then slid her hand into my palm and looked at me kindly.

"What, like right now?" I asked, puzzled. Was she waiting for her boyfriend, maybe?

"I'm a teacher and waiting for a call to tell me where to go."

"You don't teach here?"

She looked disappointed before she responded. "We get placed where we are needed. There are many. I'm a new teacher and not needed here, so I have to go somewhere else."

"Really? And you find out when?"

"Soon, then I must go, immediately."

"That's pretty short notice. And inconvenient?"

"Yes," her lips drew that *yes* out so long and so vivaciously. "But better than unemployed." She was lucky to have work; her country was in ruin. I told her I taught English in Bratislava before this pilgrim's Way.

"So, you're a teacher also?"

I gave her a silly look, rolled my eyes and spoke ardently. "Well, not exactly. It was my first job teaching. I did a course in Egypt."

"Anywhere you've not been?" she stopped me.

I was tempted to mention her house. "Too many places, I'm afraid. And worst of all, I want to go to them all!"

"There are worse goals," she smiled brightly and loudly. "I work with kids, too."

"Oh, I've taught mostly post-grads trying to improve their English. I bet you are hella good with kids, though."

She was soft, but attentive and inquisitive and a bit queer. She could be all this, but I was sure she could be tough and frank. She showed no signs of being timid.

The sooner we left this group, I thought, the sooner we could be rolling around, giggling together back in my shit-house room. I could forget about that lonesome train for a while. I could stay with her in my arms at that hotel for another week, easy, until she got her call. Maybe even find a job teaching English and put a hold on this pilgrimage. Earn some money, maybe even carry on with her after the schoolyear. A man sat beside me as these thoughts writhed through my mind. His English sounded American.

"From here, actually, but lived a long-ass time in Bah-ston. Was born here, moved there, then fifteen years later came back."

"Shit! You're Greek?"

"I practice the American accent; try to keep up so as not to lose it, you know?"

"So, Boston huh? You know Esoteric, Mr. Lif, or Akrobatic?"

"Nah, it's Hip-Hop?"

"Yes indeed, and if you're from Boston it's like knowing Common or Kanye and bein' from Chicago."

He started up a beat-box instantly, and the shit was mean. I looked over to my lady friend who was bedazzled and impressed. He kept at it.

"*Bada Pa da Pa Boom*, my freestyle got ya, *Bada pft pft Boom Bada*, my freestyle got ya goin, *Boom Bap pft snap Boom snap Boom*, on strong and like *Boom Bap pft Crack Boom Bap,* the whole crowd is getting hyped, *Ba dap Bam Bap Boom pft Bap Snap*."

He then got going harder into dub-step then back into the classic Boom Bap. Ray-O played through and I could see he tried not to lose focus as this kid carried on. But out of the blue, this guy started killing it. I became nearly hysterical

"Can you believe this kid?" I asked Hope.

"I told you, Freddi; you'll fall in love with this city!" Her hand rested in mine.

I couldn't have been happier, until our hands moved to her leg. I leaned over to her ear, "Hey, so how about we head off." Down the walkway, from the square this guy approached as I spoke. He had a round face and a very thin, trimmed beard. He looked angry and moved quickly towards us. "Hey, this guy looks pissed off."

She glanced in his direction and her mouth dropped. "Oh no." Her face lost its succulent, olive colour.

"Is it your boyfriend?"

"No worse. Embarrassing is what…" he came straight at us and started in, nearly yelling in Greek.

"Who is this?" I interrupted.

"My brother. I'm sorry, Freddi." He grabbed her arm, at the same time the words escaped her mouth and pulled her away. "I gotta go." Her words echoed in my ears as her image faded into the distance. It was so sudden and vile. The whole terrain warped. I tried to shrug it off. I tried to shake it from my nerve endings and necked my beer. I looked to the human drum machine, who had taken over Ray-O's microphone. The whole scene froze.

"What the fuck?" I mouthed towards Ray-O.

He slid me this quick look of amazement and muffled into the mic just beside him, from Boston's mitt. "I know. Fuckin' hell, mate! Cock-blocked!"

I needed to get into something. It wasn't a fucking sit-down dinner with all these head-nodding marks. I convinced Ray-O to join me. We bolted for Valouritu, where the cheapest drinks could be found. The doorman at Eightball told us it was an Erasmus party—a European exchange program—and a five Euro cover charge with a free drink.

"Fuck that," said Ray-O wisely.

"You couldn't be more right, my son," I nodded. We spun around the corner and live music seeped from a large set of windows. A folk-like sound, played from an acoustic guitar with a small, hollowed out amp for a drum. I passed my tall can of beer to Ray-O and told him I needed the loo. Back out in a hurry, blazing in a rock-star's glorified youth.

"Ray-O, the second floor is full of hunnies! The bar is lined with 'em. Whaddya reckon?"

My boy broke into a two-step. It was like a funky, Bay-Area jam had come on. Popping, amplified thumps navigating the rhythm. Mac Dre doing *Thizzle Dance*. He froze, glaring to the sky with a finger on his chin and an air of reflection. "I suppose…" with another delay, "we owe it to ourselves to get in there, or we owe it to Elpida!"

The tall cans finished themselves and the bin was an arm's length away. Up the stairs and straight to the bar, I squeezed in between a pair of ladies and a server. I looked at the bartender and shone him the most natural, confident grin my face had worn.

"Can I get two pints of draft?"

Ep. 24
A Message from James

Born naked into the world, Sub-Saharans stayed that way through infancy and part of childhood. Feet bare, raised on heat and stones, the soles of their feet grew tough. Encrusted by nature and calloused for life. Not unlike the roots of a tree, which were guided by tribal men to form strong bridges. Stronger than man's artificial constructions, these tree roots bore the weight of thousands to walk across impassable rivers. People used to cross these rivers every year, every day until the monsoon season destroyed everything. Tree roots offered a natural solution that could withstand hard rains and powerful floods.

My roots were never healthy enough, neither prepared nor forged for such a life. I lacked patience and became agitated by miscommunication. A city boy, brought into the world with a copper spoon, forced to eat with a fork, raised under the protection of streetlamps. Comfortable through tough winters, heated by layers of warmth, given everything I needed. What choice was there but to strip it all clean and burrow into dark, muggy, lime- and mildew-covered canals? Little else could be done but swim through, climb around, and stomp along unwashed brush, hoping to be infected by insects, disease, and spite until the spirit splintered and change took place.

It was more than a personal quest to find my breaking point. Years of travel called for a new method of communicating with the world. Tramping along, by foot, the interactions became more and empowering, meaningful. Credibility offered respect. Weeks along the Way, my feet became worn and leathery. The Way remained unrelenting. A piece of driftwood floating on a slow, steady stream, bobbing unceasingly, tossed from a mountain waterfall, pushed on and on, lacking the power to stop. Slowly the wood erodes, pieces scatter, broken and disintegrating, until it banks on a rock beach for crabs to scurry under. The pause in Thessaloniki let strength return, it allowed my pieces to dry and hunger for the road to return. I checked my mail before leaving.

Mr. Freddi Woomba, pilgrim, Friend, Nomad, Spartan!

"All of human happiness passes by in the end like a dream,
And I wish today to enjoy mine for as long as it lasts,
Asking pardon for our faults,
As it so befits noble hearts
To pardon them. " – La Vida es Sueño by Juan Calderon de la Barca

How are you, my friend? How was the hot spring, did you love Thessaloniki as I did, I wonder? Right away, things have changed for me and by the time you read this, I'm already in the south of Greece. How can one apologize, or offer condolences? Well, there are pieces of writing that work for us and others that don't. This man, Juan Calderon – you know how much I love Spanish – and his words completely reigned over me with treasures of great inspiration, I felt they were appropriate. My regrets for not being with you brother, out there in Macedonia, I know if we were together at that point things would have been different. But the same goes for all the other experiences. It was not meant to be easy for you.

I believe that together, we may have had a great journey, but at the same time we are pilgrims. What does that mean, pilgrim? I am speaking about the internal and external quests, soul seeking to be cliché and also culturally invigorated, adventure, mountains, ruins, large unbound campaigns. It is also possible that after a few days we would have become irritated by one another. I cannot say, but I didn't force the Way and hoped with sincerity we would cross paths. And likely we still will, my dear Freddi.

I look back over my time on the road and most of it, walking as a pilgrim. There is definitely a sense of setting out and finding myself swept along, at times unable to control the tides or where the winds take me. This is, of course, the nature of a long journey and the joy of it. Who can say what the future holds? Or how we will change over time? Or if we will forge ourselves, unify ourselves, strengthen from the Way? And yet, we are always planning, the mind forever drifting to the future, for a reality that does not yet exist. I have lost count of the number of times I have been asked what I will do when I stop, where I will settle down. There is an assumption that we can map out the future, and when it doesn't go as planned, we become agitated. I think you understand.

You look to me for companionship along the Way, Freddi, and I am sorry we didn't make it work. I know how hard it is because I am on the Way, alone, too. You spoke about your lack of patience. You see that I have this. You spoke about compassion and sentimentality for others, a strength to look the other way and not get frustrated. You say I have this. You've said that I am more reasonable, less confrontational. You have everything you need, Freddi. Don't let your mind take over and convince you that you are any less than fantastic. And if these attributes are what you seek then take the time to build them. They are inside of you, like they are inside of me. Sometimes, we lose touch with ourselves, you know this. We have to find our other selves, the love and compassion for ourselves as well as others. The Way, this is meant to bring us closer, time for meditation, time for silence and reflection. But I see a different me than you do, and I suffer as well. Plus, we write, and we create through our suffering! Still,

230

how much can we handle before the teapot overflows or the steam builds and the kettle cracks?

You are strong in your determination and virtue. Your goals, you fix them, and you have a will to live. I have met few people so determined in my life. Your story, your years in Asia and Oz, Europe, Africa. These begin to toll on our bodies, and we need rest. Well, now is not the time for rest perhaps, but try to steal some where you can. And above all, enjoy the Way, my brother. Love surrounds us, even when it seems that the world is pissing down on ya!

As for me, I know I want to walk to India. Yeah, that's a great idea. I can go and see all those places I've always dreamed of, impress myself, do what few have done. It is a great idea, and it set me on a good path. But I became so attached to the idea of walking that I have often put myself through hell, just to maintain that original ideal. I am not trying to deter you my friend, this is me.

I met a German cyclist in Albania pedalling the Egnatia Way like us. He was so focused on biking everywhere in the world that he had become so miserable. He felt he couldn't go anywhere unless he was biking. He had become so fixated on the need to bike, his brand, and to prove himself as a cyclist that he ignored beautiful opportunities. And I must confess that there are times I was the same and you as well. It created misery and suffering, all because of some crazy idea in our minds.

The journey has a life of its own, and in trying to control it, I was simply trying to hold on to an identity, my perception of myself. When I found myself looking in the mirror, I was still trying to understand all this. I still wanted to be out walking, as I had dreamed of. But somehow everything was pointing to a new road, and all the signs were saying it was time to stop a while. Then this boat from Kavala to Athens presented itself and I won't stop walking, just take a break. I want to explore the islands and maybe pick grapes on Crete. The season is soon, money is good even if it is not good money!

And we are both after unique experiences aren't we? So, I am excited for this new chapter of the pilgrimage and I am sorry we didn't meet. Actually, I am sad we didn't, but you know, the Way has its own plans sometimes and it is up to us to try our best to 'listen'. But most importantly, listen to ourselves and decide if this matches that course you hear the Way offer you. God damn! That is a lot of listening. Am I being too serious here? Listen, up to you, but if you get on that boat in Kavala, I will be waiting for you somewhere. I know how hard it has been across Greece. The Way is just so rubbish and the south... is, well, likely something else, no? If you decide to carry on for Istanbul my brother, I wish you the best, really, and stay strong. No one Way is better than another. Maybe we'll meet in ol' Constantinople and finally share a few stories, hey! I will still arrive there, no doubt in my mind, and likely on foot, but I guess not by this road from Rome.

     Suerte, Buen Camino pilgrim,
     Yours, Sincerely,
     Brother James

Ep. 25
A Reflexologist

"Somewhere in the last hundred kilometres, hundreds of fuckers will join the Way, so they can get the certificate," was a near constant refrain that started during the first few days of the Camino.

"You get a certificate?" It confused me as I asked the question. I was stupefied. "Why would anyone care about a scrap of paper?" Could one buy new shoes or food or cooking oil with this certificate? Coming to grips with the fact that people bothered our Camino de Santiago for a certificate astonished me. 100 kilometres on a straight, trodden road sounded boring, like child's play. My grandma could do that, even after her second chemo treatment. However, if a person chose the Way for personal reasons or because they walked the first few sections over the course of a few years, well that was something else. But for a certificate, I honestly couldn't have dreamt something more absurd or pathetic.

The Way suffered an invasion of gate-crashing infidels. Some in groups, children on class trips, droves dragging their feet hurriedly with intrusive, disrupting voices. Sherpa types arrived. Elderly people hired cars for their luggage. This spectacle suffocated the mantra I had built. Honed appreciation, the trees that surrounded me exhaled a lifeforce. The trail became a home.

I felt attached to it. It was a part of me—no, I was a part of it. Suddenly, barrages of sprinting footsteps took over. Unhinged crows racing, squawking alto and baritone pitches. My sensitive, pacified ear drums suffered a violent assault. I abandoned any idea of staying in albergues. We had to alter our regimens. The influx of tourists brought out creativity in my compatriots. Somehow, weekend fishermen with wide wallets and fat chins created a void that absorbed joy within me. Deep loneliness bred its spores and spread untamed. Fortunately, I had my brothers and sisters beside me and forests to dwell in.

Love rose from the notion that we had nothing ahead of us but to wake and stride. This peaceful romance inspired great resilience. It rid us of any form of anxiety that existed before the Way. Most of us celebrated that. We took to small villages. We chased the horizon at Cruz de Ferroz to beat sunrise at the iron cross. Some stayed with the Templar's community to avoid traffic. Most of us halted before Ponferrada in a park to swim.

A rustic, beige, cobblestone bridge at the base of Cruz de Ferroz crossed the river. We congregated under a set of trees. I put my tent in the garden park after a long, afternoon session. Around 2 a.m., the sprinklers came on and smashed my little house so hard, I feared the seams would tear. It took a few doses of water before I got my pegs out and tent away. The last hours before sunrise, every dog screamed like it was being tortured by a villain in a horror movie. I pushed and kept walking until my tank was bone dry. I collapsed into a heap in a shaded area. The rest of the journey was similar. Minding the crowds and staying to abnormal hours. Lounging on my mat, reading a book within coniferous walls. By mid-afternoon, the One Hundreds finished, like I had before they arrived. Instead, I would walk the hours until sunset and finish my day. It was the Way it should have always been. I stayed in my tent full time. There was a beautiful, uphill corridor. A gallery of dense forest before Sarria. It climbed to a great, open space. A field with an unkempt band shell. Up on the stage, I fried up vegetables as the sun crashed. In Sarria, the One Hundreds brought an incredible amount of foot traffic.

"Freddi! Let's go, brother. A new day is upon us! The One Hundreds await us!" said Amos. His voice had grown more familiar than my mother's. And he was waking me earlier than she ever did growing up, the bastard.

"Thanks buddy, love you too."

I caught up with him after packing my tent. We burrowed and weaved through congregations. I stopped. My eyes bulged at the sight of a bridge crossing a lake. Portomarin was on the other side.

"Come on, man! We gotta check how deep this baby is!" I said excitedly. I stroked the handrail, sliding my hand along while staring down in fascination. I raced to the water and dove into the lake. It might as well have been the Philippine Sea it was so warm. Unlike all the bone-chilling rivers, this was a tub of radiant, fresh water. I backstroked with long, outstretched arms. At the middle of the bridge, I stopped. With my arm up straight to the sky, I tried to touch the basin floor. I rose quickly and sprang from the water like a bobbing pencil.

"It's so fucking deep, bro!" I howled hysterically.

The moment I came back up to cross the bridge, Cosimo came walking over. I marched quickly toward him, feigning panic.

"Cosi," I sped at him. "I cannot, any longer..."

He approached me and reached out, since I had done the same. Just before we touched hands, I grabbed the railing and pulled myself over. He yelped in horror.

"Non! Che cazzo!"

"Yewwwwwww!" I shouted as I fell 15 metres.

"Hey!" shouted Amos from below. "Jump! Come on, it's safe!" he called to the One Hundreds, too afraid, calling them to wait. If a few stopped, we took turns running up to prove that it was all good. Our normal clan gathered along with a few others. At one point, the beers had gone down so smoothly, the Irish flute-wielding gent suggested a boating excursion. Two, wooden rowers floated nearby. We devised a plan. We would return the boat, no harm done. The beer and wine had everyone drunk. We had more than a dozen people egging us on until we conceded. We crept up to the boats from the shoreline. My Irish companion hesitated, then refused to get into the water altogether. I took his knife, climbed in, and went to cut the rope. Once I had a boat in my hands, keeping low to the water and floating back towards our group, the game got salty.

234

"Hey! Alto! Basta ya! PUTA MADRE!"

The moment I heard Spanish coming from the main road uphill, I relinquished the boat and swam to shore. I passed my colleague running backwards, barefoot, ignoring the brambles everywhere.

"Come on, bro! Let's go!" I said, squealing with laughter. "He's fuckin' on us, brother!" I bolted to the pier where everyone watched. Quickly, I changed into dry clothes and rubbed my hair with a towel. Up to the top of the stairs and into a barbershop I went.

"Quando tempo por," I paused, "haircut?" I decided to shave my well-grown beard. He told me it would be 30 minutes. I sat down and grabbed a magazine. I fidgeted nervously, thinking this guy could walk by and notice me. I went back outside. The road was silent with no irregular movement. I looked down the long, cascading stairs from above. It was as I left it, a bunch of drunk pilgrims.

"Freddi, you dumb, lucky sonfabich cazzo!" Dani filled me in, stroking his beard violently. The man had looked for me but found nothing. He shouted at them, demanding, but the group shrugged. "We told him the people had run off. He stormed away, cursing in Spanish," Dani explained disapprovingly, while Amos tapped me on the shoulder.

"Irish just left to check into an albergue."

I grinned. "Glad I didn't shave my beard for nothing then."

"Ya had to try it, eh."

The pilgrims disbursed. The party shifted to an albergue for dinner. Cosimo, Amos, and Dani decided on another night walk.

"It's worth staying ahead of the One Hundreds," suggested Amos. "Plus, last time you guys had so much fun, I feel like I missed out."

"Only for you, Amos. But we have to roll a spliff first," Dani interjected, looking at Cosimo with the usual gesture. "We can't go walking after sunset without one of those. Should we eat?"

I looked at Dani smugly. "What you're really asking is, 'Freddi, you gonna cook before we leave?' Isn't that it?"

"Well, I don't want to be presumptuous, but you know none of us can cook so easily as you," he flattered me.

On the Way, we filled up on bottles before the shops closed. Our headlamps did much better this time. Mostly thanks to Amos. He may have been young and inexperienced in the game of life, but he had a knack for navigation. Together, like when we'd first forged this small brotherhood on the Way to Roncesvalles, we walked on until well after midnight. A light appeared in the distance, and we went for it. It was hard to tell where we could sleep. This time a park bench didn't simply appear, nor a bus stop. This light, however, may have given us something.

We followed that light like calves after milk. It hung from a nameless building. The slate window drapes were all closed. I tried the knob. Inside, there was a kitchen area, perfectly tidy, and a big, sitting room with a large table. I walked through a corridor and up a set of stairs. A three-tier rack held a couple dozen shoes surrounded by white walls and a door. Pilgrims, sweat, and snoring, they were almost as brilliant to see as the empty beds. The boys had cupboards open like mice. They beamed at me, leeringly. I pulled out my little Henkel knife and plastic chopping board. There was garlic and onion in my bag already. I collected balsamic vinegar, two tins of tomato, and boiled some water.

"There's mushroom here!" Dani called from the open, illuminated fridge. He had already found the dried pasta. We slept until the cleaning lady moved us along in the morning.

* * *

I fell to my knees at the pier in Kavala as I watched the ferry to Athens depart. My mom told me often to watch out for signs, pay attention to signs, and listen to the universe. It was a long week before the next boat. It was now, more than ever, essential to see this thing through to Istanbul. James had his own path. He was right. If I wanted to find patience and empathy, I had to find it on my own, not through him. Long streets and narrow alleys waited.

Outside of Kavala, headed for Alexandropoulos, I had a far road ahead. A football park lit by high, powerful bulbs greeted me at the edge of Komotini. Though late, people were playing. I found their coach, or he found me. He worked as a neurosurgeon when he wasn't coaching. He told me they would be finished soon, and I could sleep there, even in the change room if I wanted.

"Do you know about the Greek Toe?" he asked me in a neutral tone. He'd stuck around after everyone else had changed and piled into their cars. We shared a few beers left over from scrimmage.

"The Greek Toe?" I asked.

"Yes, let me see your foot, Freddi. Although, the amount you walked, the power it took, I don't have to look, I know," he said confidently.

"Know what?"

"If your second toe is longer than your big toe, that means you've got a Greek foot. And if you have this Greek foot, then it means that in your distant bloodline, there is Greek ancestry. I mean there are lots of Greeks in Canada, yea?" I showed him.

"I knew it," he celebrated. "Now you have to wear our jersey, you are a Greek!" Greece ruled the world before Romans. This stood to say that many, if not most Europeans would trace back to Greece 200 years before Christ.

"And people in Greece deny it, but if they were from Athens," he continued, "their family bloodline would go back to Africa. Bourgeois Greeks in Athens were once sent away. What remained were freed slaves from Africa." He paused for me to take it in before carrying further.

"We have a lot to be proud of historically. We introduced democracy and developed modern medicine. The first free-thinking philosophers. Now, we are ruined. There is nothing here, a sinking ship. No jobs, inflation. We are second-rate citizens in the European Union. We have been discarded by them."

In Alexandropoulos, I walked the well-lit main street, looking for food. This was such a chore in Greece. At a small park, I made orzo with fried eggplant and tomato. I found a small slab of beach nearby. The first time since Albania, I got to sleep to the sea's tranquillity. I could see an island. The neurosurgeon spoke to me about it, too. "Alexander the Great's parents holidayed there. It is the same island that Homer wrote about in the *Iliad*. Nothing but goats, full of goats, even today."

With October approaching November, it was better to keep moving.

In Feres, the border town nearest to Turkey, I sought the local church for my tent. The priest's understudy met me.

"Let me ask," he suggested. Instead of that, though, he came back. "Why don't you stay with me, at my house?"

I nodded exuberantly.

"It's a small place and you'll have to sleep on the couch, but…"

I interrupted him, "That would be perfect, if I could only get a shower," I said with my hands up. "It's been a while." I smelt my armpits.

Alesandro told me his story. He wrote poetry and played guitar and recently decided to follow God passionately. He spent nine months at Mt. Athos and looked to return.

He spoke earnestly. "I almost died, Freddi." He lived in Belgium for a few years, studied there, and started in with party drugs. "Of course, I experimented here before that, but curiosity grew for darker and deeper things," he confessed. He got started on heroin. "Then I overdosed; my girlfriend basically revived me." My face contorted.

"Heroin is some serious shit, eh. It's not a weekend of MDMA," I added.

"Yea, I came back and went to Mt. Athos. Best thing I could have done." He told me he had to go out to meet friends. "You can come, but I guess you'd rather stay here and chill?"

"Thanks for understanding," I reassured him.

"Help yourself to tea, food, whatever you want, Freddi. Take a shower and consider this your house now."

The neurosurgeon in Komotini spoke of many things during our time together. He was excited to meet such an "adventurer," as he called me.

"Freddi, I should have had adventures of my own like you. That is what life is for," he smiled broadly. "It is something everyone should do. Experience different cultures, challenge ourselves before we have kids."

It was a perfect night with an open sky. This was the kind of person I wanted to meet and interact with. The type who provided insights into Greek life, the Way they saw it and the Way in which they were taught. He spoke of art, culture, and history. His insights into Greek life seemed equally applicable and relevant to the universal human condition.

"You'll see, when you cross the border to Turkey, his face will be everywhere," the neurosurgeon's face never faltered from its upbeat, sweeping contentment.

"Who's that?" I queried.

He looked at me with a twinkle in his eye, "He's the dictator they had. They call him AtaTurk. His face is hung up in every shop like Stalin or Kim Jung-Il. You'll see."

This was the first time I heard this name. I said nothing, just nodding in agreement. I was excited to see this kind of thing. In India, one couldn't go anywhere without seeing Gandhi. In the Northern territories, it was the same with the Dalai Lama. In Albania, I didn't once see Hoxha's face glamourized. In most countries I had visited, modern leaders had short lifespans. But AtaTurk, he was the Godfather of Rap, the KRS-One of Hip-Hop for Turks. He saved them from colonialism. His actions alone made sure that Turkey had its own country; at least that's how they saw it.

The man did many things, and some of them were great improvements. He gave women the right to vote. But, as a minority in his Turkey, life was far from glorious. He washed his land of all minority groups. All while attempting to create the impression of western progress.

"He shifted the alphabet to Latin and abolished all traditional garments worn by Ottoman Turks," the neurosurgeon expounded.

AtaTurk empowered a legion to fight back after the end of WWI. As a commanding officer, he helped hold the shores of Gallipoli against England and the Allies. His most important move after consolidating Turkey was the full abolition of the Ottoman Empire. In 1923, he became Turkey's fearless leader and president until his death 15 years later.

239

"You'll see how they venerate him. Just be careful not to speak poorly of him. You don't want to end up in jail."

Of course, his sentiments were a little outdated, but it was true not so long ago. His advice added an element of intrigue to my upcoming visit to this nationalistic, westernized, yet Orthodox Muslim country, mostly in Asia. I knew so little about it, but what I had picked up sounded confusing.

"When he was a child, my father's parents' generation was forced to move their families back to Greece. People on both sides moved back to their respective countries. They'd occupied Greece for 400 years. We are two and the same now. But we don't share the same religious background, and I guess this is where the problem lies. We cannot have peace between us," he said, dejected. That was the only time I saw him sulk. "This is what is so great about Canada. Over here, there has been so much continuous war. There has always been warring and feuding and power struggle. Did you visit Philippi? You must have, if you walked the Egnatia Way?"

I looked at him confused. And irritated, as I knew once he mentioned it that I had missed an important piece of the puzzle.

The Roman Egnatia Way across Greece was mostly a Hellenistic road. Philippi was one of the main centres and surrounded by gold mines. Philip II protected them with an impregnable garrison called Crenides before renaming it after himself. After the Macedonians capitulated, the city became Roman, and the Roman period eventually led to Civil War after the assassination of Caesar. The largest number of troops in Roman history up to that point fought in this Civil War. Nearly 50,000 men died in the battle at Philippi. Mark Antony and Octavian triumphed in their reverence of Caesar. Octavian became Emperor of Rome and was named Augustus. Once the dust settled and St. Paul got on the move, he established the world's first Christian church in Philippi. In the 5th century, a much larger cathedral was consecrated along with space for pilgrims. A huge gate opened to the Via Egnatia.

"Freddi! Are you relaxing? Everything is good?"

I thanked Alesandro for the incomparable shower. I applauded one of his poems. We sat down, and he noticed I was repeatedly rubbing my shoulder.

"Are you okay, Freddi? You got a sore shoulder?"

"I got a sore everything," I laughed. "So, before all the junk in Belgium, you said you studied, yea?"

He confirmed, then moved to the kitchen. "You want ginger tea?" he offered.

"Sure man, that would be great."

"I studied physiotherapy and worked for a long time." He turned back toward me as he filled his kettle.

"Is that right?" I asked encouragingly. "Physical therapy?"

He brought the tea over. "I'll put you on the massage table after you finish this tea, and we'll have a look at your shoulder, okay?"

My heart palpitated like a toreador facing off against a belligerent bull. "That would be so great, man. My body is wearing thin, and this shoulder is getting harder to cope with."

"I could tell. I think I can help," he said.

Once I was on the bed, he started. My face contorted and my body grunted. He told me to relax. I struggled. He picked up a plastic roller with long, stiff ribs. He took my foot in his hand.

"So, how long have you been walking?" he asked.

Before I could respond, he pushed the roller against my foot. I jostled on the bed in agony. My words, already committed, came out like sputtering hogwash.

"Thu-thu-thu-fuck! What the hell was that?"

He stopped with the roller, laughed, and waited for me to lie back down.

"That was crazy, whatever you did. I just got this massive pain in my shoulder? You didn't even touch my shoulder, what the fuck?" I exclaimed.

He grinned and apologized. "Everything is connected to your feet, or your feet are connected to everything else in your body. It is probably your feet that are causing the pain in your shoulder. I am going to continue, okay?"

I agreed hesitantly. Again, the pain erupted in my shoulder as he applied the satanic device to the ball of my foot. "Holy shit! Damn son, what the," I barked in shock. "Wow, wait, wait, wait!"

He stopped again. I took a breath. "You ready, Freddi?"

"Oh Jesus, baby Jesus, no!"

He laughed again as he pressed down with the roller. He rolled the device over my foot a few more times. Every time, the same painful, convulsive aggravation. The anguish slapped me. Then, he moved to my legs and back. The sharp, daggering rush into my shoulder only happened when he pressed my right foot.

"Freddi, you're putting a lot of stress on your feet. It's not getting better as long as you continue walking. You need to stretch regularly and stop for a while. Your body's calling out. It is obvious. You have to do back stretches for your shoulder and feet to heal."

Once I got up from the bed, I felt relieved. The pain in my shoulder subsided. He put another tea in my hands then picked up his guitar. Istanbul was just eight long days away.

Ep. 26
Turkish Delights

The bridge from Greece to Turkey was fortified by heavily armoured military vehicles on both sides. The Greeks, much as they may have wanted to, wouldn't let me cross by foot. I hitched a truck ride for a whole kilometre. At customs, the Turkish guard was in no mood for cordiality. He said no more than four words in English.

"Where from?" he demanded.

"Canada," I responded through the cut-out windowpane.

"Fifty euro," he snapped.

Caught off-guard, I glanced into his eyes, concentrating. "Huh?"

"Fifty euro," he repeated in an unchanged, irritated tone.

"Woah, huh, nah, that can't be right, bro. It's too much!" I panicked. I considered going back to Alesandro's place. 50 euros was a lot. Ten euros a day and another 200 until I found a job in the biggest, busiest city of Europe. This had to be wrong. All along the Way, through all the conversations, no one mentioned 50 fuckin' euro. I thought Visa fees didn't exist in Europe.

"You're not exactly in Europe over there, are ya?" I said to myself. Perhaps he was demanding a tip? I was halfway to India. The Way was teaching me the patience I sought, right here.

But instead of remaining composed, I insisted he was wrong. He challenged me immediately, like he'd been waiting for me, excited. An entourage of vowels and consonants poured out like alphabet soup.

"Greece," was his last word, the only one I understood. I turned my head, following his finger as it pointed behind us. I demanded to speak to a higher-ranking officer. He waved me off aggressively. Anxiety had stifled me. I stormed back toward Greece. The officer seemed to feed off my despair, revelling in it. I was desperate and lashed out. And instead of accepting my request to speak with his supervisor, he heard disrespect. He saw a contemptuous prick. After deliberation, pacing to ease my nervousness, I returned to a different booth.

"There, English, go," an agent ordered bluntly. In the office, it was the same: pay 50 bucks or head back to Greece. But for Americans and Europeans it cost 20. When I returned to the booth, with my 50-euro note, I noticed a big, golden frame. A portrait of a moustached man photographed in a big, fuzzy hat. Thick, dark clouds collected over enormous, cascading flags behind the border. These huge, towering flags instilled a sense of fear, a premonition of upcoming inevitable conflict. Even though we remained on European soil until the Bosporus Sea, essentially, politically, people were obviously Republican. A westernized, religion-free state was Ataturk's vision for a European Turkey.

20 feet across the border, I was dumbfounded and tense. Aside from the huge, draping banderols that choked my panorama, the road ahead was less gripping. Yellow grass on a plain. Flat as a moth's wing. Five kilometres off the main highway, the township of Ipsala began. A village city, hollow as a grave robber's heart. Miserable as far as I could tell, shanty cafes with mouldy corners. The streets would have been great if they were dusty. Rounding it off, a university, attracting the third string of Istanbul's students. A crumbling, neglected, souring building. The walls stained yellow as my mom's living room ceiling from nicotine. Age, the mere passage of time, wasn't what made it all miserable. Abandonment and forgotten homes had charm. But Ipsala lacked an identity. Stuck in the crossfire of life. It was robbed of its distinctive character, stripped and neglected by the urbanization of larger city centres.

Shortly after my arrival at the central cafe, a crowd of men encircled me. Beside them sat a small group of students from the university. One young woman stood out. She was short, slim at the waist with pushed up little breasts swelling out of a low-cut shirt. Large, green, pointed eyes, covered in eyeliner. Her skin glowed a cream colour. She had soft, plump lips and a small, button nose. Her long, light brown hair was tied into a bun revealing her long neck. She managed the most English out of the lot, smiling constantly at me. Just enough English to send one of her friends off the veranda. He returned with a young man who shook my hand graciously.

"How can we help you?" he inquired calmly.

"I need a place to sleep tonight."

"You mean like a hotel?"

I shook my head. "Like a park, for my tent."

He translated to the others as I spoke.

A server came and brought tea for everyone. I was elated by the unexpected Turkish delight. No longer did I have to drink murky, brown coffee or pay a ridiculous price for imported tea. Served in small, glass lava lamps, it arrived on glass saucers with little, baby spoons. The ruby liquid glistened as clear, small bits of black leaves sank to the fat-bottomed glass. For 30-euro cents, I got local tea leaves from the Black Sea region of Trabzon. Beside it, a stack of cubes in a white ramekin. I dropped one inside. My spoon sang off the sides of the thin, bulbous glass. The energy mounted around me, and curious people gathered. We couldn't communicate through anything but laughter. An older man came from his table, anxious to meet me. The English novice introduced him to me. He grabbed my hand and shook it vigorously. He spoke animatedly in Turkish, with the impression I would catch on. He kissed his teeth. I quivered. Shortly afterwards, another lava lamp of tea arrived for me. People kept drawing each other's attention by kissing their teeth.

"This is going to drive me mad," I thought.

The old man settled in with the students. He took me by the hand and led the Way. A few hundred metres through town, he ordered my first, true Turkish kebab. It was less than spectacular. Every corner of the world did it better. Nothing more than half a loaf of white bread stuffed with shaved, roasted chicken. The mosque's megaphone pierced my senses, blocking

244

out any further teeth kissing sounds. I had almost forgotten about that thing. It called for evening prayer. I cringed at the thought of waking up to that loudspeaker every morning. My old friend continued to speak with me in Turkish as he walked me up the stairs of a hotel.

Behind a butchered desk stood a tall, slim, tanned young lad in slacks and a collared shirt. If there was an inexpensive room in this town, he'd brought me to it. Soiled carpets, walls blackened by decay. I didn't even have local currency yet. A group sat inside another room with their door open.

"You guys speak English?" I asked.

"Yes, yes of course," one said.

"Of course," I thought. "Well, look, my friend here has brought me to a hotel room, but," my face became desperate. "I do not have any wish to pay for a hotel, see. He continues to speak with me excitedly, but I don't have any idea what he's saying. I just wanted to find a park for my tent."

The stranger rolled chocolate hills of words together for my elderly friend. Their lips pursed dulcet melodies to one another, syllables dancing like stones, skipping off the sea.

"He paid for room. He wants invite you breakfast tomorrow. Be ready, 10 a.m."

I waited in the morning. The man didn't arrive. I had to get some cash, or lira, as they called it. Again, no one could speak English, and the students were off at school. One place had a pastry stuffed with spinach, cheese, and ground beef. They called it Burek. Not nearly as cheap as the Albanian one, it was less oily and in a rolled pastry tube. Someone called to me from the garden cafe I'd arrived at. He pulled a chair out. We smiled at each other long, until mine became awkward.

"Istanbul, I must go."

He nodded energetically to my words. He then kissed his teeth. I squinted at the sound. A small, porcelain cup with swampy, thick liquid on a saucer arrived. I recognized it.

"Turkish coffee," he declared confidently. "Corba?" he asked.

I had no idea what he meant by corba, so I shrugged apologetically and grinned with a half-smile.

"This is Albanian coffee," I giggled.

245

"Turkish coffee," he said sternly.

No point in mentioning Macedonian or Greek coffee. He finished his cup, then turned it over. Afterwards, he pulled the cup off the saucer and looked at it for a moment. The inner part of the cup was streaked with brown lines.

"Sorry," I shook my head.

"Corba?" He asked again as he kissed his teeth at the waiter. Five minutes passed of moderate silence. He spoke in his unfamiliar language. I shrugged until we smiled at one another and shared some awkward laughter. A bowl of very thick, dark orange soup arrived. A lemon on the plate and three slices of bread. The soaked bread was incredible.

"I could live on this," I thought to myself. "Um shukran, I mean," I paused. "How do you say thank you in Turkish?" He nodded and smiled.

"Afiyet Olsun," he said.

In Kesan, I found a real money exchange. The rain didn't let up that night. Two different mosques refused to let me sleep inside or even camp beside them. I cozied up in a ditch, full of rubbish, on the side of a busy, little street. Kesan was another town of destitute ugliness. I walked out in the morning needing to trek a couple kilometres back to the main road. This time, for breakfast I entered a shop called, *Cig Kofte*—raw meat. The young lady rolled it tight and passed it to me. "Afiyet Olsun," she said with a gracious smile.

I walked a straight line for hours. It became dark, quickly. The days were getting shorter. Rain came more frequently, splashing down in heavy torrents; the Way curved into a village. The first structure I encountered was an old barn with a fenced door and protruding roof. The low-lying barn held a couple dozen sheep. Rain plummeted. The sheep called out. The ground stopped absorbing water. Large puddles formed. Not a great place to pitch a tent. Not far off, through the rain, I could see a house with large, bay windows. Inside, a living area and dining table surrounded by happy, warm, dry people.

They were eating dinner. Two kids, a set of parents, and a granny. Despite being silent, I could hear them. They spoke the same words my family did when we all gathered for

Thanksgiving or Christmas. They laughed at one another's jokes. The kids spoke of their aspirations and projects coming up. The parents patted them encouragingly. At any moment, I could have sworn they would bring it in for a big, family hug. Everyone appeared so happy. They all looked so warm and clean and full. Most of all, not one of them had a spot of rain to worry about. I thought about the hot, thick soup and cig kofte. My stomach grumbled. Walls white as Rocky Mountain powder, white platters passed around, white plates refilled. My stomach grumbled again. My hands vibrated from the cool, night air, while intermittent commotion passed between the sheep. Like the towns people of Ipsala, they spoke a language I couldn't understand, yet they carried on. From some of those sheep, I heard sentiments of dolorous compassion.

"Why don't you have a rain jacket?" I heard my own voice ask.

"Because I don't have any extra money, idiot," I said aloud.

"You didn't prepare yourself right," the voice retorted.

The family had moved to their sitting room to watch television. My depression swelled as the rain continued. Everywhere was dark. All, except for this house, refreshing the western vision of what love looked like. And benevolent as the sheep were, they didn't tire, just like the rain. One option sat in front of me, so I walked to the door of the happy family. Mom opened it. I smiled as the door widened enough for her to see me. I didn't want to startle her.

"Merahba, afedersiniz, but I," I tried to be polite in Turkish. She looked so stunned, I expected her to shriek. Instead of closing the door, she waved her hand at me to wait. Her husband came to the door, timid and calm.

"Hello? Are you okay?" he asked in English.

I let out a sigh of relief. "I'm really sorry man, but I was up there," I pointed to the little house full of noisy sheep, "and been there for a long time. The rain doesn't stop," I sulked and smiled in unison.

"Please, come in," he led me to his foyer, covered by high, thick glass windows. There were a couple of white couches. Everything was white. Shortly after I sat down, mum brought a wooden tray of food and lava lamps of tea. I looked at him and his wife, my eyes sparkling, holding back, trying to conceal my sentiments.

"Afiyet Olsun," they both said.

"Thank you so much, really, I can't," I stuttered. "Don't know how much…"

My new friend interrupted me, "Afiyet olsun is like, 'enjoy'. Please, enjoy."

His wife nodded before leaving.

I had spent an hour minimum overcome by this dreary, pathetic, miserable notion of myself. A grim fool, I forgot in an instant that I was a pilgrim on a bigger mission. I saw a family, one I could never have, one that someone in my past told me I could never have. I saw a man who took care of business and his healthy, wonderful, happy kids. He took care of his stepmother and rarely complained. Without hesitation, this man grabbed my shoulder tight and pulled me in from the cold. His wife, following his lead, accepted me as family. This kind, tall, pale, blond-haired man sat on the opposite couch. He looked at me empathetically with wide, blue eyes. The small table held a spread of food similar to the many that were extended to me across Albania.

"Why, sorry, my English," he paused and shrugged. "What you do? Where from you?"

I explained that I was Canadian after thanking him a handful of times and hugging him. His kids came in and his daughter jumped on his lap. The glint in his eye was heartwarming. I told him and his kids that I walked from Rome. He called his wife over. They spoke in Turkish, and both looked at me again.

"Walk by foot?" He asked for me to repeat.

I nodded. "I'm going to Istanbul to teach English," I reiterated. "I hope, I mean, I guess, well, I don't know."

He introduced his kids and wife. I picked at the cheese blocks, tomato salad, black olives, and bread. In between his broken words, I took spoonfuls of tiny ravioli pasta covered in yogurt, paprika, olive oil, and cumin. This yogurt pasta, so bizarre and wrong, was fantastic. Once I finished, he tapped my knee.

"Come with me, okay, bring your stuff," he suggested.

I followed him. Handfuls of men were gathered in a low-roofed teahouse. Many rose after I came down the stairs and into the hall with their neighbour. They jostled and jolted. He must

248

have said Canada three or four times. Every time I heard "Istanbul," I heard "Rome" before it. More than once, many gasped. Mouths were agape. Multiple men came to shake my hand and welcome me in delightful, Turkish syllables. They also bought me rounds of a hot, sweet orange drink. Also served in little lava lamps. And finally, my host pulled me back outside. The rain had subsided. I imagined myself bundled beside the bellowing sheep in misery, then laughed out loud.

"What, you are okay?"

"Yes, no problem, just very happy. Thank you so much."

We went up a set of stairs and into a building. The second floor had two rooms, each with a bed inside. It resembled a pilgrim's dorm.

"Please, sleep here tonight. Relax, sleep. Tomorrow morning come, breakfast with family, okay?"

I shook my head in disbelief. I turned to him and grabbed his hands, shaking them. "This is so great, so great, thank you so much," I blurted. My head became vertiginous from this whole event. Hardly did my book cover open before I was sawing logs.

At breakfast, there was a motorbike outside. I didn't recall it being there before. The man, in his broken words, told me he had gone on trips. He also told me he'd studied economics, but his father became very ill.

"After that, I became farmer."

He drove his motorbike a couple times a year to remote parts of Turkey. He loved his bike and being on the road. He put his arm around my shoulder and the other into my hand. I opened it and there were a few folded notes. It was about thirty euros worth of lira. I refused, he insisted. I refused, he insisted. I caved. He didn't look at me as a stranger or strange. He envied what I had as much as I envied him. He thanked me for keeping up with the road.

"I have kids, you know?"

I agreed. Lovely kids, and both would grow up to be great parents.

"Once I get settled in Istanbul, maybe I can come back and give lessons to her."

He smiled ear to ear, nodding in agreement. He walked me out after I shook hands with his kids and hugged his wife. Outside, I admired his motorbike before pulling him in close.

"Good luck, brother. Thank you so much, really."

"You too. Good health to Istanbul."

Ep. 27
The Way Home

Boredom, conflict, and tension burgeoned like cysts. Wine, beer, raki, and ouzo were my anti-inflammatories. All of which landed me in a ditch. I resented myself for not planning more, for not investing in a smartphone, for insisting on remaining off-grid. Cheated by poor trail markings along the Via Francigena Del Sud and ancient Egnatia Way, bitterness was my constant companion. Hiking trails and deep forests waited in Norway. Homestays held the magic. These simple interactions with real people in their homes clarified the knowledge I sought. Divided by borders, religions, languages, and history, there was still something universally human in us all.

The Way from Rome began in mid-July. It was near the end of October. The whole pilgrimage, and for years before this, I chased adventure and excitement. This sheep farmer with his family embraced my struggle. Humanity was revealing itself. The soul of Turkey was laid before me in that sheep farmer's foyer.

The rain only got worse, but every hour I neared the fortress walls of old Constantinople and Hagia Sophia. These people who took me in were far more exhilarating than any temple could ever be. They were remarkable. Cornerstones of communities, ignored by average people who never stopped to consider that all one needed to do to find humanity and love was knock on a stranger's door.

I told them I was walking to Istanbul. "How dare you lie to them?" I snapped accusingly at myself as the rain soaked my Crocs and feet.

They sacrificed for me. They made this journey an epic one. At times, I thought I walked to prove to myself I had the strength. I wanted a hike worth remembering. But for a long time, I had been walking for them. No matter how much rain poured

250

down, I had to do it. That farmer gave me more than just 30 euro by showing me love and compassion, he offered strength. He gave me what I needed to push forward through the heavy rain.

I was a selfish, only child who grew up with suffocating love from a mother who would sacrifice everything for her son. Unfortunately, I looked everywhere for that same kind of sacrifice, and at the same time, the paradox of proving I didn't need it. This Way hadn't finished yet; there was a week ahead. Walking out of this farmer's little village, I knew I had reached my end of this journey. Inside those dining room windows, I saw the true value of love, and the beautiful disaster I was. Those last few days, I pushed onwards for that farmer.

"How many times did you reach for love with women that you met on the Way?" The voice activated in my head.

Before any of this walking, before the Camino, before I arrived in Europe, I chased adventure, specifically involving a female partner who would sacrifice it all. In return, I promised her safety and the time of our lives. There were times when I thought, or hoped, that a real lasting relationship would develop.

Her name was Lisa, the heartbreaker who led me to St-Jean-Pied-De-Port. Slightly older than me, and on a journey of her own. She bailed on an internship in Kuala Lumpur. Then, on a whim, flew to Jakarta. Took a room over a bar in Yogyakarta. I happened into this same bar in Yogyakarta with my mate Will.

Will and I had hiked up a volcano for sunrise. When we returned to town, we were destroyed, dirty, and most of all, parched. I took a beer in a bar and watched this woman pass by a few times in her long, red dress. I reached out and asked her to sit. After a few days together in her bed, I left as I always did, remorseful and empty. I liked this woman. Her words rang in my head. She squeezed me and told me how perfect we fit together.

I received a message from Lisa. "I've been thinking about you, Freddi. Can't get you out of my mind, in fact. And maybe, well, if you might like, I would like to join you. What do you think?"

We met at a train station near Bromo National Park the following afternoon. I embraced her with both arms, and we shared a kiss I was sure never to land from. The sequence of fantastic events erupted from there. We spent incredible weeks together, and later months. But there was more to it. I asked for her devotion, and I did keep her safe. But I didn't tender enough in return. My yearning for the road stood between us, and unknown adventures, like a nice, shiny, golden coin. Lisa wanted to be my precious. That was, until she knew that she wasn't going to be that for me.

I refuted myself out loud. "She told me to light the plane ticket on fire, forget the whole thing, and fuck off. She told me to get lost."

"With reason, no?"

I wasn't prepared or equipped to cope with something as cosmic as a co-existence where I gave as much as I received. Spoiled and selfish, I thought only of myself. And to be honest, this wasn't entirely true. I thought about her so often and offered my power and energy. Still, I couldn't put anyone, not even her, in front of my own desires. And for a woman who had other ideas for her life, this was an unmistakable warning.

"I want kids, Freddi. Plain and simple. And you are still a kid yourself." I could still hear her saying that. "I found a real man with a real job and a real place and a real car. Go have fun and enjoy your life. Forget about me."

It was so mean and blunt and hard to swallow. It took a long time to process. I mocked life for months after that, wallowing in self-pity. Soaked in the wormwood of a chalice, I waited on hallucinations of a better life. One that I was worthy of, because I failed this one. Every chance, I took it and fucked my way into forgiveness. Penance and atonement, I couldn't do before the absolution. It was then I remembered my old friend from Hungary who'd told me her stories from her Camino Way, who'd often called me "Pilgrim." Reflecting, Lisa had done the same, in a more cutthroat way, with other words. She wanted to be in a co-operative relationship. Unfortunately, I was already in one with the Way. And so, feeling betrayed and stupid, she called me every name in the book.

"So, what the fuck were you doing drinking and philandering around Berlin grovelling over her after you broke up if you knew she had a point?"

When I arrived at St-Jean-Pied-de-Port, the amount of people caused me a small amount of anxiety. I doubted my Hungarian friend's advice. That was, until I met Amos, Cosimo and Dani, staring at the bulky Pyrenees summits, and I began to forgive myself. This was the first day of accepting that my uncontrollable need to follow the Way meant that I might need to let go of any dream of sharing the Way with a lover. Realizations force one to grow. Kinship with my fellow pilgrims gave me the community, even if temporary, that I needed to become myself again. Every step followed another and led to another day of walking beside them. It was perfect.

"So, now you're chasing adventure again heading to Istanbul, no? And what for?"

"Is it really about the adventure?" I asked the voice.

This time, I had to forgive others. I had to be patient with others. I found myself. I'd become open-minded, cultured, understanding. But how long would it take before I accepted others for their views? Before I accepted them being closed-minded or selfish or ridiculous or self-centred? So what if I had gone through it and come out the other side wiser? My challenge was to endure their points of view even if they didn't correlate with mine. If I couldn't accept it, I could at least move on without anger. The job that lay in front of me was to find compassion and patience even for those who I didn't really believe deserved it.

"But how long is this going to take, for fuck's sake?"

By reaching out for a love I felt only a woman could provide, I held myself back. I hoped to inspire that kind of love in Anya, for a few days or a week. With the same grip, I tried to grab onto Nikki as she walked off to bed. And Elpita, the mirage of perfection, who left without even a final hug. Each one had a message or story that meant something. Whether for a reason, a season, or a lifetime, the sheep farmers were everywhere. At every turn, I looked for exactly what I ran away from with Lisa. The Way gave me every chance to recover.

"I forgave myself for being miserable, and now I'm trying to make up for it with every female I meet?" I questioned the voice.

But the answers lay with strangers. It was overall compassion I needed to find. Patience to turn the other cheek. I had to remind myself to breathe, instead of letting anxiety cause friction through communication gaps. And most of all, to embrace the love all these homestays offered. They deserved commemoration. The sheep farmer, as he looked at me with his blue eyes and German chin. The same compassion I was searching for; he had found the answers.

I saw Lisa inside his bay windows. She was passing the serving platter to her son. She beamed at her husband, who rubbed his son's head after saying thank you. Her carpet clean, with table and chairs, couches, and kitchen all in the comfort of her home. Her circle of life was nearly complete, but for white hair and grandkids. The cold, the smelly, disruptive sheep, inflated my timorous depths with burden and sorrow. Fears from my past rekindling. Famished and dirty, worn and sore, rejected by the life I watched in those bay windows. I watched what would have happened if I had decided to put shoes on like *she* once suggested. Laced shoes and fitted pants. And if I continued to walk the Way, I would only get as close as the foyer. But at least I had the courage to knock. And I was happy for her and her marvellous family, safe in their living room. She wanted children. Her Way brought her there. She gave birth to a wonderful son and had a loving partner. She deserved that. Still, I felt dejected seeing her in there so happy without me.

With the Way to Istanbul complete, daily life wouldn't offer answers so vividly. People wouldn't be as empathetic. Instead, I needed to be the stronger one, clearer, calmer. And let love come, instead of chasing a forgiveness I already had. The Way had given me so much, yet every time I became lost, I became frustrated. And every time I got lost, I was welcomed into something else. It wasn't smooth sailing. The trail was ugly. But that was life, essentially. And the Way, this was life as well. A pilgrim walked along as everyone else drove, with no obligations other than to walk. Enjoyable and enlightening as it was, no one could walk forever. One had to return to society at some point, or risk talking to themselves for decades. I hoped that I could "re-join society" at my whim, then live amongst others with compassion and patience until the next Way called me to join it.

In Florina, I tried hard to get the museum to offer me answers and solutions. When they didn't, I became angry. This happened again, with the gatekeeper at the hot spring surrounded by tourists. And again, at Kavala as I watched James and the ferry depart. I was done with all that. I kept blaming others and kicking the dirt instead of accepting the Way. It was time to accept the Way and forgive others. Life was like a walk in the rain, after all. I could hide from it and take cover, or I could simply get drenched. And clearly, if I was going to make it to Istanbul, I was going to get drenched.

* * *

Aymeric Picaud, a French monk, scholar, and pilgrim, wrote the first ever tourist guidebook on El-Camino-De-Santiago-De-Compostella. He wrote it in the mid-12th century. From the second day at Roncesvalles, my ego snubbed the guidebooks. The closer we got to Compostella, the more crucial that choice became. Most of the group I called family gathered in a forest 20 kilometres from the great cathedral of Santiago. The idea was to reach Compostella for sunrise, and the church on Friday morning ahead of traffic. Most pilgrims attended on Fridays because of the huge ceremony. A bell swung from the roof, smoke circulated, and so on and so forth. My Camino finished three days later, at Fisterra. I planned to put my tent there, on a beach as Ali suggested, so I could bury my watch.

Candles lit our camp. Everyone stretched out on their mats. We huddled around, telling stories of the Way, rejoicing in comedic moments and their follies. Cosimo sang a cappella, Irish weaved out rhythms with his flute. Dani farted. There was a father and daughter team from Bretagne, France, whose eyes reminded me of my recklessness. The Italian kindergarten teacher and the Dane I met on a park bench back in St-Jean-Pied-de-Port. And then, there was the only proper Christian I met on the Way, from New Orleans, Leah's friend. In spirit, Elena also lay beside me, laughing wholeheartedly. I had egged everyone on since the first, cold, brash night in Roncevalles. A month had passed, and nights had gotten warmer. I managed to gather most of my family together for a good old Canadian camp out. Most of the group considered this their last night on the Way. Amos was missing. It was the last night that Dani, Cosimo, and I would be together. Our kindergarten teacher rose first. As motivated as her first day of class, with a pile of games under her right arm, she got us going. The night walk had become a ritual at this stage. Despite having a whole gang, we wound up ass backwards, looking over the city of Santiago from a distance. When we realized how fucked we had become, the young Frenchie from Bretagne unpacked a cake to celebrate our last night walking the Camino together.

Sunrise was upon us, and the others rushed the main streets of Santiago to reach the Cathedral. Deterred, I noticed a cafe open. As I ordered a tortilla de patatas, Cosimo entered and ordered two beers from behind me.

"Buen Camino, Freddi, good brother," he declared, as he put his arm around my shoulder.

I wrapped around him laughing. "No Cathedral?" Behind him was the kindergarten teacher. She tried to refuse, but we ordered her a beer anyway.

The packed Cathedral square bustled. All the people I'd walked beside for a month had collected, awaiting the ceremony. Bodies cuddled each other in celebration. It resembled a time when a Canadian team had finally won a hockey championship. The plaza crammed together a mob of crying men. I could not shed a tear. Instead, I found some shade and rolled my mat out for a nap.

A street cleaning zamboni startled me awake. The cobbled alleys that poured from the Cathedral were familiar mazes in Spain. At siesta, walls and windows closed, then silence. The old town widened to a park with a theatre area. Large, drivable roads with cars passing quickly. I found in the park a large gang of familiar pilgrims. Alistair's big red hair and flag immediately stood out. Gathered in circles, they passed wine around and spoke of the Way.

"Remember how Amos broke a chair in Astorga?" Alistair chuckled hoarsely. "He fell right back!"

"That actually hurt, you bastard!"

I interrupted, "It's because he was hung over as fuck from our night walk, eh guy?"

Amos turned, "Yea, that was a big one. Where you been man?"

256

"Just woke up. Street cleaner almost drove right over me."

All the nonsense with the church ceremony, the certificates and stamps and the overly demonstrative public outpourings of self-congratulation, finished in the late afternoon.

Dani hurried over, "What a deal guys, cazzo! This place is amazing!"

We moved across the road from the park to a cafe called *100 Montaditos*. The café had tiny sandwiches for a buck, but more importantly, they had beers for a buck, too. I sat down at one of the metal tables outside. I couldn't believe my eyes. Elena was walking the brick laneway towards me.

"You're still here," I threw myself around her. "I was sure you were gone."

"I couldn't leave without saying bye to you guys. I knew everyone would show up today, so I stretched it out one more day."

"So, you're leaving with the others tomorrow, back to Madrid?" I asked, half sullenly.

"Yea, back to reality. We can't all be like you, Freddi," she said happily. "We might like to be, though."

"No, you wouldn't."

She winked, squeezed me again, and whispered, "You're probably right."

"Anyway, this café has one-euro beers. One bloody euro baby, baby, c'mon, baby c'mon!" I sang with a cheeky smile.

She shook her head, "Is that a good thing?"

I threw my arm around her shoulder and moved her closer.

"It's a great thing. Everyone's gathering here. It'll make the goodbyes much more manageable for me," I paused. "And fun."

"You're crazy, Freddi, but I love you. And goodbyes are not forever," she said with a sense of formality and sincerity.

I looked back at her, my eyes sparkled, excited for the coming drinks, but also struck by her words. "I love you too, little lady. You're one of the good ones. But, some goodbyes are forever." I grabbed Dani by the shoulder. "Let's make some room for sexy pants, yea?"

The singing erupted after sunset. I hugged every one of my family members as many times as I could. We shouted into the sky with everything we had, to Roxanne and to Queen, for Freddi Mercury and for us. We were champions. We were free. We locked arms. We lip synced. All the brick walkways around the Cathedral were packed in tight. Gridlocked, with people in stretch pants and waterproofs, cargos, sweaty t-shirts, and button ups. Wild, unkempt hair, ungroomed beards, unwashed faces. We were pilgrims and fucking happy about it. Musicians appeared with accordions and guitars. They played in front of our cafe terrace. We danced in a huge circle and kicked our legs to the gypsy sounds. Elated, we lashed out in excessive cheers. The euro beers kept pouring. My freestyles got longer. The glasses clanged against one another. The singing got louder and more atrocious. We carried on until the very last shop closed. Back at the Cathedral, I returned to where I had napped, holding onto the night, looking for someone to share my bottle of wine. I wasn't ready to quit. This time, the square was empty, noiseless, and illuminated by urine-coloured street lanterns. Two girls sat across from one another. They sounded English and familiar.

"Freddi! Get over here," Elena hollered out. "You still alive?" she asked as she laughed and pulled me in. I wrapped my arms around them and kissed each of them on the cheek.

"What would I have done for a nice threesome?" I thought, and then blurted out, "Jesus, that would really finish things, wouldn't it?"

"What would?" the Dane asked.

I shrugged, "If you guys walked the last three days with me to Fisterra," I said, passing my bottle of wine to Elena.

"I'd love to," Elena responded, "if only I didn't have the real world calling me back."

This was the hardest part of travel for me. It reminded me of journeys past, in love and friendship where roads bent in opposition and the Way separated us. I knew this bond had to be broken. We couldn't be anything other than distant acquaintances who shared something in the past. We might message each other once a year, like my friends back home did. The problem was, I refused to let go or move on. I buried my fear of being alone and sheltered it with annoyance.

"Fuck the real world. I mean, of course. Priorities, responsibilities, it makes sense. I got it."

"You won't be walking alone, Freddi," Elena had taken my hand, holding it tightly against her chest. "There will be others, and I will also be with you still, out there. Just call on me when you need to, I'll respond," she consoled me with a big squeeze.

I looked back at the Cathedral. "That thing doesn't finish this for me, you know? That, I guess, is the real issue. The coast. Take me to the fuckin' coast," I murmured, fading off.

"'Take me to bed,' is what you should be saying."

I passed out beside Elena, in their room, holding her as closely as I could. She would leave me for Madrid in the morning. They would all leave.

Ep. 28
The Republic

The rain continued, only this time I found a small, neighbourhood market. Under the awning, I watched slivers of rainfall. Surrounded by huge buildings, it was dark again. Tekirdag might have been a small community once, but as the populations around Istanbul swelled, so did each of the places I passed. Building contractors loved this. And investors were anxious to fund soulless apartment complexes until occupants appeared. Tekirdag corresponded to any medium-sized city in Canada. Perhaps I ignored or missed the light, but I noticed zero flair for European architecture. No sign of the 18th or 19th centuries. I had hoped to leave Tekirdag, but the highway was no better, with huge trucks blowing past at all hours. A young man exited the shop and passed me. He turned around.

"Merahba," I replied. "I don't speak Turkish, sorry."

"Are you okay?"

"Relatively, yes," I snickered, unimpressed by the rain.

"Where are you from?" led to, "What is a Canadian doing in Tekirdag?"

"I'm walking to Istanbul."

He laughed and asked why.

"I made promises to people, and I gotta follow through."

"Huh?" he asked with a confused glare. "Where did you walk from?"

"The Vatican in Rome," I retorted without animation.

"Seriously?" he straightened. "Are you Christian?"

I shook my head vehemently, "It was just a landmark."

"Are you Muslim? We are Muslim here, you know."

I conceded with irony.

"All of Turkey," he said strictly.

"I don't pick sides," I smiled and shrugged, "I'm, I dunno, Agnostic I guess."

He lived with his parents but offered me space for the night. It was a short walk and ten floors up one of the faceless, cubicle buildings. I felt sorry for the miserable architects who were stuck building these monstrous towers. I built similar structures out of Lego with no instructions when I was seven. His parents greeted me. Neither spoke English. He explained the situation to them. His parents went to sleep, and he opened up. He studied engineering at university. His English was tremendous. The first thing I mentioned was AtaTurk.

"He is the father of our nation," he commented proudly. "A great man."

"I noticed," I responded ironically. "His portrait's everywhere."

"We love him very much," he declared again, proudly. I asked him about the Armenians, Kurds, and Greeks who lived in newly formed Turkey during that time.

"They tried to kill us. We only fought back."

I listened calmly. I heard the voice of a young, English-speaking, university-educated Turkish man. The first I had met. This fascinated me a great deal. This allegiance that many Turks held for one man astonished me. Through all the Americanization, consumerism, branding, and media, he remained iconized in the squares of so many different parks. People here gripped tightly to their father, as well as local pop music and the local film industry. If one looked around, they would see the streets of any Canadian town, but for so many hijabs. Still, everything remained proudly Turkish.

At home, most people knew John A. McDonald, our first prime minister. But at the turn of century, when a poll aired on television for "The Greatest Canadian of All Time," Neil Young destroyed him. We rinsed and blamed and cajoled our political leaders. Complaining about our leaders was a favoured pastime for Canadians. Most European countries saw politics in a similar context, except with more personal accountability. But in Turkey, this picture, this veneration, his face with daggering eyebrows, clammed my hands. The whole thing gave me shivers. And most Canadians, tragically, weren't nationalistic enough to buy Canadian products, listen to Canadian music, or watch Canadian television. Most of which was pretty rubbish anyhow. This was why I had such a hard time with national pride.

In Turkey, they projected a pride like Americans, and they built towers like Americans, dressed like Americans, and learned to speak like Americans, but remained proudly Turkish. And Turkey, because of its right-wing political views regarding traditional roles, spoiled me with hospitality.

Two main highways ran from Tekirdag into Istanbul. The motorway I avoided and a coastal road, which merged with the former. I wanted to stay on the coast and relish the occasional swim while evading traffic. As in Albania, it was difficult to go hungry. Every day, a door opened with a man there, holding a bulb of tea. A worker selling melons from the back of his pickup pulled out a stainless-steel knife. He waved and called me over. I hesitated but crossed the busy, four-lane road. He sliced off a piece of a melon. I worried he would charge me or insist I buy one. He pushed the piece into my hand while shaking the other. His face bobbed with excitement. The flavourful liquid dripped over my hands and mouth. He offered me a towel from his truck.

I shook his hand. "Tesekurlar." I repeated it a few times, thanking him for the best damned honeycomb melon I'd ever tasted.

He locked the door and took my hand. Traffic passed, so he put his arm across my chest. When the lights changed and cars stopped, he lifted his arm, and I walked the busy road again. He led me into a cafe. We sat and he ordered two corba and cay. By this time, I understood corba meant pureed lentil soup, and cay was tea. He sulked when I started to remove money from my shirt pocket. He pushed my hand back with his hairy, brown forearm. He crossed the street again, after tapping my head with his. I learned later that this was common among Kurdish men. Turks,

261

or Turkic people, migrated in flocks from the Eastern Caspian Sea of Central Asia in the 13th and 14th centuries. Kurds descended for millennia around Asia Minor. They lived in bits of Iran, Iraq, and Syria, but the largest portion were settled in Turkey. Many called Diyarbakir the newest Kurdish capital.

Glamorous, luxury-styled, multi-level apartment buildings saturated the coast. Most of them white as clouds with sandy, yellow panelling. Kilometres of housing blocks, empty, kidney-shaped swimming pools, and empty outdoor tables. Thousands of condos. I couldn't have imagined the whole coastline to Istanbul being eaten by housing, but after hours on foot, it became obvious. As I walked a sandy patch, it turned to grass and fencing. Gated partitions continued appearing along the footpath. I happened upon a man in his yard.

"Do you speak English?" I asked.

He nodded and smiled.

"Where are all the people that normally live in these houses?"

He laughed a little before responding, "They are at home."

"So, these are not homes?" I smirked whimsically.

"These are holiday homes. Everyone's gone back to work and school, mostly in Istanbul. It's October now, winter is coming." He spoke with patience and pronounced each word.

I glanced around. "All of them? Geezus, I can't," I stuttered. "What about you?"

"I came to collect some things. I finished work and came by on my way home," he said before pausing silently for a moment. "I think there's a bottle of whiskey inside hiding somewhere, what do you think?"

I beamed. "Best idea I've heard in a long time."

"I know you are walking. I mean, you could stay here, but I have to lock the door. And the gatekeeper. It's simply too complicated. You can have dinner with us. Maybe another glass of whiskey is over there," he said, inviting me to his house.

"You don't shy from the drink, my good man. I like it. I'd be honoured. But before you go off to work in the morning, could you drive me back here so I could continue my walk?"

262

"Why not? I love your devotion," he said frankly, laughing a little. "It is very impressive. What was it you did before all this walking?"

"I trained as a chef," I replied to him quietly. "I loved cooking," I looked down cowardly. "Still do actually, just lost my Way from the kitchen." I rolled my shoulders. "Who knows. I taught a half-year of English, and hopefully, when I reach Istanbul, I'll do that again."

"English teacher and a chef, maybe we'll have you stay, you can teach my children and cook dinners. Although you'll see tonight, we have great food in Turkey." We finished our last mouthfuls of scotch.

Inside his large, 20th-story apartment, his wife brought platters onto his terrace. I could have spoken with this man for years, yet we existed in different classes. He lived in the upper tier of Turkish society. Unlike the young, ambitious student back in Tekirdag, he was careful not to pick sides in politics. Strangers from different paths, we shared some things in common. We both loved salty cheese and were won through our stomachs. In the morning, after walking from an incredible, massive, comfortable bed, I realised he had two wives. He had his stomach filled by two fantastic cooks. One, I felt without asking, was an ex-wife that stuck around.

Each day, someone stood above the crowd to help me a little. Entirely unexpected. Just like in Albania, I thought to myself. Westernization, I thought, built fences, and Orthodoxy created closed minds. In these countries, one could hardly feel that, at least when it came to the lone pilgrim who passed through town unarmed and soiled. If they offered pity, I would think otherwise. They held compassion and pride that I considered visiting their country in this Way. Their honour to have me was the greatest contributing sentiment. That thought boggled my unpatriotic mind. But wars had been won with that kind of devotion. And Turks had fought long, hard wars.

The Istanbul experience began through a hundred suburbs before arriving in the old city. It began in Silivri, 75 kilometres from the city centre, where city folk escaped for fried fish on Sundays.

I walked to a high cliff with two faces. One rested in shadow from town, covered in grass, sand, and small pebbles. I settled into my camp for the night until two, drifting young men sat on a nearby bench. Like me, they had tucked into shadow from the Townies. Excited to be in some decent company, I abandoned my camp to join them. Both single 21-year-olds, neither had any plans for their future. I could relate.

"Except the army," Altay said. He was being shipped off in two days for a year's enlistment. "After that, years down the line, they can call on us for reserve training."

I thought about home. "My grandfather was in the reserves… until he crashed a Jeep, drunk as a pirate," I joked. We shared our first laugh together.

"Well, tonight we celebrate like your grandfather," Altay said, rising and passing me a beer.

"Yes," I agreed, standing. "We have to send you off properly!"

Altay's friend said something in Turkish and also stood.

"Freddi, today is Turkey's birthday."

On October 29th in 1923, Turkey became an independent nation. And I just so happened to waddle into Silivri for the festivities. I insisted on buying the next round of bottles.

At the boardwalk, thousands poured in from side streets on foot. The party rumbled. Traffic stopped, people marched, and a huge light shone on a massive, billowing, cherry-coloured flag. Instead of fireworks, like on Canada Day at home, a few public speakers took to the microphone. Audacious, proud, intense voices spoke with gesticulating body language. The whole time through the speeches, people waved sticks with the moon and star in blistering white dye. I had two flags stuffed into the top of my pack. People adored this and tapped me on the shoulders with enthusiasm. Once the voices stopped their announcements, a powerful, dubstep-remixed, Stalinist marching song began.

"This is our Republican anthem!" Altay said, invested. The new version appeared as out of place as this election campaign, rallying votes during a birthday celebration. Despite the techno beat, to me the sound was exactly what so many American movies portrayed at Communist gatherings in Russia. Gallant, brusque, hardened as fortress walls, only now with a steady electronic crowd pleaser.

264

"Lenin meets Skrillex?" I thought to myself. And after the anthem played four times, the whole assembly finished like someone had pulled a single plug. Everyone went right back to the streets they'd shuffled in from an hour earlier. The streets drained and stores closed. Within a few minutes, we were the only ones remaining, standing there with beers in our hands.

"There was a strong chance for a great party here, what the fuck?"

"We're in Turkey, Freddi. There's no party. We have our own party," Altay's voice became astute. We went to his flat after saying goodbye to his friend. He offered me space in his room. His mother greeted me, ready as usual to feed us. I said hello to his grandfather in a rocking chair. Altay's room was no different than mine as a teenager, except he adored football and I skateboarding. He weighed his time living with his mom. He grabbed things as he spoke. He stroked his comfy double bed and jumped on it before rising again. He rolled his fingers across a poster. He was no longer a teenager but knew that he had not yet become an adult, either. This year, the army promised a transformation. Blown away by the idea of a full year away, being pushed around and belittled, he wasn't bothered by this like I would be. Before we could continue our chat, shouting erupted from another room. Unimpressed, Altay returned with a flat grin.

"So, my grandfather also lives here. He is different, Freddi. You know what I mean?"

I shrugged, supposing that I did, though I didn't. I grabbed his knee as his face sulked in shame, "It's alright, brother, it was nice of you to offer. I have my tent. There's that spot where I met you. It's a good spot. No worries, seriously."

His grandfather howled and hollered and demanded I leave.

His mother shook my hand apologetically. Her eyes sparkled with a hint of humility.

"It's your beard, Freddi. He thinks things because of your beard," Altay tried to explain.

There were three things that flared the tailfeathers of the Republican Turk: anything negative about the founding father, Armenian sympathizers, and lastly, any talk of Kurds, especially their independence. Many, I noticed, considered Kurds separate, and yet refused to let them be just that. They were also convinced that all Kurds were terrorists, full stop. And Kurds wore thick, black beards just like mine.

"Let's go grab another beer at the shop and forget about it," I said as I threw my pack on like so many other times, ready to go.

Outside, Altay looked back at me, shuffling through the narrow, dirt streets between people. "I know a good spot we can go, okay?" he said, leading the way.

He spoke quickly to a few people. I had picked up a few sentences and simple remarks; a wave of tender-voiced, scrutinizing faces, and nursery rhymes. The words carried like bubbling parodies of a drunk girl back home speaking to a friend who had arrived unexpectedly to a house party.

"Yar-da-mar-la-war-ma-bir, ya doin here?"

Altay turned to me after a few discussions. "I found a place we can buy beers," he remarked. I patted him on the shoulder.

"We can't send you off to the army sober, can we?"

We took seats on a long channel of rocks with a bag of large, Efes bottles. Colourful lights weaved an electric rainbow from somewhere in the distance. Somewhere I had come from. The night sky generated an unprecedented spectacle. The stars glittered with a spellbinding grip. The water was calm but for light ripples against the rocks. The city at our backs and put to bed. It was hard to believe that just hours before, a huge gathering shouted their proud anthem in unison, waving their flags as football fans.

"I'm not prepared for this," he confessed, taking another swig of beer.

"Few are, my brother from another mother," I quipped. He laughed a little at my colloquial term. "But, really, man, you gotta find that strength from deep inside, know what I mean? You think it was easy for me to walk here from Rome?"

"I guess not," he replied. I clutched his collarbone.

"Look, man, the first few months will be very tough, but you'll get through it. You might want to leave, run, escape, whatever. But it will get better, normal, routine. I promise that." He nodded along. "And you'll walk away from it more disciplined and readier for what lies ahead. I'm sure the accomplishment will lift your head high."

"You think?"

"I dunno, bro. I'm glad it's not me," I laughed and tapped his bottle. He adored his Republic, and if not, he acted like he did because he had to, at least for the following year.

Ep. 29
Diamonds Covered in Dust

Istanbul expanded as I left the fishery village. Not a patch of grass the rest of the Way on a map. I targeted a small patch on the seaside called City Park for the night. That left a mere 30 kilometres between me, Blue Mosque and Hagia Sophia.

This region, not so long ago, had sloping swaths of countryside sparsely populated by a few homes. It was surrounded by water with beaches to both sides. With the Black Sea to the north and the Marmara in the south, it would have been pockmarked with small, wooden fishing boats and men rolling their nets in little, red square hats. The unoccupied spaces between the two seas would have been used as vast grazing fields for goats to produce fresh Ayran.

Ayran was a cultural point of pride for Turks all over the country. Many dishes were provincial, but Ayran was national. A yogurt drink. Certainly not European. Ottoman colonialism brought it across their empire to the Adriatic. The tradition of this drink began even before the Ottoman, out on the Eurasian steppe, where Turkic nations still drink cold fermented horse milk from large, wooden drums. Before the buildings that ran from Silivri, I would have heard silence 150 years ago. Only the sounds of squawking gumboots, farm animals, and the odd mother hollering for her children. Every few hours, a humble prayer would sound from the single nearby mosque. Later, church bells would chime through the air. And wheels rolling over pebbles on their way into little Istanbul's city walls. Then, finally, surrounded by a minstrel variety of languages and noise. Stills of Antoine Melling's eye, tiny settlements on wide waterways. Big, dirt carriage roads lined with green fields and fetching, healthy trees. But, as I walked down through traffic never before seen, not a blade of grass or twig.

The road from Silivri climbed and climbed, then rolled down and up again. Rain poured. I walked into a shop to swap my wet socks for a fresh pair, unnoticed. Traffic built until it became relentless. The road bent down again. My heart pushed forward. It pumped for my legs and thighs and kept my mind assertive. A line of auto shops appeared. Oil stains and puddles, body parts, the smell of grease and petrol. The road went down a good couple hundred meters. Sidewalks narrowed further. My nerves rattled as cars neared. And after the bridge, more bustle. I contemplated winding through side streets, getting stuck, constantly asking directions from people who didn't speak English. I knew the consequences. After the congested area came malls and markets. Nameless stores by the thousands. The malls linked university campuses grey as monsoon clouds. In one huge, outdoor strip mall with high, encased walkways, I came to a tourism office. It shocked me so much I froze before entering. My body was a soaked handkerchief. Inside, air conditioning blew hard and cool. I pointed my face at the chilly vents. My eyes squinted and spread the salt from my ducts and stretched the salt from my hairy cheeks until I scratched them in relief. This was the closest I would get to a windy breeze. The woman almost fell from her chair.

"Are you okay?"

I nodded. "Yes, just very hot." I struggled for words as I cooled off.

"You look like you've been hiking up mountains or something?"

"Almost," I said, turning away from the air vents. "Do you have a map by any chance?"

She had an old, hand-drawn representation of the old town area. Short bits of road came out from it, but no clear way from this office down to the Blue Mosque and Hagia Sophia.

"I'm sorry, best I can do," she toiled through pamphlets. "You know, you could take the bus from here. It's quite cheap, only a couple lira. It's a short ride." She thought for a minute and continued, "It's a long walk from here, *very* long."

"You're telling me," I laughed. "Thanks for the map. Have a good one, tesekurlar and buen camino."

Her large smile could have eclipsed the moon as she waved. "You should take that bus!"

Concrete ate the whole sky. Pavement suppressed all vegetation. I counted steps, pushing my legs until the City Park. By the time I reached it, night ruled, and parked campers filled it. Not an inch of space to pitch my tent. A food truck sat up front on the main road. I had a sandwich. The airport was in front, which I had to pass. Nothing remained but a solid road. The road widened to sixteen lanes and the traffic headlights appeared as long lines of diamonds and rubies, as far as the eye could see. I pushed on and on.

The rain started again, and I rushed into a heated food truck. I ordered soup and tea and threw my pack down aggressively. I wanted to scream in frustration. Nothing but cement, rain, and steady traffic. I had no play. I went out to pee. And there, I noticed a massive, empty parking space behind the food truck. I went back inside. The man asked someone eating what I had asked him. The guest shrugged. They both looked at me with mysterious gazes. All I could think of was the grilled, marinated meat I smelt, the fat dripping down onto hot coals. Beautiful meat rolled onto long, metal swords. I couldn't remember the last time I had soft, tender, grilled beef striploin. I pulled my tent out and showed it to them pointing at it vehemently, shaking. I was off the deep end with exhaustion. And sleeping on those stones, in my tent on the wet ground, was the worst fucking plan going. What I wanted was one of them to suggest I sleep in the heated truck. I put my tent up and passed out quickly. My intensity went so far into a land without time, I didn't realise I had set my tent on a big pothole. And through the night, rain filled it so much the puddle soaked through before it woke me up. Nothing was untainted after that. My only chance was a blow dryer in a breakfast café. I spent the whole morning there, watching rain fall without pause.

* * *

The clear, turquoise sea, crystalline majesty all the Way to the Americas. The end of the Old World. The brisk, fresh air slapped my face, and I could feel the water wrapping around my naked, sweaty body. A couple hours remained; Fisterra neared. I could hear Alistair's voice in my head, his red moustache rubbing his upper lip, his green eyes sparkling in the sunlight.

269

"You'll love it there, you really will. You'll find some resolve. And time to really reflect on all this, my friend." I needed that. But I also wanted to do it with my family.

"They're all gone," I told myself as the Way reached a cliff and then down to a white sand beach. A familiar group of Israeli faces stood together on a slab of cement. Cosimo rushed from their core with the smile of a circus clown. He leapt onto me, and I fell to the sand, giggling.

"Porchodio, Cosimo, che cazzo!"

"Hey brother!" he hollered repeatedly. "We now Madrid Israelis go. Good see you brother." His English had improved in a month.

On my feet, I shrugged in disapproval, "You're going to leave before we party and share at least one sunset at Fisterra? How did you get here?" I asked.

He frowned. "We bus yesterday."

A beach waited for us all to create more memories and build stronger bonds. In my eyes, I saw more time. I became confused. It surprised me to see him, as I thought he was long gone.

"And Dani?" I asked desperately.

"He Fisterra, bus seven," Cosimo watched my disappointment. "He go France."

I gave him a look of shock. It couldn't be. I had three hours to reach him before his bus left, and that was 15 kilometres away. I decided to run some of it. If anything, I could convince him to stay. Plus, Alex Garland wrote about a place that tickled my fantasies in the late 90s. Two decades had passed imagining what it would be like to live on a beach. He had to share that with me. Cosimo made his decision. I could see that, but surely I could convince Dani. We had walked 900 kilometres. Well, I had walked 900, to get there. Suddenly, Dani, the closest male partner I'd had in years, was going to leave all this, again. This madness had to be stopped, and I was prepared to run for it.

Snaking bends. Every bend brought another bend, jogging and speed-walking in intervals. A very long, very thin, very white beach appeared.

"Dani's leaving paradise! Come on, legs!" I said, trying to motivate myself. I made it to the pilgrim's office, where I

270

found the kindergarten teacher. She'd taken a bus there with the Dane. I arrived panting heavily and visibly distraught.

"Has he gone?" I asked maniacally, completely out of breath.

"Who?" she asked, laughing.

"Dani, has Dani left? I saw Cosimo a couple hours ago," I grabbed my knees. "I've been racing to reach him. Bloody, fucking hell."

"Sorry, Freddi, he just left."

I sulked and breathed in and out, staring at the cement. "Fucking bastardo," I said softly through all the breaths. "He had to leave. What a shithead." I looked up to the sky and grabbed my back. "I fucking tried, though. I fucking tried to reach you, you sonfabich."

Alistair arrived from around a corner then. "Freddi! We're at the beach, Amos is there, we're gonna have a fire. Sunset is coming," he smiled. "You made it," he said proudly. "900 kilometres, brother. It's a long Way, isn't it?" He grinned with congratulations.

"Let's go. Get some supplies and follow me." I picked up a couple bottles of wine and some food. The girls came too, with some cheese and bread and a bottle between them.

Up a long hill, I struggled. My body was finished, and the hill wouldn't stop. We came to a forested area and trail. High trees covered the sun with shade. A wide, dirt path fit Alistair and I, side by side. I opened a pack of cheap olives and threw one in my mouth. The trees parted. The Atlantic was first, then the long, golden, empty belt of tawny sand. The small waves coiled. Every tense muscle in my body eased. The beach bent on both sides and created a secluded cove.

"What I tell you, Freddi! This is, The Beach. Not bad, huh?"

It was a mint. It was ours. It was so isolated and perfect and near enough to the shops.

Alistair got in front of us before the path went downhill. "So, welcome guys. This is Mar De Fora." He pointed at the rocky slab to the far-right side of the beach, "That is the dragon, which protects us from oncoming danger," he said, grinning. "We are safe here. So, come in peace."

There must have been a dozen pilgrims lined up as the sun dropped down. I put my tent up beside a couple others.

"We should have camped here, instead of checking into the albergue," the girls said to one another.

"You can still stay, why not?"

Those who did stay collected around a well-defined, well-used fire pit. Wood stacked in a loose pile beside it. Ali sparked the fire and I chopped everything for my puttanesca sauce. The fire going, I cooked a large pot of pasta.

Amos put his arm around me. "Freddi, baby, how do ya feel, bro?"

"Like I'm exactly where I'm supposed to be." I looked out to the last moments of light left. "But I miss Dani very much."

"Your paths will cross again. And there is still family here."

Alistair came over with Polish Stan. Stan put a wine box in my hands. "And there are plenty of stimulus packets tonight!" he giggled playfully.

"But," Alistair interrupted, "it won't be the last goodbye, I'm afraid. We all go onto our own Way from here."

I squeezed my lips together and squinted my eyes and swigged from the box. "I don't know how much more I can take, though."

"And that's fine. You're not a robot. We all have limitations. The Way helps us find what they are."

I nodded, still saddened by those already gone.

"Be proud and celebrate your accomplishment. Never mind the rest, my brother." He squeezed me again and put the box back in my hand. Alistair climbed a piece of rock face and stuck his flag of hearts into the cliff. "Back to where I found it." He put his arm around me. "Welcome home, Freddi."

Ep. 30
The Wallflower

Historical Constantinople gained importance and held it because of the Bosporus strait. Surrounded by sea and ultimately fish, settlement was easy. Simple fortifications held shores. A life source for hungry pioneers and later, a stronghold for Empires.

This waterway proved the perfect solitude for a royal Pasha's *yalis* – mansion. Tucked away with his harem, built into the hillside, parallel to the water itself, like a floating house perfectly isolated. Istanbul's position on the Black Sea brought Peter the Great and much later, the climax of WWI. A raging nine months of gruesome, relentless battle before the allies returned to Greece. The Turks gave every ounce of grit and fire to protect their precious city and the Bosporus. The Ottoman flopped afterward and the yalis, made of wood, one by one burned to the sea in ash. Crashing freighters in thick clouds, intentional fires or poor infrastructure, slowly the Empire's rich remnants perished.

Still north of the Bosporus and technically Europe, streets blended continents without apology. Narrow and confusing apartment clusters wound like any old, European city. Bodies clogged sidewalks and endless storefronts. But the lack of road signs crystallized the continental shift. Horns rushed along traffic. Money and connections bypassed virtuosity. An amicable chaos, a finely aromatic fuse of dementia. Corners filled with people dressed to accept any role, who had deferred their once promising street dreams for a hustler's survival.

I settled on one grilled kofta sandwich instead of two. In the late evening, one could hear an owl hooting until the ruckus began again at sunrise with morning prayer. Nearing the great temples, my heart palpitated. My legs quivered, pleading for relief. The Way wound through inefficient, local instructions. My impatience grew to apathy. I resisted the urge to chuck my pack into the Golden Horn. The four, pencil-thick towers of the Blue Mosque appeared. Thousands of tourists created a noise that rattled my ears. The clicking of picture-takers was unnerving. I panicked, surrounded by couples and families snapping selfies. Dread and claustrophobia urged me to run. The celebratory moment dissipated to irrelevancy. Every one of them had a bed for the night. Each person I approached for a single photo waved me off as a beggar. Once the site of a Pagan Temple, Hagia Sophia after 1200 years was no more than a museum. Too cluttered with bodies, every impulse shouted, "Escape!"

A hostel in Taksim posted online for volunteers, but the article's title remained nameless. The posting had the suburb marked and a photo of the building at night. A bridge took me away from all the overbearing trenches of tourists to Galata

Tower. Muddled again with consternation by the hordes. There was no escape. The Way mounted steeply to a massive, pedestrian tarmac called Istiklal. This time, the mobs of tourists came at me in huge, wide lines. The people might have made it harder by locking arms. Beyoglu, with its small tourist trolleys rolling up and down like San Francisco or Lisbon. A gargantuan strip mall, the colour came from street musicians and men who sold mussel shells stuffed with rice. At Taksim Square, a Hilton rose many stories, and a Starbucks glowed beside it. Across the road, handfuls of flower vendors. Men in the sun, dark with tight, rough skin, sold toasted chestnuts that perfumed the air. Little red flags flapped everywhere around Gezi Park. Downhill, Taksim's gentrified portion dipped into Tarlabasi. Dilapidated, overcast, moody, and neglected.

"What the fuck are you doing, Freddi? How the fuck?" It had already taken a few hours to arrive, and suddenly I was surrounded by high-reaching hotel towers of a thousand different names. "Push on fucker!"

What I knew: the place was a hostel, not a hotel. And by an initial glance of all the buildings around, there were few that shared that title.

Hours passed, the same streets trampled time and again. I approached front-desk clerks, pedestrians, shopkeepers, and a little underground restaurant for corba. Inside, I had to kneel for my table. Tables nearly touching the carpet, like a kindergarten workstation. I couldn't wait to squeeze lemon into my soup and bite into the green, pickled chilies. My mouth watered as the cay arrived. I dunked the bread into the corba impatiently after it hit the table. It was soon only saucy remains.

Downhill, a long, horizontal sign appeared, written in playful lettering. Large front windows. A desk inside had a woman with wildly tied, curly, dark auburn hair and light freckles. Left of her sat another young woman in one of two old armchairs, also looking wildly rustic in second-hand clothing. A small desk between the two chairs supported her cay.

"Sorry, hi, I mean, how are ya, sorry, but is this a hostel?"

The woman giggled at me, "Yes, yes, how are you?" she asked, enunciating the last word.

"Are you looking for a volunteer by any chance? I saw it on a website called *Workaway*?"

She paused and hummed her voice in her closed mouth. "Maybe, yes, I think so, maybe?"

Exhilarated, I let my pack swing off my stressed shoulders. The thump jolted the three of us. My legs gave out. My arms shook on the counter before I collapsed. I fell backwards into one of the high, thick, pin cushioned chairs.

"Hi!" I said glancing over. "Sorry to be so abrupt."

"Are you okay?" she asked sympathetically.

In a low, raspy voice, I replied, short of breath, "I get that question a lot. But yea. Just very, very tired."

The clerk with the dyed, scarlet hair came around, "How about a cay? You know, tea?" Her voice was high-pitched but scratchy. "I'm gonna smoke, so, now or after? You gonna have to wait for the boss, anyway."

"Please," I struggled to answer, "cay would be great." I reluctantly continued. "And a glass of water, maybe, please." One owner arrived. His name was Mehmet, like a great, brave ruler of the Ottoman. In this case, his ruling was shared with his sister. Both had obtained master's degrees in Portugal. And like the receptionist, they spoke tremendous English. I filled Mehmet in, through my genuinely battered voice. Once his sister arrived, they agreed. I found a spot to dump my pack. A four-bed dorm for the receptionist and me. I fell asleep on contact with the mattress.

"Sorry, sorry," she said hurriedly after turning the light on.

I paused and rubbed my face, looking at the metal bunk above. "Hey, all good. Wow, was that nap nice, so great to be finished." I stroked my cheeks, "Sorry if I was indifferent to you earlier. What I mean is, sorry I didn't introduce myself."

She grinned acceptingly. "You walked a long way. I guess you're pretty tired. Don't worry, take rest. My name's Emine." She spoke hastily, distracted. She wore this cute, short, cobalt dress covered in pink and white flowers. It hung from spaghetti straps off her thin, bare shoulders. And her thin, long legs were covered in odd, maroon pantyhose. She was a sparkplug with unabashed character. Her hair was tied up with a yellow, embroidered scarf mismatched except the big, fresh, white gardenia stuffed in her hair. She was impossible to ignore. And she stood fidgeting, swinging her slim waist and bony hips

275

side to side as we made introductions. Like a rocket ready to head into orbit.

"I just needed," she said as she bent down into her stuff, "something."

"Grab what you want, take your time. Where did that flower come from? It's gorgeous."

Emine turned. "Oh, you like it? Thanks. Muge, the morning cleaner, brought it for me. She is so sweet. Always flowers."

The pair running our hostel looked like they were Persian or Indian. Emine on the other hand, had olive, Mediterranean skin. "Where are you parents from?" I asked.

"They are in Adana, near to Syria. My father is Armenian, though." That explained Turkey. Her bloodline combined orthodox Christian and Muslim and Caucasus with the Middle East. Coarse, bronzed, freckled by the blazing sun of Southern Turkey, her skin was the product of her beautifully flawed identity crisis. She relished in it brilliantly.

"So, you are quite a mix then," I commented.

"Most of the Turkish are stuck in the middle," she laughed between her words hoarsely before talking again. "I'm gonna watch anime now," she said swiftly in a garbled, North American accent. "It's *so* good."

She had exquisite features. Long, thin fingers with maroon-painted nails to match her stockings. Her eyebrows were thin and darted around her pointed, dark Middle Eastern eyes. Her high, regal cheekbones complimented her bright, thin, paint-free face down to her narrow chin.

Upstairs, a man named Yunus worked the night desk. He was the resident Kurd. In Tarlabasi, a Kurdish neighbourhood, they needed to have a local staff member or two. His beard was like mine: thick, matted, long, and jet black. But he groomed it to length, and unlike me, he had very dark eyes. Cheerful, he was like Emine, laughing as he spoke. And his laughter came from the pit of his big, round belly. There were a couple of travellers in the common area and two French lads who lived down the road. They were in university on a student exchange. Everyone had come to know about my journey and sat curiously. Miles was halfway through his year abroad. I'd arrived right in the middle of a community. Something I'd craved for months, rambling to myself

276

on the long stretches. Miles came from California and had a west coast, killer calm attitude. We unified through our love for Mac Dre, Living Legends, and other Bay Area Hip-Hop.

"I think you are the guy, Freddi," he said to me cheerfully. I looked back at him inquisitively. "I'm looking for something different than simply travelling around, you know?" He paused for a moment. "I've been doing it a while, it's great, it's fun. But like you, I mean shit, you walked across Europe!"

"And pretty damn happy to be finished," I confessed, feeling all the pains and aches in my body. "But yea, I feel ya, for sure. That's what put me on the pilgrimage. I needed change, new perspectives. A chance to really create, time to create and connect with the Way."

"The Way?" he asked attentively.

"It's like, the road, you know? It's the path, the people, the journey, the details, the problems, the moments of thrill and peace. It's the whole package. If you think of traveling as simply, just that, traveling. Well then, you likely don't give a shit about the Way. But," I said excitedly, "*if* you see this as a lifestyle and make it into a unique, tailored one, well, it becomes more of a spiritual Way. An esoteric guide through your thoughts and ambitions and life that relishes the Way itself. After all, it's not the destination, right? but how one reaches it that matters."

"Wow, yea. I mean, I can dig that for sure. It, I mean, I want it to be more than just a trip. I want it to be a kind of Way for me, too. But it's hard to break free from tourism. I want to get closer, you know? Not just Thailand Full Moon Parties n' shit," he said repugnantly. "I'm headed to South Asia, and I know it's there. But maybe Japan," he spoke earnestly. "What are your thoughts?"

I groaned from shoulder pain and looked around. "That we grab a few beers from the shop and talk about the 88 Temples pilgrimage in Japan."

I helped prepare breakfast for the staff with Muge. She wore a hijab and had a very pleasant face. One that missed the sun often. We set a brilliant spread of food I came to know. I learned that the ravioli was *manti*, pronounced 'maen-te,' and the bulgur salad was called *kisir*, pronounced 'ki-ze'. In the afternoon, I passed a few light hours helping Muge, again with

277

the cleaning. Emine was in and out, smoking her rollies and playing with the kittens outside. Aside from chain smoking dodgy, local, cheap rolling tobacco and wearing mustard-coloured or baby blue stockings, Emine obsessed with anime and *Game of Thrones*. With the programs she watched, once they flicked on, she flicked right out of our world. My curiosity toward her insisted on glancing looks. A compulsion grew to know more. She seemed staggeringly different and careless of it. Her body language and appearance screamed, but her words were few. She looked so immaculately blended between Asia, Arabia, and Europe. When she wore a pair of black and blue tights covered in yellow skulls, I noticed her ass. The perfect Sub-Saharan apple. Her whole body was tight and thin and slim except this abnormally fantastic butt. At night, the city rocked, full of lights and great adventure I couldn't afford. From the transvestites to the Saudi tourists and Syrian refugees, stimulating personalities roamed. After a week, Emine promised to take me out.

"My parents wanted me to be a housewife like my sisters. Learn to sew at school. I got good grades. I worked hard on purpose. My teachers praised me. My parents had no choice but to send me to university. Far from home, I applied to Izmir. My place, Adana, it's pretty traditional Muslim, ya know?" I nodded. "I had to get out. I didn't know what to study. I picked English cuz I liked to read Tolkien." She laughed boisterously and pulled at her limp little, yellow-stained rollie. "But I really learned about drugs. It took me seven years to get my bachelor's," she said with another spritely laugh. Though it was a tone-deaf, obtrusive cackle, her laugh and flair stoked my fire, because she didn't care at all. We went into a neighbouring part of Tarlabasi.

"Don't worry about money here. Let's get some beers and enjoy, ya?"

I nodded shyly.

There was a group of people in a mildewy, airless basement apartment. Hotboxed with smoke, psytrance played while one guy held a guitar. Everyone was smitten by Emine's arrival. An uproarious cheer, the Turkish became louder and faster as everyone shared a hug with her. I squeezed into a corner. There was no distinction between them. A tonal fusion of nations. Tall and short and dark and pale, round and slim, but none as thin as Emine. A bunch were different from any I'd met before in Istanbul. The government claimed that some 97 percent of Turkey were Muslim. In this room that number became propaganda. Nor the owners of our hostel, nor anyone I met in the city. Most claimed the religious decree, as I saw it, to avoid conflict. The smooth function of business depended on it. But in this room, eight wallflowers lived differently. They wanted nothing to do with Western diplomacy nor an Islamic state. The whole room had studied in Izmir, the Republic's Anatolian heart. And all came to Istanbul for more freedom.

Emine was a transient. She lived with little besides laptop and clothes. I found great appeal in this. The first woman I met that really personified it. She could have been ready to leave in a matter of hours. She was DeNiro in Heat:

Don't let yourself get attached to anything you are not willing to walk out on in 30 seconds flat if you feel the heat around the corner.

"I've travelled all over Turkey, Freddi. But, leaving. I want to go to Norway and get my master's." Right away, I thought about escorting her there.

"I noticed your pack. You seem like a wanderer. I did the same thing in Canada. I wandered like crazy. But no master's. You got a chance there. It's worth it."

She spoke to me between conversations. I was a fly on the wall otherwise, unavoidable but perfectly ignored. The group spoke in wild syllables, ignoring that I couldn't understand. I came to recognize a few words. The Turkish language had its complexities, but the vocabulary wasn't vast.

Yok, one would say. This meant anything from "no" to "never mind." I would hear repeatedly, *guzel* or *chok guzel*. This ranged from "beautiful," to "incredibly amazing." Spliffs were spun in rotation, and the beers, too. My head was tainted. Everything reminded me of my first flat back home, except that my boombox pumped Hip-Hop.

"Take this slowly," someone said from my right side, "really." It was the first time someone had spoken to me, except Emine. I pulled on the spliff. I dragged off it a few times, eager to escape. He waved his hand for me to slow down. The room faded quickly after that.

279

"Freddi! Freddi! Come back!"

All I could see was Emine, far away, like I was in a deep coffin. Her words were clouded. I could barely hear her. I was in *Poltergeist*, trapped in a television. Panic spiked when my mouth refused to produce sound. My eyes flared and my mouth opened, but words were unheard. I kept falling until I saw raindrops head on.

"Come back, Freddi, baby, Freddi, come back," like a soft whisper in a distant wind. The rain hit and the sounds got louder, the drops fell harder. Her gentle voice reached me, saved me, wrapped me up and comforted me. I flew up from the ground.

"Holy fuck," I gasped. The room went silent.

"Come, come, take it slow," Emine said as she guided me into the bedroom. She laid me down and stroked my face with her hand. "It's okay," she repeated softly.

I shook my head vehemently, "It's not okay. I have no clothes, no boots, no jacket, no money, no job. Winter is nearly here, it's getting colder. How can I show up to a school like this and get work? In these clothes? I've been so lonely out there, so weak. What have I done with myself? Maybe I'm too far gone, and lost, *and…*" I raised my voice from shrill self-pity to fright before continuing with delirious babble. "What the hell happened to me? I thought I'd never speak again, fuckin' hell!"

Emine opened her hand onto my head to lower me against the bed, then moved it under my shirt and against my chest. "Relax, you gotta relax. It's okay now. There was a cannabinoid, very strong. It's very strong. Have to go slow with it. But you're fine now, right?"

I spoke about my clothes and self-professed poverty and ugliness.

"We can get you clothes, together. I can help you. You're far from ugly Freddi, you're just tired, exhausted. You walked a long way. You are stressed and broken," she observed. She moved her hand into my pants and my mid-frame choked up. "Let me help that stress a bit, huh?" My body jolted as she moved softly downwards. She stroked my ambition until stiff.

"Relax baby, let your body loose, you need it," she said in my ear as her hand continued caressing. I softened and moaned. "Don't worry about anything. I'm here to help, no problem. It feels good, right?" Her cheek bones were in front of my face, sparkling, her eyes open and gentle.

"So good."

She stroked gently, quickly, and smoothly until I relaxed and threw my hands around her beautiful face. We kissed. She climbed onto me, and I pulled my face towards hers. "Don't stop. Push hard, let me feel you, please, let me feel you."

Every chance we got from then on, we went for her bottom bunk. I couldn't wait until her shift ended and we could lose ourselves into each other's sweat. She experimented with LSD, mushrooms, DMT, and ayahuasca, reaching out to a spiritual world her social environment couldn't provide. She went deep in, digging for Rumi, listening to the long breaths of a Shaman's tune her people sang centuries before, out on the steppe from Turkmenistan until Mongolia. We got lost out there. She taught me of herself with my fingers all the Way along her skin until I could easily open her from inside. I felt every part of her and listened for more of her life. The physical kisses ripped inside of me and pulled my spirit to the surface. Her energy drained from her stomach and into me. She let me put all my pressure into her. All the suffering and struggle of the past months, we moved through it all. And—and I was able to let it go. We wrapped our legs and arms around each other like monkeys. I yearned to see her eyes every morning. I craved and craved, and she gave and persisted. The harmony came with our panting breaths. This social outcast, this lover of mine, this beautiful wallflower was everything I could have hoped for. She had me.

Late one evening, Yunus and I talked outside. I had just convinced California Miles to grab a beer.

"Kanka, last night, Emine came upstairs late, strange," he said, grinning contently. I nodded. "She had sex with me right there. Out of nowhere," he grinned again, but this time with surprise. "Out of nowhere, kanka."

The whole scene shook and vibrated. I became dizzy. I held my emotions back. Instead, I nodded and smiled, happy for him. We had kept our affair quiet. I wanted to rush down and shake the woman awake, but instead I grabbed Miles. We were on our Way to this Reggae and Hip-Hop bar, Nia. Ten minutes up the road, I stopped him.

281

"How could you!"

She rolled over with sleep in her eyes.

"How couldn't I?" cackling sarcastically as always. "What did I do?"

"I'm serious, how the hell. Why the, would you, what the fuck, Emine? Yunus? Why?"

"Why not?" Her face had little emotion, less than I had ever seen from her in past days. She was normally bursting with facial expressions and body language.

"That's it? This meant nothing?"

"When did we say that we were some kind of couple, huh? We are free, aren't we? Isn't that what you really want, anyhow?" Her face had lifted again, "You wanna get serious? You don't! You'll leave, and then I'll be the poor local with the broken heart, huh? Is that it?"

"But Yunus? Our co-worker, come on!"

"Freddi, I'm bad news, can't you see that? A beautiful disaster. And you are no better. We are bad for each other. That is it. We should stop. That's it."

"I don't care about your shitty self-destruction or how bad we might be suited for the long haul. We feel right together. I know it. I feel it like nothing before. And yea, we don't know what is gonna happen in two days, let alone two months, but what we have is fucking, bloody special. Why the fuck throw it away right now? We all have insecurities. So, take me down there with you, Emine. And follow me to the bottle, so we can figure it out like broken, unstable, self-mutilating adults. I've been completely open, finally."

I looked at her with deep intent. "I've had a hard time being that in the past, trusting people who couldn't understand, coming from a different lifestyle. We share that intimate relationship of nomadic impulses. I wanna be open and honest and spirited and spacious with you. We aren't fragile dolls, we are two people who need love, that is all. I want to give you love." I lay down beside her.

She rolled away from me. "I don't know, Fred, this can't end well. How do you know you want me, huh? Because we are fucking and it feels good?"

"Yes, it can be that. But it's more than that, for sure. I can feel this thing inside my stomach, this ugly thing that insists you

282

be around me as much as possible and that you are the light, the sunlight that brightens me up. Just let me in, and let's forget about yesterday and last week."

"You'll be here for me?" She asked, speaking to the wall. "I don't believe it."

I rolled her toward me. "One hundred and something days I fucking walked. The whole time, I looked for sunlight, a transient life source that could be like mine, that could live and see life like me. I believe you do."

"Maybe," she said shyly.

"We have nothing but our backpacks. And our naked, sweaty bodies." I busted into light laughter. "Which seem to really like each other right now! Right?"

She nodded, grinning auspiciously.

"So, let's just try it out then."

She nodded again, but with wounded eyes, still wet. Her body sagged and her face lay onto my chest.

"Hey, this is not a time for tears," I said, wiping her face.

"What about yours?" she replied plummily again.

"I know, right? See what you do."

She shook her head in disapproval.

"I don't want to possess you, Emine, really. Do what you want, please. Just don't do like that to push me off our little private, happy island. You want me, right? And you like this, right?"

She wrapped herself inside of me. I slid two of my fingers down her throat as I pushed against her. She moaned hard as I thrusted my thigh muscles and wrapped a hand around her outstretched neck. An hour later, she woke me up.

"Baby," she said excitedly.

"You okay? Everything fine?" I asked, worried.

"Thank you." I smiled and squeezed her close to me. "One more thing," she grinned playfully, gently beside my face.

"Yea," I looked at her, my hand on her face. "What's up?"

"Your feet move. Your toes I mean, your toes, they move while you're sleeping. Like you're still walking.

ABOUT AUTHOR

 Relish In the Tread is Steve Hunter's first publication. He studied at college to become a Chef, then apprenticed around Canada before flying over to Australia, and working as a Chef De Parti. One day, his grandma passed away and his girlfriend dumped him shortly after. From there, he committed himself to the road. With no background from university or classical writer's training, he spent 20 years training himself, honing his craft. Out on the road, living in a tent and working many random jobs, he found lots of time to read many of the great classics. Stacks of journals sit in his basement today. Collections of diaries first and then more like short stories from 88 countries and over 120,000 kilometres of hitchhiking.

While he loved hiking mountain trails, in 2013, on the advice of a friend he decided to walk across Spain on the famous – and flat – Camino de Santiago. In 2014, inspired by that overly commercialized trail, he forged his own path attempting to follow ancient routes from Rome to Istanbul. The year after that, he walked across half of Portugal. And later on, across the east coast of Taiwan. And later still, the Lykia Way in the south of Turkey. The road could teach us everything we needed to know. And then, through our own practice we could hone a craft worth sharing. If it was honest, pure, and from the core of our soul, the pages would have merit. If the work was for anything except sharing truths, if it was to monetize ourselves, then that craft had no purpose. Hunter's words came from years of living hand to mouth, from a 12-kilogram backpack with little desire for more than to learn about the diverse cultures of our planet, the people movement that has shaped us, the colonial impressions that have been left on us and the wholehearted belief that our future lay in minimalism.

Growing up in the lower, middle class of a lunchbox town in the western world, it was easy to be engulfed by a bubble. *Relish* has been written for all those people who remained in their bubble. It's for all those people who want to know what it is like to live on our planet, at the cliff edge, walking, slowly taking everything in. It is for all those too afraid to leave their comfort zone. And those who despite their best efforts live from an entitled perspective. *Relish in the Tread* is also for all Hunter's long-termers out there that have been living the same kind of life for years and years, grabbing life by the nut-sack, never giving up, thirsty for knowledge and willing to sacrifice it all for the road. He's met very few along the Way after 15 years. But when he did, he felt their souls connect. And he hopes that this book here does the same thing. It takes the soul of a road warrior and brings it into each reader. Especially, the lonely ones out there walking the planet that know the hardships, but recognize the value far more than any external, fictitious comfort that society either tells us to have or suggests we invest in. *Relish in the Tread* is an attempt to keep those people company who are in their tent right now, reading with a headlamp on, ignoring the howling cries of coyotes.

Made in the USA
Columbia, SC
18 April 2023

15536151R00171